When

Stars

Align

When Stars Align

A Novel

Bruce Genaro

When Stars Align

Published by Remington Publishing
New Canaan, Connecticut

www.RemingtonPublishing.com

ISBN: 978-0-578-48312-2 (paperback)
ISBN: 978-0-578-48313-9 (ebook)
LCCN: 2019937482

For Thomas David Johnson
(the one and only),
who makes all things possible and inevitably more fun and
interesting.

When Stars Align

Chapter One

Megan Walker watched her students scribble notations into notebooks and clickity-clack comments into micro-thin laptops as photographs of skyscrapers, cathedrals, thatched huts, and pyramids flashed past their eyes in a series of blurred colors and bright lights. Standing in front of them while they stared languidly past her, she could only pretend to be interested in the images being projected onto the screen with metronomic constancy. She heard herself utter the words "skin," "façade," and "vestibule" as she interpreted each of the photos that emerged on the flat white screen behind her. Illustrations of columns began to appear: first Doric, then Ionic, then Corinthian. She had designed the lecture so that it would culminate in a final photograph that was a composition of all three types of columns: the unadorned alongside the fluted, flanked by the florid. She focused a red laser beam pointer on one image after another as she acquainted her students with the origins of each.

"There is nothing quite as simple as a column," she told

them. "What could be more straightforward, more utilitarian in its use, than two cylinders positioned under a plane? And yet today, society feels the need to embellish them, to hide them, to disguise them in some way."

She turned her back on the students and faced the screen. She paused briefly for effect before turning back to make her final point.

"Function. Structure. Support. As simple, and in many ways as important, as the wheel."

As she closed the lid on her laptop, the students, most only a dozen years her junior, scooped up their textbooks and computers, wriggled into light jackets and thin sweaters, and shuffled quickly but systematically out of the lecture hall. To Megan, they appeared eager to get on to the next thing, whatever that might be. They seemed to her to have already gone there, mentally, long before the class had officially come to an end. *If they only knew*, she thought, *that life will do with them what it will, regardless of their plans, irrespective of their intentions, independent of their dreams.* At times she had to bite her lip to keep from lecturing them about the dangers of assumptions or the randomness of destiny.

Megan had been teaching art history at Emerson College for seven years. It was a popular class, and she was an admired instructor. She understood that the students saw her neither as the woman she had been nor as the woman she saw herself as but rather as the woman she had become: refined, worldly, polished. It was a persona she was reluctant to embrace. The disparity between how others perceived her and how she perceived herself never failed to amuse her, primarily because her transformation, as subtle as it was, had not been intentional. No, it was happenstance. Serendipity. The luck of the draw. She had simply put one foot in front of the other and, without meaning to and with no harbinger of what was to come, stumbled into a life she had neither coveted nor pursued.

After locking up her classroom and leaving campus, she found her brother, Tommy, sitting in the driver's seat of her Mustang, which was parked on Boylston Street. The windows were up, and he was fiddling with the radio. She rapped on the glass with her ring finger, and the noise startled him.

"Jesus!" he said as he pressed the button to lower the window.

"You're rather tightly wound for someone about to leave on vacation," she said.

"Well, I'd be a little more relaxed if I hadn't spent the better part of the morning tying up your loose ends." He pointed to a plastic Walgreens bag on the back seat as evidence. "Did you have to nearly break the glass to get my attention?"

"Sorry, I wasn't thinking. I guess I'm a bit nervous about our trip. I just want to get to the airport and be on our way." She motioned to the rear of the car. "Pop the trunk, would ya?"

"No room," Tommy said. "You'll have to put your stuff in the back seat."

"Did you overpack again? We're only going for a long weekend."

"I like to have options. Now get in the car, we're running late."

"You've got—"

"Yes, I've got boarding passes, phone chargers, passports, and disinfectant wipes. And I've even converted a few hundred dollars into Euros."

Tommy resumed playing with the radio dials as Megan settled into the passenger seat.

"You need a new car," he said. "Something from this century. Something that plays Bluetooth or SiriusXM. I need traveling music, and I can't get anything on this piece of crap."

"Oh, shut up and drive," she said, and pressed the radio dial with her open palm to turn it off. "How about I sing 'La vie en Rose' or 'La Marseillaise' to get you in the Parisian spirit?" She cleared her throat and began to sing. "*Allons, enfants de la Patrie*—"

"Okay, okay, you win. A top forty station it is," Tommy said, his eyes wide in mock horror.

He switched the radio back on and punched in a random station. He started the car, checked the mirrors, and eased into traffic. As he slowed down to stop at a red light, a dream catcher suspended from the rearview mirror began to sway back and forth. He reached a hand out to keep it from swinging.

"What's up with this?" he said. "These things don't work. And who dreams in their car?"

"Oh, Tommy, my sweet, cynical sibling. If they don't work, then please explain to me how it is that we are heading off for a weekend in Paris, first-class, all expenses paid."

"You *know* why. And it's not because of some tacky souvenir you bought in an Arizona gift shop. Anyway, I'm not going to argue with you about it."

"Good, because you'd lose. Have you heard from Lauren and your husband?"

"Yes, of course. Gregg made sure that they got to the airport three hours before our flight leaves, so we need to step on it. And by the way, for the record, he said your buddy Lauren is bringing twice as much luggage as I am."

"God, it's no wonder you and she bicker so much. You're like two peas in a pod."

"Oh please, don't insult me. I'm nothing like her. That girl is more self-centered than a gyroscope."

"I rest my case," she said.

"Hey, don't let me forget to stop by the newsstand before we board."

"Oh, no you don't. I will not sit next to you in first class if you're going to read those trashy tabloids all the way to France. You can pick up a novel or a self-help book—Lord knows you could use one of those. But *People* magazine and trash like *Star* are off limits to you."

"Spoilsport!" he said, turning up the volume on the radio to indicate that the conversation was over.

They drove to the airport in silence, oblivious, by choice and by habit, of the ways in which the past could still impact their future.

Chapter Two
(Four Years Earlier)

It was Megan's third day in Paris and the first without rain. She had spent the better part of the previous two days wandering around the Louvre's various levels and endless rooms, making notes, taking pictures, and occasionally pausing to do a quick sketch in a tattered Moleskine. But on that third morning, when the sun broke through, she planted herself at a table in a café packed with Europeans. She was happy to be sitting there by herself, relaxing, observing, and absorbing the sound of glasses tinkling, newspapers shuffling, and rapid-fire conversations in a profusion of foreign languages.

For years, she had dreamed of visiting the City of Light, but there had always been something more pressing, more important to attend to, more fiscally responsible to do with her meager savings than to spend it on a European vacation. But the past twelve months had been a particularly trying time and had presented her with numerous opportunities and reasons to reevaluate her life. There were the usual challenges of academia, along with the added pressure from the new dean to publish; a bad breakup with a boyfriend; and her mother's cancer diagnosis. And while her byline had appeared in several prestigious periodicals, while she was actually relieved to be romantically unencumbered once again—partly to be free to devote her full attention to her mother's recovery—these events had left her with a feeling of uncertainty about her life and her future. While her mother's cancer hadn't been terminal, she felt as if her rapidly approaching thirtieth birthday just might be, if only metaphorically. And so, even though her first trip to Paris had as yet been uneventful, she couldn't have been happier, sitting there alone, away from the pressures of work, relieved of the complications of family, and free from the accommodations and entanglements of a relationship.

Cosimo Garibaldi had been wandering the streets for over an hour, searching for a place to land. He wasn't exactly sure what it was that he was looking for, only that he would know it when he found it. He walked slowly, casually across Pont Saint-Louis, his new ankle-high black leather boots slipping every now and then on the damp brick pavers. He stopped, leaned against the bridge, and tightened the belt on his mohair coat to ward off a damp chill that still lingered in the air. His head was lowered and his eyes focused on his feet as they often were in an effort to avoid being recognized.

When he looked up again, he spotted a vacant table at La Brasserie de l'Isle Saint-Louis, empty but for the remnants of the previous patron's *petit déjeuner*. He hesitated, unsure if it was a suitable place to sit and relax, given his current mood, and uncertain whether he could handle the crush of people with their arms outstretched, reading that morning's issue of *Le Monde*, or tolerate the chatter of a few dozen people engaged in lively, animated conversations. As he tentatively made his way across the cobblestone walkway, two gentlemen stood and left the café. Their vacancy revealed a young woman sitting alone under the red awning, wiping crumbs from the corner of her mouth with the pointed edge of a starched white napkin. Oblivious to the fact that she was being watched, she took another bite of a flaky croissant and a delicate sip of a large café crème. She breathed a deep sigh and gazed out across the Seine, the view no longer cloaked by inclement weather. She seemed content to be sitting there by herself, eating breakfast, drinking coffee, and quietly observing the ebb and flow of Parisian life.

Cosimo was transfixed by the sunlight as it danced around the highlights in her hair. There was something vaguely comforting in the sight of her, something that demanded a much closer inspection. It wasn't her beauty that was drawing him to her, as her physiognomy was nearer to pretty than it was to beautiful. And though she did exude an air of uncomplicated sophistication, he wouldn't have classified her as elegant, an inherent attribute in all of his previous paramours. Most notable to him about her presence was that she wasn't wafer-thin. And that was perfectly fine with Cosimo, who had become bored by the embrace of emaciated women, all of whom mimicked the style and fashion of contemporary *Vogue* cover girls, all striving for that one-dimensional, airbrushed, and famished look.

He wanted to turn away, but he couldn't. He tried to resist the pull of her energy, to be indifferent to the magnetic force field that was drawing him toward her. But he was caught in a vortex that was all the more enchanting because of the coin-sized lights flickering on the building behind her, cast there as if on purpose for dramatic effect by the sun's reflection off the Seine. The light show, both playful and haunting after so many days of gloomy darkness, gave the scene an ethereal glow. Momentarily spellbound, he shook his head as if he were trying to wake from a dream. Only it was too late for that. The forces that had been set in motion were impossible to stop. It would have been easier for him to catch a falling safe in his bare hands than to walk away from such an obvious yet inexplicable attraction.

Megan, having finished her croissant, wiped the crumbs from the side of her mouth and took another sip of coffee. Her delicate sips and tiny bites were contrary to her usually hurried, messy, gulping manner. She wanted to linger there indefinitely, if not forever, with the faint smell of the Seine, the frequent wisps of cigarette smoke, and the gray melancholy of Notre Dame's flying buttresses all a permanent part of her reality. While her first trip to Paris had not been without complications, like weather, neither had it been a disappointment.

She was captivated by a tableau on the other side of the river and decided to try to capture its essence on paper. She withdrew a pen from her purse, spread open her black leather notebook on the wobbly metal table, and began to render the cluster of buildings in thick black ink. She was concentrating on the task, her eyes darting from the structures to the page and back again, her hand rapidly making bold, sweeping strokes punctuated with tiny flourishes, when her concentration was interrupted by the arrival of a tall, tanned, boyish-looking gentleman. With a measured, purposeful gait, he gave the impression that he was heading straight for her, approaching her as if he knew her, as if he were intent on picking up a previous conversation from where they'd left off. And although he carried himself with dignity and grace, she also got the impression that there was an air of tension about him, like a fully compressed spring that had been tenuously secured.

Megan, usually oblivious to fashion trends or how people dressed, couldn't help but notice the paisley silk scarf that was hung about his neck in the shape of a triangle. It reminded her of the bandana masks worn by actors in old TV westerns that she used to watch when she was a child. His thick mop of chocolate-brown hair looked as if it were moving in several different directions at once, and the pair of sunglasses balanced on his nose added a layer of mysteriousness to his sudden, stealthy arrival.

"*Scusi,*" he said as he squeezed in behind her, "*buon pomeriggio.*" And then, with an air of elegance and poise reminiscent of another era, he relaxed into a weathered cane chair at the table next to hers. His mannerisms seemed choreographed—not so much theatrical but rather polished and refined. She offered him a half-smile and then returned to adding black pen marks to beige paper that were meant to represent limestone buildings on *Le Rive Gauche.* She took another sip of coffee and used her napkin to blot away a speck of rogue foam from her top lip. Cosimo extended his arm, checked his watch, then absentmindedly scanned the patio. Megan wondered if she had mistaken his interest in her, as his manner now seemed to indicate indifference.

Cosimo looked away out of habit. It was a trick he'd

learned to keep even the most avid of star-fuckers at a safe distance. Before ordering his usual double espresso, he engaged the waiter in a frenetic tête-à-tête about restaurants and nightclubs, all the while taking covert glances in Megan's direction. He was trying to come off as aloof while at the same time mildly interested. Initiating conversations wasn't his forte. He was enough of a celebrity, at least in certain parts of Europe, that the ability to end a discussion and move on, without appearing ungracious or elitist, was a far more requisite skill than knowing how to start one in the first place.

Cosimo could usually tell from a person's initial response if he'd been recognized. Acknowledging smiles were often followed by averted eyes, which were usually followed by another terse, apologetic smile that eventually retreated in embarrassment once eye contact had been made. Either that, or he was the target of more frequent and longer stares with the unadulterated intention of engaging him in a dialogue or asking him for a photograph. He took comfort in knowing that even as the world was getting smaller because of air travel and the internet, and even though many individuals were inclined to assume a certain familiarity with the rich and famous because they followed them on Twitter or liked them on Facebook, being a prince still inspired a certain amount of awe and respect. And although the antisocial wall that he was prone to erect occasionally left him feeling alone or lonely, he was, more often than not, grateful for it. As for the woman with the sketchbook, he was incapable of reading her body language, of ascertaining if her quick peeks at him were due to recognition or shy flirtation. Was it possible that he had found the one woman in Paris of a certain age who did not recognize him and perceive him as her own personal lottery ticket to wealth and notoriety?

Not one prone to infatuation or flirtation, Megan found it unsettling when she realized she was stealing sidelong glances at him as well. She turned the page in her journal and made a few more quick, concentrated scratches with her pen. Those new, seemingly random black markings, all curvy lines and deft dashes, had a remarkable resemblance to a slender young man with curly hair, sitting in a café, wrapped in a scarf.

To her, the gentleman's clothes implied contradictory statements about him. His jeans were formfitting, faded and frayed in spots, and haphazardly torn so that in certain places, his furry thighs were exposed. He wore a white crepe shirt unbuttoned halfway down his chest that revealed modest sun-kissed pectorals, a thin patch of brown hair, and a gold medallion that sparkled in the sunlight.

While his clothes were contemporary, his watch was obviously an antique, likely an heirloom that had been handed down for generations; the crystal cloudy, the silver scratched, the leather band faded and scuffed. The sunglasses perched upon his nose were the perfect stylistic touch, the lenses probably polarized, and the frames likely crafted from a scarce new material and ubiquitously appliquéd with the initials of some young, up-and-coming fashion designer. He removed his shades and placed them on the tabletop, revealing a pair of green eyes that seemed to both penetrate and devour. Oddly, she also noticed that the sunglasses, now resting alone on the table, looked like any other pair of cheap plastic frames one might find on a drugstore carousel crammed into tight aisles next to shelves stocked with postcards, sunscreen, and paperback books.

As the bells of Notre Dame struck twelve, Megan leaned back and nestled into her chair while Cosimo and the waiter continued their enthusiastic exchange.

"*Puissé-je vois?*" Cosimo said to Megan after the waiter had walked away.

"*Je ne comprends pas*," she answered automatically with a practiced reply. "*Je ne parle pas français.*"

"*Desole*," he said. "May I see?"

When her response was a confused expression, he pointed to her journal. Megan was caught off guard by the prospect of a stranger flipping through her personal sketches and intimate thoughts, yet for some reason, she was compelled to do as he requested. With an apprehensive smile, she reluctantly handed him the notebook. He accepted it with a knowing grin. Leafing casually through the pages, he was careful to display that he was simply admiring her artwork and not reading her private notations. He came to rest upon the rough outline of the buildings across the Seine, the drawing she'd begun before he'd arrived but hadn't yet finished.

"You have captured them well," he said. "You are an artist?"

"Me? No!" She waved a hand in the air to indicate that the very idea of it was a ridiculous one. "I'm a teacher. History. I teach art history."

"You are visiting?"

"Yes. From Boston. Only for a week."

Cosimo's hand lingered on the top of the page as if he were about to move on to the next.

"Your first visit here?" he asked.

"Yes. Is it that obvious?"

"No! No," he said, dismissing her comment with an exaggerated shake of his head. "With your sketchbook and your intensity, you fit right in with all of these other aesthetes." He slowly, teasingly, turned the page to the likeness of himself. "Now *this* one I like," he said. He studied it quietly, thoughtfully for a few seconds. "But I think it needs a caption."

"A caption?"

"*Si, si.* A bubble with words." He pointed to her fountain pen. "May I?"

She removed the cap and handed it to him. He set the journal on the table and drew a large, irregular circle above the line that represented his head. He finished it off with a point that was directed to a mark that implied a mouth. Inside the circle, with surprisingly erratic lettering, he wrote, "Will you have dinner with me tonight?" and then handed the journal back to her. She took it, read his comment, glanced up at him, and then looked back down at her book. On the next page she made another sketch, this one of a nondescript woman seated under a patio umbrella. She drew a bubble over that head, and inside that circle, she printed in a neat, refined script, "But I don't even know you."

He borrowed her book again and drew another circle under his first one. In that one he hastily scratched the words, "But that is the purpose of the dinner." When he handed it back to her, she laughed.

"*N'est-ce pas?*" he asked.

"*Je ne sais pas,*" she said and shrugged her shoulders.

She put the journal away in her handbag. "*Je…*how do you say…" She quickly abandoned any pretense that she could speak French fluently and said, "Why don't we start with coffee and see how that goes?"

Cosimo, unaccustomed as he was to being infatuated with others, was not sure how to proceed. He was not used to having a woman be so distant, so indifferent toward him. He was thrown off-balance by the notion of a woman who didn't jump at the chance to join him for dinner. In the circles in which he traveled, women were not so coy, demure, or foolish enough to squander the opportunity to spend an evening with the last prince of Italy. However, at that moment, there remained the possibility that this woman had no idea that the person with whom she was conversing was the last prince of Italy. But there was also the possibility that she *did* know and that she was toying with him. Either way, he continued to try to persuade her to let him show her a Paris that could not be found in any guidebook.

"It will give you some interesting stories to tell your class," he said.

"And what do you do?" she asked, anxious to change the subject. "For a living, I mean?"

Their conversation was interrupted by the arrival of Cosimo's coffee. His tapered fingers grasped the tiny handle, and he took a sip.

"My family has several businesses," he said, placing the cup back onto the saucer. "They keep me on a retainer." He spooned a cube of sugar into his espresso and then twisted and dragged a sliver of lemon rind along the rim of the cup. The oils from the citrus skin shimmered in the dark liquid, creating an effect similar to the one that the sun had upon the Seine. "Technically, it's more of a *restrainer* than a retainer," he said as he slowly stirred his coffee. "In effect, they pay me to stay *away* from the businesses."

Megan, unable to discern if his comment was serious or sarcastic, suppressed a laugh and took another sip of coffee. Despite the fact that it was officially summer and the days were lingering well into the evening, there continued to be a nip in the air. Cosimo noticed that Megan's arms were covered in goose bumps and that she was rubbing them briskly with her palms from time to time. He stood, smiled, removed his coat, and draped it over her shoulders.

"May I?" he asked, pointing to the empty chair at her table. She nodded. He sat down and immediately took hold of her hands. He turned one of them over and examined her palm.

"I have a friend," he said. "She is a…what is the word?…fortune-teller. She reads palms, tea leaves, some numerology, things like that. But," he said as he peered intently into her hand, "she believes that the essence of a person lies in their aura. That tells her more about a person than all of those other things combined." His index finger slowly, methodically traced her lifeline. He fell silent as he studied her palm with intense concentration.

"What do you see?" she asked, barely able to conceal her growing discomfort.

"*Me?* I cannot read palms. I see only your fair skin and the essence of life that is coursing through your veins." He let go of her hand. "*Auras?* Those I can read sometimes."

"I'm going to use the facilities," she said, standing, not

really having to and not completely certain that she was going to return.

"*Pardon?*"

"The ladies' room," she said. And then, failing to consider the consequences, she added, "Would you mind ordering me another coffee if the waiter comes back?"

"*Absolument!*" he said. "*Café crème?*

"*Oui.*"

Megan weaved around the tightly packed tables as she made her way to the front door of the café. She glanced back to find Cosimo engaged in a dialogue with a couple at a nearby table. He was animated once again, like he had been with the waiter: hands flying, words flowing, his facial expressions exaggerated. Inside, she descended a cavernous passageway with worn, slippery stone steps that led to a subterranean washroom. She washed her hands and then studied her face in a murky, gold-flecked mirror. She accepted a paper towel from a short woman in a white uniform and then placed a few Euros in a tarnished silver tray on the vanity.

On her way back upstairs, she debated whether or not to phone her brother, Tommy. When she remembered the time difference, she realized he would still be at work. She thought about calling her friend Lauren, but then she already knew what Lauren would say: "Go! Go! You're on vacation. Live a little. Oh, and take lots of pictures." Then she considered texting Tommy a description of the man she'd just decided to have dinner with. That way, in a few days, if they find her mangled body floating in the Seine, they'll at least have some idea of who the perpetrator was. But she quickly abandoned that plan because with Tommy, a message that even hinted at trouble was likely to stir up more drama than it was meant to prevent.

Intrigued as she was by this stranger, she was also wary of him. His energy and his focus were all over the map, and he was a bit more forward than she was used to or comfortable with. Yet she couldn't deny that she was attracted to him, oddly drawn to him, unusually receptive to him. *It's only dinner*, she thought as she made her way back to the table. *I can handle dinner.*

After a light meal that night in a quiet bistro in the 14th arrondissement, they went to a small jazz club recommended earlier by the waiter at the brasserie. There they drank wine while they listened to a large Brazilian woman in a flowing caftan sing songs of unrequited love. Megan told Cosimo about her loosely drawn itinerary for the rest of the week and asked him if he had any other recommendations.

"You must see Mont-Saint-Michel," he said, emphatically, insistently. "It's eerie in a way. It's both calming and captivating. One cannot visit the place without being affected by it. You leave there in an altered state."

"Have you seen the movie *Mindwalk?*" she asked. "It was filmed entirely at the abbey." As she began to tell him about the philosophical ideas behind the screenplay, she noticed his eyes racing about the room, his fingers riffing on the tabletop. "Anyway, ever since I saw it I've wanted to go there, but it's not an easy place to get to."

There was a lull in the conversation that was quickly followed by Cosimo enthusiastically saying, "I will drive

you. We shall go together in my convertible." He winked
and added, "It is much faster than the train and a lot more
fun."

～

At midnight they walked the few blocks back to
Cosimo's haphazardly parked Carrera Cabriolet. While
Megan admired the clean lines and the hidden horse-
power of the German automobile, she made no connection between what she knew the car probably cost and the
amount of money her date might have in his bank account.
Her father had been a mechanic most of his life, so she'd
spent the better part of her childhood around men who
lived at home with their parents well into their twenties
in order to afford a souped-up Corvette or a tricked-out
Testarossa. She knew that to most men, a cool coupe was
far more essential than a posh pad.

En route back to Megan's hotel, Cosimo took a few
detours to point out his favorite buildings and streets, a
hidden little gem of a park, and a quick spin past a few of
the more popular tourist attractions: the Tuileries, the Place
des Vosges, and the Louvre with its glass pyramid glowing
so dreamily with an amber light that it demanded one be
in awe of it.

Megan was equally terrified and exhilarated as Cosimo
raced his convertible through the streets, weaving in and
out of lanes at speeds well over the city's limits. After a final
lap around the Place de la Concorde's obelisk, he raced back
to the Latin Quarter through streets that, at one o'clock in
the morning, were still intermittently clogged with traffic.
The tires on his 911 screeched as he maneuvered the gear-

shift back and forth to squeeze into an open space. She ran her hands through her wind-blown hair as he walked around to the passenger side to open her door. She was somewhat shaken from the drive, which had more to do with her general discomfort at being a passenger than it did with the vehicle's velocity or his skills as a pilot.

"I'll have to get back to you about Mont-Saint-Michel," she said. "I've only got a few days left, and there's still a lot I'd like to see."

"Of course," he said, "of course." Cosimo's mouth unconsciously morphed into a childish pout which softened into a smile as he gently touched her elbow and whispered, "I promise not to drive so fast next time. *Si?*"

"Yes," she said with some reluctance. "*Si.*"

The dimly lit lobby of Megan's hotel was vacant but for a desk clerk flipping through a copy of *Paris-Match*. She approached the desk, and the clerk, barely acknowledging her, handed her a large brass key dangling from the end of a braided red rope. With a cordial but tender kiss on her cheek, Cosimo bid her good night and wished her a pleasant evening. And then, when he was halfway to the exit, he stopped, turned his torso in her direction as if he were about to walk back to her, and then just as quickly turned around again and vanished into the revolving doors.

Back out on the dark, deserted street, Cosimo took in a few deep breaths of the chilly night air. He walked briskly, his pace getting faster, his strides getting longer, even though he was moving forward with no definitive destination in mind. He was so high from the evening's conversation and the invigorating fresh air that he had forgotten that he'd parked his car around the corner from her hotel.

A half hour later he was still walking, still humming, still floating, oblivious to the hour and immune to the cold. Reflections of the evening and the rare anticipation of the day ahead propelled him forward. Whenever his spirits soared like this, he neglected to take his medication, either because he forgot to or because he didn't feel the need to. Either way, the pills in his coat pocket were likely to remain where they were until or unless something catastrophic happened.

His euphoria started to wane about the same time his feet began to throb from walking all day in new shoes that were stylish and aesthetically pleasing but not very comfortable. So he hailed a taxi and directed the driver to his flat in the Marais. An hour later, after a valiant attempt at sleep, the comforter on the floor, the sheets tangled about his legs, he was still wide awake. Even the white-noise machine in his bedroom, with its soothing sounds of the sea and its quiet calls of gulls, failed to calm his mind.

He got up and tried to write in his journal, but his thoughts were too fleeting to be captured on paper. He tried to read. He spent a half an hour playing Brahms on the baby grand piano. Nothing made him sleepy. Nothing calmed him down. Nothing took his mind off the woman who, for some reason, for the first time in years, had given the young prince a reason to live.

Chapter Three

Princess Maria-Carmella Stefani Garibaldi di Sorrento comfortably occupied the head seat at the end of a long, mahogany conference table. She shuffled a small stack of papers while ten men in dark business suits and pinstriped ties waited patiently for her direction. A petite woman, a mere five foot five in heels, she managed to command the attention of anyone anywhere near her orbit, from waitresses to heads of state, from hobos to the hoi-polloi, and, much to her dismay, the occasional paparazzi. She closed the cover of her leather portfolio, walked over to a window that overlooked the jumble of buildings that is Milan's business district, and, with her back to the room, stared off into the distance. Her hands folded in front of her, her demeanor deceptively pleasant, she turned around and addressed the board.

"Gentlemen," she said, "you're telling me that with all of the brain power in this room and with all of the resources at your disposal, the only recommendations that you have for getting us out of this economic tailspin are to sell off a few buildings and close one of our textile plants?"

The ten men, most of them in their midfifties, CEOs and CFOs of their own multinational corporations and millionaires many times over, sat there, mute. Maria-Carmella scrutinized their faces one by one, silently daring each of them to offer up another suggestion, an apology, a sacrificial lamb, or a scapegoat.

"Well, I'm not at all surprised," she said, when no answer was forthcoming. "Short of extortion," she added, her eyes lingering on Count Rimaldi, "or blackmailing our business partners," she continued, shifting her attention to the duke of Westchester, "I would say that your recommendations are well thought out and pragmatic."

The count cleared his throat. The duke blotted his forehead with a silk handkerchief. The two firmly believed that Maria-Carmella had the knowledge, the power, and the wherewithal to carry out both extortion and blackmail. In fact, when her husband, Prince Leonardo, disappeared ten years earlier, the board of directors openly debated in a private session whether she had done him in herself (a pistol being the favored weapon, with arsenic poisoning a close second) or whether she'd hired someone else to do the job for her. While the press still occasionally ran stories that either lamented the demise of Cosimo's father or professed to have knowledge of his whereabouts, it was only Maria-Carmella and Prince Leo who really knew what happened the night that he went missing.

"As you know, gentlemen, I often defer to your judgment, finance being your area of expertise," she said. "But in this instance, I'm fairly certain that my idea of leverage and your idea of leverage are two decidedly different things. And while I have the utmost respect for each and every one of you, the difference between success and failure lies in knowing which interpretation will be the most advantageous."

She strode back to the conference table and sat down. She opened her portfolio, put on her reading glasses, and made a few quick notes. She removed her glasses and carefully placed them back into their case. She closed her portfolio and returned it to its designated spot in her valise. She then pushed a button on the console in front of her and ordered a secretary to have her car brought round.

"I guess this means we're adjourned," said the junior member of the group, Marcus Baldduchi, as he reached for his phone.

"Yes, Marcus," Maria-Carmella said, with a little more venom than was necessary, "you're finished." She donned her coat and left the office. "But *my* work is just beginning," she murmured to herself in the elevator as the heavy, gilded doors closed behind her.

It took close to an hour of staring out the window of the limousine as it wound its way through the Italian countryside before she could summon the resolve to pick up the phone. The call was a last resort—one she had always intended to make, but never under such circumstances. Not when the stakes were so high. Not when the difference between yes and no meant the difference between success and failure. Not when the outcome of everything she held dear was dependent on the cooperation of her only male heir, Crown Prince Giuseppe Cosimo Garibaldi di Sorrento, whom, even at the age of twenty-four, she still considered to be, in many ways, a child. But she had the necessary leverage: her title, her money, and the ear of Cosimo's confidante—his sister, Regina.

The Garibaldi family fortune had diminished over the past several years, thanks in part to the world economic crisis, a few market trend miscalculations, and a couple of unfortunate partnerships. However, it was not the amount of money that had evaporated that troubled Maria-Carmella (she still had more cash, assets, and buying power than many small countries); rather, it was the loss of influence and power, real or perceived, that disturbed her. She had no need for another yacht, another villa, another private jet. What she needed more than anything else was to feel—to *be*—significant.

She was nervous about making the call because of the timing; it seemed equally too late and too early for such a proposition, even though the subject of marriage between the two families had been a topic of discussion for years.

"Paulo, I think the time has come to iron out the details and implement our little merger," she said when he answered the phone.

"Hmmm. If it were anyone but you, Maria-Carmella, I would accuse them of being cryptic."

"And I would be, if I thought that would get me what I want."

"I like a woman steadfast in her pursuits, who grabs with gusto all that life has to offer."

"I'll be in New York on the twenty-fifth. Annabella? She is still agreeable to—"

"Yes, Maria, she is still agreeable," he said, mimicking her. "And Cosimo? He is still…?"

"I'll see you on the twenty-fifth, Paulo."

She made one more call before the town car arrived at the family estate. It was to Cosimo, who, as usual, didn't answer. He was another one who needed to be dealt with cryptically but firmly. Her message commanded him to return home immediately. Maria-Carmella was a master of subtext, each word laden with demands, every pause peppered with a threat, each inflection bearing an ultimatum, and all of them intricately hidden beneath her polished, aristocratic pronunciation. But in this instance, she made certain that this one call to Cosimo left nothing open to interpretation. At least as far as she was concerned. In her mind, her sense of urgency could only mean one thing: it was time for him to fulfill his familial duty and get married.

As the car made its way up the long, winding driveway, her eyes surveyed the exterior of the estate. The family villa looked faded, tired, old, and a little rough around the edges. It occurred to her that she had been spending too much time there alone, that she, too, was beginning to look and feel a little old and tired herself. She made a mental note to have her assistant book her the rejuvenation package at her favorite spa in New York and a dinner reservation for three at Per Se. If Columbus Circle was to be her battlefield, then Juvéderm and foie gras would be her weapons of choice.

Chapter Four

At nine o'clock the next morning, Cosimo called her hotel. A groggy and decidedly hungover Megan answered the phone.

"*Bonjour?*"

"I've woken you," he said apologetically.

"No, no. It's okay. I'm glad you called," she said, stifling a yawn. "There's a good chance I would have slept through the rest of my vacation if you hadn't. What time is it?"

"A little after nine."

"That's not *so* bad." She waited for him to speak, but there was only an awkward silence. "Thank you again for dinner. I had a nice evening."

"*Moi aussi.* Might I see you again? And if it's not too, what is the word…*présomptueux*…this afternoon?"

"If you like. So long as you remember my French is, well, rusty at best."

"Rusty?"

"*Oui,*" she said, then searched her brain for an alternative, less American word. "*Vieux et ... et fatigue.*"

"*Si.* Évidemment. I mean, *je pron désolé.* I mean, I'm sorry," he said, struggling to communicate using three different languages. "*C'est tres difficile, n'est pas?*"

"It's okay," she said. "*D'accord?* I'm planning to visit the Musée d'Orsay this morning. Then l'Orangerie in the afternoon, if I haven't overdosed on impressionism by then." When he had no immediate response to her itinerary, she added, "Wouldn't you be bored?"

While she had told him of her plans the night before, he had, in his enthusiasm for seeing her again, forgotten what they were. He knew that he shouldn't have been drinking, as the interaction of alcohol with his medications drastically and unpredictably altered his moods and compromised his fluctuating sanity. But when he was with her, he felt so normal, so ordinary, so sane, that he completely and conveniently forgot his promise to himself to abstain. Quite the contrary, it encouraged him to overindulge.

He was groggy himself that morning due to his excess consumption of vodka and a complete lack of sleep. But hearing her voice and the thought of sitting next to her in his Porsche as they cruised along the countryside toward Mont-Saint-Michel re-energized him. As much as he wanted to see her again, the idea of spending an afternoon meandering through an old, repurposed train station pretending to admire paintings and statues by artists long since dead, especially in a collection he had already seen a dozen times, seemed tedious and dull. The museum, with its dour security guards, bright lights, and hordes of T-shirt-wearing, camera-wielding tourists, was a risky venue for him.

He would get bored, then anxious, then irritable. It was anyone's guess as to what might happen next. It was entirely possible for him, in such a situation, to spiral in a matter of minutes from a passionate, interested companion into a maniacal, mutant miscreant.

"Perhaps you are right," he said. "You will want to go at your own pace, to linger, to sit, to sketch a little." He picked up his watch from the table and tapped its crystal with his finger as he pondered his options. "Dinner, then?"

"Yes, that would be nice," she said, wiping a bit of sleep from her eyes.

"*Vingt heures?* I will pick you up at your hotel? *Oui?*"

"Okay, but you have to promise—"

"Yes, English, I know. And I have already promised the other, remember?" he said, laughing. Then quietly, conspiratorially, he said, "I will drive so slowly you will not even realize the car is in motion."

∽

Megan hung up the phone and propped a couple of pillows behind her head. Her room was the typical middle-class tourist fare: a small writing desk, an armoire that housed a television and a minibar, and a nondescript side chair barely large enough for a child. There was an ordinariness about the place that plush towels and goose down comforters couldn't disguise. *This is not like me,* she thought. *A spontaneous dinner with someone you strike up a conversation with in a café is one thing—but this—this is a date. A second date if you will. And what is he after that he calls me less than twelve hours after we had dinner?*

Had it been anyone else, anywhere else, or any other

time in her life, she would have been cordial but kept him at a distance. She would have continued sketching in her journal and enjoyed a nice, quiet evening by herself instead of allowing him to riffle through her notebook and engage her in a one-sided conversation about her life. *What is it about him? Why am I so looking forward to seeing him again that I dread the thought that he'll cancel or stand me up?* She picked up her journal and, in black ink and perfect penmanship, relived the previous evening, from coffee to good-night kiss, and tried to make sense of it.

That morning the line to get in to the Musée d'Orsay snaked around the building and moved at an excruciatingly slow pace. And, as one tourist after another cut in front of her with neither an explanation nor an apology, Megan wondered if she was truly up for another day of stale air and prerecorded messages about the life and loves of French painters and Italian sculptors. She decided to walk over to the Tuileries instead and have an early lunch before checking out the crowds at l'Orangerie. She knew she wouldn't miss seeing the Art Deco furniture displays or the miniature replica of the Paris Opera House at the D'Orsay, but she couldn't fly back to Boston without seeing the water lilies by Monet that filled the better part of l'Orangerie's basement. The same images that filled a dozen books she had read in preparation for her trip. They weren't paintings so much as they were moments in time, captured for eternity, made even more real because what had been captured for posterity never actually existed; they were only an artist's *interpretation* of a moment in time. Yet, in an odd way, she knew that those moments actually did exist, now that they were in the form of stretched canvases, wild drawings, and dollops of paint. And it was taking those existential thoughts and sharing them with her students that made being a teacher so rewarding.

She was sitting in a green metal chair that fronted a small pond eating a *jambon buerre* and watching a young boy steer a miniature sailboat across the water when her phone rang.

"*Bonjour*," she said in to the black box, her voice displaying a lilt that she had unconsciously appropriated after several days of listening to the conversations around her.

"My, don't you sound as if you belong there, answering the phone in French, and in that Parisian way that makes every statement seem like a question," Tommy said. "I guess you're enjoying yourself more than you thought you would."

"You guessed right, little brother. And I owe it all to you."

"Hey, all I did was lend you my Rosetta Stone CDs and convince you that, even by yourself, you would have a good time. On second thought, you do owe it all to me."

"That's the narcissistic Tommy I know and love."

"Where are you?"

"Some museum. You know, Greek statues, impressionist paintings, Egyptian sarcophagi. The usual high-culture, low-entertainment stuff."

"Fess up, sis. You're either at the top of the Eiffel tower or in the Tuileries waiting in line for a crepe smothered in Nutella."

"You think you know me so well."

"Which one?"

"Nutella."

"I knew it! I'd kill for one of those. I'd ask you to bring me back one, but they don't travel so well. Bring me back a cute little French boy instead. You know, the gift that keeps on giving."

"So how's life at Saint Elsewhere?"

"Dull as usual. Nothing as exciting as dinner in a little bistro with a tall, dark Frenchman."

"He wasn't French, smartass, he was Italian. And how did you know?"

"Oh, you slut. I just knew it. Ask Lauren. I bet her fifty bucks that by the end of the first day, you'd have some handsome foreigner as your own personal tour guide."

"Well you're wrong. I didn't meet him until the *third* day. And it was dinner, nothing else. So, if you wagered on anything more than an entrée and a glass of wine, you lose."

"Ahhh, the week is still young, and you, my dear, are putty in the hands of a cute guy with a compliment." Tommy's phone beeped and Megan heard him swear under his breath. "Just when things are getting good. I'm on call, and Nurse Ratched just texted me. I'll ring you back later. Be prepared to give details. And not that coy bullshit you usually pass off as gossip, either. I'm gonna want juicy tidbits about my slutty sister's first trip to Europe."

Chapter Five

That night, Cosimo arrived at Megan's hotel on rue Saint-Séverin in the Latin Quarter at eight o'clock sharp. He waited in the lobby in an overstuffed chair that had dull patches on the velvet upholstery. He rubbed his hands back and forth against the worn fabric in nervous anticipation.

The nervousness perplexed him, because it wasn't a condition he was familiar with, especially when it came to women. Except when it came to Maria-Carmella, and with her, there was good reason. When Megan stepped out of the elevator, he almost didn't recognize her. Her hair was longer and fuller. The day before it had been pulled back and pinned up. Now it framed her face and accentuated her bright-blue eyes and her high cheekbones.

As she approached him, she offered up a small wave. He kissed her on the cheeks and told her that she looked beautiful and that she radiated a certain glow.

"Radiant? Me? Really?"

"*Si, si.*"

Megan shifted her body toward the full-length mirror near the front desk. She tilted her head as she evaluated her reflection. She was different from most of the women she knew in that she was content with her looks and her body, comfortable in her own skin, and not overly concerned about her outward appearance. She wondered why someone as handsome and as cosmopolitan as Cosimo would say that she was radiant when, in reality, she simply looked nice. Cosimo's hand cupped her chin and steered her gaze from the mirror back to his face.

"It is not how you see yourself, it is how others see you."

She took a couple of steps to back away from him. She looked perplexed and slightly uncomfortable. Realizing that he had unwittingly wandered into a perilous situation, he said, "The light within us is only visible to others, not to ourselves. To me, you are radiant. But then you don't know me well enough to know my intentions, to know if my compliment is genuine or if there's an ulterior motive."

The word *gigolo* rushed to the forefront of her thoughts. If it was money he was after, she had nothing to worry about. If it was sex, well…

"*Is* it a come-on?" she asked.

"This is dangerous territory," he said.

"How so?"

"If you do not accept my compliment, then you question my honesty, and you insult me. And if the reason you doubt my sincerity is because you deem yourself unworthy, then you insult yourself. Either way, dangerous territory."

"Hmmm. I see what you mean."

"There is only one remedy for this. You must go," he said, pointing to the elevator. "We must start the evening over. I will go outside, and you will go back to your room. We shall meet back here in five minutes."

When Megan emerged from the elevator for the second time that night, Cosimo reacted as if he were seeing her for the first time. She smiled as she made her way across the lobby to where he stood, jauntily leaning against a marble column. He took her hand and a small step backwards.

"You look nice," he said. "*Very* nice."

"No, I do not look nice," she said, freeing her hand and moving in the direction of the revolving doors. "I look *radiant.*"

"I stand corrected," he said, smiling and sprinting to catch up with her.

⸎

As they walked from the Left Bank to the Right, they talked about current events. They discussed politics, art, religion, and the effect of the internet on modern-day life. They did not, however, tell each other about their families or their distant pasts, their successes or their failures, their disappointments or their regrets. They unconsciously knew that to do so would break the spell that they were under. It would shine a light on the fact that the evening ahead, so full of promise, was no ordinary night out for the two of them, because their days together were numbered. Soon, she would be going back to America, and he would be leaving for parts unknown; their lives about to return to their previously scheduled programs.

Having arrived early for their reservation, they resumed their conversation while strolling along the waterfront and watching the bateaux-mouches float by, their bright lights illuminating the grand façades of the limestone buildings that lined the quai. Cosimo could tell that Megan relished the opportunity to peek into those highlighted apartments with their high ceilings, their crystal chandeliers, their tall bookcases, and their air of lives well lived. She told him that she pictured herself living there one day, shopping for bread at the corner patisserie, selecting gladiolas and tiger lilies at the crack of dawn from the local flower-mart, and arguing over cuts of beef at a charcuterie on rue de Buci. They circled past the café where they'd first met and then doubled back down the street that divides the Île Saint-Louis in half, arriving once again at the restaurant.

During dinner, the topic of conversation changed frequently, from the ambiance of the restaurant, to the flavor of the food, to the opera music playing a little too loudly. And somehow, Cosimo always managed to circle back to his favorite topic of the evening, Megan Walker. She couldn't remember the last time she'd been on a date with a man who didn't ultimately (and predictably) try to keep the conversation focused on his job, or on sports, or, occasionally, on his job *in* sports. But Cosimo never once brought up baseball or football, or how hard he worked, or how important he was to the success of whatever business he was in. He was more interested in finding out about her than he was in regaling her with tales of his latest conquests, real or imagined. And he liked that Megan didn't seek his counsel or approval while choosing an entrée and that she wasn't disappointed with her selection after it had been served. He liked watching her because she reveled in the food itself. She enjoyed every bite and ate every morsel, never once voicing a concern for calories or carbs.

It was eleven o'clock by the time they finished their meal. When they stepped out into the street, they found the promenade dense with people. While they had been dining, rue Saint-Louis en l'Île had been transformed in to an island-wide block party. As they neared Île de la Cité, the crowds grew thicker and drunker, the bands bigger and more boisterous. Megan and Cosimo were absorbed into the mass of people, and with no plans of their own, they allowed themselves to be swept up and carried away by a buoyant group that was drifting slowly toward Pont Louis Philippe. The raucous crowd, all laughing, singing, and drinking, stalled in front of a courtyard to listen to a troupe of musicians perform their own version of *La Vie en Rose*.

For most of the night, Megan vacillated between giddy and reserved, singing out loud in mangled French one minute, then quietly observing the scene the next. But Cosimo sensed an uneasiness about her, so when the crowd moved past an establishment that served alcohol, he gently guided her into the dimly lit room. The safety of the bar served a secondary function as well, for he had just spotted a rather disreputable tabloid photographer indiscriminately snapping shots and heading their way. The last thing he needed was to be photographed with a mysterious woman on his arm. Again. He was enjoying the evening, in part, because of his anonymity, and he wanted to keep it that way for as long as possible.

He slid over a barstool for her to sit on and ordered two French 75s. When the cocktails arrived, Megan took a tiny sip. She found the taste pleasant and the carbonation refreshing. She took another sip, and another, until her sips bordered on slurps. Cosimo ordered another round.

Halfway through the second cocktail, Megan tugged on his lapel and drew him closer so that she could whisper in his ear.

"You know, I *was* a little tense earlier," she confessed. "This was a good idea."

"A little Cognac and champagne always helps me to relax."

"Well, this shertainly did the trick," she slurred. "What's going on out there?" Megan waved to the revelers as they passed, the roar of their merriment only moderately diffused by the thickness of the plate glass window.

"All the people?" he said, waving and smiling along with her. "It is the celebration of the solstice of the summer."

"Oh," she said, still not knowing why the French celebrated the longest day of the year in such a grand manner, but pretending his response had answered her question.

By the time they had finished their drinks and rejoined the party, Cosimo was even more smitten with this American woman, who, slightly intoxicated, conversed openly and readily with strangers, drank when libations were offered, and sang along with a band of teenagers who had gathered together in a semicircle in front of the Hotel de Ville to hear a three-piece band clumsily bang out their rendition of *Je ne regrette rien*. When the song was over, Megan seemed to deflate slightly. Suddenly tired and a little drunk, she fought to keep her head up. With her inhibitions loosened and her defenses down, she wrapped an arm around Cosimo's waist and rested her head on his mohaired shoulder.

"What a perfect way to end a day," she said, "singing about having no regrets…with a bunch of Parisians…in Parisia."

When she tried to lift her head, she wobbled a bit. He took her arm to steady her.

"In Parisia?" she giggled. "I meant, in Parish."

The clock on a nearby church tower struck twelve while, at the same time, the Eiffel Tower lit itself up like a Vegas showgirl, filling the night sky with flickering beams of golden light as its deceptively durable structure stood shimmering in the distance.

"It's so sparkly," she said, her hands moving to his face and cupping his jaw in her palms. She was close enough to kiss him. And she did. Cosimo let himself be kissed, but he resisted the temptation to kiss her back. He knew that she was swept up in the moment, a woman on vacation, a little more adventurous and a little more inebriated than she would ordinarily be at home. He wanted more than anything to kiss her back. To keep kissing her. He had thought of little else all day. But he needed her to want him, and he wasn't confident that she would. She had thrown him off his game to the point that it no longer seemed like a game. He wasn't trying to be seductive, or mysterious, or unavailable, or any of the things that he thought were appealing to the women he dated. In fact, for the first time in years, he wasn't *trying* to be anyone or anything but himself.

The sheer unpredictability of the situation made him practically euphoric. Who was this creature with the power to make a prince's knees quiver with anticipation? What was it about her that made him want to linger, to talk, to listen to her babble uncomfortably, or sing out of key, to be happy simply to be in her presence without the need or the expectation of anything more? He knew what an intricate dance it was with women—that first kiss, that first act of lovemaking. He was not about to make a misstep where she was concerned.

They sauntered back to her hotel through city streets that were nearly back to normal—the bands dismantled, the noise dissipated, the crowds dwindled down to a few couples and the occasional ménage à trois. She was a combination of calm, tired, and inebriated. Cosimo stood with his back against the hotel's façade and pulled her close. She was layered on top of him, chest-to-chest, nose-to-nose. He tilted his head and moved his mouth towards hers, almost imperceptibly. When their lips touched, it felt like warm water running through his body. It felt like floating, like flying. He had to concentrate on something else or he could lose control of his passion, allow his libido carte blanche. The kiss had to be tender, not passionate; intimate, but not sexual. Their tongues gently, briefly comingled. And then he pulled away from her and placed his hands upon her face.

"I would like to see you again," he said.

She inhaled deeply and exhaled slowly, hesitating because she was afraid of what might happen next. Or what might *not* happen. If she were in America, she'd know what to do. But the rules in France were different, the boundaries blurred, the roles not so rigidly defined, the subtext too subtle. She had forgotten how complex the game was, how emotionally wrenching it could be. If you went too far, or if you didn't go far enough, you lost everything. It was then, while she was peering into the depths of Cosimo's bluish-green eyes, wondering how she would answer his question, that she heard the voice of Lauren. Actually, what she heard was Lauren's lame impersonation of Ruth Gordon, her face scrunched up, her finger waving in the air to press home her point, saying, "If you don't get out there and play the game, ya got nuthin' to talk about in the locker room." So Megan decided to roll the dice.

"Do you want to come up?"

Cosimo moved his hands to the back of her neck and pulled her toward him. He kissed her again, this time more passionately, more provocatively. After their lips parted, neither of them said anything for what seemed like an eternity.

"I think you may have had a little too much to drink," he said. "Your judgment…*peut-être*…is not so good." He placed his chilled hands in his coat pockets and rattled his keys. "I should go."

Megan stifled her first response, which would have been a slap followed by, "Yes, I think you *should* go." Instead, she calmly backed away from him and turned her attention to the hotel's entrance. She was about to press the night button and alert the desk clerk when Cosimo turned her toward him.

"I see you *domani?*" he said in a way that was both promising and pleading.

"I don't know whether to be insulted or impressed," she said, backing away.

"*Je ne comprends pas.*"

"*Ça ne fait rien!*" she said. "You're right." She extended a hand to him. "Well, good night. I mean…goodbye."

He took her hand and, instead of shaking it, kissed it.

"You are tired, and you drank a lot of wine. You need a good night's sleep." He took and held both of her hands. "I will see you tomorrow."

"You know, I'm not in the habit of—"

"You don't have to say anything. Your aura, see, I told you
I can read them…it glows with a bright light. It shimmers
like the Eiffel Tower. You are beautiful inside and out, and
I hope that I am fortunate enough to see you again."

As a clock tower on the corner struck two, they awkwardly embraced, neither of them sure if they had played
their cards right. They lingered there a while longer under
the frosted glass canopy of a hotel in the 5th arrondissement,
neither wanting the moment to end. When they could no
longer postpone the inevitable, they shared one last, tender
kiss beneath the diffused glow and the knowing smile of a
waning crescent moon.

Megan turned on the TV as soon as she entered her
hotel room. She needed to see something, to hear something,
anything at all to take her mind off what just happened. Or
hadn't happened. But CNN's continual loop on rising gas
prices and declining property values did little to help her
forget that she was a woman alone in a foreign country
who had just invited a complete stranger up to her room.
And worse than that, he'd declined her offer. Still, there had
been that kiss.

She changed the channel to Canal+ and strained to
understand the dialogue of a French hospital drama. While
getting ready for bed, she decided to leave the TV on, an
experiment to see if her French would improve overnight
by hearing the language spoken subliminally. But sleep she
couldn't, and at three o'clock in the morning, she called her
brother in Boston. When he didn't answer, she called her

best friend, Lauren. Lauren's boyfriend, Robert, answered the phone.

"So, a few days in Paris and you're already homesick?" he said. "Or are you calling to say you're never coming back?"

"Both. I'm homesick, and I'm not coming back."

"You're kidding, right?" Robert seemed genuinely concerned as he called out Lauren's name. "She'll be right here. She's probably doing laundry." He called out Lauren's name again. "You're not really going to stay there are you? What about your job? What about your—"

"Robert," she said, "slow down. I was only kidding."

"Oh, good, because Lauren will—"

"Yes, Lauren will strangle you if you don't come home," Lauren said, taking the phone from Robert. "She'll hop on the next plane and fly all night for the sheer pleasure of hunting you down and skinning you alive."

Megan picked up the remote control to lower the volume on the TV; only she pressed the wrong button, and now the actors were screaming at each other in French.

"Hold on," she said. She walked over to the TV and manually lowered the volume. "That's better. Now, what was that about strangling someone?"

"You have to come back, because…" Lauren took a dramatic pause before finally saying, "because I want you to be my maid of honor."

"Your what?"

"You heard me. Maid…of…honor."

"Robert proposed? Really? You've known him, what…six months?"

"Now wait a minute. You're the last person I would

expect to get all nineteen-fifties suburban housewifey on me. Whatever happened to congratulations?"

"Yes, of course. Congratulations. I'm surprised, that's all. I didn't know the two of you were that serious."

"I didn't, either, until I saw the size of the rock he gave me. Are you having…ouch…stop it, Robert. I was just kidding."

Megan could hear them gently slapping each other in the background.

"He's so gullible," Lauren said. "Are you having fun? Have you met anyone?"

"Yes," Megan said. "And that's all I'm going to say on the subject."

"Hey, no fair. I give you the scoop of the year, and all you have to say is no comment?"

"I'll call you in a couple of days. Tell Robert I said congrats."

"But—" Lauren said.

"I know. I shouldn't have called. I guess I just needed to hear a familiar voice. I'll call you back in a few days."

Megan abandoned her experiment of learning a foreign language while sleeping and turned off the TV. With the room suddenly quiet and the lights off, she fell asleep instantly.

When Cosimo returned to his flat, Jeremy and Reeva, two friends from his days at a Swiss boarding school, were in the living room, transforming his foldout sofa into a queen-size bed.

"Some things never change," Jeremy said. "No matter

how late we stay out partying, good ol' Coz will always walk in the door after us."

"Yeah, but while we're out partying, he's out moping," Reeva said. "Likely taking long walks by himself along the river, I imagine. Isn't that right, Sweetie?"

"You're both right," Cosimo said. "It all depends on the day, the moon, and how many drugs I've taken. Or not."

"And how much alcohol you've added to the mix," Jeremy said.

"You know me all too well, brother."

Cosimo walked over to one of the gilded antique bois-serie panels positioned between two tall windows and lightly pressed a finger against one of its edges. The panel eased open to reveal a wet bar stocked with a variety of glassware, beverages, and mixes.

"I neglected to tell you about this before I left this after-noon," he said. "Please, help yourselves."

He pressed the side of an adjoining panel, and when that one popped open, it revealed a shallow linen closet. He removed two fresh pillowcases and a couple of towels and handed them to Reeva.

"I just adore this place," she said. "The limestone walls, the high ceilings, the herringbone floor, the marble fireplace with the gilded mirror over it. It's lovely!"

"You don't think it's too much?" Cosimo asked.

"The antiques mixed with a few modern pieces. The stark white walls and the ebony floors. It's minimalist and overdone at the same time," she said as she stuffed a goose-down pillow into one of the cases. "It's so you!"

"That's me, cliché and novel, groundbreaking and traditional," he said, realizing as he said it that he was ready for something new, some*place* new.

"You *are* coming with us tomorrow, aren't you?" Jeremy said. "We've hardly seen you at all this trip."

"We're driving out to Giverny," Reeva added as she struggled to put a fitted sheet onto the mattress. "We went to Musée Marmottan today, and now I just *have* to see those gardens again. Do you ever get that way? Something crosses your radar and you can't think of anything else?"

"Me? Never."

Reeva looked baffled until she saw Jeremy shaking his head.

"You had me there," she said. "For a second I thought you were serious."

"Truly," Jeremy said, "if anyone is distractible, it's him."

"I have no idea what you two are talking about," Cosimo said. He grabbed an edge of the sheet that Reeva was wrestling with and secured it to a corner of the bed. "Sorry, I won't be able to join you in Giverny. I'm afraid that I'm currently preoccupied with another shiny object that's got my full attention. And this one, I'm convinced, is worth holding onto."

Chapter Six

The next morning, Paris was what weathermen call partly cloudy. As was Megan Walker. The digital clock on the nightstand informed her that it was 9:45 a.m. The unlit light on the phone sitting next to it implied that there were no messages waiting for her. Even though she barely knew Cosimo, she thought she knew him well enough to concede that if he hadn't called by then, he wasn't going to. A few Tylenol, a pert CNN newscaster, and a hot shower helped keep her from rehashing the events of the previous two days. But then, looming ahead of her was the tedious, unavoidable task of second-guessing her every move. On the heels of that would come self-flagellation for ignoring her instincts that tried to warn her that even the concept of Cosimo was too good to be true.

She randomly opened her guidebook to the section on Montmartre. There was only one thing of interest to her there on the pages that morning: the basilica of Sacré-Coeur. She knew that she would need a far greater diver-

sion than she'd get from a few stained-glass windows and
the images of Christ with his twelve apostles rendered in
mosaic tiles. Photographs on another page, of green grass
and bronze statues, of Edith Piaf and Gertrude Stein, persuaded her that a walk through Cimetière du Père Lachaise
was more in keeping with her current emotional state. She
put a pair of sunglasses and a collapsible umbrella into her
purse because the weather, like her mood, seemed unpredictable.

She had no patience for the terminally slow elevator
that morning, so she took the stairs. The winding staircase
led to a lobby that was frequently crowded with Germans
and Americans trying to check in, check out, or exchange
currency. But that morning, instead of a roomful of tourists,
the foyer was empty and quiet—deserted but for a solitary
figure, sitting on a sofa, his feet propped up on an ottoman,
his eyes tightly shut.

She stopped by the front desk on her way out to check
for messages. In response to her question, a disinterested
clerk silently extended his chin, pointing it in the direction of an alcove by the gift shop. There sat a disheveled,
unshaven, but well-dressed Cosimo, his arms folded across
his chest, his ankles positioned one on top of the other, and
an empty espresso cup balanced on his lap. He looked like
a tired young man. He looked like a sleepy little boy. He
looked like the rest of her stay in Paris.

"How long have you been sitting here?" she asked,
pushing his feet aside and sitting on the ottoman. He
grabbed hold of the coffee cup before it fell.

"Since eight." His hands grasped the china cup and
saucer to quiet the clatter.

"Why didn't you...never mind."

"Where are you going?" he asked.

"The cemetery."

"Sounds serious."

She gave his leg a light smack with her purse.

"Going to pay homage to Gertrude Stein?" he asked.

"And Alice B. Toklas, Oscar Wilde, and Jim Morrison. How did you know?"

"Lucky guess." He leaned forward. "Kiss me."

"What?"

"*Kiss* me."

"Here?"

"Kiss me."

And in that one kiss, forty-eight hours after they had first met, the remainder of Megan Walker's first trip to Paris was decided.

∽

That afternoon Megan did the unthinkable. At great expense, and with a surprising lack of trepidation, she called the airline and extended her trip for another week. Since Jeremy and Reeva had moved on to the next leg of their journey, and since Megan had a few more days to get to know Cosimo intimately, it made sense for her to stay with him in his small, sparsely furnished flat in the Marais. The apartment, which he had been subletting for a few months, had been completely renovated with all the modern conveniences and the finest finishes to an exacting standard, with the intention that it look as if it had never been touched at all. To Megan it was old, rustic, funky, but with a fresh coat of paint. It was tiny and cramped if you compared it to American apartments. But since she had no other Parisian flat to compare it to, she had no way of knowing his one-bedroom pied-à-terre was actually quite grand by Parisian standards.

They spent much of their time together in the area surrounding Cosimo's flat. They enjoyed an afternoon in the Musée National Picasso with Megan providing a running commentary. She'd been excited about seeing La Chèvre in person, and she shared a story about the various materials Picasso had used in its creation and the reactions of the critics to the mixed-media sculpture when it was first presented. Teaching was just one of those things she couldn't resist doing.

They had dinner two nights in a row at a place called Camille, where they sat outside and conversed over the noise of rattling cars and pedestrian chatter. She ordered steak frites both nights. The following evening they dined at Au Gamin, where Cosimo coaxed her into ordering a different entrée. She admitted that the *margret de canard* was the best she'd ever had. Especially since it was the *only margret de canard* she'd ever had.

Megan dragged Cosimo to Les Deux Magots against his wishes. He conceded to the venue but insisted that they sit inside. She accepted his terms, but with a few conditions of her own. He had to pretend that he was Jean-Paul Sartre, and she, with her journal in one hand and a fountain pen in the other, Simone de Beauvoir. Once seated, she pulled her hair up into a bun. Her demeanor and countenance instantly mutated into something more serious and determined. Her eyes scanned the other patrons as she puffed away on a pretend cigarette.

"And people say I'm crazy," Cosimo said, immediately abandoning the charade.

When Simone began to wave enthusiastically to a woman across the room while whispering to Cosimo, "Look, Jean-Paul, there's Zelda," he took away her glass and shook a finger at her.

"No more wine for you," he said.

When Simone frowned, he handed the glass back to her. When she asked him for a refill, he acquiesced.

"Zelda, she was the crazy one, yes?" he said.

"I guess you could say that," Simone said and then whispered, "All of the great ones are."

"I have read some of her letters to Scott. She was a good writer."

"She was an amazing writer." Simone stared dreamily across the café; then, with a sigh, she added, "She didn't live long, but she lived well."

"That reminds me of one of my uncle's favorite sayings," Cosimo said. "He claimed it was Winston Churchill who said it first. ''Tis better to live one day as a lion than a lifetime as a lamb.' Or something to that effect."

"I like that," she said. "But it's easier said than done."

"*C'est vrai*," he said. "*C'est vrai*."

While Cosimo was more than happy to accompany Megan to a few of the predictable and highly trafficked tourist spots, he insisted that they also patronize establishments where the stock in trade was coffee and pastries, not T-shirts, baseball caps, and miniature brass replicas of the Eiffel Tower.

And it was in one of those places, on a cloudy day, on a side street in the Latin Quarter, a week after they met, that

they had their first argument. It was about nothing. It was
about everything. And it was simply time for them to have
some friction. Twenty minutes later, neither of them would
remember what the heated discussion had been about.
Cosimo did what he did best in those situations: he sulked.
He grew silent and sullen. He became annoyingly agreeable.
"Fine!" "Whatever you want." "If that will make you happy."
And Megan did what she did best: she waited it out. It was
she who finally broke the silence when she noticed a tall,
blond woman gracefully striding toward them.

"That woman," she said, nudging Cosimo, "is stunning.
She also looks familiar."

"That is not just any woman," he said. "That is Catherine Deneuve."

Megan furrowed her brow, concentrated her gaze, and
tried to process that possibility. No, it couldn't be. But the
closer the woman got, the more she had to concede that
Cosimo was right.

"It is her," she said, picking up her cell phone. "Would it
be tacky if I took a picture?"

"Do you even have to ask?"

She shook her head and placed the phone on the table.
Catherine broke into a smile as she approached. Cosimo
stood, they exchanged kisses, and then they rapidly conversed in French. Megan remained seated, unable to take
her eyes off the statuesque actress. After a few minutes,
Cosimo responded to one of her questions in English.

"She's fine, she's fine. I'll give her your best." Then he
introduced Megan, apologizing for not having done so
earlier. The three of them chatted briefly. Then there was

one more round of kisses before Catherine continued on her way.

"She seems nice," Megan said. "I've never been that close to a celebrity before." She watched her as she walked away and then turned around to face Cosimo again, her eyes still wide in amazement. "She's more than a celebrity, you know. She's an icon."

"To me she is just Catherine."

"I can see that. How do you know her?"

"Paris is a small town. Everyone knows Catherine, and Catherine knows everyone. It is like that. Nothing so special."

"You know, when you introduced us, she spoke to me in English. Why does everyone here automatically assume I speak English and not French?"

"It is most likely your fashion sense."

"Excuse me?"

"Your clothes," he said.

"I know what you meant. I think you just insulted me."

"*Mais non*. The American clothes are different. The colors, the style, the…"

"Not as good?"

"No, I never said that. Not good or bad, just different." He put his hand up to his face to force a grin, indicating to her that she should smile. She did. "Do you think I would be seen with someone who wasn't chic? You, I have no doubt, would look magnificent no matter what you wore." He picked up a paper napkin and held it up as an example, then he took some Euros out of his pocket and placed them in the glass on the table with the tab.

"You weaseled your way out of that one pretty easily," she said.

"What can I say?" he said, shrugging his shoulders. "It's a gift."

Chapter Seven

The remainder of Megan and Cosimo's time together in Paris flew by like some sickly sweet, overproduced romantic comedy montage, with images of couples walking hand in hand along moonlit quays, cozy dinners for two in candlelit restaurants, and lots of long, interesting conversations about nothing of any substance. Truth is, Megan and Cosimo weren't exactly like that, but they came pretty close. Both were smitten, but cautiously so. Each was living in the moment, their past of no consequence, their future entrusted to providence. And both of them were delighted to be in the company of someone who made them forget who they were, who saw them as the person they wanted to be.

Megan's last morning in Paris was a blur of packing and repacking; of checking and double-checking confirmation numbers, seat assignments, that her passport was in her purse; retracing their steps to try and recall where they'd last parked the car; a final café crème at a corner patisserie; and a parting view of the Eiffel Tower as they sped out of town. There were long, tender kisses that conveyed detailed messages mere words could have only hinted at. There was a Porsche 911 flying through the streets of Paris, nimbly operated and pushed to its limits by an overly caffeinated Cosimo attempting to get to the gate on time. And there was the sprawling, cavernous, concrete airline terminal that served as the backdrop for their final farewell.

Cosimo rarely used his influence to receive special treatment, but in this instance, he pulled a few strings so that he could be with Megan right up until she boarded. It was there, among the people movers, ganged seating, industrial carpeting, and overpriced junk food, that they had to say their goodbyes. Huddled together in the busy terminal, they shared an awkward silence. Up until then there had been no promises and no expectations. No plans to meet again. No urging of the other to call regularly. For the previous week they had lived a rarefied existence; two people headed nowhere in particular, both free of confines and conflicts, both ready for new experiences; two people traversing disparate paths that somehow cosmically intersected at a little bistro on the Île Saint-Louis.

He asked her to stand back a few feet so that he could take a photo of her.

"I don't think so," she said. "I hate having my picture taken. Besides, the last thing I want is for you to have a memento of me with my eyes all puffy from lack of sleep and sad goodbyes."

"But why?" he said. "You look lovely all dressed up in your new Parisian outfit."

Megan, not one used to compliments, blushed and turned away while acting satirically coquettish.

"I do feel kind of glamorous, thanks in part to a rather sexy Italian with a good eye for fashion who helped me pick it out," she said. "In fact, I feel a bit like Camille Beauchamp standing here at Charles de Gaulle airport with my passport in hand, a new smartly tailored outfit, and a handsome young man with a foreign accent bidding me goodbye."

"This Camille, she is a friend of yours? You have not mentioned her before."

"No, no," she said, laughing. When she realized she may have hurt his feelings, she touched his arm and said, "I'm not laughing at *you*. It struck me as funny, that's all. I'm used to hanging out with the same group of friends who automatically get my references."

"So you are *not* a friend of this Camille?" he asked, still not sure what the joke was.

"No, Cosimo," she said, laughing even harder. "Camille is not a real person. She's a character in the movie, *Now Voyager*. Bette Davis plays an ugly duckling who is sent away to a sanatorium and ends up on this cruise ship where she meets a handsome stranger."

"This plot. It sounds vaguely familiar to me," he said, smiling.

"Don't be smug; it doesn't suit you. Anyway, she falls in love with a man whom she can never have because he's already married." She inched closer to him, grasped his medallion between her thumb and forefinger, and rubbed it the way she had seen him do so often that past week. "The movie ends with my favorite line ever. It's late at night, and she's standing in front of a window with the man she loves but can never have. She knows he's heartbroken because he can't give her more, so to convince him she's content with what she has, she says, 'Let's not ask for the moon. We have the stars.'" Megan took a deep breath and held it because she could sense she was about to tear up. "Is that not the most beautiful thing you've ever heard?"

"Perhaps not the *most* beautiful, but yes, it's a nice philosophy, a practical approach to life."

Megan was not surprised that Cosimo did not find the sentiment as meaningful as she did. For one thing, he was a man. And for another, it was bound to lose something in the translation.

"I'm afraid I'm not a very good actress," she said. "I didn't do it justice. But my favorite scene is when she returns home to Boston and astonishes her friends and family because they see that she's been transformed from an unattractive spinster into a beautiful young woman. Kind of like how I feel now."

"I don't understand," he said. "Why do you think you are like this character? You were beautiful when I met you."

She looked away from him, stared down at her feet, and shook her head. She wanted to believe him, but she also hated that it mattered, disliked the idea that someone else had the ability to make her feel good. Or bad. Cosimo could tell that she was uncomfortable being put on a pedestal, but he wasn't sure why. Every other woman he'd ever known had always demanded that she be placed on one. But before either of them had the chance to process their emotions, the airline began announcing the departure of Megan's flight.

She walked over to the seating area and retrieved her carry-on bag.

"I'm afraid you've spoiled me," she said. "When I get home, there won't be anyone who would even think of saying such nice things to me, much less say them."

"That will be *my* job, *si?* I will call you every day and remind you how beautiful you are."

"Stop!" she said. "Be serious." She watched her fellow travelers queueing up to board. "My friend Lauren always calls things bittersweet. I never really knew what she meant by that until now, standing here, having to say goodbye to you."

"But unlike the characters in your movie, there is nothing keeping us apart. In our case, the bitter is only temporary."

"You seem to have forgotten about a little thing called the Atlantic Ocean."

"A minor detail. I will come see you in Boston. And then we can stand together in front of a window, like Camille and her friend, and write our own ending."

Then, while being jostled by too many passengers with too much luggage, they shared one last embrace as an airline representative's amplified voice reminded them that flight 422 was now boarding at gate 53.

Chapter Eight

As the Porsche sailed around the treacherous curves of the Amalfi coast, Cosimo smiled when he saw the stretch of aquamarine ocean because it reminded him of the eyes of the blond American woman he'd said *adieu* to only yesterday. He shifted the car down to third gear to maneuver around a particularly dangerous bend in the road. Normally he was not so conscious at the wheel, or so cautious. But it was less than a year ago that he'd totaled a brand-new Alfa-Romeo taking that very same hairpin turn. And were it not for the fact that he hadn't been wearing a seatbelt and been ejected from the vehicle into one of the few shrubs that dotted the rocky hillside, he would have been totaled, too. At the time, the risk of pushing a sports car to its limit had been its own reward. And back then, the thought of plunging down a jagged cliff into the cold, deep water of the Mediterranean seemed like an acceptable way to go. In fact, it seemed like the answer to a good many things. But that was before he knew of her existence, or before she knew of his. And even though he hadn't been in the market for a serious relationship, since he'd found one, he intended to do everything within his power to keep it.

A long family history of mental illness had designated Cosimo the unfortunate beneficiary of depression, bipolar disorder, attention deficit hyperactivity disorder, and a recently diagnosed case of mild schizophrenia. Because of those, his life consisted of accommodations and trade-offs, of having to examine every situation, every opportunity, every decision, and to try to find the path of least resistance.

Burdened with erratic episodes of psychosis, his life could be difficult, and decision-making the equivalent of a roll of the dice. There was always a psychiatrist with a prescription pad at the ready, eager to dole out an assortment of medications to try to thwart whatever his symptoms happened to be. And there were so many symptoms and so many pills that he'd come to think of the process as a game of one-armed bandit, but instead of the ubiquitous fruits and numbers popping up when he pulls down a lever, he is confronted with a colorful display of capsules, tablets, and the occasional syringe. Those doctors, with their fancy offices, their fifty-minute hours, and their walls crammed with ancient medical books, all told him some version of "Trial and error is the best, if not the only, approach to battling psychosis." Cosimo's arsenal of medications, which he took on a regular basis, included, but was not limited to, antidepressants, antipsychotics, antianxiety medicines, and mood stabilizers. He'd become so dependent on them that he hid emergency caches in so many different places that he often forgot where those hiding places were.

And because the road he was on would eventually deliver him to the family estate, to Villa Vita Fortunata, to the matriarch, to the mother, to Princess Maria-Carmella Stefani Garibaldi di Sorrento, the thought of skidding off the road and coming to a fiery or watery end still held some appeal. But the destruction of another high-priced, high-performance vehicle could only hamper any negotiations he would have with her. It was a toss-up as to which would be more painful: driving his car off a cliff and plummeting to a near-certain death or confronting Maria-Carmella with his plan to move to America to pursue a relationship with a commoner. He couldn't even begin to fathom her reaction to the news that the woman he would be wooing was neither Catholic, nor wealthy, nor royal. He tried to erase the picture of Maria-Carmella from his mind by replacing it with memories of a few days spent in Paris with the American woman he had too quickly, uncharacteristically, and possibly fatally come to love.

It began the instant he spotted her sitting under the red canopy of La Brasserie de l'Île Saint-Louis. At first he'd simply forgotten to take his afternoon appetizer of lithium and Wellbutrin. And later, as long as she was around, he didn't want to be perceived as the kind of person who had to pop pills in order to function like a normal human being. Neither did he want her to see him swallow, to see him *have* to swallow, a handful of brightly colored capsules and chalky oblong tablets several times a day. Nor did he want to have to sneak off to a lavatory to do it in private, like they were an illicit, dangerous drug and he, a pathetic, barely functioning addict. Unfortunately, those rather innocent and naïve justifications for skipping his meds led to the more conscious acts of rationalizing his behavior and to bargaining with himself, and with whatever gods were listening, about when, or even *if*, he would resume taking them.

Between Cosimo and his demons, there was a constant battle for control. And no matter how valiantly he fought it, he knew the chance existed that he might never win, that he might never be cured. It was of little comfort to him that the pills actually did, occasionally, alleviate some of the symptoms, ameliorate a modicum of pain. But depression, mania, anxiety, and a multitude of voices were as much a part of who he was as was his noble birth.

Even then, in his twenty-fourth year, Cosimo trembled at the sight of the family estate that had the power to transform him into a six-year-old boy, desperate to run away from that place, from that palace, from that prison, down to the peaceful, unstructured, uncompromising world of Uncle Giuseppe's vegetable garden. As the gates swung open, the Porsche, idling in neutral, purred. Then it roared aggressively as Cosimo floored it, testing the manufacturer's claim of zero to sixty in four-point-three seconds. The road leading up to the mansion was a half mile long and paved with a thick layer of crushed granite and salmon-hued pebbles. The spinning tires of the car sent the small rocks flying, transforming the beige granite surface into a cloud of pink dust.

He knew he should have called first, that he should have confirmed their meeting before driving all that way, but he didn't want to alert her as to the exact time of his arrival. His mother had her own cornucopia of issues to deal with, which caused her persona to alternate between accommodating and accusatory, between pleasant and petulant, between indifferent and defiant. A nervous breakdown a number of years ago, after the passing of her brother Giuseppe, guaranteed that any future confrontation with her might be a loaded one.

As the sports car approached the front entrance, he imagined himself in a game of Russian roulette with Maria-Carmella. After pulling the trigger on the shiny silver revolver, she spins the chamber; then, grinning, hands the weapon over to him. "Your turn," she says. He takes the brightly polished gun in his hand, admires the bizarre beauty in something so utilitarian and dangerous, and then, just before he holds it up to his own temple, he closes his eyes and prays. Going back home for him was like that.

Cosimo lived off a trust fund and a black American Express card, each controlled and meticulously monitored by his mother. He could usually persuade her to grant him whatever it was he needed, but never without a struggle, never without a concession or two. He understood that with her brother, his uncle Giuseppe, gone, her children grown and living on their own, her husband no longer in the picture, and a dwindling staff to order around, she needed to seize every opportunity to demonstrate, to remind them, that she was the one still in control.

Though he had not seen her in almost six months, he had done everything that she had requested of him: he had stayed out of trouble, kept his doctors' appointments, and, until recently, regularly taken his medications. She had to know, to acknowledge, that he had been making every possible effort to be responsible, reliable, to live up to the family name. He hoped that, for the first time in his life, she would treat him like an adult, like a human being, like her mature son. She would commend him for his efforts and make available to him the funds necessary for his relocation to Boston. *In some alternate universe,* he thought, for he knew that with Maria-Carmella, nothing ever had been, or ever would be, easy.

The house stood high on a hill, surrounded by olive groves, overlooking a vast, verdant piece of land. From a distance it looked miniature, inconsequential. But as one got closer, with its mammoth limestone and timber façade, its massive arches and the steel gate covering and guarding the front door, and the intricate iron grillwork emblazoned with the Garibaldi family crest protecting the leaded glass windows, it began to resemble a fortress.

He pulled the car up to the front entrance and turned off the ignition. He opened the glove compartment to look for some pills, hoping to find at least a few Valium nestled there among the papers and the parking tickets. But all he found was an expired prescription for Zyprexa and an empty bottle of Advil. He knew that there were several prescription bottles buried in his luggage, but digging them out would take more energy than he could muster.

He walked up the front steps, bewildered that no one had heard the car on the gravel, that no one had come to greet him or take his bags. The moment he entered the house, he was confronted by the massive foyer with its

high ceiling and golden frescos and greeted by the unmistakable aroma of marinara sauce with its secret blend of
herbs and spices that his uncle Giuseppe jokingly claimed
had been stolen from him by the resident chef. It reminded
him of his structured but not altogether unpleasant childhood, when there was always a cook on staff preparing a
stew, grilling up fish, or roasting some pungent game. And
always the essence of garlic, lemon, rosemary, and lavender
lingering in the air. He followed the scent, which took him
through several rooms, the furniture in each covered over
as if the house was about to be closed up and vacated for
an extended period.

While the kitchen had retained most of its original
architectural details, the appliances were new, and a recent
renovation had replaced the dated black-and-white tile
backsplash with more contemporary glass mosaics in warm
browns and cool greens. He passed under an archway, and
as he moved farther into the kitchen, it occurred to him
that his entire flat in Paris could easily fit into one corner of
that room.

He noticed a couple conversing by the walk-in freezer.
For a second he thought he was having another hallucina-
tion because the woman standing there with her back to
him, talking to someone in a chef's hat, looked an awful lot
like his sister, Regina. But as far as he knew, she was still in
New York. He turned away from the cook and the mirage
of his sister to head toward the library, then the conserva-
tory, then the music room, to anywhere Maria-Carmella
was likely to be. When he heard someone calling his name,
he slowed his pace but did not stop. Now, in addition to
hallucinations, he assumed he was hearing voices again.

"Coz! Where are you going?"

He stopped a few feet before the archway and spun around to confront the mysterious voice.

"What are you doing here?" he said to Regina, who now stood a few feet away. "I thought I was seeing things."

"What am *I* doing here? What are *you* doing here?" she asked as she wrapped her arms around him.

"I came to dance with the devil," he said.

"Very funny. Why are you really here?"

"What happened to Manhattan?" he asked.

"Cash flow. I'm finally in a position to launch that clothing line of mine, but I could use another backer or two," she said, leading him outside to a small patio under a wisteria-laden trellis. She sat down on a slatted wooden bench partially covered in moss and patted the spot next to her.

"So, you came to dance with the devil too?" he said, taking a seat.

"Mother's not here. That's why *I* am."

He opened his mouth, but nothing came out. He wasn't sure what to say, what to ask. He experienced a feeling of relief, as if he'd just loosened a tie and a shirt collar that had been too tight. But he knew it was only a temporary reprieve from a confrontation that was inevitable.

"You thought she was here? No, she left for New York yesterday. Something about buying a hotel. Or was it *selling* a hotel?"

"You're kidding, right?" he said. "She summons me home with thinly veiled threats, and then she flies off without a word?"

"I wish I was. The last time she came to the city, she

stayed with me for a month." She placed a hand on Cosimo's head and playfully ruffled his curls. "She's not pushing you to marry Annabella again, is she? Is that why she's looking to raise capital?"

"What else could it be? Why else would she demand a face-to-face?"

"Because she can," she said. She reached behind her and broke off a sprig of rosemary, ground it up in her palm, and let the scent fill the space between them. She brushed her hands together and let the gray-green bristles fall to the ground. "You know the worst part of coming home? It's knowing that Giuseppe will never stop by again with an armful of produce or a bottle of wine pressed from his own grapes." She scratched a thin line in the moss with a fingernail. "This whole place is going to ruin. I can't even bring myself to walk down to the garden. You just know she's let it go to weed."

"Maria-Carmella in New York? She detests Manhattan," Cosimo said.

"Not anymore. Evidently, she's become the darling of the socialite set, if you can fathom that. For some reason she's on *everybody's* list this season." Regina exaggerated the word *everybody* as if the idea that her mother was on anyone's list was unthinkable.

"Good for her. Ever since Father vanished, she's done nothing but work," he said. "But yes, it's hard to imagine her enjoying herself. Enjoying anything." And then, because he was afraid of the answer, he hesitated before asking, "When is she coming back?"

"Who knows? She's appropriated my place as her own personal pied-à-terre. Can you picture the two of us in that tiny five-thousand-square-foot penthouse?" Regina made exaggerated gestures and wild, crazy eyes. "I'm afraid to have a cocktail for fear I'll lose control and toss her over the balcony."

Cosimo chuckled at the thought of the two of them wrestling in their sequined designer gowns, their necks and arms laden with jewelry, their perfectly coiffed and colored hair hardly moving, and each trying to push the other off the patio and down into the stream of speeding traffic that traverses Central Park West.

He tried to convince himself that his mother's desertion changed nothing, that he would stand his ground and demand his independence, regardless of her stalling tactics. All that her early departure had done was delay things indefinitely. But Cosimo's predilection for instant gratification guaranteed that he would never be comfortable with "indefinitely." And he preferred to deal with his mother on his home turf. If the conversation were to take place in a foreign environment, any advantage he might have had would be compromised. She would dominate and confuse him, trick him in to thinking that her suggestions, that her opinions, that her vision of what he should do with his life, were actually his. She would remind him of things he had said, although he had never said them; of pledges he had made, which, in reality, were promises he'd never uttered. And as much as he would like to confide in Regina about his dilemma of having fallen in love with a woman his mother would never approve of, he feared that even she, his confidante and occasional savior, was not immune to Maria-Carmella's influence or threats.

Cosimo leaped to his feet as if he'd been stung by an insect or had a brilliant idea that needed to be immediately implemented.

"I'm going to walk down to the garden before I unpack. I've been sitting in that car for two days, and I need some exercise." He held out a hand to her. "Come with me?"

She shook her head no and then stood and kissed him on the forehead.

"Do you think that's a good idea?" she said. "Maybe it would be better to remember it the way it was."

"I'm sure I can handle it."

"I'll have to pass on this one. But don't say I didn't warn you."

"How about dinner, then?"

"Can't. Not tonight. I've got a big meeting with money people." She rubbed her hands together the same way she had with the rosemary, but this time to indicate the concept of cold, hard cash. "Tomorrow?"

"I'm not sure how long I'll be around," he said. He started to walk in the direction of his uncle Giuseppe's garden, then turned around to say, "I'm going to take a nap after my walk. Wake me when you get back from dinner."

He gave her a childlike wave as he began his journey along the once-beaten path that led to a small garden that sat at the bottom of a hill on the outskirts of the family's villa: to tomato plants, to basil, to green and yellow peppers, and to a youth that was no more. The farther away from the house he got, the more constricted his throat became. He hadn't been down there since his uncle had passed away, and this solitary, meditative walk down to a veritable speck of agrarian land was a pilgrimage to one of the few good things he could recall from his childhood.

As he made his way down the densely overgrown path, he was reminded of one afternoon in particular. He was about six years old and sitting on the perimeter of the small vegetable garden located on a far corner of the estate. It was so far removed from the villa that the three-story house was barely visible from his vantage point on the ground, where he sat among the peppers and the escarole and the fava beans. He wore sandals, seersucker shorts, and a starched, white, short-sleeved shirt. He was filling a small metal pail with soil that he'd dug up with a tiny plastic shovel. Uncle Giuseppe, in a torn and faded undershirt and mud-splattered pants, was on his knees, in the dirt, inspecting the leaves of a few dozen plants.

"Catch," his uncle said as he tossed a yellow heirloom tomato at him.

Cosimo dropped his shovel and reached out with both hands. The plump fruit landed safely in his outstretched palms.

"May I eat it?" he asked.

"Yes, Cosimo. That one I grew especially for you."

Cosimo pulled out a handkerchief and began to wipe the tomato off with such careful attention that he may as well have been polishing a jewel. He held it up to his mouth but didn't take a bite. He merely stared at its dimpled flesh and its green stub of a stem.

"Something wrong?" Giuseppe asked.

"No, Uncle G. Only…what about Mother? What if she finds out that I had something to eat before lunch?"

"You let me deal with her. I can handle your mother."

Giuseppe brushed the dirt from his knees, walked over to Cosimo, sat down, and placed an arm over the boy's shoulder.

"Your mother, you know, she's not as tough as she pretends to be. Growing up, she and I were very close, like you and your sister." Then, as an afterthought, he added, "Sometimes."

"But you're not anything like Mother. She doesn't even like it when I come down here to visit you. And she really hates it when I get dirty."

"Yet she allows you to because you are with me, and she knows you will be safe. See, she is not *so* bad."

"I guess not, Uncle," Cosimo said. He tossed the tomato into the air and caught it in his open palm. "She is much nicer when you're around. I wish you could live with us all the time."

"You know, she is not one to show her emotions, so I can't help but tease her once in a while. I like to tell her how much I love her and how much she means to me. And then I try to hug her," he said, smiling mischievously. "A little thing like that can drive her crazy."

"Why?"

"I don't know exactly, but I do enjoy seeing her get so flustered that she has to walk away." Giuseppe intercepted Cosimo's tomato in mid-air. "Your mother is rarely speechless, so sometimes I do it because she irritates me. That's the quickest way I know of getting her to shut up." He winked and gave the boy a gentle, conspiratorial jab to his ribs.

"Why do you think it is that she never says things like that?"

"So you've noticed. It's not you, son. I doubt that she's ever been able to express such thoughts. Some people are just that way." He took a small bite out of Cosimo's tomato. He wiped away a drop of juice from the corner of his mouth with his forearm and handed it back to his nephew. "But just because she doesn't say it doesn't mean she doesn't love you."

"I know," Cosimo said. He smiled at his uncle, and then he took a big bite out of the tomato's yellow flesh.

"Still," Giuseppe said, "it makes me sad to see her have so much of everything, except that which is most important: the capacity to love and be loved."

"If it makes her crazy when you say those things, why do you do it?"

"Because she needs to hear it. Everyone does."

"*I* don't need to hear it," Cosimo said and then took another bite of the fruit.

Giuseppe laughed and ran a hand through Cosimo's curly hair.

"*You*, my sweet prince," he said, "you need to hear it most of all."

The closer Cosimo got to the diminutive plot, the harder it was for him to keep from crying, and the clearer it became that the situation was much worse than he had expected or could have predicted. The garden was not filled with dead and dying plants as he'd envisioned it would be. It had not been overrun by tall grasses native to the area or ravaged by rabbits and deer. It was simply gone. Obliterated. Vanished. It was as if it had never been. As if a large piece of machinery had been brought down there to dig up the earth, to push things aside, to remove every last trace of the only spot on those many acres where things were once cultivated.

It was a long walk back to the house, but the time passed quickly because the tears that were on the verge of spilling over had morphed into rage. He repeated, over and over, first to himself and then out loud, "She had no right." The more he said it, the angrier he got. He had to find a way to release it. His therapists had told him on more than one occasion that depression is anger directed inwards. But what was he to do with that anger? How was he to let it go? The garden was gone. Uncle Giuseppe was gone. Maria-Carmella was gone, at least temporarily. Megan was gone. Even Regina would be gone, if only for the night. He had no one to vent to and no one to console him. When he arrived back at the house, he was startled to see it still standing there, as if it had snuck up on him while he hadn't been looking.

It was a stately residence, not a house. It was not meant to be lived in; it was meant to impress. Villa Vita Fortunata was not a home and never had been. It was a state of mind. And it was a relic. Cosimo's room was as it always was—pristine. A suite at the Four Seasons would be more comfortable, more inviting. There were no pictures or mementos anywhere in sight: no school trophies on a shelf, no framed diplomas on a wall, no tower of books haphazardly stacked in a corner on the floor. And even if he were to add any of those things, the next day he would find the room just as it was and a chambermaid quietly closing the door behind her.

He started to unpack. The first thing he did was unearth a bottle of Xanax from the neat pile of clothes and swallow two of them without water. He was hopeful that, in addition to calming his nerves, they would also dissipate some of his anger. As he transferred his shirts to the first drawer of the bureau, his hand brushed up against a foreign object. It was a plastic bag taped to the top of the inside of the cabinet. It took him a moment to recognize what kinds of pills he had stashed there inside of a wrinkled Ziploc bag. He had ingested so many pills in his short lifetime that he often popped things into his mouth without ever knowing or caring what they were. Each one was branded with strange letters or numbers, depending on their milligrams or their purpose. Each had a unique color or shape that differentiated it from all the others. But usually, if they weren't in the bottle that they came in, it was anyone's guess as to what they were. These bright beauties, however, he did recall. They were the sweet, reassuring, unmistakable red of Seconal. *This is serendipity,* he thought. He opened the packet into his palm and stared at them as they rolled around in his hand. And even though he was exhausted beyond measure, he knew that he wouldn't, couldn't sleep. He swallowed two of the capsules with a glass of water from the bathroom tap and then walked the few feet back to his bed and sat on the corner of it, the mattress and box spring so thick that his feet dangled a few inches from the floor. He began to scroll through his phone for something to do, unconsciously rereading messages from the past few days, when he came across a text from Jeremy that he had overlooked.

reev & I are back in states.

thx again for place 2 crash.

nyc is where its hapning. Y dont U join us.

BTW ran in 2 MariaC 2nite @ dinner.

Lookd like she had Annas dad in a headlock. LOL

C U soon. J

He tossed the phone onto the bed, not knowing what to make of Jeremy's note. Maybe he was joking. Or maybe Maria-Carmella was finally putting her plan into motion. Either way, there was nothing he could do about it, so he went back to unpacking his clothes. As he was zipping up an empty suitcase, he noticed a gray piece of paper sticking out from under the inside strap. Since the lining was practically the same color, it almost went unnoticed. As he read the letter that Megan had slipped into his satchel the night before they went their separate ways, he became agitated. He should have felt comfortable and safe there in his old room, but he felt anything but. He had finally found someone he could be himself with, someone he could trust not to judge him, betray him, or have unreasonable expectations of him. And there was Maria-Carmella stirring up trouble again, jerking him around, and having a tête-à-tête with the Bollettieris behind his back. The note wasn't a pleasant reminder of the previous week; it was a stark reminder of his mother's ability and proclivity to turn his world upside down.

Cosimo experienced a rush of emotions: anger, resentment, love, fear, loneliness, regret, all of them pouring forth and mixing together like a soup in his nervous system. The thought of Maria-Carmella and Annabella conspiring against him and planning his future made him furious. With no one around to absorb or deflect his rage, he scrunched up the note in the palm of his hand until it was an unrecognizable piece of debris and flung it across the room. Then he swallowed two more Xanax and another Seconal. He needed a period of time when he wasn't required to think or feel, plan or pretend, when he wouldn't career or crumble. If he stayed in his present state of mind, he would endlessly speculate about what might or might not happen in a future that was beyond his control. He was already starting to obsess about the prospect of some of them. With the possibility of sleep still a faint idea in his head, he swallowed a few more Seconal. He couldn't remember how many he had already taken, and quite frankly, at that moment, it didn't matter. Besides, what was one more? Or one more? Or one more?

Regina glanced at her Cartier wristwatch. It was a gift, but she couldn't remember from whom. It could have been the Duke of Something-or-Other, or the Earl of Such-and-Such, or the Sultan of This-or-That. Though she was fortunate that she hadn't inherited the psychosis that had plagued the Garibaldis for generations, she did experience symptoms of ADHD, which she considered, under certain circumstances, to be more of an asset than a liability. The hands on the Roman numerals indicated that it was later than she thought. Even though it was a business dinner, she had decided she'd invite Cosimo to join her after all. It had been months since they'd seen each other, and when he was in the right frame of mind, he could be an engaging and persuasive asset.

She knocked on the door to his room, but there was

no answer. She called his name and knocked again. Still no answer. She turned the doorknob and found it unlocked. The room was dark, the lights off, the paneled windows tightly shut. The home phone, which had been unplugged, rested on the floor in the middle of the room. There were numerous plastic pill bottles, empty or almost, scattered on top of the bureau and around the bed. The monogrammed sheets lay in a crumpled pile on the floor. There was no sign of Cosimo anywhere. She spoke his name several times, calling him, willing him to surface, to come out of hiding. She looked on the balcony, in the bathroom, and in the closet. It wasn't until she saw the mass of sheets on the floor in the middle of the room begin to move that it occurred to her to look under them.

"Cosimo!" she shouted as she tried to untangle her brother from the thick yards of fabric. He gave no response, and he made no effort to assist her. If he was moving, she thought, he must be breathing; so she tugged even harder at the twisted mass of linen. Slowly he was revealed, first leg, then torso, then head. She asked him a series of questions: "How many did you take? When did you take them? Were you drinking alcohol?" Her inquisition was met with silence.

She propped up his limp body, and from behind him, she inserted her arms under his armpits and tried to stand. Cosimo was thin, but he was mostly muscle, and a limp Cosimo was a heavy Cosimo. Too heavy for Regina to lift by herself. She grabbed hold of a corner of the sheet, and with her brother still unconscious, she slowly dragged him across the floor and into the bathroom. She lifted his head and tried to get him to drink some water. He didn't. She turned him over and tried to induce vomiting. She couldn't. She ran cold water and dunked a towel into it, and then gently placed the damp cloth over his face.

She left him lying there with a cold compress on his forehead and returned to the bedroom. She sifted through the few things she found in the bureau, but these failed to provide any clue as to how to handle the situation. She made a few guesses at the four-digit passcode on his cell phone, but after several failed attempts, she abandoned that idea. Somewhere he had to have contact numbers for psychiatrists or physicians or other practitioners who'd treated him for any number of things. She found a doctor's name on one of the plastic bottles, but no phone number, no address, and nothing to indicate what the medication had been prescribed for.

She bent down to pick up the home phone, not knowing whom she was going to call first. It was then that she noticed the miscellaneous items scattered around the room: his little black journal, a plane ticket, and a crumpled piece of paper. She was hoping to find the number of his doctor, but there was nothing in the notebook but a few stray thoughts and some crude sketches.

She dialed her own physician in New York and got his service. There was only one other person she knew she could rely on in a situation like this. And while she could think of a dozen reasons not to make that call, there was one that demanded she must.

If I don't call her and something happens to him, she pondered, even as she dialed the number, *how would I ever forgive myself?* When the voice on the other end offered a gruff greeting, Regina slapped her cheek with her own hand to force herself to be present, to shift her focus from reactive to proactive.

"I'm sorry to bother you, Mother, but it's Cosimo. He's taken some pills. A lot of them, by the looks of it. I'm not positive, but I assume they were sedatives."

Maria-Carmella asked her several questions about his condition: Was he conscious, had she checked his vital signs, did she have any idea as to how many he'd consumed, had any members of the staff seen him in that condition?

Regina had to put the phone down and run to the bathroom to take Cosimo's pulse. It was weak, but it could have been worse.

"Yes, I made sure his breathing passages were clear. I tried to—"

Maria-Carmella cut her off, told her that she had done the right thing by calling her, and that she would call Dr. Wyckoff and have him dispatch the appropriate, discreet personnel to come and assist her.

Regina sat in the middle of the doorway, half of her body splayed out on the bedroom floor, the other half trembling on the cold marble tiles of the bathroom. With one hand she held the crumpled letter written on stationery from a three-star hotel in Paris. With the other, she gripped Cosimo's hand and gave it constant rhythmic squeezes, like little heartbeats, her breath going in and out in sync with each tiny pulse.

Dr. Wyckoff called and explained what would happen next. Very shortly another doctor would be arriving with a medical team in what would look like an ordinary limousine. Cosimo would be carefully and discreetly removed from the villa through a side entrance. He would then be situated in the vehicle, which would be equipped with everything necessary to keep him stable and comfortable while they transported him to a private, full-care facility. The only things left for Regina to do were to wait and to make sure that none of the staff wandered anywhere near the designated exit door.

She laid the crinkled piece of paper out on the floor and pressed it flat to remove the creases that distorted the tidy handwriting it contained. It seemed to her that this note, written with a woman's dainty hand, so deliberately mangled and so cavalierly cast aside, *must* have something to do with Cosimo swallowing an unknown quantity of pills. And while it might contain the answer as to why he did what he did, it clearly wasn't going to be of any use to her in trying to revive him. But with nothing to do but wait and hope, she began to read her brother's private correspondence. It was all she had to go on to try to help him. At least that was how she rationalized that rare breach of privacy. The beautifully transcribed letter covered both sides of the paper. There was something about the penmanship— slanted, feminine, neat—that felt familiar and somehow comforting, like a distant memory or a pleasant dream.

Chapter Nine

The door made a faint whooshing noise as it slowly closed behind her. The anteroom that she found herself in was awash in pastel colors, terry cloth fabrics, and the nearly overpowering aroma of French lavender. The soothing, dulcet tones of Enya that were being piped into the room were a little too much for Megan to endure on top of all that other feminine crap.

"The problem with these places," she said, as she sat down next to Lauren on a towel-draped chaise, "is that they're all the same. They're so cliché. The colors, the music, the smells." She removed a towel that was wrapped around her head and fluffed her hair with her hands. "Just once I'd like to go to a day spa that has bright-orange walls and rock 'n' roll music."

"I agree," Lauren said. "The atmosphere in these places does lack a certain inspiration. But somehow I don't think that listening to the Rolling Stones belt out 'Sympathy for the Devil' would do anything to enhance the massage experience, either."

"Anything would be an improvement over Enya."

"Celine Dion?" Lauren asked.

"Point taken," Megan said, pouring herself a glass of water from a pitcher filled with sliced cucumbers and lemons.

"Thank you for this, but really, you didn't have to," Lauren said.

"I know that. It's my small way of thanking you for picking me up at the airport, for getting my mail, for being such a good friend in general." She pointed to the pitcher, and when Lauren nodded, she poured another glass. "Besides, I thought it would give us a chance to spend some quiet time together to talk about your wedding plans."

"Well, it helps that this is a cell-free zone."

"What's that supposed to mean?"

"It means," Lauren said, "that for the first time in weeks, you won't be distracted by constantly checking to see if your little Paris fling has left you a message."

"Has it been that bad?"

Lauren took a sip of the tepid water and grimaced.

"It needs ice," she said. "And mint." She placed the glass down on a side table. "I've just never seen you like this before, so preoccupied, so concerned about whether or not some guy was going to call you. It's out of character."

"I'm perplexed by it too. It's just that he insisted he'd call. Even after I told him he didn't need to, after I said I knew he wouldn't. Even after I said, 'Look, it's been great fun, but you and I both know this is one of those whirlwind vacation romances that will diminish with as much intensity as it began,' he insisted he'd call. After that he became even more adamant, promising that before too long, he'd fly here to see me."

"Have you tried calling *him?*"

"No. I haven't had the…it was on my…I mean, I thought about it. But…"

"So then, no?"

"The truth is, I don't know what I want. Sure, we had a great time in Paris, but that's part of the problem. He lives in *Paris.*" Megan picked up a plastic bottle and spritzed the scent of eucalyptus into the air. "And even if I were ready for another relationship, which I'm not, it wouldn't be with someone who lives on another continent. And then I've got school starting again…"

"And yet?"

"And yet, he's pretty terrific. So should I be worried about him or pissed off that he hasn't called?"

For Cosimo, the panorama of the verdant, jagged, craggy Swiss Alps through the windows of the doctor's paneled office was not an unpleasant view. Neither was it an unfamiliar one. However, it had been a few years since he'd last seen them from this vantage point, and the difference between his earlier visits and this one was that the earlier ones had been made with his consent. But this time the panorama of lush mountaintops and calm blue lakes was not so much pleasing as it was a reminder of how little control he had over his life.

The silence in the room was getting to him. It always

did. And it inevitably happened more than once during each session: the psychiatrist staring at him expectantly, tapping his ballpoint pen against a yellow legal pad, and Cosimo fidgeting in an uncomfortable chair, looking everywhere except in the therapist's direction—High Noon at the I'm Okay, You're Okay Corral, each waiting for the other to speak. Cosimo, as usual, was the first to concede.

"Seriously," he said, glaring at the doctor, one of the many psychiatrists he'd been seeing for more than a decade, "don't you ever grow tired of this game? Don't you find it the least bit tedious?" He waited for a response, and when enough time had passed that he knew there wasn't going to be one, exasperated, he added, "I know *I* do."

"So what we do here is all a game to you, Cosimo? Please, explain."

"Yes, it's a game. It's *all* a game. Including that annoying habit you have of answering a question with a question." Cosimo shifted his weight in the winged-back chair, but no matter how much he contorted his body, regardless of how he positioned his arms or his legs, he couldn't get comfortable while he waited for another response. "And then there's *that*," he said, unable to stand the silence any longer.

"And then there's what?"

"That game you play of not answering a question at all, of just staring at me, expecting me to do all the work in this relationship."

"First of all, you didn't ask me a question. You simply made what I assumed was a rhetorical statement."

"You know very well what I mean. Don't go twisting my—"

"Cosimo, Cosimo…what am I to do with you? There are so many issues wrapped up in your previous statement that I don't even know where to start."

"Please, explain?" Cosimo said, smugly crossing his arms over his chest for emphasis.

The therapist shook his head as he scribbled notes on his pad. When he was finished writing, he squinted at a tiny crystal clock that was resting on a shelf crowded with ancient medical books and dated periodicals.

"I'm afraid we'll have to continue this conversation tomorrow," he said, placing his hands in his lap as he often did to further indicate that their session was over.

The next day was more of the same: questions and silence and stalemates, followed by even more intolerable periods of silence.

"Yes, Dr. J, I blame my mother for everything," Cosimo said in response to one of his previous queries. "I blame her for my father's disappearance. I blame her for my huge ego and my feelings of worthlessness. I blame her for the economy, volcanic eruptions, global warming, and the trouble in the Middle East." He glanced over at the clock on the shelf, hoping that their time was up. "I know it's nonsensical, but it's just easier that way."

"Cosimo, you have so much misplaced anger. Is it conceivable that—"

"Enough!" Cosimo shouted as he bolted out of his chair. He walked over to the window and watched the other patients for a minute as they roamed around the grounds in bathrobes and slippers and various states of stupor. He rested his backside on the windowsill and addressed the doctor. "Why are we playing this little game anyway, Doctor? Yes, game. You know as well as I do that my problems are more biochemical than they are psychological. And yes, a little maternal…but that's beside the point."

"And what exactly qualifies you to make such a diagnosis?"

"Years and years of study at the feet of Dr. J, the renowned and revered psychobabblist."

"Tell me, Cosimo, how exactly—"

"No, Doctor, you tell me—how much more of this bullshit must I endure before I can get back to my normal life? It's not like I'm still some teenager who can put his life on hold to spend a few weeks at a clinic regurgitating the minutiae of his life so that you can dissect it and speculate on the repercussions. I'm an adult now, with responsibilities. There are things I must attend to."

"You know very well that it's not as simple as that."

"What I do know, Doctor, is that you are *going* to return my things to me. Immediately. I insist that my passport, my wallet, and my cell phone be in my room within the hour." And just before he slammed the door on his way out of the therapist's office, he demanded, "And have your staff make arrangements to get me to Manhattan by tomorrow evening."

The psychiatrist's office was on the third floor of a 1960s precast concrete building. It was sparsely furnished with beige leatherette club chairs, a glass coffee table, and teak bookcases filled to overflowing with hardcovers bearing titles like *An Unquiet Mind* and *The Drama of the Gifted Child.* Most of the books were without jackets and looked as if they'd been published in the 1950s and purchased at suburban garage sales. The rest of the furniture was straight out of a *Scandinavian Design* catalogue, circa 1966.

Megan sat on a sofa, also beige, with padding that had deteriorated to the point that it sagged beneath her, forcing her to slump forward like a stuffed animal on a child's bed. Dr. Enowitch, Emerson College's resident therapist, sat across from her in a beat-up knock-off of an Eames chair in matching beige leatherette. He was humming to himself and wiping smudges from his eyeglasses with a static-free cloth. After a long hesitation, he cleared his throat.

"What would you like to talk about today?" he asked, as if this weren't her first time seeing him as a patient.

"I'm not sure where to begin. Or how you could possibly help."

"Why don't you say the first thing that comes to your mind? We can start with that."

"Okay. Well, like I said on the phone, I'd gotten involved with this guy on vacation, and everything was going along fine. But then I didn't hear from him for several weeks, which normally wouldn't have bothered me, but…"

"But?"

"He was adamant that he would call. Anyway, a few weeks ago I found out why he hadn't. It seems he couldn't because he'd been institutionalized, locked up, committed."

She was playing with the buttons on her blouse, wrapping a thin thread around and around one that had come loose, when she realized how her comment must have sounded.

"I'm afraid I don't know any genteel way to say that. No matter how I phrase it in my head, it comes out cold and condescending." She waited for Dr. Enowitch to say something, but all he did was clear his throat. "Anyway, he was at home when he had some sort of meltdown. So his family shipped him off to a loony bin...I mean...hospital in Switzerland. They kept him there for a month, cut off from the rest of the world."

"How did you find that out?" Dr. Enowitch asked.

"He called me, finally."

"Go on."

"He's in New York now, under the care of a different psychiatrist."

"And how does that make you feel?"

"Bad for him, for what he's had to go through." She gripped the end of the thread she'd been toying with and snapped it in two. "What concerns me is that this guy that I care about is apparently bipolar and borderline schizophrenic."

"And you didn't suspect anything before this? You didn't notice any aberrant behavior when the two of you were together?"

"Not really," she said as she dropped the torn thread into a waste paper basket. "Everyone has their little quirks. I did suspect that he had ADD. He reminded me of one of my former students, a brilliant young man who lacked the capacity to stay engaged on any one topic for more than a minute or two. But the rest of it—no, I never would have guessed."

"What exactly did he say when he called?"

"He said, 'I have a mental illness.' And then he told me

that his sister had found him unconscious after he'd had
a bad reaction to some medication he'd taken. His family
was under the impression that he had intentionally tried to
harm himself, so they sent him to a clinic where he could
be monitored and evaluated while he recuperated."

Megan picked up a small plaster statue that was sitting
on the table and became absorbed in the task of rotating it
in her hands. It was the sound of Dr. Enowitch clearing his
throat again that brought her attention back to the room.

"See? ADD. It's rampant."

"Did he say anything else?"

"He said that he's been on and off various medications
his entire life and that he'll likely be on some combination
of pharmaceuticals for the *rest* of his life."

"And how does that make you feel?"

"Part of me wants to run like hell, and another part of
me wants to take care of him, to fix him. Not change him,
mind you, but help him get better. If that's even possible."
She set the statue back on the table, taking care to place it
exactly where she'd found it. "*Is* that possible?"

"Anything is possible. But you have to ask yourself: Is it
probable?"

She contemplated the doctor's statement, her eyes
squinting as her brain tried to process the information, to
project herself into an unpredictable future.

"I asked him why he hadn't told me in Paris. He said he
thought he had it under control. Something about a new
prescription he'd been taking that seemed to be working.
He said it's not unusual for him to stop taking a medication
once it starts working because he doesn't feel the need to
take it anymore."

"I'm afraid that *is* a fairly common side effect. It tricks them into thinking they're better. It's a consideration for you, especially in light of your comment about wanting to help him get better." Dr. Enowitch stood, retrieved a book from the shelf, and handed it to Megan. "It's extremely difficult for anyone who has to navigate their way through this world when their instrument panel is constantly malfunctioning. But it can also be difficult for the individual who signs on as first mate."

"What's with all the nautical references?" she said as she flipped through the copy of *Manic-Depressive Illness* he'd just handed her.

"I like a good metaphor. So sue me. There's a section in there about how to live with someone who's bipolar without losing yourself. It's worth reading."

Megan perused the back cover and then slipped the book into her purse. She sat there quietly, not knowing what else to say.

"And after his revelation? What did you say to him?"

"I thanked him for being candid with me. And I said that it didn't change the way I felt about him." Her attention shifted again as she became preoccupied with a torn cuticle and the delicate task of removing it.

"Did you mean that? Or is that what you thought he wanted to hear?"

"I meant it. I meant it at the time." She tore the cuticle away from her thumb. "He reminds me of a wounded nightingale; he can't fly, but he can still sing. In a strange way, I think that's part of his charm."

"And what is it that *you* want?"

"I can't stop reminiscing about that week in Paris. It was

fun, it was passionate, but most of all, it was uncomplicated. I wonder if it's possible for us to have that again."

"Is that what you'd like?"

"Yes. But to be honest, I'm not sure what I'm willing to
risk to try to get that back."

Chapter Ten

Cosimo leaned against the filigreed metal railing that wrapped around the terrace of Regina's New York apartment. He watched as an endless stream of cars rushed past twenty stories below. He wondered why everyone was in such a hurry. He raised his head and looked out across the street to the mass of green that was Central Park, and he noticed that the leaves had begun to change color. It seemed too early for that, but then it also seemed that he had lost all track of time. He wasn't even sure what season it was. And even though it had only been a couple of months, for all he knew, years had passed since he was in Paris with Megan. He could recall their goodbyes at Charles de Gaulle and his arrival at Villa Vita Fortunata, but the rest of the summer was a thick haze. What he did remember was a hospital in the Alps; nurses in starched white uniforms; doctors with thick German accents; and lots of injections, pills, and questions, followed by endless circuitous walks around a grassy compound. And now there he was in New

York, back under Maria-Carmella's watchful eye and formidable thumb.

"You should come in now; it's getting cold," Regina said, taking his elbow.

"Take your hands off me. I don't need you telling me what to do." He yanked his arm away from her grip. "Really, I'm fine."

"Of course you are. I know you are." She twisted a gold band around and around on her finger. She couldn't look at him. "Coz, I said I was sorry...like a million times. What would you have done if you were in my position? If you had found me on the floor, unconscious, unrespon—"

"Okay, okay, I get it. I regret that I put you in that position. Next time I'll make sure you're nowhere around when I accidentally overdose on prescription drugs."

"More than a dozen sedatives in the course of an hour is not an accident. Why won't you let anyone help you?"

"I *was* getting help. Two talk therapists, a psychopharmacologist, a physician, a nutritionist, a fitness trainer...need I go on?"

Regina continued to rotate the ring around her finger as she turned her attention from her brother to the treetops of Central Park. She made no attempt to speak, to answer his question.

"And do you know what?" he said. "None of them made me feel any better. Nothing they ever did, or prescribed, or suggested, or fed me made one bit of difference. Nothing in their collective bag of tricks ever made me feel any better...ever made me feel normal."

"I know that, Coz," she said, still looking out at the park. "I know you've tried everything. I wish I could..."

"Could what? Go back in time? Not make that call? Don't you see how she is with me? Living under her constant supervision is simply another form of death for me. The long, slow kind."

"Believe what you want to about her, but I know that she did what she thought was best."

"For her!"

"For *you*, Coz. And you're just as bad. You think everything that happens in the world is about you. I called her because I didn't know what else to do. And because there is no one better in a crisis than her."

"Agreed. But you have to admit that in any situation, what's best *to her* is what's best *for her*," he said, turning his back on his sister.

"Look," she said, placing a hand on his shoulder, "in this whole awful situation, there is only one thing that I'm certain of. Her main concern at the time was seeing that you receive the best care possible."

Maria-Carmella appeared behind them with her platinum-blond hair lacquered firmly in place and a pair of black, oversized sunglasses masking her dark-brown eyes. Her arrival had been quiet and stealthy. She hadn't approached; she'd materialized. She was like an apparition, and her surprise factor was, in all likelihood, premeditated. She startled them both when she spoke.

"She's right, you know," Maria-Carmella said, inserting herself between the two of them. "Although I don't know why I care. Your reckless and thoughtless behavior has serious, and need I say negative, consequences. And yet somehow you remain either oblivious or indifferent to the fact that we are all affected by those actions."

"You mean *afflicted*, don't you, Mother?"

"Don't be flippant. There is nothing amusing about any of this."

"Mother, I'm sure all he meant was—" Regina began to say before being cut off.

"Now you're talking for me?" Cosimo said, daring her to go on.

"Enough!" Maria-Carmella demanded. "Do you think I like phoning people in the middle of the night to ask them to help my son who's tried to kill himself? Are you so delusional that you think I enjoy concocting stories for the mayor and his wife when they ask me how my son is? Do you have any idea how much I—"

"It's all about you, isn't it, Mother? Well, I'm sorry I'm such a disappointment to you. I'm sorry I'm such a burden," he said, momentarily forgetting where the balance of power lay.

Maria-Carmella raised her arm, and a dozen bejeweled bangles and the nubby pink fabric of her Chanel jacket caught Cosimo's eyes as the palm of her hand made contact with the right side of his face. The slap stunned him, physically and emotionally.

"Have you lost your mind?" she said. "I don't care what you've been through; you don't talk to me like that…not ever!" And then, practically whispering, she added, "Do you hear me?"

"Mother, was that necessary?" Regina said, stepping in between them.

"Don't you have business to attend to? Meetings to schedule? Calls to make?" Maria-Carmella pointed a finger in the direction of the French doors. Regina did as she was directed and left without a word.

"I have been very lenient with you the past few years," Maria-Carmella said once the doors to the apartment had closed. "You come and go as you please without any restrictions, without any responsibilities."

"But, Mother, whenever I show any interest in something, especially the business, you dismiss it."

"I will admit that you are intelligent and well educated; I've made sure of that. And while at times you have exhibited a small degree of enterprising spirit, it is abundantly clear to me that you are neither suited for, nor prepared for, a foray into the world of business."

Cosimo avoided his mother's eyes by playing with his wristwatch, twisting the crown to change the date, rotating the outer bezel, polishing the crystal with his shirtsleeve. When he began to tighten the wristband, Maria-Carmella grabbed hold of his arm and squeezed it, pressing gradually harder with each passing second.

"Your latest little diversion is a case in point," she said as she released her grip. "Everything has a price, and your lifestyle doesn't come cheap. Not for any of us." Her palm reached for Cosimo's cheek again, and he backed away. "What must you think of me?" she said, inching closer and moving her palm gently, maternally across his jawline.

As he watched her face attempt a look of contrition, he couldn't help but calculate the amount of money she was wearing in jewelry alone, or wonder why she seemed to place a higher value on material things than she did on him. While he knew that her touch was as close as she would

ever come to apologizing or to providing him with any
semblance of emotional sustenance, her words and actions
did demonstrate that committing him was indeed an act
of compassion, at least for her. He knew that she would
never be the kind of mother he'd read about in novels, that
this was the extent of her ability to comfort or nurture.
But even sadder to him was the utter transparency of her
behavior. He got the sense that his mother's sudden change
in demeanor, that her lame attempt to comfort him, was
simply Maria-Carmella compensating him for the harm
that she herself had just inflicted.

"I'm obligated to dine with people like the mayor's wife,
who, in her off-the-rack clothes and blue eyeshadow, feels
the need to educate *me* about the inner workings of status
and class in America," she continued, substantiating for
him the price that *she* was paying for *his* lifestyle. "I have
the villa to manage, a constant stream of charity events
to attend, board meetings, fundraisers. It's unending. And
what have I ever asked of you? Only that you stay out of
trouble, stay out of the papers, and stay out of our way.
Is that so much? And in return, I give you everything you
could possibly want."

Not everything, Mother, he thought. It was sheer instinct
and unconscious self-preservation that kept him from giving
her a retaliatory slap. But he knew that, while it would have
been liberating, it would do nothing to improve his current
situation. His savings had dwindled to a few hundred
thousand; he had no marketable skills and no foreseeable
way of earning a living. There was no way at the moment,
as he saw it, of surviving without her. That would change,

though. Somehow. But for now, sadly, she still controlled his destiny.

"I didn't mean any disrespect, Mother. It must have been the medication talking," he said, all the while imagining himself smothering her in her sleep, drowning her in the tub, poisoning her Gimlet.

Chapter Eleven

It was mid-September, and an enormous Atomic FireBall candy sun hung low in the sky, illuminating the entire eastern seaboard. And that same sun, the one that was browning Cosimo's skin while he listened to music on Regina's terrace, was annoying Megan in her Boston apartment while she tried to sleep in after a long night of grading papers.

Megan reluctantly got out of bed and squinted through the partially closed curtains at the red star that was disturbing her sleep by shining through them. She tugged on the edge of the thin drapes to close them, but they didn't budge. She tugged again. And again. And finally, that last jerk of her wrist was forceful enough that it brought the whole thing crashing down upon her. She stood there in front of the naked window, buried under a mound of beige drapery and ecru lace liner, and cursed the heavens. She struggled to untangle herself from the rubble of fabric; once free, she got back into bed, pulled the covers over her head, and prayed for sleep. She lay there for a while in that in-between state, unsure if she was awake or dreaming, when the phone rang. She was so exhausted that before she could even think of answering it, the call went to voice mail.

Cosimo lowered the volume of the portable stereo as he waited for Megan to answer, but once again, she did not.

"*Merde!*"

He didn't leave a message. He wanted to talk to her, not to some anonymous voice on a machine. He placed the phone on the end table and cranked up the volume on the portable stereo.

"Lunch in fifteen minutes," Regina called from inside the apartment.

"Don't make me come out there and get you," Maria-Carmella said, her voice breaking through the strains of piano, saxophone, and drums drifting up from his tiny black headset.

He ignored both of their requests. Instead, he walked to the edge of the balcony and hung his head over the railing. Cars sped by. Pedestrians ambled along with their children, with their dogs, or with both. While the thought of climbing on to the ledge and leaping off had crossed his mind, he dismissed the idea when he realized that the building was terraced, and that below Regina's flat were other patios jutting out at various depths. If he were to jump, he wouldn't end up on the pavement twenty stories below, a mass of bleeding, dying human pulp, as was the plan. It was more likely that he'd walk away with only a few broken bones after landing on the tiled floor or the chaise lounge of the apartment two stories down.

"Cosimo, ten minutes," Maria-Carmella announced

from her air-conditioned sanctuary. "And I expect you to put on presentable attire if you're to eat with us in the dining room."

Cosimo continued to stare at the street below. This time it was not jumping that he fantasized about but rather shoving. He envisioned his mother's mangled body on the broken remains of Mia Farrow's all-weather dining table. He delighted at the thought of her twisted form slumped over Diane Sawyer's brand-new B&B Italia lounge chairs. He daydreamed of dragging her paralyzed body from the Viennese inspired deck, past the gourmet kitchen, and through the spartan living room of Meryl Streep's starkly furnished flat.

He knew that he'd better get inside before she came out looking for him. They seemed to have come to, by no formal agreement or even conversation, a truce. For the past couple of weeks, all interactions between them had been eerily amicable, and it wouldn't be prudent for him to screw that up. Not on the day that he intended to tell her he would be moving to Boston. He turned off the music and headed to his room to change. He needed to put on an outfit suitable for lunch with Princess Maria-Carmella Stefani Garibaldi di Sorrento. "In the *dining room*," he mumbled to himself, shaking his head and his index finger as he closed the French doors behind him. "And don't be late," he said, admonishing the empty space in front of him as he continued to perfect his impersonation of Maria-Carmella.

⌒

At two o'clock in the afternoon, Megan threw the covers off, sat up, and hung her legs over the edge of the bed. She glared at the pile of curtains on the floor as if they had intentionally betrayed her. She had neither the time, the energy, nor the inclination to deal with such a mess. She rubbed the sleep from her eyes and reached for the phone on the nightstand. The glowing numbers on the face informed her that Cosimo had called at eleven forty-five. She was disappointed that she'd missed him. She'd have answered it if she'd known it was him. He'd been calling daily, but never until the evening, and usually not until after nine. She went to the medicine cabinet, retrieved a bottle of Tums, and chewed on a few antacid tablets to calm her stomach. She poured herself a glass of water and picked up the phone again, pushing the little envelope icon to speed dial her voice mail. There was only one message. But it wasn't from Cosimo. It was from her brother, Tommy.

Even though she had just woken up, she was still tired. The little sleep she had gotten was fitful and interrupted. As she moved about the apartment in her typical morning routine, she noticed that her usual fastidiousness had been replaced with something that bordered on slovenly. Her apartment was a mess. And it dawned on her as she surveyed her apartment—the mass of curtains on the floor, the crumpled comments to her students' papers overflowing from the trash bin in her living room, slash guest room, slash office—that so was her life.

Chapter Twelve

Cosimo pulled on a pair of beige Zegna slacks and slipped into a form-fitting Prada shirt. He analyzed the outfit in a full-length mirror and wondered if he could get away without wearing a jacket. After all, it was only lunch. With his family. In his sister's flat. But then again, with Maria-Carmella, the tactical thing to do was to overdress. Her idea of casual was a tuxedo without a cummerbund. After sifting through an assortment of jackets, he chose an unstructured black linen blazer. He applied more gel to tame his mound of roving hair and then inspected himself in the mirror to confirm what he already knew. All things considered, he looked and felt pretty good. Almost back to normal. Whatever that was. "I just need to get out of this house, away from her," he whispered to his reflection as he tugged the shirt cuffs past the jacket sleeve, exposing the perfect amount of cream-colored fabric below the tightly woven threads of the coat. One final touch was all that was needed. He retrieved his gold chain from a satin-lined drawer and adjusted the clasp behind his neck. The metal was cold, the weight substantial, the relief on the medallion reassuring. The nurses in Zurich had confiscated it upon his arrival and only returned it to him with the rest of his personal possessions upon his departure. He hadn't worn it since, even though it had always been a kind of talisman to him. Whenever he got nervous, whenever he was the least bit unsure of himself, his fingers would automatically, intuitively, find their way to the pendant resting on his chest. He knew that the necklace had no tangible powers, no curative traits, no real ability to ward off demons, but he'd come to rely upon it anyway. It was one of the few things that was always with him, regardless of where he happened to be on the planet. It was the only thing that gave him any sense of continuity, of stability. And, because it was the last gift he'd received from his uncle Giuseppe, it imparted a sense of self-worth.

He dashed out the door and jogged down the hall. He arrived in the dining room winded, but still in control.

"You're late," Maria-Carmella said. "You've kept us all waiting."

All meant Maria-Carmella.

"Just a few minutes," was what Cosimo had wanted to say. But instead, his sense of self-preservation kicked in, and he said, "My apologies, Mother. I needed to take a quick shower so as not to offend your guest."

The guest was supposedly a renowned poet who lived on one of the lower floors, whose invitation and presence was in fact unknown to him. Smiling at his mother, he walked over to the gentleman seated on her right. He extended his hand and said, "Hello, I'm Cosimo."

"Billy Cooper," the man said, offering a pale, fragile-looking hand in return.

"A pleasure, Mr. Cooper. Again, my apologies for keeping you waiting."

"Please, call me Billy."

Cosimo nodded, then walked behind the poet and kissed his mother on the cheek.

"You look nice," Maria-Carmella said, patting the hand he'd rested on her shoulder.

Regina stared at him from the other side of the table, her eyes wide in mock surprise, her lips tight in a restrained smirk. She seemed befuddled by the sudden shift in temperaments, by the apparent but unexpected rapprochement between mother and son.

The chef, in a starched white uniform and toque, entered the room through a pair of black-lacquered doors. Maria-Carmella bristled at the noise they made as they swung back and forth behind him. He announced the menu and asked if there were any questions or special requests before his staff began serving. Maria-Carmella requested that he substitute the Cabernet Sauvignon for the '82 Bordeaux and that he make certain that his staff clear the table completely after each course. The wine substitution was made out of habit, out of the need to orchestrate everyone and everything. The bit about the staff clearing the table, an obvious and rote aspect of a wait-staff's function, was the type of conscious ploy she routinely used to remind everyone that it was she who was in charge, that it was she who ruled.

The conversation wandered from topic to topic. Cosimo was in awe of Maria-Carmella's ability to talk intelligently, in depth and at length, about any subject. It had been a while since he had seen her in a social setting, since he'd had the opportunity to watch her cast her spell. There was none of the exaggeration and bravado he had come to expect. None of the conspicuous name-dropping that so many in her position were likely, albeit unconsciously, to employ. There was no hint of sarcasm, no condescension, no reference to class. There was no belittling or baiting. Her laughter was engaging, intimate, inclusive. He could tell that Billy was smitten with her. And for the moment, Cosimo was, too. *That's how she does it,* he thought. *She seduces you with smart, witty conversation, endearing touches on the arm, a perfectly timed appreciative laugh. Then, once you are all warm and fuzzy, intoxicated by the warmth of her attention, telling her your innermost secrets, divulging details about yourself that even your closest friends don't know, she thrusts her stinger deep into your abdomen and releases a poison that instantly paralyzes you. Once you are immobilized, stunned, and stupid, she swoops in and, with great relish, methodically devours you from the inside out, never once spilling a drop of blood on her immaculately tailored haute couture creation from Christian Lacroix's current collection.*

With the lunch over, Cosimo decided to take advantage of Maria-Carmella's jovial mood and broach the subject of Boston. With his fingers tracing the outline of the pendant beneath the thin fabric of his shirt, he requested a moment alone with her.

"Well, precious, I'd love to sit down and discuss anything you like, but not right now. I've a salon appointment, and I mustn't be late." She patted his cheek with a gloved hand. "Tonight, dear. Before dinner. We'll talk then." She walked over to Regina and kissed her lightly on the forehead. A moment later, the only thing that remained of her in the dining room was the faint smell of her signature perfume.

"She's going back to her suite. That's what she calls it, you know—her suite," Regina said to Cosimo as they lingered over cappuccinos.

"Shhh," he said, then chuckled. "Just be glad she lets you stay here."

"I know," she replied, laughing. "I could say the same to you."

"Has she said anything about her plans to return home?"

"No. But I've begun to scatter Manhattan real estate brochures all around the apartment. She simply ignores them, though. I can't decide if I'm being too obvious or not obvious enough." She pointed to a small table in the hall with a neat stack of glossy flyers. "So, you and Mother are planning a tête-à-tête? I'd be happy to provide moral support if need be, or," she said, winking, "play referee."

"Thanks, but no thanks. I wouldn't want to give her the impression that I'm afraid to confront her on my own. Besides, I was trying to spare you the bloodbath."

"Confrontation? Bloodbath? Sounds serious. Tell me more."

"It's nothing you haven't already figured out for yourself, Reggie. I can't stay here indefinitely. I'll be twenty-five in a few months. I've got to...well, you know."

"Where will you go? You've been so secretive and distant since you got here."

"Not intentionally," he said, pausing for a waiter to leave the room. "But she makes me see that damn interrogator twice a week."

"The therapist? I thought he was helping?"

"Really? How? By dissecting and cross-examining me with a list of questions amply supplied by you-know-who?"

"I'm sorry you have to go through that."

"I'm so drained after those sessions, I don't even feel like calling Meg…" He caught himself and stopped mid-moniker, but that half-name lingered there in the air between them, limply floating like an old helium balloon. He was so disappointed in himself for letting that slip that he was reluctant to say anything else. So he just sat there quietly and stared across the room at the vista of black and gray skyscrapers with their mirrored façades reflecting each other's reflections.

Regina was baffled by her brother's unwillingness to confide in her. They had always been close, partly because they had no other siblings and partly because they were a united front against the whirlwind that was their mother. But she could feel they were drifting apart a little more each day. She surmised he was still angry about her call to Maria-Carmella after his overdose. But when he made that slip about calling someone else, she flashed back to that awful night and to a piece of stationery from a Parisian pensione. She had all but forgotten about the note until he uttered that name. By her recollection, the letter was nothing more than the ramblings of a woman infatuated with her brother and her reminiscence of an affair that was in the past. She'd concluded, from the way it had been mangled and discarded, that his response to the note was either anger or indifference. Either way, it implied he'd moved on from whatever brief encounter he'd had with the anonymous woman. The trouble was, there was no way she could ask him about it without confessing that she had infringed on his privacy.

"Perhaps I can help," she said. "Maybe if you told me—"

"No. Not now. Not yet. There isn't a part of me that hasn't been dissected, autopsied, and analyzed to death. I'm tired of putting every single detail of my life out there for public consumption. No offense."

"Fair enough, but I'm on your side, you know."

And even though he knew and appreciated that, he couldn't risk revealing sensitive information to her. Not when Maria-Carmella had already begun to implement *her* action plan for *his* future. If Regina's loyalty was ever put to the test, there was no doubt which side she would choose.

"Thanks," he said, and then excused himself from the table and walked out to the terrace.

The only thing he'd done all day was have lunch, and that had left him exhausted. Emotionally spent, he plopped himself down on a chaise that was shaded from the sun by a startlingly white patio umbrella. His solicitation of Maria-Carmella's time and his conversation with Regina had left him shaken. He would need all the confidence and self-assurance he could summon to engage in a battle with his mother later. And at the thought of that, at the idea that a conversation with his own mother could evolve into something epic, he laughed out loud. *Battle?* How ridiculous. Perhaps it was the new drug cocktail he had started taking, or that he was once again sporting his treasured amulet, or that he simply viewed his mother with a new perspective after their three-hour lunch with the poet. *Battle?* That word, as it rolled around in his brain, struck him as being ludicrous and melodramatic. Whatever the reason, he was momentarily optimistic, unafraid, prepared for anything. She might make him beg for whatever it was that he wanted, but she would never jettison him out into the world without sufficient means to support himself. Would she? Could she? But what if she did? He had friends. He could find work. It wouldn't be easy, but he'd get by. He was nothing if not resourceful. In fact, he was downright enterprising. Maria-Carmella had said so herself.

But he wouldn't need to resort to manual labor. No, he would never have to wear a uniform or work in an office, because he knew her Achilles heel: the tabloids. There were three things that Princess Maria-Carmella valued above all else: money, power, and image. Cosimo pictured himself directing a member of his mother's own staff to help him with his plan of Photoshopping jpegs of himself into stock photographs and laying out pages in InDesign. He envisioned one with him standing behind a counter at Burger King, his head wrapped in a cardboard crown and a nametag with Cosimo spelled out in white letters dangling from his lapel as he scooped French-fried potatoes into a small paper bag. He pictured another image, this one with him wearing an ill-fitting green vest covered in buttons embellished with humorous slogans while he stood behind a counter at Starbucks, topping off a grande Frappuccino with tall swirls from a can of whipped cream. Or better still, he thought, a snapshot of him in a trendy restaurant, wearing a tuxedo shirt and a bistro apron, serving entrées to a well-dressed clientele.

He'd approach her in the study without saying a word and hand her a manila envelope that contained his mocked-up versions of *The National Enquirer*, *The Star*, and *The New*

York Post. Upon opening it she would find the headlines, BURGER KING FINALLY STAFFED BY REAL ROYALTY and COFFEE CHAIN HIRES CROWN PRINCE OF CAPPUCCINOS. And finally, LADIES, YOUR PRINCE IS WAITING... TABLES! As she casually sifted through each one, he'd say, as nonchalantly as he could, "What have I got to lose, Mother? Besides, you should be proud of me. Once the three-month probationary period is over, they've promised to put me on the management track." He imagined her look of disgust. She had to realize, though, that her relentless effort to establish and maintain dominance over him was just as likely to train him to employ those same techniques against her. It should come as no surprise that over the course of time, the manipulated had become the manipulator.

I am not without ammunition, he proclaimed to the darkening clouds hovering over West Seventy-First Street. He took in a few deep breaths to calm and center himself. The world felt lighter, brighter, bursting with possibilities. It was amazing, he thought, the things you allow yourself to get used to in life, like the crippling, exhausting, ever-present fear of being pierced by Maria-Carmella's stealthy, poisonous stinger. But he knew how quickly his positive state of mind could lapse. Or collapse. His emotional states were perpetually transitory. His confidence, his outlook, his self-esteem were as changeable as the tides, only there was never any moon to inform him, nothing to herald its inevitable fluctuation, no way of predicting what might come next. If only his feeling of confidence would last a few more hours, he thought, he would be able to stand his ground and use his mother's own tactics against her.

Just before he closed his eyes to visualize a successful

meeting with her, he noticed an alert on his cell phone. It informed him that he had missed a call, and he recognized the number as Megan's. There was no little icon lit, which meant no message was left. But at least she'd been thinking of him. He wanted to call her, but he was too shaken from his conversation with Regina and too anxious about the upcoming showdown with his mother. He would call her later. Then she could congratulate or console him, depending on the outcome. Either way, he would need to hear her voice.

Chapter Thirteen

Megan stood on a small ladder that she'd borrowed from the Harvard law student who lived next door. He had offered to come over and help her, but she merely thanked him and said that she could handle it herself. Once she had begun the process, though, she wished that she hadn't dismissed his offer so readily. The curtain rod extended well past her shoulders on both sides, causing her to wobble, first left, then right, then back again. She hoisted the cumbersome curtain above her head while she tried to maintain her balance on the narrow metal steps. The swaying made her feel like a tightrope walker inching along an impossibly thin line. She stood on her tiptoes and leaned into the window. She strained to hook the brass metal bar into the two coordinating C brackets. Her first few attempts resulted in a mass of curtain all twisted and tangled on the carpet, tired wrists, and a wrenched ankle. She tried again, stretching herself a fraction of an inch higher, but that only managed to send a dull pain coursing through her previously compromised foot. She extended her arms again until she thought her shoulders would pop. She gave one final heave-ho with the expulsion of all the air left in her lungs and successfully hoisted the curtain rod back into its metal clips.

She stepped into the hall to return the ladder to her neighbor. While she waited for Mitchell to answer the door, she noticed that the carpet was dirty and worn in a few spots, the paint was peeling in certain places, and that the one flickering fluorescent light suspended from the water-stained ceiling barely illuminated the narrow hallway. She made a mental note to call the management company and complain.

"That was quick," Mitchell said, taking the ladder from her.

"Yeah, luckily I didn't do too much damage," she said. "If that thing had been a half an inch shorter, I'd still be at it. Or on the floor writhing in pain."

"You know, I'm usually locked up in here studying, so don't hesitate to knock if you ever need anything. I can always use a break from reading torts." He leaned the ladder up against a wall and crossed his arms over his chest. "Hey, don't let the Good Samaritan act fool you, I've a selfish motive. I'm trying to bank extra karma points to compensate for all those criminals I'll be defending once I pass the bar."

She gave him a smile that she hoped conveyed appreciation for the use of his ladder and acknowledgement of his altruistic piggy bank. The transaction done, the pleasantries dispensed, an uncomfortable silence descended over them.

"Well, you definitely earned some bonus points today.

Thanks again. I might actually get to sleep in tomorrow," she said as she turned to leave.

"Hey," he said, "I've noticed we keep similar schedules. How about getting together for dinner sometime? You know, something casual, not like a date or anything."

"Sure, okay," she said, more out of a sense of obligation than of interest. And, because she was still trying to process Cosimo's recent revelation, the prospect of getting involved with someone else, especially someone who lived across the hall, made her heart palpitate. And not in a good way. Why he didn't consider her date-worthy—unless, of course, that was just a line he used on women to get that first date—was another matter altogether.

"I'm leaving town for a few days," he said. "My parents just finished renovating a place on Martha's Vineyard. They're getting the whole family together for the weekend. I'll be back Sunday night. Does Monday work for you?

"I think so. Yeah. That'll work," she said, hoping her lack of enthusiasm wasn't as obvious as it felt.

"Perfect. I'll see you then."

Megan walked the few feet back to her front door as Mitchell closed his. She tried to pinpoint her hesitancy regarding him. She made a mental tally of his attributes: he was pleasant, attractive, polite, and educated. Then she wondered how old he was. Twenty-six, she guessed. She'd lived in that building for over a year, and that was the longest conversation they'd ever shared. She'd always thought that he was good-looking, maybe even too good-looking, but for whatever reason, he wasn't her type. He was tall (at least six feet), his shoulders broad, his jaw angular, his hair a thick mop of strawberry blond, and he had a chest that thrust the Harvard logo on his maroon sweatshirt so far out that it looked three-dimensional. Megan typically favored thinner, darker, more bookish types. Like Cosimo. Strangely enough, she couldn't say if he was bookish or not, since the subject of literature had never come up during their time together. But she had to admit that Mitchell, while big and blond to an extreme, did emit a rather bookish aura. That was confirmed earlier as she waited in his living room while he retrieved the ladder from another room. In his absence she perused his shelves. She expected to find a stack of law reviews, a few business books, and a shelf or two dedicated to sports and fitness. Instead, she found well-worn copies of Faulkner, Carver, Dostoevsky, Nabokov, Maugham, and Camus.

When he walked back in to the living room, Mitchell found her thumbing through a heavily notated and dog-eared copy of *Sirens of Titan.*

"Not his most popular novel," he said with a sad, somewhat reverential tone, "but it is one of my favorites."

"Mine too," she said. "Now would be a good time to reread it. I could use a good literary diversion."

"I know what you mean," he said, taking the paperback from her and placing it back in its spot between *Welcome to the Monkey House* and *Slaughter House Five.* "You can borrow it if you want. That is, if you don't mind seeing all my lame comments in the margins." He reached for the book again.

"Thanks, but I'd prefer to pick up a copy of my own to fondle and scribble in," she said. "I can't tell you how sad I was when I heard that he'd passed away. You would have thought I'd known him personally."

"In a way, you did," he said. "For me, all those hours I spent reading his texts, reflecting on his ideas, laughing at his characters and their situations—it was like I was in his presence. His voice and his words were so strong, so unique, even years after he wrote them."

Megan and Mitchell stood in the doorway and looked at each other silently, awkwardly. Then she left with his ladder and a new opinion of the jock she'd only previously shared an occasional elevator ride with.

Chapter Fourteen

Cosimo was in his bedroom, the door locked, the shades drawn, and the contents of the closet spread out in unorganized piles atop the king-size bed. The dresser drawers were perilously stacked on the ebony-stained floor, one on top of the other, and the artwork, the objet d'art, and the lampshades were all askew. He sat in a sleek, modern club chair covered in a yellow bouclé fabric with his feet propped up on a matching ottoman and scanned the wreckage. His heart was beating rapidly, and his breathing was labored. His fingers moved across the gold medallion, stopping occasionally to feel the stones, to touch each of the eight small diamonds. He counted them aloud as his fingertips passed over each one: one, two, three…seven, eight…again, and again, and again. This had become his mantra.

He tried to catch his breath, to complete one deep inhale, but he was unable to fill his lungs with oxygen. His eyes frantically surveyed the ravaged room as he tried to remember where he'd stashed a bottle of Xanax. He couldn't talk with his mother like he was, not in the state he was in. And he couldn't *not* talk with her, either, after having specifically requested a conference with her. Eventually it popped into his head where he'd hidden them: in a pair of socks in the recesses of the top left drawer of the bureau. He'd been searching so manically and haphazardly that he'd neglected to inspect the rolled-up hosiery. He had filled up the empty portion of the bottle with tissue paper so that if it were ever moved—by the maid, by his mother—the pills wouldn't rattle around and announce that they were hiding there. Thus, they made no sound when he'd emptied the contents of the drawer onto the floor. He unrolled several pairs of black socks until he came upon the one with the hidden cache.

He quickly swallowed two, even though just having the pills in his hands, knowing that they could be coursing through his bloodstream in a matter of minutes, relaxed him, reassured him. His heart rate slowed, and his breathing became more measured. He knew that it was unnecessary to hide the prescription from his mother or the housekeeper, but he couldn't help himself. The very idea of not having them, of them being lost or stolen, clouded his judgment.

Except for the chorus of voices, which hadn't returned since he'd left the hospital, he could endure almost all of the symptoms that his faulty brain chemistry inflicted upon him. He had no trouble gambling and carousing the night away, engaging in anonymous sex, and squandering away heaps of cash when he was having one of his manic episodes. And while it was considerably less enjoyable, he could just as easily go for days without eating and bury himself under the covers to block out the rest of the world during those longer, seemingly endless periods of depression. What he couldn't endure were the panic attacks with their debilitating surge of irrational and unrelenting anxiety that made him irritable to the point of rage. It was that aspect of his illness that made him dependent on a combination of prescription drugs, illicit drugs, and alcohol, and made stability of any kind for him a pipe dream.

"Coz, Mother rang a few minutes ago," Regina said, as she gave a gentle rap on his door. "She was at the club and ran into Charlotte Something-or-Other. She said she's decided to join her for dinner." She rapped on the door again, but there was still no answer. "Coz? Are you there?"

"Thanks, Reggie," he said, acutely aware of the rising panic in her voice. "Did she say when she'd be back?" He looked around the disheveled room and then inched his way toward the door to confirm that it was locked.

"No, she didn't."

"I was about to step into the shower," he said. "Do you have plans tonight? Do you want to have dinner?"

"No plans," she said. "Meet me in the living room when you're done. I'll get us a nice table somewhere."

"Great. Give me a half hour."

He laid his head back down on the mattress in the one spot that was free of crumpled clothing, and he closed his eyes. It occurred to him that Maria-Carmella's impromptu dinner date might be a ruse, a power play to throw him off balance. She was both fond of and adept at coercing even the simplest of circumstances and conversations into a psychological chess match. He considered bailing on his dinner plans with Regina by faking a migraine. He could use some time alone, possibly to search his mother's suite. But in all likelihood, there was nothing of value there anyway, no important documents or keys, no blank checks or credit cards, nothing that would tide him over financially if she cut off his trust fund. Not in a place where someone, especially Cosimo, could find them. He once spent a few hours trying to forge her signature but then abandoned the idea after realizing that, in addition to her autograph, he would need pin numbers and passwords to gain access to any of her accounts or safety deposit boxes. Searching her room, he decided, was not worth the risk of her wrath, and possible execution, when the odds of uncovering anything of value were negligible. And, since Regina was the best person to keep his mind off things for a few hours, he decided to keep their date.

He popped another pill into his mouth, walked into the bathroom, stood under the rain shower, and let the warm water trickle down his body, relaxing him, soothing him, cleansing him. *Ahhh,* he thought, *the Xanax are starting to kick in.*

Megan and her brother Tommy were seated in a red leather banquette at Giorgio's, a new restaurant in the north end of town. It was as kitschy as kitschy could be, with red-and-white checkered table cloths, fake crumbling frescos painted on the walls, and green wine bottles in straw baskets with long tapered candles that dripped multicolored wax. The waiter delivered their antipasto plates, and Tom's eyes followed the beefy, redheaded Irish boy all the way back to the kitchen. Megan took a sip of wine and snapped her fingers to get his attention.

"Hello? Earth to Tommy."

"Sorry," he said, turning to look at her. "What can I say, I'm a butt man."

"More like butt*head*," she said.

She grabbed a breadstick from a glass on the table and took a bite out of it.

"Better watch your carbs," Tommy sneered.

"Then why did you drag me to an Italian place?" she said and then took several more bites in quick succession. "Mitchell asked me out to dinner. What do you think that means?"

"Who's Mitchell?"

"You know, that guy in my building. The one across the hall?"

"Hunky next-door-neighbor Mitchell? The big, beefy blond?" he said. Then, fanning his face with the red vinyl menu, he added, "The Nordic god with the killer pecs?"

"That's the one."

"Wow, I'm impressed. Jealous, but impressed."

"Yeah, he is more your type than mine."

"He's my Barbie dream date if there ever was one."

"So what does it mean? He did say it wasn't a date."

"I don't know. Dinner could mean anything. Lunch, though, that's a different story," Tommy said. "Trust me, you don't want to be on the receiving end of a 'Let's do lunch' invite."

"When were you ever dumped?"

"Me? Are you kidding? I don't *get* those calls, I *make* those calls," he said as he slathered butter on a piece of focaccia. "Anyway, nothing against you, Love, but how the hell did you snag that one?"

"Don't be mean. It's a hetero thing. You wouldn't understand."

"And what about that Italian mystery date of yours? When do I get to meet Mr. Mysterioso?"

"Speaking of irresistible, how is Gregg?" she said.

"He's good. The same," Tommy said as he moved the condiments around on the table, rearranging them according to height and color. "Although I get the sense he's planning something big. I have a sneaking suspicion that he's going to propose. How weird is that?"

"Propose? Marriage? To you?"

"Yes, to me. *Now* who's being mean?"

"I think it's sweet," she said. "It's nice that you finally have the option to get married. Why should we straight people be the only ones who suffer?" She jabbed the remainder of her breadstick into the air to make a point. Then, with her best New York Jewish accent, she said, "You could do worse."

"And I have," Tommy said, picking up a couple of breadsticks and pretending to bang them on a drum. "Budump-bump!" he said before taking a bite out of one. "But you know Gregg; it'll never happen. All the planning, all the preparation. Everything he does has to be perfect. He's probably on the phone right now booking a choir of angels to sing the Hallelujah chorus the instant I say yes."

Megan, frustrated by Tommy's propensity to turn even the most painful of subjects into a stand-up comedy routine, and the most joyous of occasions into a dramatic *Lifetime* movie of the week, let loose a sigh of exasperation.

"Seriously, though," he said, putting the breadsticks down. "He may be fanatical, but I'm still crazy about him. I'd still marry him. If he ever asks."

She raised a glass to toast, although to what, she wasn't exactly sure.

"So, we've covered the stud muffin next door and my boyfriend, and yet you continue to avoid the subject of Cosimo the Magnificent, Cosimo the Invisible, Cosimo the..." Tommy, having run out of one-liners, fell silent. He picked up the wine bottle and refilled Megan's glass. "Exactly how many carafes of this cheap Chianti is it going to take to get you to start talking?"

"Seven," she said and took a large swig that emptied a third of her glass. "Honestly, there's nothing to tell. The last time I spoke to him, he was all excited, like he was dying to tell me something. And then, instead of telling me, he said he would call me later, and then he hung up."

The waiter delivered their entrées and sprinkled Parmesan cheese and cracked pepper over them. Megan watched Tommy intently, surprised to find that his eyes stayed focused on hers, even when the waiter dropped a spoon and bent over to pick it up.

"How long has he been in New York?" Tommy asked.

"Two and a half weeks. Maybe three. I'm not sure what's happening between us, and I'm beginning to wonder if I'm ever going to see him again," she said and then emptied another third of her glass. "Is it possible that he's a figment of my imagination? That I fabricated this whole scenario out of boredom?"

"Maybe he *can't* come see you. Maybe he's under house arrest."

"Stop it!"

"No, really. Maybe he got busted for money laundering or armed robbery or pedophilia or something, and now he has to wear one of those Martha Stewart thingies around his ankle."

"Thanks for that, but I think I'll stick with my theory."

"All I'm saying is, if I were you, I wouldn't wait forever for any guy. Especially with Thor next door polishing up his hammer." He shook his head at the thought of letting that big, beefy blond go. "You don't want to end up as a cat lady, do you? And I don't want to have to break into your apartment one day to find you sitting alone in the dark, dressed in an old, tattered Filene's Basement bridal gown, and staring at a wedding cake covered in cobwebs." The whole idea of it amused him, and he let out a chuckle. When neither the comment nor the laughter got a rise out of her, he added, "Remind me again how old you are, Miss Hammersmith?"

"It's Havisham, you twit," she said, pouring herself more wine. "Why do I even bother talking to you?"

Chapter Fifteen

The Manhattan sky was peppered with cumulus clouds that moved briskly across a background of renaissance blue. The sun appeared, disappeared, and then reappeared again and again, transforming Regina's kitchen into a kaleidoscope of sunlight and shade. Cosimo was at the Wolf range, stirring grated cheese into an omelet pan and laughing at one of Regina's stories, when Maria-Carmella entered, wearing a bright red outfit that neither of them had seen before.

"Good morning, children," she said, retrieving a glass of pink liquid from the refrigerator that had been prepared and left for her by the previous day's pro tempore chef.

"Morning, Mother," Cosimo and Regina said in unison like grade-school children greeting their teacher.

"Mother, that suit is gorgeous," Regina said as Maria-Carmella joined her at the breakfast table. "That color is so intense." She leaned in closer to appraise the stitch marks, the buttons, the pleats. "Is it Bill Blass?"

"One of the very last pieces he designed himself," she

said, picking an invisible speck from the sleeve and folding it into a cloth napkin. "Even for me though, this color…it's a bit strong, wouldn't you say?"

That was a loaded question. Regina had to not only formulate her answer carefully, she had to do it quickly. If she agreed, her response might be construed as placating or patronizing. If she disagreed, Maria-Carmella might interpret her comment as contradictory and disrespectful. Cosimo jealously watched her deft performance as she proved that she was more like her mother than she would ever care to admit.

"Yes, it is a *little* outrageous," Regina said. "But you're the one woman I know who can pull that off, whose presence can't be overshadowed, not even by such a bold color choice. I love it."

"Thank you, dear. I must say I agree with you. One shouldn't be afraid of color. I don't know why I haven't worn it before. Personally, I'm of the opinion that Bill's designs have always had a timeless quality."

Cosimo tilted his head slightly and gave Regina a private wink. She had managed to display the ideal qualities of independence and respect by conjuring up, in a fraction of a second, a response that both contradicted and agreed with Maria-Carmella.

"Mother, can I get you anything?" Cosimo said, transferring the pan from the stovetop to the oven. "An omelet? Some coffee?"

"Nothing for me, dear, thank you. But that little talk you wanted to have yesterday—why don't we have it tomorrow, over lunch?"

"I won't be here tomorrow, Mother. I'll be gone all weekend."

"Did you clear that with Dr. Wyckoff?"

"No, Mother, I cleared it with Cosimo Garibaldi," he said. And then, before she could respond, he added, "There's nothing left for him to say. Or for me to say to him. I need to live my own life, Mother. I can't...I won't have the people on your payroll making decisions for me. Certainly you can understand that?"

"I only meant that—"

"I will not hang around indefinitely waiting for Wyckoff, or you, or anyone else for that matter, to tell me how to live my life," he said, trying to come off as confident and definite without being overly aggressive.

"What's so wrong with your life? What could you possibly be lacking?" she said as she stirred a spoon around in the thick, pink shake.

"I'm not like you and Regina. I can't go shopping every day and then mingle every night at mindless dinner parties, club openings, and fund-raisers. I need more than that. And that's part of my problem. I have nothing to do all day, nothing to occupy my time or my mind. So I ruminate about the past, and I worry about the future. And if you think that shackling me to this apartment and requiring me to get a permission slip for every move I make is some kind of panacea for my disease...let me assure you...it is not." He walked over to the table where his mother and sister were seated. "I've decided to go back to school, Mother." It was a lie that just slipped out in the heat of the moment. He panicked and fabricated the idea of continuing his education because he feared the questions that a spontaneous trip to Boston might provoke.

"I can arrange—" she started to say, but Cosimo interrupted her once again.

"No, Mother. This is something *I* need to do. Something I need to evaluate and execute by myself...to succeed at or to fail at on my own," he said, a little more forcefully than he'd intended. There was a long pause while he waited for Maria-Carmella to respond. In his frustration and impatience, he had made a drastic misstep, and he knew it. He'd raised his voice, he'd challenged her authority, and he'd repeatedly interrupted her. He tried to gauge, from her expression, by the look in her eyes, by the contraction of her lips, whether she was pondering the degree of punishment she would inflict upon him, or if she was merely orchestrating a sense of tension to shake his confidence. She was too proficient in such matters to ever reveal her cards before she was ready. He mentally braced himself for an eruption, an explosion, a spewing forth of venom. He began to emotionally curl up like a bug.

Regina left the table and carried her coffee cup to the sink. The silence was thick, the tension palpable as she tiptoed towards the hallway. She stopped long enough to whisper, "I'm going to excuse myself while I still can." And then, in her normal voice, normal walk, she added, "If anybody needs me for anything...like triage...I'll be in the solarium." She gave Cosimo a sympathetic wink and left.

Cosimo watched his older sibling walk away, her stride confident, her posture elegant, her presence commanding. He saw Maria-Carmella smile to herself as she, too, witnessed Regina's unconscious poise and composure under pressure. His stomach churned as he watched his mother's expression morph into something more sinister when she brought her attention back to him. He slumped in his chair, and his head drifted slowly forward as he silently, nervously, awaited her decree. He tried to adjust his posture, to sit up straight, but his earlier burst of confidence had dissipated, and his insecurities had resurfaced. His mother's steely, fixed glare was the physical manifestation of the reality of the situation: that Cosimo did not have, nor had he ever had, any real control over the situation. Or his life.

"I will give you anything you need," the matriarch said, quietly, unceremoniously. "Although it should go without saying that if I allow you to do this, if I allow you to pursue once again whatever whim or dalliance strikes your fancy, there will be stipulations that you must agree to. And there will be things expected of you in return."

"Annabella Bollettieri," Cosimo said, his body slumping forward again with resignation.

"Annabella Bollettieri," Maria-Carmella parroted back to him, imitating his inflection and tone. "It pleases me to know that this comes as no surprise to you. It had occurred to me that you might have forgotten."

"How could I forget, Mother? You've only been planning this since I was sixteen."

"There was always a chance you were operating under the delusion that my plans for you had dissipated or that I had had a change of heart."

"No, but I naturally assumed that you would one day realize that this is not the 1600s." He lifted his head, not so much in defiance as in disbelief. "I don't love her, Mother.

I barely know her. What kind of archaic system forces two people together who don't love each other?"

"You are twenty-four years old, Cosimo. It's time for you to grow up. Do you think that I loved your father when I married him? I was introduced to him three days before our wedding."

"Is that some kind of justification for continuing such an antiquated custom?"

"What if it is?" she said. "And don't you dare condescend to me. I am well aware that we are not living in the Middle Ages."

"That's a relief."

"Don't be smug. Even you, with your skewed vision of the world, can comprehend why such customs have endured for centuries. And you know very well that you and Annabella will be free to lead fully independent lives, so long as you do so discreetly."

"I just don't see why—"

"Cosimo! Honestly! Grow up and accept your responsibilities. You can't possibly be oblivious to the opportunities that will present themselves once our two families have commingled. Power and prestige are fleeting things, dear boy, and we must take advantage of every opportunity that presents itself. We must prepare for the future." Her tone shifted, and Cosimo got the distinct impression that, even though she was addressing him, she had forgotten that he was still in the room, sitting just a few feet away from her. "The greater the unity, the greater the power. Remember that. Together we will create a dynasty of epic proportions. Our families will become legendary," she said and then paused to give her remarks the weight they deserved. "We owe it to ourselves. To the world. You should consider the historical impact that the merging of our two bloodlines will have, and your part in it. Imagine the offspring, the lineage."

"Imagine the *crazy* offspring," Cosimo mumbled.

"What was that?"

"I said they'd be *amazing* offspring."

"Yes. They would. They would indeed. I'm glad you see that, Cosimo. Do you have any idea what's at stake here? Can you comprehend that this is your duty—no, your *privilege* to carry on this line? The Garibaldis are…*were* the oldest ruling class in Europe. A thousand years. And Italy will not stay a republic forever, I guarantee you that. It's only a matter of time before…" Maria-Carmella said, and then she drifted off.

She continued to peer into his eyes, but he got the sense that she was looking through him, not at him. He could tell that the dialogue, or rather her monologue, continued, but that it was playing itself out silently in her head. And try as he might to read her mind, her penetrating, unblinking stare was too impenetrable to reveal her innermost grandiose thoughts. Maria-Carmella was not devoid of, or entirely resistant to, a few delusions of her own. Cosimo, unable to make sense of her peculiar behavior, was at a loss for words. So he sat there and said nothing while he waited for her tirade and her reverie to come to a formal, and hopefully hasty, conclusion.

"We can discuss this in more detail later," she said, snapping back to reality. "But right now I must get ready for a charity auction. Where is it you're heading off to tonight?"

"Tomorrow. I'm leaving in the morning for Boston, to

see some friends, maybe visit a few campuses. To see if I'd like it there," he added, as if it was just one of many options he was contemplating.

"Boston is a lovely city. Quaint and still somewhat provincial. I haven't been there in ages." She stood, walked around the table, and gently but purposefully placed a hand on his shoulder. "I think it will suit you," she whispered in an oddly maternal way. "Well, I'm off. You have fun this weekend," she mock-ordered him. "I'm sorry I was out so late that we missed our little chat." She started to walk away, and then she suddenly swung around again. "Not to worry, dear; whatever you need, you let me know." As she made her way down the hallway to the foyer, her back to him and her voice getting fainter with every word, she added, "I'm happy to see you taking charge of your life, Cosimo. It's about time."

He watched as she weaved her way through the apartment, slithering and silent as a sated serpent. Still in a state of shock, he'd been unable to offer a thank-you or say goodbye. He sat there in the kitchen, his mouth agape, wondering what alien life form had switched mothers on him, or which one of his prescription medications were deluding him into imagining his mother as congenial. Or worse yet, what kind of sick, twisted prank were the gods playing on him, and how long would it last? He walked out to the patio and leaned over the railing that overlooked the front entrance. He saw the black town car pull up and the driver get out to open the rear door. He watched Maria-Carmella in her crimson Bill Blass suit slip gracefully into the back seat. Cosimo, having seen her once more in the light of day going about her usual business, felt fairly confident that

what had just transpired between them was not a halluci-
nation, an illusion, or a hologram, so he made his way back
to the kitchen to finish his breakfast. He spent the rest of
the day on the phone and on the internet making reserva-
tions, confirming flights, and hiring drivers. The thought of
seeing Megan erased all of his troubles, all of his conflicts, all
of the petty doubts from his mind. He even forgot, at least
temporarily, about his cafeteria list of mental disorders and
that his mother had just introduced a new stumbling block:
a fiancée in the form of one Annabella Bollettieri, heir to
the Dolce Vita Gelato fortune and a descendant of one of
Europe's oldest governing families.

Chapter Sixteen

Megan sat at a table under a black-and-white awning at an outdoor café, anxiously watching an eclectic parade of shoppers and strollers wander up and down Newbury Street. Either her Timex watch was running fast or Cosimo was already a half hour late. She took another sip of iced tea and resumed drawing thin, dark lines on beige notebook paper that were meant to depict a brownstone building on the other side of the street. She focused her attention on one crumbling corner of the caramel-colored exterior. It was the most interesting detail because it was bathed in the amber light of the afternoon sun, which exposed and enhanced the façade's numerous flaws. Its angles were visually compromised, the stone so softened and feathered by weather that the surface had been rendered multilayered and blurry. She tried to capture its imperfections, the essence of the stone, in the equally fuzzy medium of charcoal. But her sketch didn't adequately convey the contradictions that the building did. She had failed, in her estimation, to recreate a sense of solidity while simultaneously exposing its weakness. Frustrated with her meager artistic talent, she closed the notebook and put it away with a sigh of resignation. She leaned back, sipped her tea, and tried to relax. It was a perfect Boston afternoon, she thought as she surveyed the pedestrians ambling past her on that unusually warm September day.

One of those pedestrians was Cosimo Garibaldi, who, with his measured gait and deliberate stride, was rapidly approaching the café. His hair, which stuck out from underneath a knit cap, bounced wildly as he walked. His scarf, this time draped loosely about his neck and over his shoulders, flapped lightly in the breeze. His large, tortoise-shell sunglasses were meant to serve as both sunscreen and disguise, to shield him from the sun's glare as well as the paparazzi's lens, if there happened to be any lurking about. As he approached the restaurant, Megan watched him with a mixture of curiosity, anxiety, reminiscence, and antici-pation. They had not seen each other since that last day in June when he'd wished her bon voyage and adieu at Charles De Gaulle airport.

They had spoken on the phone almost every day since he'd arrived in New York, and it was during their last con-versation that Cosimo confessed how he felt.

"I can't take it any longer; I must see you," he said. "I am coming to Boston tomorrow. Where can we meet?"

"Cosimo, I can't…I have…I need—"

"No?" The tenor of his one-word question unmasked his insecurity, his fear of abandonment, his quiet desper-ation. He lacked the ability to filter his thoughts or to pretend that things were other than they were. Even when the stakes were high. Despite having grown up in a household where deception and manipulation were the norm rather than the exception, he was incapable of being mendacious or of keeping his cards hidden. Whatever came out of Cosimo's mouth was the truth, at least at the time, at least as he saw it.

"I have to work. And I have a drawing class in the afternoon," she said. "Tomorrow's not good for me."

Since Cosimo had experienced the world as duplicitous, having learned at a young age to anticipate, to expect a hidden agenda, he wondered what it was she was really trying to tell him.

"What about Saturday? I'm free on Saturday," she offered.

"Yes. Yes, I can do that," he said, before she'd even finished her sentence.

And so it was decided that they would rendezvous at a café in Back Bay early Saturday afternoon.

She had thought about a reunion often during their separation, of what it would be like to see him, of how it would feel to hold him, to be held by him, to run her fingers through his wavy hair, to caress his chest while her hands traveled back and forth across his hips. She had replayed it over and over again in her mind. And in each instance, the vision had a different outcome. What was it that she wanted? What did she need? What could she accept, forgive, dismiss, avoid, tolerate, endure? So many questions had been percolating in her mind after he had explained, or rather tried to explain, his disappearance. But she had to admit that during all of their phone conversations, he came across as the same man she had fallen for in Paris. There were no weird outbursts. No talking in tongues. He hadn't been hearing voices or seeing things that weren't there, at least as far as she knew. And he'd always called when he said he would. Still…

Cosimo saw her sitting on the patio and stopped short to watch her, to admire her, to prolong their reunion in a weird masochistic way, anticipating what it would be like to hold her in his arms again. He had waited so long. A lifetime, it seemed. She was the same, yet she had changed. Her hair was shorter and the cut somewhat different. It had the effect of framing her face, of highlighting it and complementing her physiognomy, which made her even more beautiful than he remembered. He found it hard to believe that it was really her sitting there, glowing from within. And without. And the thought occurred to him that in some cosmic and metaphysical way, it was for her that the sun shone. It was *because* of her that the sun shone.

His feelings for people or possessions had always faded in the past, his passions dissipating, evaporating, diluting over time. But for her, every day his desire grew stronger, grew deeper, gained velocity and intensity. And as much as he feared the idea of being controlled by another woman, he could neither resist nor deny how he felt about her. He removed his sunglasses so that he could see her unfiltered.

Megan had her own justifications for being wary of getting more deeply involved with Cosimo. It never occurred to her that a few days in Europe with a man—a fling, for lack of a better word—would ever evolve into something else, something substantial, something permanent. As much as she'd enjoyed being with him, she never dreamed that it might lead to something more. She had never wanted to find herself in the very position she had found herself in: falling in love with someone who might not be available to her. And while she hadn't as yet used the *word* "love," she had admitted, begrudgingly to herself (as well as to him during a phone conversation), that she did have feelings for him, that she hadn't been able to stop thinking about him during his absence.

Cosimo entered the café through a small metal gate flanked by two potted shrubs. Megan smiled and stood to greet him. She was about to say "Hi," but the greeting got stuck in her throat when he placed his hand on the small of her back and slowly, gently, consciously, as if time had forgotten to show up for work, pulled her body close to his. Their eyes locked together in a silent hello as he drew her closer to him. Oblivious to all else, his breathing rapid, their hips touching, he leaned in, hesitated for the briefest of moments, and then kissed her.

He could feel the blood pumping through his veins and the inner workings of his heart. He could sense his neurons firing and his synapses igniting. It was as if, in a matter of seconds, the world had shifted from black-and-white and monophonic into Technicolor and stereophonic. After months of deprivation, the world was alive again. And it occurred to him, as he pressed his lips against hers, that she had been what was missing from his life all along, that it was she who held the key to whatever it was that was locked inside of him.

"Hello," he said, once he'd released her from his embrace.

"Hu…hu…hi," she said. "That was *some* greeting."

"I didn't plan to do that," he said, blushing, his eyes drifting to the pavement. "I planned *not* to do that," he added, looking up. "But when I saw you, it was like my mind was hijacked. No…wait. That's not what I meant. What I meant was—"

"Cosimo, it's okay. You needn't watch everything you say to me. I'm not going to scrutinize or judge you. Not yet, anyway," she said, grinning. She leaned forward and gave him a tender, albeit slightly less passionate, kiss on the lips. "Did you drive?" she asked as they settled into their seats.

"No. I took an early flight."

"What have you been doing all morning?"

"It's a surprise. I'll tell you later. Maybe tonight after dinner. For now, I want to tell you how beautiful you look. More radiant than I remember. But if I recall correctly, the last time I tried to do that, it did not go so well."

"Don't worry about it. At least now I know what to expect." She reached across the table and brushed away a lock of his hair. "And you—you look nice, healthy. And tan. Maybe I should check myself into that hospital in Zurich. I'm a little bonkers myself these days."

"Did you say *Boinkers?* That sounds like a child's game. Or better yet," he said with a lecherous grin, "like something we should play after dinner?"

"Slow down, cowboy. As happy as I am to see you, I'm not sure I'm ready for any more games."

He wasn't sure what she meant by that last comment, and neither was she. So they both chose to ignore it.

"There's one thing you need to know about me," she said as she waved to get the waiter's attention. "I hate surprises."

"What about birthdays? What about presents?"

"Surprises are only enjoyable for those planning the surprise, not for the surprisee," she said. "And while we're on the subject, I'm not so fond of secrets, either. The same rule applies to them. They're a lot more interesting for the person keeping them than they are for the one they're being kept from. So, you're not really going to make me wait until after dinner now, are you?"

"I know, I will give you hints. You're smart. You'll figure it out." He rubbed his palms together briskly and pondered the situation. "Okay, I've got it. Your first clue is...view."

"Fine, don't tell me. But I'm going to remember this when you want to play Boinkers later."

"I am so happy to see you," was his only reply.

They talked. They laughed. They ate Salade Nicoise. They drank wine, held hands, kissed occasionally, and reminisced. They left the café two hours later and walked leisurely in the direction of the Commons.

Chapter Seventeen

As they walked through town, Megan directed Cosimo's attention to the stately maple trees and to the forlorn weeping willows, to the green Esplanade and the grayish Charles River, to the Federal-style row houses perched on Beacon Hill, and to the golden dome of the State Capitol holding court over the Boston Common. They stopped to admire the Hancock tower and its mirrored surface reflecting sunset-colored clouds. And they paused to listen to a tuxedoed trio huddled together in front of Trinity Church playing *Le Quattro Stagioni* for spare change.

"It's not Paris," she said, "but for my money, it's the next best thing."

"Were you born here?"

"Yes, although I wasn't raised here. I grew up over there, just past that neon CITGO sign," she said, pointing in the direction of the large, triangular logo in the distance. "Brookline. My folks still live there, although they recently bought a condo in Florida. They're calling it investment

property, but my guess is they'll move there before too
long. Anyway, as soon as I was old enough to take the T
by myself, I came here every chance I got." She watched
Cosimo as he took in the full panorama of the city, from
the modern skyscrapers of the Financial District to the
Gothic churches of Back Bay. "What do you think?" she
asked. "About Boston, I mean. It must be rather provincial and boring to you. Compared to the Upper West Side,
anyway."

"New York has never been my favorite city," he said.
"Too many people. Too much noise. It's dirty, the people
are rude, and everyone is in such a hurry. But this…this
feels more civilized, friendlier, livable."

"I agree. I've never wanted to live anywhere else," she
said. "Except maybe Paris."

"Parquet," he said.

"What?"

"Parquet. It's your next clue."

"Why don't we walk over to the Gardens and see if the
Swan Boats are running?"

He took the hint and dropped the subject. They
strolled through the Commons in silence; then, dodging
and weaving through a steady stream of traffic, they crossed
over to the Public Garden. As they approached the water,
they saw that the Swan Boats were tethered to the dock.
They stopped in the middle of a bridge and admired them
as they bobbed up and down in the shallow pond. The way
that the fading sun sparkled on the water, glistened on the
white painted birds, and shimmered off the polished brass
railings reminded Megan of the day they'd first met, and the

way the light, reflecting off the Seine, had danced across the limestone buildings.

"Don't be mad at me, okay, but I have one more clue for you," he said.

"I'm not mad, Cosimo. I'm just not very good at games. I never have been. With that understood, what's the clue?"

"Your third clue is…" Cosimo paused, not to create suspense, but because he hadn't thought the whole thing through. He had felt compelled to do what he was about to do since he'd boarded the plane at Kennedy that morning. He hadn't been able to think of anything else all day. He searched her eyes for a sign, for some indication that what he was about to do made sense. Her perplexed expression failed to reveal her thoughts, and it made him want to retract the whole business about clues, to put a stop to whatever it was he had set in motion—to stop everything. He would have given anything to be back in Regina's guestroom, buried under a mound of blankets, the phone on mute and the shades tightly drawn. He wanted to call Dr. Wyckoff, to get his opinion, to run the idea by someone, anyone, before he made a complete fool of himself.

His hand nervously searched around in his coat pockets for a Xanax, even though he knew there weren't any there. And even if he did find one, it was too late to take it. He slipped his other hand in between the buttons of his shirt, his fingers instinctively trying to find, to feel, to fondle the gold medallion that rested on his breastplate.

"Your third clue is…" he said, hesitating again as he counted the gems embedded in the necklace. The edge of the medal was smooth from years of wear, from a decade of being massaged, but he gripped it so tightly that it still dug deep into the flesh of his forefinger. The pressure and the familiarity of it calmed his nerves long enough for him to say, "The final clue is…I love you."

They stood quietly together on the bridge as strangers strolled by, as tourists snapped photographs of the Swan Boats, and as parents chastised unruly children while simultaneously attempting to buy soft-serve ice cream from a vendor in a truck. When the hint of a smile finally surfaced on Megan's face, Cosimo made a hand gesture to preclude her from speaking. After such an uncomfortable silence, he needed more time before hearing her response.

"I can't believe I said it," he said, still squeezing the gold talisman between his thumb and forefinger. An agonizing silence evolved into an unbearable one. The awkwardness of the situation caused him to ramble. "It's okay if you don't feel the same way. I didn't say it to have you say it back. Me, I have always been this way. I can't help myself. I say whatever's on my mind, and I rarely stop to consider the consequences." He looked into the murky water, hoping it contained some message or omen that would inform or enlighten him as to what he should say next. He shuffled his feet in a way that reminded Megan of a teenage boy on his first date. "The way that I feel about you, I have never felt about anyone. And I don't know what to do with those feelings. Is there some policy, some protocol, some set of rules one should follow?"

"No, Cosimo, there's no protocol. There's no map, no manual, no tour guide, no textbook. We're all left to figure out that lifelong secret on our own, to muddle through it independently, as best we can."

"So it would seem."

Cosimo spotted a vacant bench a few feet away and moved in that direction. He motioned for Megan to follow. Once seated, his fingers began mindlessly peeling off a skateboarding decal from one of the wooden slats.

"I have been doing a lot of thinking lately," he said. "And not necessarily by choice. And I have come to the realization that it is entirely possible to have everything that you need or want, and at the same time, have nothing at all."

"That's rather profound," she said. "*Sad*, but profound."

"Unfortunately, that predicament is not unique to me. *That* is what's sad." He closed his eyes, leaned forward, and kissed her on the forehead. His warm lips lingered there while he paused to catch his breath, to steady his pulse. He pulled away from her and said, "I didn't...I don't expect you to say it back, although I do hope that you will feel that way someday." He looked away from her and turned his attention to his fingers as he tried to peel away the pieces of the shredded decal that had become stuck to them. As he transferred the sticky strips of paper from his fingers back to the slats on the bench, it occurred to him that what he'd said could easily be misconstrued. "I meant, I hope that someday you feel that *love* thing, not that having everything and nothing at the same time, thing."

"Yeah, I got that," she said with the hint of a laugh.

"I know that it was too soon to tell you. But I also knew that I couldn't make it through the weekend *without* telling you. I just...I needed...I only wanted you to know. Good or bad, having been raised by wolves, when I see a moon, I howl at it."

"You are so very sweet. A little bizarre, but sweet. And

you should know—I think you do—that I'm crazy about
you."

A grin spread across Cosimo's face.

"I haven't stopped thinking about you since I left
France," she added. "Try as I might." Cosimo tried unsuc-
cessfully to stifle a joyous laugh, but it burst forth from his
lips like a baby's bubbled burp.

"And while I'm happy that you're here, even you have
to realize that we've only just met, that we barely know
each other."

"But what does duration have to do with anything?" he
said. "I feel how I feel."

"Look, I've been in and out of love more often than I
care to remember, or am willing to admit. And if there's one
thing I've learned, it's that it's best to take things slow. If you
move too fast, you can get whiplash or the bends."

"I thought you said there were no rules?"

"Exactly."

"But—"

"Call it a guideline. A very vague, very flexible guideline."

Megan was drawn to Cosimo, to his vulnerability, to
his openness. The sight of him deep in concentration, his
eyes narrowed and his mouth pursed in a mix of wonder
and befuddlement, aroused an equal amount of compassion
and affection in her. And inexplicably, but undeniably, lust.

"Don't try to figure it out, Cosimo. Honestly, there are
no right or wrong answers, no schedules to follow, no gurus
to guide you. What works in one relationship inevitably
won't work in another. We are all slaves to the heart beating
in our chest and to that mythological winged cherub with

the bow and arrow and regrettably bad aim. Just do what your heart tells you to, which you did."

Her eyes drifted back to the swan boats as she reflected on her concept of love and wondered if she truly believed her own words. Looking back at him, she said, "By the way, you're not the only one who has a secret."

"You are obviously wise beyond your years," he said. "As for the secret, I'll play along. Do I get a clue?"

"No clues. No games. I'd rather just tell you."

She leaned in sideways, cupped a hand behind his head, and teasingly, seductively, whispered in his ear, "I don't really want to wait until after dinner to play Boinkers with you."

He flashed her a playful, lascivious grin.

"You know, I hate to admit it," he said, "but your secret is much better than mine."

And without any further discussion, he put his arm around her waist and led her through the Public Gardens toward his suite at the Four Seasons.

Chapter Eighteen

Megan, freshly showered, stood in front of the marble vanity and applied moisturizer to her face from a basket of tiny complimentary toiletries. She peered into the magnifying mirror and wondered if the European facemask, toner, and moisturizing cream she'd just used had minimized any of the fine lines she'd begun to notice around her eyes. She didn't know if it was the Swedish skin-care line or the bathroom's flattering pink lighting, but her wrinkles were less noticeable. She added a touch of her own lipstick and a dab of bronzer from a sample that a saleswoman at Macy's insisted she try. She repackaged the amenities so that they looked untouched and returned to the bedroom to find the king-size bed empty. The thick down comforter was draped over one corner of the mattress, and a dozen pillows were stacked haphazardly against the damask headboard. And Cosimo, who had been lying in the middle of that rumpled mess earlier, was now missing.

She slipped on a plush, white Egyptian cotton robe

that she found hanging in the closet and walked into the living room, expecting to find him reclining on a sofa, watching TV, or reading a book. But the parlor, like the bed, was empty. Vast and empty. The room seemed so cavernous that she felt uncomfortable being there without him. As she walked through the living and dining areas, she scrutinized the soft, ultrasuede fabrics, the nubby silk throw pillows, the highly polished mahogany dining table, the oversized flat-screen TV. She imagined an insistent rap on the other side of the thick paneled door, followed by a security guard bursting into the room and grilling her about her presence there and then ordering her to get dressed, to gather her belongings, and follow him out into the hall.

Standing at the window, she traced the steps she and Cosimo had taken only a few hours earlier, backwards from the hotel's entrance on Boylston Street, through the Public Garden, dark now except for the dim glimmer of street lamps, and ultimately back to the bridge where they had stood as the sun began to set. The same bridge where Cosimo, the missing Cosimo, had declared his love for her. The hotel phone by the sofa rang, but she made no move to answer it. As the ringing continued, the noise seemed to get louder and more insistent with each *briinnnggg*.

She made her way to the bedroom again and changed back into the outfit she'd been wearing earlier. The full-length mirror and the overhead lighting exaggerated the wrinkles in her clothes, which had been lying on the floor untouched for several hours after she and Cosimo had tossed them there in a fit of passion. She heard her cell phone's distinctive ring emanating from her purse. She retrieved it and found that the caller's ID was restricted. Normally she wouldn't answer such a call, but this one she did.

"Where are you?" Cosimo asked.

"I'm in the hotel room. Where are you?"

"Why didn't you answer?"

"It didn't feel right, not being my room and all. I had no reason to assume that it would be for me. And it didn't occur to me that it would be you. Are you coming back soon?"

"Yes. I'm in the fitness center. I had a sudden urge to swim."

She had no response to his comment. She didn't know what it meant, or how she felt about him deserting her to partake of a few laps in the hotel pool.

"It's late; you must be getting hungry. I thought we could eat downstairs in the hotel," he said. "Is that okay with you?"

She sat down on a corner of the bed and took in the luxurious details of the opulent suite as she carefully deliberated the answer to his question. She sighed as her gaze moved from the sepia toile draperies and the salmon-hued velvet club chairs down to the wrinkles in her cotton slacks and the scuff marks on her Ferragamo knock-offs.

"Coz…I'm not really…" She wasn't sure how to finish the sentence, so she didn't.

"I'll be right up."

She sat there with nothing to do but wait for him to come back. She picked up the robe from the bed, draped it over a satin hanger, and hung it back in the closet. On the floor was Cosimo's empty suitcase. His shirts were all neatly hung, seven or eight of them at quick glance, as were an equal number of pressed pants that hung upside down from special wooden hangers. Five pairs of shoes lined the floor, all polished and shoe-treed. On the overhead shelves sat a neat stack of jeans and a small pile of sweaters. The exposed sleeve of one of his shirts had an interesting pattern on it, and she was curious to see it close up. She separated the shirts to get a better look at it, and when the front came into full view, it was not the pattern that caught her eye; it was the label: Prada. She slid that one aside only to find that the next shirt in line was also Prada. The one after that was a Dolce & Gabbana and the item after that, Armani. Those were followed by a couple of designers she'd never heard of before and a light-blue buttoned-down linen number by Ermenegildo Zegna. With her curiosity piqued, she knelt down on the floor and pulled a cedar shoetree from a black loafer. It did not shock her to find a Prada insignia there as well. Next to them were a pair of cordovan lace-ups embossed with the name Bruno Magli. The next pair were a dark-brown suede that bore a red and green tab that even she recognized as Gucci's trademark. And the last pair she checked were a supple, buttery, brown leather that bore a familiar signature on the interior heel: Ferragamo. As she slipped the final shoetree back into place, she muttered, "I bet *those* Ferragamos aren't knock-offs." When she heard the door to the suite open and close, she shut the closet, sat down in one of the club chairs, and waited for Cosimo to enter with his hair still wet and the scent of chlorine emanating from his skin.

～

Megan and Cosimo sat quietly at the dining table while

they ate room-service Caesar salads and steak au poivre. Other than the intermittent clack of cutlery against china, the only sound in the spacious suite came from the rhythmic tapping of Cosimo's fingertips on the glass tabletop.

"I'm going to put on some music," he said. "Any requests?"

"Whatever you like is fine."

He retrieved an iPod from his pants pocket and walked over to a wall in the middle of the room. He inserted the device into a Bang & Olufsen BeoSound 5 and pressed a couple of buttons. Instantaneously the beauty of Simon Standage's violin performing Concerto in E Major, *La Primavera*, Opus 8, from Vivaldi's *Four Seasons*, replaced the silence in the room.

"Ahhh, she has remembered how to smile," he said, taking his seat again.

"It reminds me of this afternoon, that trio on Boylston Street. They were playing the autumn concerto. That seems like weeks ago."

"It was, in a way. You want to distance yourself from it."

"That's not true."

"Really? I don't see you for months, and the first thing out of my mouth is…" He couldn't bring himself to say it again. "It's just that you were all I thought about the whole time we were apart. And seeing you again…I couldn't help myself."

"Cosimo, you should never apologize for loving someone. It caught me off guard, that's all. And then this." She extended her arm in a sweeping motion, like Vanna White presenting a motor home or an Amana Radarange to a studio audience. "This suite is bigger than the house I grew up in. And your closet…all those beautiful, expensive clothes."

"I know. I always pack too much. I'm a slave to my moods, so I prepare for anything and everything." He picked up his knife and fork and cut into a piece of asparagus. "Eat. Eat. Your steak is getting cold."

She sliced off a piece of buttery, pepper-encrusted meat and chewed it slowly. Her head bobbed back and forth in rhythm to Vivaldi's second Allegro, Danza Pastorale.

"You know, you never did tell me *your* secret," she said. "And if you give me another clue, I'll fling this filet at you."

"Bearing in mind how this afternoon went, and considering what it is I have to share, I think I'll opt for the flying beef."

Megan pierced the steak on her plate with a fork and gave him a menacing stare.

"Okay, okay, you win. But I can't tell you. I have to *show* you. Tomorrow."

She raised the steak into the air and intensified her glare.

"Okay, okay, tonight. But may I finish my dinner first?"

She walked around to his side of the table and sat on his lap. One of her fingers played with a spiral of silky, chestnut-colored hair on his head. Her lips found their way to his, and she kissed him, closed mouth; more tender than romantic, more loving than lustful.

"Yes, you can finish dinner," she said, "but no more stalling."

Megan stood in her stocking feet on the newly waxed parquet floor and admired the view from the bay window. She delighted in the new perspective, in a view that looked down on the treetops that dotted the Commons, at the people in miniature as they dashed about, at the blur of glowing headlights and red taillights of cars as they zig-zagged up Arlington Street.

"What floor are we on again?" she asked.

"The top floor," he said, grinning.

She smacked his arm with her palm.

"Twentieth," he said as he rubbed his elbow and faked being injured.

"I'll bet the sunrise from this window is amazing."

"I might be able to arrange for you to see that at some point," he said.

"This place is gorgeous, Cosimo. And the view is stunning. It's so much more intimate than looking down on it from the Hancock Tower." She kissed him tenderly on the cheek. "Thank you for sharing it with me."

He had explained the excursion by telling her that he knew she was an architecture aficionado. And since he'd been given access to the place for a few days, he thought she'd appreciate it for its interesting layout, its sophisticated design, and its inspired use of materials: the marble, the limestone, the teak. Not to mention the spectacular view.

"Come on, tell me. Whose apartment is this?"

"And right now I wish I'd let you throw that steak at me instead of showing you this place."

"Why won't you tell me?"

"Okay. The short answer is, it's mine."

First she smiled, then she chuckled, and then she deduced from his pained expression that he was serious.

"What do you mean, it's *yours*?"

"Well, clarifying that would require the long answer."

Cosimo understood her confusion as well as her frustration. His declaration of love hadn't gone as he'd planned, so he couldn't imagine how she'd react to the revelation that he'd bought the apartment they were standing in, and that he was moving to Boston.

"I get along beautifully with my sister, but I can't live with her forever. And then there's my mother, who for some reason is also living there. And she's, well...she's...a topic best left for another time."

"And what has that got to do with this...this...what is it? A three-bedroom luxury condominium at the Parkhurst?"

"I was getting bored with Paris. And New York...it's not for me long term. And I can't go home because, well, I can't. And since I haven't been able to get you out of my head, as a lark, I called up a few realtors to ask about apartments here."

"You were *bored* with Paris?"

His only response was a shrug of the shoulders.

"I know what I said earlier about the two cities," she continued, "but that's what you call a rationalization. It's how you placate yourself when you don't have a choice." She moved over to one of the sofas and took a seat. "And it didn't occur to you to tell me about this until now?"

"It was one of those things that took on a life of its own. Before I knew it, I was getting daily emails with links to websites and virtual tours of properties. When I saw this one, I made a ridiculously low offer. Even my agent was shocked they accepted it. Suddenly I'm in escrow and ordering inspections." He paced back and forth a few times before taking a seat on the sofa. "I swear, none of it was real until I saw the place this morning for the first time."

"I don't know what to say other than it was awfully

presumptuous of you to…how could you even…*who does this?*"

"I know you're upset, but you were just one of the factors behind my decision."

"Is that supposed to make me feel better?"

"Look, I had to move somewhere," he said, making his way to the wine cooler. He opened the glass door of the Sub Zero and removed the bottle of champagne he had placed there earlier. "And Boston presented itself as good a place as any. Honestly, I could have moved to New Zealand or Zimbabwe or Zihuatanejo if I'd wanted to." He sat down next to her and placed two glasses on the coffee table. "I chose to be near you."

"I'm flattered, I really am. But you're making a lot of assumptions based on a week in Paris that wasn't even real."

"I am aware of that. And I have no intention of putting any pressure on you. If things work out between us, great. If they don't, they don't." He twisted the hook on the wire cage and removed it. "So you can either help me toast to a new beginning…" he said, prying the cork lose and letting a faint pop escape from the bottle, "or I can call you a taxi and consume this entire bottle by myself in my new flat."

"Is that what *you* want?" she said, leaping to her feet, her face flush with fury. "Because I'm quite capable of calling my own cab."

"No. Of course not. Haven't you heard anything I've said today?" He patted the tanned burgundy leather seat cushion next to him. "But I get the impression that that might be what *you* want. And if it is, then I want to make it easy for you, make it…" He couldn't continue. He was trying to be cavalier about it, but the thought of her leaving was causing his stomach to churn and his throat to close up.

She sat down on the sofa again, close enough to him so that their knees touched.

"You've got to give me some time," she said, accepting the glass of champagne he held out. "I don't see you for months, and then suddenly you *have* to see me. The next thing I know, you're declaring your love for me and moving here."

"I know. I came on too strong. I'm irrepressibly impulsive."

"And then the Four Seasons," she said. "Why the hotel if you own this place?"

"Still in escrow. The current owners live in Saudi Arabia. It just so happens they are friends of the family. They gave me a key so that I could start making arrangements with decorators and contractors. It's not officially mine until the end of the month."

She sat there quietly, trying to process what was happening. The more she thought about the incongruities she'd managed to ignore, the more they began to seem obvious. And consequential.

"I don't know how I didn't see this coming," she said. "I had no idea."

"No idea about what?"

"That you were so well off. In Paris you were living in this small, sparsely furnished flat in the Marais," she said. It was then that she recalled reading somewhere that often the grander, the more noble a person is, the more they are inclined to downplay it. "And you had roommates or something, didn't you?" she asked, still hoping her instincts hadn't betrayed her.

"Every apartment in Paris is small and sparsely furnished. I was merely subletting the place for a few months until I could figure out what it was that I wanted to do, or where I wanted to be long term. As for those roommates, they were friends from school who were staying with me for a few nights. And I was content in that tiny apartment for a while, but…"

Cosimo became abruptly and acutely aware of his environment, of the fact that, very soon, he would own all of that stuff. And conversely, all of that stuff would own him.

"You're more fortunate than most to have those options," she said.

"I am fortunate in many ways, not so much in others. It's nice to be able to swim a few laps in the Four Seasons' pool if I'm so inclined. But when I get out of the water and dry myself off, my problems are still there. Just like yours."

"Only your towels are Egyptian cotton, and mine are terrycloth. Look, I'm happy for you. I'm glad that you can afford nice things. But when you asked me if I wanted to eat in the hotel earlier, well, it made me feel awkward and uncomfortable."

"Why?"

"Because I don't belong there. I keep picturing the other guests scrutinizing me as we walk through the lobby, staring at my synthetic blouse, snickering at my plastic watchband, sneering at my pleather handbag. I imagine some hoity-toity maître d' giving me the once-over before leading us to a dark table in a corner by the kitchen. I feel out of place."

"You shouldn't care so much about what other people think," he said.

"That's easier said than done. And what about your perception of me? You met me in Paris. That was a rare trip that ate up most of my savings. I know I wasn't staying at the George V, but still, I may have given you the wrong impression."

"And what impression might that have been?"

"That I was someone other than a middle-class working girl living paycheck to paycheck. You have to understand, my people don't live in penthouses. We rent small apartments near public transportation and wash our clothes in coin-operated Laundromats. An evening out for us is a combo platter at TGI Fridays followed by an action-adventure movie at the local Cineplex. Our linens are not real linen; they're purchased on sale at Target, and as for threads, well, all I can say is, there's not enough of them to bother counting." She raised her glass in a mock toast to the reality that was her life.

Cosimo placed his glass on the coffee table; then he took hers and set it down next to his.

"Why do you tell me this? Do you think any of that matters to me? Have I ever given you the impression that I care about money? That I care whether or not you have money? Yes, I can afford nice things, so yes, I have nice things. It is what I know. Until today, I never once thought about how much money you might or might not have. I don't judge you for not having money; why would you judge me for having it?"

"I'm not judging you. You're sweet and kind and

generous, and if anybody deserves to be rich, it's probably
you."

"Then what is the problem? Is there a problem?"

"Honestly, I don't know. But it proves my point that
we barely know each other. I'm afraid that I don't fit into a
world of French leather furniture, Porsche 911s, and Cristal
champagne served in Baccarat flutes," she said as she reached
for the glass of Cristal on the coffee table in what she now
automatically assumed was a Baccarat flute.

"You think you don't fit in, but I assure you, it is all a
game. I do not fit in, either. The only difference is, I was
raised to believe that I belonged, that I was entitled to a
share of everything that the world has to offer. And I was
taught certain formalities and protocols that afford me a
degree of comfort in most situations. I can teach you those
things, the small graces, the little nuances, the correct fork
to use, so that you too can feel comfortable and *know* that
you belong."

"I don't know what to say," she said, lifting her glass high
in the air, "except, A *votre santé*."

Cosimo reached for his glass, brought it to his lips, and
took a sip. He raised his hand and made a toast of his own:
"*Tout vient a qui sait attendre*."

"Okay, no fair. You know my French isn't that good."

"*C'est vrai*."

"Don't be mean," she said, playfully smacking the side of
his head. "What did you toast to?"

"I said, loosely translated, all things come to those who
know how to wait."

"I like that. And it's so much more elegant in French."

Megan walked over to the floor-to-ceiling window. She

seemed to be scrutinizing the park and the distant skyscrapers that were crowded into small clusters in the financial district. Her intense concentration implied a quest, a search for something in particular. Cosimo placed his empty flute on the coffee table and then walked over and stood behind her. He wrapped his arms around her waist and rested his chin on her shoulder.

"What are you searching for?" he asked.

"That's a loaded question."

"I don't understand."

She shifted her body so that they were standing side by side.

"Loaded? It means…oh, never mind. No, I wasn't looking for anything in particular. I was simply admiring the view. And reflecting on how different our lives are." She hesitated before making her next comment, unsure if it was wise to express it out loud. She looked deep into his eyes, as if the truth were hidden somewhere in them, and said it anyway. "To be honest, I was wondering if there are any *other* secrets you haven't told me yet."

"I did not keep anything from you. You must know that. The money, it is not a subject I think about or talk about, so there was nothing to tell. How could I have known that it would be an issue for you? I don't lie, which in my case is more of a liability than an asset. And while I won't keep secrets from you, I can't tell you everything, either. There are things that must be discovered. You would be bored if you knew everything about me from the start." He took her hands in his, comforting, comingling, connected. "Things need to be revealed slowly, and in a specific order. You know, to protect national security."

"If I find out you're working for the CIA, I'm going to strangle you."

"CIA, that's funny. No, I am with Interpol. Wait, let me show you my badge," he said and reached into his back pocket.

She raised her arm in a mock strike pose.

"No, no, don't hit me again," he said with a convincingly thick Russian accent. "I may be foreign spy, but I bruise easily."

The lights in the ceiling cast a subtle pink glow onto Cosimo. They gave his already tanned complexion a warm hue and the highlights in his curly hair a serene angelic quality. Megan was anxious about the path they were on, yet somehow certain that this beautiful, kind creature with the warm heart and surprising sense of humor would never intentionally do anything to harm her. She shifted their positions so that his back was flush against the plate glass window, and she leaned into him. While she was looking into his eyes, she got a distinct and unpleasant sensation that something had been set into motion. Something that neither of them had the power to stop. It was a sensation of both resignation and empowerment, and it made her feel as if she had stepped off a ledge without first checking to see if there was a safety net below. Whatever the outcome, she figured she might as well enjoy the view on the way down. She grasped the back of his head and gave him a kiss that was determined and delicate, surrendering and controlling, passionate and playful all at the same time. Her mind and her body were now a bubbling cauldron of emotions, and she knew without question that she had lost whatever control she'd once thought she'd had.

"This I like," he said. "Much better than all that slapping, *n'est-ce pas?*"

"*Peut-être,*" she said, giving him another playful slap on the arm, "*peut-être.*"

Chapter Nineteen

Cosimo, heading nowhere in particular, ambled in a daze down a crowded, shop-infested, traffic-congested Fifth Avenue. He'd left Regina's flat an hour earlier and had been wandering aimlessly ever since. Nothing appealed to him. Not the latest sportswear collection in the Ermenegildo Zegna boutique, not the new Patek Philippe watches in the jeweler's window, not the French bistro on the corner with the pretty young waitress, not even the coffee and croissants at Bouchon. He wondered, why, if he had everything anyone could ever want, did he feel so empty? He often got melancholy when things went his way. Good fortune made him nervous—which for him was a problem, as more often than not, things went his way. But it did seem to him that good things, good events, even good thoughts, were merely precursors to bad ones; fathers leave, uncles die, friends move away. Good or bad, nothing stayed the same.

The previous weekend with Megan hadn't gone as he'd expected. He thought she'd be thrilled that he was moving to Boston. He hadn't anticipated the hesitation in her voice, hadn't reckoned that there might be a cap on her enthusiasm as far as he was concerned. But evidently there was. The fact that she wasn't comfortable in his new flat, or even by the idea that he could afford such a place, had taken him completely by surprise. Everything had been so easy for them in Paris, so casual, so equal. In Boston, on her home turf, he found her much more guarded and protective than she'd been when they first met. It seemed to him that his revelation had shifted the balance of power in her mind, made her feel as if she'd lost some footing and needed to protect herself. But against what, he had no clue. All he wanted was be with her, to love her. And, of course, eventually, to be loved back.

Cosimo had no tolerance for indifference, no patience for passivity. You were either fully engaged in the world, in an activity, in a relationship, or you weren't. There was nothing else, no in-between. Anything done half-heartedly was a waste of time, of energy. But even though he may have misjudged her, it was too late for him to walk away, for him to pretend—to her or to himself—that he would be okay without her.

So, while the balance of power may have shifted for Megan with regard to finances, for Cosimo, there had been an equally troubling shift on an emotional level. And that was especially troubling for him because even the most unintentional slight, the tiniest indication that he might not be everything to her, had the potential to completely undo him. The questioning, the self-doubt, the second-guessing could go on for days, weeks, years. Therapists had told him that fear of abandonment is secured early in one's life and that there is no definitive way to compensate for it. One must learn to live with it, to be aware that one's perceptions are not necessarily a true reflection of reality. It helps if one can remain rational, but it is difficult to be rational when you're dealing with an irrational manifestation of a childhood fear.

When he first met her, he felt that he could be himself: silly, capricious, intense, reserved, outgoing, shy—the full spectrum of his bipolar disorder. But now that she was back in Boston and settled into her familiar routine, she was more reserved, more inhibited, and decidedly more cautious. There were moments—a kiss, a whisper, a look—that harked back to the Megan of Paris, but with each passing hour, she became more restrained, more East Coast, more staunch. Her ability to be spontaneous and her appreciation of his impulsivity had diminished with the passing of time. What if she was right? What if he *had* made some wrong assumptions about her? Perhaps she had, intentionally or not, adopted a different persona while vacationing in a foreign country.

He paused in front of Bvlgari to admire a pair of earrings in the window. A taxi driver leaning on his horn startled him, and when he spun around, he spotted Maria-Carmella emerging from Tiffany on the opposite side of the street. She was wearing her knee-length lynx fur coat with the high collar and large cuffs. He laughed at the thought of her in it. Whenever anyone asked her what type of animal skin it was, out of political correctness, she feigned ignorance. Her response was usually along the lines of, "I'm not exactly sure, but it's quite realistic for faux, wouldn't you agree?" But in the circles in which she traveled and in the company that she kept, all of the diamonds were genuine, all of the hair was real (even if it wasn't their own), and all of their coats had once roamed the wild. It was only their breasts and their cheekbones that were fake.

He bolted into Bvlgari, praying that that wasn't going to be her next stop. With his head down in an effort to conceal his profile, he walked to the stairwell leading up to the mezzanine. Several salespeople monitored him nervously, suspiciously. Upstairs his eyes were fixated below, to the front door and to the gray strip of sidewalk in front of it. He waited for his mother to breeze in, her hands gripping numerous tiny packages, and the inevitable commotion that erupts whenever she enters a retail store. Salesclerks inevitably trip over each other to get to her first and take her wrap. They can't compliment her quick enough or steam her cappuccino hot enough before they commence presenting her with an array of necklaces, brooches, and bracelets for her to consider.

Cosimo had fortuitously managed to avoid her since his return from Boston. Maria-Carmella had made an unexpected business trip to London and then spent the better part of the week in meetings with attorneys. During her absence, Cosimo spent his days quietly reading and contemplating and doing his best to forget that Maria-Carmella would eventually, inevitably arrive back at Regina's flat, armed and loaded with her usual barrage of questions, most of which he preferred not to answer. Cosimo garnered from a conversation he'd overheard between the housekeeper and the doorman that Maria-Carmella was in one of her more foul moods that morning. He had been lucky enough and careful enough to arrange his entrances and exits so that they hadn't coincided with hers. But he knew that he couldn't, and probably shouldn't, avoid her much longer. She might notice and jump to the conclusion that it was intentional, if she hadn't already. The repercussions that would follow even such a trivial revelation were beyond the scope of even Cosimo's vivid imagination.

A young couple entered the store, and the sound of the glass doors clicking shut behind them caused Cosimo's heart to beat faster. A few minutes later, the doors were pushed open again by an elderly gentleman in an ill-fitting suit. The young couple quickly circled the first floor and then left. Cosimo had lost track of time and wasn't sure how long he'd been standing there. Two minutes? Five? Ten? A few more minutes passed as he pretended to be interested in a pair of gold and lapis cufflinks. Then, with no sign of Maria-Carmella anywhere, he felt as if he could breathe again.

Maria-Carmella's moods were often as volatile as Cosimo's, but hers came with consequences; hers came with ultimatums. On that particular day, what Cosimo was most afraid of was that she had morphed back into her caustic, critical, calculating self and was prepared to reprimand him for some minor infraction he'd made of one of her arbitrary rules. Or berate him for the slightest breach of etiquette or fashion. Or worse yet, threaten to curtail his spending. But avoiding her wasn't the answer. Getting away from her was. He regretted not having greeted her on the street earlier, when they would have been on neutral ground. That would have pleased her, to see him back in New York, out for a stroll, competent and functioning normally. At least that's what she would have seen on the surface. He slowly made his way back down to the first floor and approached a svelte, leggy, blond salesclerk.

"May I see the earrings in the window?" he said. "The sapphires?"

"Certainly," she said as she escorted him over to one of the Philippe Starck chairs. "I'll bring them right over."

He settled into the crystal-clear polycarbonate chair he had just conjured Maria-Carmella sitting in. He admired the salesclerk's long, perfectly proportioned legs as she placed a velvet pad showcasing the earrings down on a small table in front of him.

"These are princess-cut fine blue sapphires weighing one-point-nine carats," she said as her perfectly manicured nails directed his eyes to the faceted gems. "They rest in a handcrafted bezel cut setting of brightly polished platinum with eighteen-carat white gold friction backs." She took the backing off one of them to demonstrate. "I have to say, these are my current favorites. They're lovely, aren't they?" She replaced the backing. "And, as you can probably tell from the detail, they were designed exclusively for Bvlgari by Antonio Citterio."

"They're extraordinary. May I?" he asked as he reached for them.

"Absolutely, Mr. Garibaldi. Can I get you a cappuccino? A glass of champagne?"

"No, I'm good, thank you," he said to the woman whose wide grin he couldn't quite interpret. What he didn't say was, *How did you know my name?* He was accustomed to being recognized in Europe, but it always took him by surprise in America. Had he asked her, she would have told him that she'd recognized his face from a photograph on page six of that morning's *New York Daily News*. It was a blurry but unmistakable snapshot of Cosimo and Regina that had been surreptitiously captured two nights earlier at a nightclub opening she had dragged him to. The salesclerk might have also told him, had he asked, that his sister was mesmerizing in her Armani strapless gown, and that he was adorable because of the way he sleepily rested his head on her bare shoulder. But he didn't ask, and she didn't offer.

"Could you wrap these up, please? I'd like to take them with me."

"Of course, Mr. Garibaldi. Do you have an account with us?"

"No. Can you put them on my card?" He pulled out his wallet and handed her a black American Express card.

"Absolutely. This will only take a second."

He stepped out of the store and into the rush of people who were shuffling down Fifth Avenue. The wind had picked up, and there was a chill in the air that hadn't been there earlier. While he had been hiding out in the jewelry store, late summer had abruptly turned into fall. And not the pumpkin carving, multicolored-leaves kind of fall, but rather an autumn that was the precursor to an inevitably harsh winter, like those found in an Utrillo landscape of muted colors and barren trees. When he left Regina's flat, the day had an air of early spring about it—cool but sunny, crisp but refreshing—and he had dressed appropriately in a light jacket and thin silk shirt. But that outfit would not be sufficient for the walk back, which was easily twenty blocks, so he hailed a cab rather than make the trip back on foot.

As the taxi bumped, swerved, and honked its way

uptown, abruptly stopping and starting at every other light, he checked his messages. There was one email from Megan, two from Regina, and four text messages from Maria-Carmella. He put the device back into its leather holster without reading or responding to any of them. *Later,* he thought. *I'll get to them later.*

There was no one in the living room of Regina's apartment, so, as quietly as he could, he headed for his bedroom. Unfortunately he had to pass the study to get there. And it was there in the dimly lit room, infused with the strains of violins rising from the apartment's audio system, that he found Maria-Carmella sitting in a chair with a newspaper resting in her lap. She silently motioned for him to join her. He entered the room, but just barely. He leaned against a bookcase to the right of the archway and tried his best to act pleasant, to conceal his desire to be elsewhere.

"Come in, come in," she said.

He inched forward. She held up the newspaper that was folded open to a section of black-and-white photographs of people clustered together dancing, hugging, smiling, posing, most of them in tuxedos and ball gowns. They stood coupled together in theater lobbies, or in awkward groups at museum entrances and banquet halls. Names and titles in tiny lettering were printed beneath each tableau.

"Why can't my children be profiled here once in a while instead of that trash you and your sister were in this morning? Answer me that," she said as she tossed the *New York Times* society page at her son. He made no attempt to intercept it. It hit his head and then landed with an audible shuffle at his feet. Lost in thought, he stood there, staring at it. When he looked up, she was standing inches away from him. With both of her hands placed firmly on her hips, she hovered over him, even though she was significantly shorter than he was. She shook her head from side to side in a dismissive fashion. Her hair, which was pulled back tightly in a chignon, foreshadowed the emergence of darker roots along her scalp. He was captivated by those roots. He studied them. He tried to understand them, like they were a mystery to be solved, some secret to be discovered, some code to be broken. His eyes, and almost instantaneously his head, started to follow hers, back and forth, back and forth, unaware that his movements were mimicking hers. Hypnotized by the repetitive motion of the contrasting line of hair running down the center of his mother's scalp, he had stopped listening to her latest in a series of tirades. But his attention was brought back to the room and to Maria-Carmella when he felt the full impact of her hand and her twelve-carat diamond ring on the side of his face.

"It's bad enough that you disobey my requests, that you embarrass me in public, that you repeatedly disappoint me. I will not have you mock me as well!"

"But, Mother, I wasn't. I didn't mean to—" he said, truly befuddled by her response, completely unaware that the movement of his head had replicated hers.

"Enough! You…" She shook her head in disgust and an eternal silence ensued.

He dared not utter a word. He knew that no matter what he said, she would interpret it differently, spin his words around, and use them against him. Anything he said would simply add fuel to the fire. It was best to let her vent and then deal with the situation later, after she'd had a chance to calm down.

"You are my greatest challenge," she said, her tone tinted with both exasperation and resignation. She shook her head as she walked around him and the pile of paper still at his feet. "What to do?" she muttered to herself as she left the room. "What to do?" The only sound in the apartment, other than the recorded violins and the faint rumble of traffic coming from outside, was the clicking of her stiletto heels on the polished wood floor as she hurried down the hallway to her suite.

Chapter Twenty

It was a Monday afternoon, and Megan was moving about her small, frugally furnished apartment with a bucket of cleaning supplies and a temperamental handheld vacuum cleaner. She attacked each surface with foam or spray, cloth or sponge, broom or suction, vigorously scouring each area with determination. In the kitchen, she sprayed the counter with Tilex for the second time and tried, without success, to restore the gray grout to its original white. Exhausted, she went to the living room, sat on the loveseat, and propped her feet up on an ottoman. She massaged a shoulder and wondered why such a small space took so long to clean and why she could never get it clean enough, no matter how hard she scrubbed.

The sky darkened as day segued to night, making it appear as if the outside world had begun to encroach on her inside one. In the dim light of dusk, her small apartment felt even tinier than it actually was. The kitchen, which she rarely cooked in, was dingy and dated. And the living room, which had always felt comfortable and cozy, was now cold and claustrophobic. The streetlamp, which usually went unnoticed, penetrated her window with an annoying flicker. The tenants in the brick building across the alley, whom she'd always thought of as congenial, had mutated into nosy neighbors eerily ogling her through their venetian blinds. She pulled down the Levolors to obstruct what she now perceived as her neighbors' stares, but the flickering streetlamp that buzzed and crackled with each waning of its harsh light still managed to invade her space.

She tried to resist the temptation to compare her view of garbage cans, telephone poles, and beat-up cars to Cosimo's vista of manicured gardens, glass skyscrapers, and city lights. Or her dated gold shag carpeting to his polished parquet floors. Or her discount poly-blend sheets to his thousand-thread-count Egyptian cotton bedding. She knew where she stood in the grand scheme of things, that she was worse off than some and more fortunate than others, stuck in a place by birth, by circumstances, by fate, somewhere between lower and middle class. And even though she had worked hard for more and strove valiantly for better, as she'd been raised to do, she was content with being average. She could live with being average. She had, in fact, been quite happy until now being average. But she was beginning to wonder why. And how.

She was aware that a world existed that was substantially different, exponentially better than her own. A society of which she had only superficial knowledge from skimming through manicure salon copies of *Town & Country* or *Vogue* or from scanning the society section of the *Boston Globe* with its black-and-white images of people at the opera, the symphony, fundraisers, or charity events. But her conception of that fraternity changed once she'd journeyed into their world and experienced the difference firsthand. And though she tried to ignore it, that was difficult to do, because a metamorphosis had taken place in her on a neurological level.

The world and its possibilities are transmuted once you've slept on lavender-scented sheets and dreamt of giant sunflowers swaying in the open fields of southern France. Or had your skin soothed and caressed by luxurious fabrics that felt as if they'd been spun together by angels out of gossamer and clouds. Or tasted a perfectly cooked and seasoned filet and then cleansed your palate with a glass of '61 Chateau Trotanoy. After that, you are forever changed. Once exposed to those things, you yearn for something better: for sounds that are more soothing and acoustically pleasant; for textures that are deeper, softer, richer; for colors that are more vivid, lighting that is more flattering, and experiences that are just—well—more of everything. And it is then that you unexpectedly discover that there is strength in things you once thought dainty, and that the true value of something often transcends the material. Megan Walker had been content with who she was and where she was. But she was no longer certain that she was content with where it was that she was headed.

The wall phone rang, and she got up to answer it, still massaging her shoulder as she made her way from the living room back to the kitchen.

"How'd it go with Cosimo?" Tommy asked.

"Okay. Fine. He left this morning," she said in a monotone voice.

"Wow. That good, huh? He sounds like a keeper."

"Please, Tommy, not today."

"Are you okay? Do you need me to come over?"

"I'm fine. I'm just a little down, a little confused, that's all."

"About?"

"I like him. A lot. But we have nothing in common. That became painfully apparent this weekend. I wish I knew…I'm afraid that…" She trailed off, unable to finish her thought.

"That's always been your problem; you overanalyze everything. Why don't you try feeling instead of thinking for a change?" He waited for a response, but there wasn't one. "You know, for someone with such a strong work ethic, you have a rather profound fear of success. Admit it: you're afraid of having what you want."

"You've been listening to Oprah on the radio again, haven't you?" she said, circling back to the kitchen to attack the grout again.

"Hey, don't dis the O! You could learn a thing or two from her. Like, for instance, she'd probably tell you that what you're truly afraid of is happiness."

"I'm happy."

"No, sis. What you are is not *un*happy. Big difference."

She fell silent as her hand moved furiously back and forth across the tiles while white foam splattered the windows and walls. She breathed hard, her lips tightly clenched. Tommy cleared his throat to remind her that he was still on the line.

"What am I supposed to say to that?" she asked. She sat down on the chipped linoleum floor and rested her head against the cold metal of the refrigerator door. Her arms quivered from scrubbing, from trepidation, from thoughts of a dubious future.

"You can tell me that you'll stop trying to control your life and start living it. And it's not even about him. I don't care who you date or if you date anyone at all. I just want you to be happy. You *deserve* to be happy."

"I'm fine, really. And while I'd love to hear more of your theories on how screwed up I am, you've caught me in the middle of something. I'll call you tomorrow."

She hung up before he could say another word.

That was not the first time she and Tommy had had that conversation or one similar to it. But there was something in his spiel this time that made his comments about her obsessive need to control things spin around in her head. Or it might have been his timing, expressing those thoughts after a weekend at the Four Seasons and Cosimo's revelation. Whatever it was, it forced her to look at things from a new perspective.

She opened the cabinet under the sink and placed the cleaning supplies back in their designated spots. That mindless task gave her the opportunity to reflect on her past relationships and the many ways she had, in one way or another, controlled all of them. It was she who inevitably determined the pace, the duration, the level of intimacy. It was she who decided what they would do, when they would do it, and even how. And it was she who decreed when the affair was over and it was time to move on. In every one of her relationships, regardless of the length or the intensity, she had somehow managed to remain autonomous.

As she walked through the alcove between the living room and the bedroom, she felt her lips quiver. By the time she reached the foot of her bed, her breathing had become staccato, and tears were streaming down her cheeks. Seconds later she was sitting on the floor with her back against the wall, sobbing into her lemony-fresh palms. It had come on without warning, like a flash flood or an earthquake. She had been mentally circling the apartment, checking off areas she'd cleaned, planning to tackle those she hadn't, and trying to forget Tommy's comments. She didn't want to think about them, to acknowledge them, because if she did, she would have to do something about them. But Tommy's words had finally sunk in, forced their way through a barrier she'd held in place to avoid facing, deep down, what she already knew. She wept from exhaustion: not from cleaning, but from controlling, from hiding, from trying to insulate and protect herself. Those tears, which had pushed their way past her innumerable defense mechanisms, were further proof that Tommy was right.

She stood in the bathroom, staring into the sparkling clean basin that smelled of a mixture of lemon and pine trees, and washed the tears away. As she patted her face dry with a hand towel, she heard a knock at the front door. She had no intention of answering it until she absentmindedly removed a piece of lint from the drapes, which reminded her of the ladder, which reminded her of her neighbor, which reminded her of their dinner plans. She peered into the scratched peephole that rendered everything distorted and fuzzy and saw Mitchell standing there in all his blurry blondness. She caught a glimpse of herself preening in the hall mirror, evaluating her outfit, running her fingers through her hair to give it more volume. Megan, while always well groomed, was never overly concerned about her appearance, usually preferring comfort to style, practical to trendy, cotton to silk. Acceptable and presentable were all she usually strived for. So why, she wondered, was she primping to greet Mitchell in the hallway?

"How was your trip to the Vineyard?" she asked after opening the door.

"Oh, about what you'd expect. Everyone enjoyed it at first, but by the next morning, we were ready to strangle each other. Not to mention the fact that, family dynamics being what they are, everyone starts to feel, not to mention act, like they're eight years old again."

"Wait until you meet my brother, Tommy. He doesn't need a family reunion to regress. He's eternally eight years old."

"How was *your* weekend?"

"Interesting," she said. "I'll tell you about it later."

"Are we still on for dinner?"

Megan and Mitchell discussed several options before settling on a time and place to meet. With the pleasantries out of the way and the coordinates locked in, she closed the door and retreated to her bedroom. She lay down to take a nap, but her thoughts prevented her from drifting off. Thoughts about Cosimo, about Paris, about the condo at the Parkhurst Plaza, about how she wished she were having dinner with Cosimo instead of Blondie. And about the fact that it was impossible to deny that things had already spiraled out of control.

∽

A few hours later, Megan was drying dishes at the kitchen sink when she heard another knock at the door. She glanced at the faux-jeweled cat clock on the wall. It read 6:15 p.m. She thought that it was odd for Mitchell, even with the little she knew about him, to be so early. She also thought she was supposed to meet him at the restaurant around the corner. But given how distracted she'd been lately, it was quite possible that she'd misunderstood him. When she opened the door, it was not Mitchell she found waiting in the hall; it was her brother, Tommy.

"Hubba-hubba!" he said.

"What does that mean? And what are you doing here?"

"It means I just passed that creamy blondsicle on the way up," he said. "And I came here because I'm worried about you." He shuffled his feet and looked away. "And…well…I feel horrible. You know…for being such a—"

"Tommy, I'm fine. I told you that."

"Well, you didn't sound fine on the phone."

"Well, I am."

"Excuse me for worrying about my big sister."

"I know you mean well, but it's not necessary. Besides, I've got a lot going on, and right now I have to get ready for my dinner with that Popsicle next door."

"Blondsicle."

"Whatever."

"Can I come along? Can I? Can I?"

"Why, so you can sit across the table and gawk at him all night?"

"I'll have you know I am quite capable of carrying on a very intelligent, and some would say witty, conversation. *While* gawking."

"Aren't you supposed to be getting married soon? Shouldn't you be home filling out bridal registry forms for Macy's and Target?"

"Bloomies and Williams-Sonoma," he said and then gasped at the thought of wedding gifts from Tarjay. "And to answer your question, no, I'm still sans fiancé." To prove his point, he held out his naked right hand and waved it in front of her face. "What difference does it make, anyway? Blondie's straight, isn't he? What kind of trouble could I get into with him?" When she didn't respond, he asked again, this time more emphatically. "He is straight, isn't he?"

"I don't know; he hasn't completed his questionnaire yet. Besides, you're a little too interested in the answer." She pointed in the direction of the door, but Tommy didn't budge. "His sexual preference aside, how could I possibly explain bringing my baby brother along on our first nondate?"

"That's the loophole; it's a *nondate*. The more the merrier."

"Fine, but you're paying for my dinner."

"Deal! And I promise I won't embarrass you. Well, no more than usual."

After their dinner with Mitchell, Tommy went to Megan's apartment for a nightcap and a recap.

"Well, that was bachelor number one. When do I get to meet bachelor number two?" he said and began to hum the theme song from *The Dating Game*.

"Knock it off. That's my life you're satirizing, not some comedy sketch you're writing for the Townie Players."

"Ouch!"

"Sorry…I'm a little sensitive on the subject."

"No, *I'm* sorry," Tommy said.

"Well, you should be." She gave him a look that failed to reveal if she was serious or kidding. She disappeared into the kitchen, and when she returned, she sat down and tore open a package of Mint Milanos. "Cookie?"

"No thanks. So, what's your issue with bachelor number two?"

"I feel guilty about the way I treated him this weekend. It was all so different—Boston, the apartment, the money. I kept putting up walls between us. It was as if I was purposely trying to keep him at a distance. But that was never my intention."

"I thought you told me that you dragged him off for sex at the first opportunity."

"Well, there's intimate…and then there's *intimate*."

"You're saying you screwed him to keep him at a distance?"

"Precisely."

"I will never understand you straight people. But I do understand what you mean about Blondie. He's gorgeous, articulate, smart, well-read…" He paused as he further pondered Mitchell's abundant attributes.

"Don't forget buff!" she said, contributing to the list.

"Umm-hmm!" he said. "I was getting to that. You know, saving the best for last. But there's just something missing. It's like he's there, but he's not. Maybe it's his sense of humor. I don't think he has one. Is that possible?"

"Tommy, he's studying to be a lawyer. He comes from a long line of lawyers. It's not only possible; it's probable."

"*Quelle dommage*," he said. "I don't care how pretty they are—if they don't laugh at my jokes, it's over."

"Well, at least you've got your priorities straight. Still, why can't I fall for a guy like that? Simple. Down to earth. Sane."

"And he looks damn fine in a T-shirt."

"Good night, Tommy," she said. And this time she ushered him to the door.

Chapter Twenty-One

At the end of yet another long, aimless walk around the city, Cosimo lingered in front of Regina's building and tipped his head back to survey its exterior. After a weekend spent with Megan pointing out architectural elements to him, he had developed a new appreciation for façades. But it was not the art deco details of the Upper West Side building that kept him on the sidewalk with a doorman poised to ease his access. The longer he stared at the stone coping, the gray limestone, the copper cornices, the more obvious his reluctance to reenter the penthouse became. What traumatized him more than any actual confrontation with Maria-Carmella was the anticipation of one. It was bad enough that his own moods swung wildly, from suicidal to euphoric and back again, keeping him off balance, tentative, anxious. But to be at the mercy of his mother's own constantly shifting mental state was even more nerve-wracking and unsettling. While the ground beneath his emotional foundation was decidedly shaky on its own, it was made even more so by the unstable footing of the person who controlled his wealth.

A few days earlier, he had stopped taking his medications again, so his nervous system was compromised and vulnerable to any emotional upheaval that loomed on the horizon. He hadn't stopped taking his meds because he was feeling better or because they had deluded him into believing he could manage without them; he stopped taking them because they left him feeling nothing at all. He had discovered over the years that, as awful as they were, he preferred the states of anxiety and mania to those of apathy and low libido.

In the lobby, the doorman held the bronze elevator doors open and gave him a respectful bow of the head. Cosimo wished him a good afternoon. While the doors quietly closed on him, he got a queer sensation in his stomach, as if the doorman had been trying to convey something to him beyond his customary salutation. The button to Regina's floor was already lit, and as the cabin moved slowly upward, he tried to uncover the hidden meaning in the one brightly lit number on a brass panel filled with unlit numbers. Everything that day seemed to have a hidden subtext.

He heard a murmur, not so much in his ears as in the back of his head. It was like listening to a talk-radio program with bad reception, all static and fast and unintelligible. He was convinced that it wasn't in his head this time, that it was emanating from someplace far away. At first he strained to hear the dialogue, to decipher the words, but the distance between him and the source made them incomprehensible. Eventually he dismissed it, attributing the noise to the grinding wheels of the elevator's mechanical system. He refused to accept the possibility that the voices were only in his head. He had too much to live for to give into the voices or to the madness again. When the doors opened into Regina's apartment, that dull but incessant chatter exploded into a cacophony.

In the foyer, a young goth woman with a dragon tattoo, multiple piercings, and questionable hygiene hurried past him. In her rush she nearly impaled him with a large, theatrical light fixture as she moved it from one location to another. Two men in coveralls carrying an enormous floral arrangement followed closely behind her. Cosimo tentatively entered the living room. He thought he was on the wrong floor until he noticed Regina sitting on a sofa with her chestnut-colored hair wrapped around large plastic rollers and her hands propped in front of a miniature fan that was slowly drying her freshly lacquered nails. A young man was kneeling in front of her, meticulously applying thick bands of eyeliner. There were three other smartly dressed people seated on the sofa next to her. Another five or six people in T-shirts and baseball caps were rushing about, carrying cables, lights, and large white screens with an iridescent glow.

The noise and the frenetic activity irritated him. All he wanted to do was go to his room and bury himself underneath the covers. He inched his way toward a decorative pillar between the foyer and the living room. From there, he could see down the hall toward his mother's suite. Her door was closed, so he looked to the right to see if she was in the kitchen. It was then that Maria-Carmella materialized behind him.

"Did you know about this?" she said.

He gasped for air and clutched at his chest. He turned to face her.

"Mother, you shouldn't sneak up on a person. You nearly gave me a heart attack."

"You're always so dramatic," she said as she lifted a curly lock from his forehead and pushed some others behind his ear. "That's better. You're starting to get a little shaggy, dear, don't you think?"

He backed away from her to get her to stop fussing with his hair.

"No," he said. "I had no idea this was happening."

"I expected them to be done by now," she said.

"This place was empty when I left. What's going on?"

"Your dear, sweet sister is shooting an ad campaign for her new perfume. Not that she has to clear everything with me, mind you, but it would have been nice if she had informed me that she was turning the place into a production facility for this little photo shoot of hers. And her timing ..." Maria-Carmella shook her head and uttered a few tsk-tsks. "And look what they're doing to the floors. And the walls. She's going to have to remodel; that's all there is to it." She began to brush little invisible things off of Cosimo's sleeve with her manicured hand. "And that will be yet another mess!"

Regina shouted from across the room, "Cosimo... Coz...Coz!" When he finally looked in her direction, she patted the seat cushion next to hers. "Come here. I need your brilliance."

"Go ahead," Maria-Carmella said. "But as soon as she's done with you, we need to talk. *Capiche?*"

"*Si, si*. About what?"

Instead of an answer, she cast him a look that he was unable to interpret. And before he knew it, she was walking away from him. He watched her retreat down the hallway. When she was halfway to her room, he focused his eyes and all of his concentration onto her Balenciaga-clad back and then, quickly and deliberately, pelted her with wave after wave of flaming death rays. To his dismay, each one of them failed to pierce, to penetrate, to have any impact on her at all. And since they merely ricocheted off of her thick outer shell, she continued on her way, unscathed and unfazed.

He maneuvered a path through the crowd, cautiously avoiding the lights and the cables, to the spot where Regina was sitting. They exchanged a whispered greeting and air-kisses over the heads of the makeup artist and manicurist. Regina pointed to a man in his late twenties seated on her left.

"Cosimo, this is Terrance Lawford." When she got no reaction from him, she clarified her statement. "As in Lawford/Lawson. The advertising agency? Terrance is the guy who came up with this whole concept. He's a genius, I tell you, an absolute genius. And next to him is Simon Andre, VP of marketing for Estée Lauder. They have been an absolute dream to work with. If it weren't for Simon…well, I just don't know." She pivoted and directed an upturned palm at a blond woman wearing a Zac Posen Jet dress. "And this one is Penelope Winthrop, whom I presume you already know. She's doing some kind of article-profile-thingy on me for *Marie-Claire*. The two of you may have met last summer when we were in Positano." Regina then introduced him to the group in a way that brought to mind trumpets blaring, as if his arrival was ultimately what they had all been waiting for. "Everyone, I give you my brother, Cosimo."

"Cosimo, tell me—what do you think of the name?" Terrance asked. As he stood to shake Cosimo's hand, he pointed to a couple of photographs propped up on the coffee table. "It was quite a challenge for us to come up with one word, one single idea that captured the essence of Regina."

"Yes," said Simon. "We'd love to have your opinion. You know, get a first impression from a true aristocrat."

"Coz has been out of the country for a while," Regina said, reaching for the piece of cardboard on the coffee table. "I didn't want to bore him with my little project, so I'm afraid he's not quite up to speed." She held up a foam-core rectangle that displayed an image of an oval glass bottle with a gold-colored atomizer. The bottle in the photograph was covered in a thin metallic mesh and filled with a pale blue liquid the color of the Mediterranean Sea. Affixed to the netting was a royal blue medallion that resembled a thick globule of sealing wax. And there, in the center of the wax, in raised butter-colored script, was a solitary word: "Regal."

"We debated and deliberated forever on the name. Nobility was another one we mulled over," Terrance said. "That was your favorite, Simon, wasn't it?"

"Actually," Simon said, "I was rather keen on calling it Royal."

"I don't know that there is one word that can describe my sister," Cosimo said, "but regal is about as close as you can get." They were all quiet for a moment, as if they expected some priceless nugget of wisdom to usher forth from the great Coz. "As nice and as apt as those other choices are," he added, feeling obliged to continue, "there's a good chance they could end up alienating the very demographic you're trying to attract."

"How so?" Penelope said, holding a silver Cartier pen over a black leather portfolio.

"Anybody can aspire to be regal," he said. "Depending on your definition of it, people can actually *become* regal. But true nobility is decided by birth. If you're not born into royalty, then your only chance for nobility is to marry into it."

Terrance nodded his head in agreement to everything Cosimo said. Simon simply stood there with his hands in his pockets and grinned. Penelope copied down every word he uttered on a tablet that she supported with her forearm. Regina, while listening closely to his every word, continued to be prepped and prodded for pictures.

"In my opinion, all that Princess Di, Prince Charles, Camilla, and Fergie nonsense tarnished the whole notion of royalty," Cosimo said. "All of their pedestrian behavior made it seem pompous, elitist, and, dare I say, tawdry. In the twenty-first century? It's better to be a pop star than a prince. And yes, I would wager that you've made the right choice with Regal, if my opinion counts for anything."

"See, I told you he was brilliant," Regina exclaimed, as if they had all been waiting for that proclamation. She shooed away her hair and makeup people and gestured to Terrance and Simon that she was taking a break. She dragged Cosimo by the hand across the room. She stopped abruptly at a rolling rack that was partially hidden beneath an array of haute couture gowns.

"When did all this happen?" he asked.

"This? It's been going on for months. I mean *months*. I didn't tell anybody." She placed her hand on his arm. "Really! Nobody! Terrance cooked up this whole campaign. He…*we're* hoping to leverage the publicity I'll get from it for my new clothing line. Then, you know, do some cross-marketing, create various tie-ins, that sort of thing."

"Listen to you! Cross-marketing, tie-ins. You're amazing. I don't know how you do it."

"Why, thank you," she said, making a little curtsy. "Now, I need you to help me select a gown for the print ad. That's the one decision I don't trust them to make. It has to subtly scream Regal." She pulled a few garment bags from the rack and unzipped them. "There's this strapless citrus satin-chiffon Marchesa one. It's sexy, bold, maybe a bit haughty." She put that one aside and presented another. "Or this Versace tulle ball gown. Don't you just love all these crystal teardrops embroidered into it? To me it says romance. It's also a little dreamlike, maybe a bit fairytale-ish." She winked at him. "You know, subliminally evoking visions of princesses trapped in tiny towers, patiently waiting to be rescued by a dashing young man on horseback." Regina rested her head on Cosimo's shoulder and surveyed the chaos that was playing itself out in other parts of the foyer and the sitting room. "Or is it the other way round? Who rescues whom?"

"I'll vouch for your ability to save dumbbells in distress. You've certainly come to my rescue on more than one occasion," he said.

He inspected the dresses one by one. He caressed the fabrics with his hands, held them up under different lights, and viewed them from various angles.

"And last but not least, there's this Valentino number that comes with a floor-length organza cape," she said, holding it up to the others for him to compare. "To me it feels like a blend of the other two; it's sexy and sophisticated, but it's also delicate and dreamy." She waited while he evaluated each one.

He examined each of them again, carefully inspecting the intricate patterns, thoughtfully evaluating the hours and hours of beadwork meticulously applied by hand, and checking to see if the stitching and the embroidery and the fabrics all came together in a way that was both original and timeless. He had Regina hold them up one last time while he paced back and forth a few feet away.

"Versace, definitely the Versace," he said.

"Really? I was sure you'd say Valentino." She retrieved the Versace tulle gown with the teardrop crystals and reappraised it.

"You said it yourself," he said. "It's dreamlike. And dreams are what you're selling as much as anything else." He took the gown from her and held it up. He took a few steps back so that she could see it from a distance. "It's also the subtlest. It's elegant but understated. Maybe Mother can get away with wearing clothes that stop traffic, but for this campaign, you want a look that's seductive and inviting."

"Come here," she said. She returned the dress to the rack and gave him a big squeeze, like she was trying to contain him, like she was trying to absorb him. "I'm going to miss you so much when you leave. And while she'd never admit it, I know Mother will, too. She's different when you're not here. She likes having you around."

"I guess that's probably true of any parasite and its host."

"Cosimo! That's a terrible thing to—"

"I know, I know. I'm just having a bad morning. Look, I don't want to be a black cloud over your day, not when Leibovitz is trying to capture that beautiful smile of yours." He waved to Annie across the room and blew her a kiss. "I'll be in my room if you have any other fashion emergencies."

Cosimo gave an obligatory nod to Simon, Terrance, and Penelope. He kissed Regina on the cheek and headed toward his room, stepping around light fixtures, wind machines, and all of the other paraphernalia employed by the photographer.

"Mr. Garibaldi, may I have a word, please?" Simon said, striding toward him.

"Please, call me Cosimo," he said, shaking Simon's hand again.

"Cosimo, I wanted to talk to you about…well, we've been discussing the concept of…you see, we at Estée Lauder have complete faith that Regal will be a huge success. Everything about Regina, her celebrity status, her business savvy, her network…well, we're very excited."

"Yes, she's just like her mother in that regard, a force to be reckoned with."

"Terrance and I have discussed doing a men's cologne along the same lines, you know, a similar ad campaign, complementary packaging."

"That's great. Very exciting. Good luck with that," he said and began to walk away.

"Mr. Garibaldi," Simon said, placing a hand on the prince's shoulder. "Cosimo," he added before quickly removing his hand. "I guess I didn't make myself clear. The point I was trying to make is that we're interested in creating a fragrance, in building a campaign around *you*."

Cosimo's mind was reeling from a dozen different things. He was agitated by the supposedly controlled chaos of the room, by the people rushing back and forth, the glaring lights, and the incessant noise. It registered on his slight frame like real physical pressure, like a weight bearing down on his shoulders, compressing his chest, squashing him as if he were an insignificant gnat.

When he made the decision to stop taking his drugs, he stopped taking all of them, even the tiny, pink, five-milligram tablets of Xanax that he always carried with him. On Monday afternoon, after he'd returned from Boston, he gathered up every pill he could find—every pink, every blue, every yellow one, all the round, the triangular, the ovals, and the oblongs. And then, capsule after capsule, pill after pill, each and every one of them a nuisance to ingest, horrible to taste, and a challenge to swallow, he dumped them swiftly and effortlessly into the kitchen sink with the disposal on and the water running.

The complexity of his life, the numerous stresses that had been piling up day after day, real and imagined, and the trauma that his body was being subjected to in the process of withdrawing from a myriad of medications all at once, cold turkey, made it difficult for him to comprehend Simon's query. It made it onerous for him to concentrate on almost anything at all. Which, in turn, rendered him slow to respond to even the simplest of questions or requests.

"Of course, you'd have a contract comparable to Regina's with input and final approval on almost all aspects of the enterprise," Simon added.

Terrance, who had stepped away to consult with Annie, cut his conversation short to add his perspective to Simon's proposal.

"We've worked out all the numbers without trying to blue-sky it, and we're pretty confident in our projections," Terrance said. "Lawford/Lawson and a few Estée Lauder executives have formed a joint venture group to develop campaign-based merchandise. We approached Regina because our research indicated that an offering like Regal was the ideal platform to launch future products from." He rushed back to his seat to retrieve his laptop. He flashed a thumbs-up to Regina who was peeking out from behind a folding screen as her retinue helped her shimmy into the heavily weighted, skin-tight Versace gown.

"We've even gone so far as to test-market some men's fragrances," Simon said. "We believe that premiering a product like Nobility or Royal, or whatever it is we call it, on the heels of Regal, will launch the two complementary brands into the stratosphere."

"Quite frankly," Terrance said, "when it comes right down to it, it's all about marketing and packaging, not smell. I mean come-on, Aramis? Hai Karate? Drakkar Noir? Awful stuff, but they all sold well—still do—because the public has bought into their hype. I'd be willing to bet that I could put lighter fluid in a bottle and with the right label, slogan, packaging, and model, it would outsell Polo, Brut, and Paco Rabanne combined."

At a certain point they weren't talking *to* Cosimo, they were talking *at* him. Because he wasn't there. He watched them as they opened and closed their mouths while making exaggerated hand gestures. He saw them point to multicolored charts and graphs that were flashing on a tiny LCD screen. But he was incapable of fathoming what any of it meant. He tried to speak, only nothing escaped his lips. Simon and Terrance continued to ramble on about market penetration, brand strategies, statistics, and focus groups, never once realizing it was falling on deaf ears.

Maria-Carmella, on her way back to the elevator, came up behind him and whispered in his ear. But the only thing he heard was the ominous sliding trombone of a cartoon character's "whaa-whaa-whaa." He watched her enter the elevator cab and then disappear behind the closed doors. As he thought about her in the lift traveling slowly down to the lobby, a scene replayed itself in his head: a tape of a conversation he had unintentionally eavesdropped on a few days earlier:

Standing behind a Japanese folding screen, Cosimo heard Maria-Carmella praising Regina: "Now you, you were born with it. But Cosimo, he lacks the killer instinct."

His sister attempted to put things in perspective: "You at least have to give him credit for making a valiant effort, don't you?"

Maria-Carmella countered her defense with, "He's my son, and I love him, but there are days when I question if he even has the survival instinct."

Regina conceded: "He has always been a slave to his emotions."

Maria-Carmella added, "I keep challenging him to be tougher, to fight back, but he never does. He's just like your father."

Regina came to his rescue once again: "He stood up to you last week about Boston, didn't he?"

Maria-Carmella ended the conversation with, "Regina, dear, you're mistaking desperation for passion and power. He was simply at the end of his rope, and somehow that manifested itself into an all-too-brief episode of bravado. I'm afraid he will never be anything more than he is."

~

Penelope, who had missed the bulk of Simon's sales pitch thanks to a call from her editor, rejoined the group who were huddled in a corner.

"What did I miss?" she said.

Penelope's reemergence interrupted Cosimo's reverie, which brought his attention back to the three people gathered around a laptop discussing various metrics and ROI.

"Don't you think marketing Cosimo and Regina as two separate but related brands under the theme of royalty would be a smashing success?" Simon asked her.

"Now you're putting them both on the spot," Terrance said. "Please, allow me to apologize for Simon's—"

It was Cosimo who, suddenly present and miraculously lucid, interrupted Terrance.

"Can you give me those statistics again? In English this time."

Terrance referred back to the colorful pie charts and multihued graphs neatly organized on his computer screen. He made sure that Cosimo paid particular attention to the highlighted row of numbers and the list of percentages.

"We anticipate worldwide sales of around a hundred and fifty million the first year," he said. "Just for the cologne. That doesn't include line-extensions like moisturizers, soaps, or shaving cream. Those we'd roll out nine to twelve months later. Our research indicates that a large segment of the male population has already embraced revitalizing skin care products, and that number will continue to grow as they age." Terrance handed his laptop to Simon, and, without missing a beat, his demeanor shifted from ad-man tossing out creative ideas to pitchman ready to close the deal. "We're not talking about a product here; we're talking about a lifestyle. The opportunities are limitless. But all that aside, Cosimo," he said, pointing to the screen one more time, "here is what your compensation for the first year alone would look like. If we meet our projections."

Cosimo paused to consider his sister, presently hidden by the Japanese screen, who was about to launch her own line of clothing in addition to a new perfume venture. He tried to visualize himself behind that screen being tucked and fluffed, poked and prodded, tweaked and torqued for just one of many photo shoots. His reflection prompted a question about the viability of it all.

"And what's *your* opinion, Penelope?" he asked. "You're exposed to thousands of brands every day, all vying to be the new 'it' product. Would this appeal to your readers?"

"Simon's absolutely right," she said. "And the timing couldn't be better. The way people feel about the current state of affairs and the people in power…I think they're ready for leaders with class, with sophistication, with style. They yearn for something to inspire them. For *someone* to aspire *to*." She looked at Terrance as if she expected him to finish her thought. "Camelot and Princess Di, they're gone for good, but the royal and elegant Garibaldis? Wow! What a pair. Those product lines, along with your combined celebrity, will eclipse everyone else's. At least for a while. But…"

"*But?*" Cosimo said, exaggerating the word, eager to hear her thoughts.

"Only that the promotion and the hype that has to go into a venture like that to make it successful…well, it would change your life forever." Her voice wavered as if she were hesitant to continue. "Cosimo, I don't know you all that well. Regina I do know. And while I've never seen her actively seek the limelight, I've never seen her shy away from it, either."

"Yes, it's perfect for her. No matter what happens with Regal," he said, "the publicity will be good for her other businesses. But for me, the bottom line is…what?"

"Monetarily, you can't lose. The question is, what do you value more, money or privacy? And which one are you willing to sacrifice for the other?"

"Thank you, Penelope," he said. "I was pondering the same question and wondering if Reggie knows what she's gotten herself into."

A hush came over the room as Regina emerged from behind the screen, her hair cascading down in waves of chestnut brown with strategically placed highlights and makeup that had been applied with an artist's touch and a jeweler's eye. The cream-colored gown conformed to her body as if she'd been sewn into it, which in fact she had. The crystal teardrop beads, hundreds of them perfectly positioned around her in a swirling pattern, reflected the sunlight pouring in through the windows. And as she began to move about, her dress manufactured a light show of miniature little rainbows that flickered and flashed around the vast open space of her apartment.

Cosimo was mesmerized by the thousands of tiny colored spectrums as they danced about the ceiling and the walls. He found it a delightful distraction from all that talk of business. His attention was brought back to the scene by the whir of Leibowitz's camera as it captured images of Regina against a backdrop of cables and crew, strobe lights and scrims, tall canvas backdrops and large metal fans. Annie continued to shoot as Regina made her way through the crowded and cluttered room, over to an eight-foot cardboard cutout of the perfume bottle emblazoned with a three-dimensional image of the medallion bearing the scripted **Regal** logo. He watched his sister comfortably navigate her way through the space, oblivious to the camera, to the crowd, or to the team that followed her making last-minute adjustments. Her beauty and her presence astounded even him. It was as if he were seeing her for the first time, how confident and unencumbered she was, how in her element she seemed. And he, Cosimo, crowned prince of nothing, ached to feel that way, too. If only he could feel that way himself, he thought, even for a moment, he'd be okay if that one moment was also his last.

"May I?" he said, reaching for Penelope's pen.

"Certainly," she said, blushing as her fingers grazed his hand.

Cosimo gestured to Regina to get her attention, but she couldn't see him standing there in the corner surrounded by her business partners. And she was engulfed herself by a different team, one that was buffing and fluffing, pinning and poking, polishing and poofing. He knew that committing to Terrance's project was just the first step in a long series of negotiations. Lawyers would need to be hired, terms negotiated, contracts drafted. But this was his chance for independence, his get-out-of-jail-free card, and he was anxious to make his intentions clear, to signal, more to himself than to anyone else, that he was taking control of his life. So, in a gesture that was meant to lighten what had become a rather serious conversation, he held up Penelope's pen like a sword, like a knight preparing for battle. He slowly, silently scanned the trio, purposely creating a bit of dramatic tension as the group waited for his decree.

"Gentlemen," he said, "where do I sign?"

Chapter Twenty-Two

In the lobby of the Parkhurst Plaza, Megan was nearly overcome by the overpowering fragrance of lilies emanating from an enormous vase of flowers sitting on top of a cherry reception desk. She tried to keep her gum-soled shoes from squeaking and slurping as she moved across the polished marble floor toward two uniformed doormen. But the more she tried to quiet them, the louder they announced her approach. In that grand room of high ceilings, original artwork, and ornate furnishings, the small Phalaenopsis orchid that she held in her hands looked miniature, pathetic, out of place.

"I'd like to leave this for Mr. Garibaldi," she said to the younger of the two gentlemen manning the desk. "I know he hasn't moved in yet, but I wanted to leave this to welcome him when he does. Is there any way that you can deliver it to his apartment?"

The doorman took the plant and placed it on the desk

next to the tiger lilies, which dwarfed and overshadowed the small orchid.

"Did you want to leave a note so he'll know who it's from?"

"Of course." She reached into the depths of her purse and pulled out a square white envelope with Cosimo's name written in neat black cursive on it and handed it to him.

"Will that be all?"

"Yes, thank you," she said as she backed away from the desk. When she turned to face the entrance, she bumped into a smartly dressed older woman with an ineffable air of wealth. The impact jolted and startled Megan, and she wobbled a bit before she regained her footing. The older woman, whose manicured hands began methodically brushing away things from her jacket, things that weren't even there, appeared unfazed.

"Oh, my goodness, I'm terribly sorry," Megan said. She extended a helping hand. "Are you all right?"

"My fault, dearie," the older woman said, ignoring her outstretched hand. She gave her a quick scan from head to toe, followed by a grimace. "I wasn't aware that I had come in through the service entrance." She uttered the word "service" as if it were an affliction or something equally distasteful and pedestrian.

"It's her again," whispered the doorman who had taken Megan's orchid.

"Who?" asked the other.

"The woman who was asking me all those questions earlier about the penthouse." He poked the other one in the ribs. "Who do you think the babe is?"

"No idea, but it looks like they're about to get into it," he said, straining to hear their conversation.

"I said I was sorry," Megan said, her face flushed with embarrassment and anger. "It was an accident. There's no need to be rude." She spun around abruptly, walked past the woman, and headed for the exit.

All the older woman could do was utter a hushed, but chilling, "Humph." Then she straightened an outfit that needed no straightening and approached the desk.

"It's a pleasure to see you again, Ms. Garibaldi," the doorman said to Maria-Carmella as he picked up Megan's orchid and retrieved a set of keys from a desk drawer. "Do you need access to the penthouse again?"

Megan stood in the doorway, unable to leave. She managed to get one last look at the woman she could only speculate was Cosimo's mother. For a woman of such small stature, her bearing was rather imposing. But how on Earth, she wondered, could such an abhorrent person produce such a sweet child?

On her way to dinner, Megan happened to pass a Coldwell Banker office. She stopped to peruse the flyers in the window and daydream over the glossy sheets that touted townhouses and flats for sale in Back Bay. A nicer place to live was one of the few luxuries she ever allowed herself to fantasize about. A stack of *Homes* magazines sat in a metal rack by the realtor's front door. She took the second one from the top and flipped through it, not really expecting to find what she was looking for. But there it was, smack in the center, two full pages of color photographs showcasing the interior of Cosimo's new penthouse. The shot of the window with the view of the park reminded her of Cosimo's arms lightly hugging her waist and his breath tinged with the musky smell of wine as he whispered in her ear. She held the magazine closer to her face to read the small black print beneath each image. A few sentences in the lower right-hand corner were filled with words and phrases like "world-class," "gourmet kitchen," "granite counters," "concierge," "teak," "terrace," and "unobstructed view of the Commons." And below that, in bold italics, were the numbers $4,200,000.

She wandered through the streets of Boston with those seven figures running around in her head, animated and with a musical soundtrack, like some clip from an old Warner Brothers cartoon. Even after a few unconscious wrong turns, she managed to arrive at Joe's American Bar & Grill just in time to meet Tommy for dinner. The hostess grabbed a menu and led her to a four-top where a gentleman was already seated, his face hidden behind a large leather-bound wine list. When the man heard the hostess say, "Enjoy your meal," he closed the leather folder and greeted her.

"Gregg. What a pleasant surprise," Megan said.

"That didn't sound very sincere," Gregg responded.

"No, really, I'm happy to see you. It's just that I've reached my surprise quota for the day."

"I didn't know surprises had quotas."

"Neither did I, Gregg, neither did I." She looked toward the entrance, but there was no sign of Tommy. "Where's my brother-slash-your-better-half? Or are you his stand-in this evening?"

"I haven't seen you in ages, so I asked if I could join you. He'll be here soon." He stood and gave her a kiss on the cheek. "Now *that's* a proper greeting," he said.

"That was sweet. Tommy never would have done that. You know he doesn't deserve you, right?"

"I tell him that constantly. Sometimes I'm convinced that don't I deserve him either...if you know what I mean?"

They both laughed, and then the laughter was followed by an uncomfortable silence. The lull in conversation was filled with Musak's instrumental interpretation of Barry Manilow's "At the Copa," to which Megan began to hum along.

"You smell nice," she said to break the tension. "What are you wearing?"

"Eau Savage. I've got about twenty sample bottles at home. One of the few perks of being a retail queen."

"Belated congrats. Tommy told me that Neiman's finally promoted you to head buyer."

"Yeah, they gave me a big title and a little raise," he said, holding his thumb and index finger together to indicate something minuscule.

"Oh, don't be so modest."

"It's nice of you to acknowledge it," he said. And then his expression grew solemn. "Can I ask you a question?"

"Sure, ask me anything."

"I don't know why I'm so nervous." He took a handkerchief out of his breast pocket and began dabbing his forehead with it. "Your brother...he makes me crazy."

"Welcome to my world," she said.

"I want to ask him to marry me."

"And what? You think you need my approval?"

"You know how he is. It's hard to get him to be serious for more than a minute. Living together is one thing, but I'm afraid this will scare him off. Or he'll start doing things to sabotage the relationship so he doesn't have to deal with it."

"Gregg, I think you underestimate him. Lord knows I do." She looked behind her to see if he was coming. "I know that he can act frivolous, but that doesn't mean he lacks depth. And just because he's less serious than most of us…okay, *all* of us…doesn't mean he's incapable of committing to something. To you." She took a sip of water and then picked up a wine glass. "I've often wondered why these are always on the table, and then the minute you order wine, they take them away." He started to say something, but she cut him off. "That was a rhetorical question. As is this. How long have you two been living together?"

"Close to three years now."

"Doesn't that tell you anything?"

"I know. Look, I'm not normally this insecure. But even after all that time, I can't tell what he's thinking or feeling." He reached into his coat pocket and pulled out a small, green, velvet box. "I'm afraid this might push him over the edge." He placed the box on the table and slid it toward her. "Quite frankly, the thought of 'till death do us part' even scares me."

Megan opened the velvet box. Inside was a brushed platinum band cradling a large Asscher cut diamond surrounded by a polished bezel edge.

"Gregg, this is gorgeous," she said as she took the ring out for a closer look.

She slipped it onto her finger, but it was several sizes too big, so it kept sliding around. She made a joke about having it resized and then held it in place so that the diamond floated on top of her index finger. The lights in the ceiling shot colored sparkles out from the center of the stone onto the walls of the restaurant. She took another sip of water to wet her throat, which had suddenly become very dry. When she spoke again, her voice quivered with emotion.

"Look, if he's neurotic enough to run away because of this, you're better off without him."

"Yes. And no. Do you have any idea how hard it is to find a guy like him?"

"Sadly I do, Gregg, sadly I do." She placed the ring back in the box but continued to stare at it. "He would be a fool to screw this up. I've known him my whole life," she continued, shifting her stare from the ring back to Gregg, "and while he may act like a flake, Tommy's no fool."

He stood up and gave her another kiss on the cheek.

"Now, can I ask *you* a question?" she said. "How long was it after you two met before one of you said 'I love you?'"

"I expect that to happen any day now," he said, deadpan.

She tossed her napkin across the table, purposely missing his head.

"Okay, honestly? It was four days."

"You're kidding me, right?"

"I remember it perfectly. I was having drinks with a friend in a bar in West Newton when I noticed him standing by himself on the opposite side of the room. There was this instant, I don't know, magnetic force field between us. I turned to the friend I was with and said—I remember the exact words—I said, 'Dave, I think I'm in big trouble.' I went over and introduced myself shortly after; then we finished our beers and went back to my place."

"You guys don't waste any time, do you?"

"Not usually." He lowered his head slightly, a little

embarrassed. "We spent the next three nights together, going out to dinner and stuff."

"And stuff?"

"Yeah, *stuff*. So the fourth night we're at this party in Marblehead, standing in someone's backyard, a friend of a friend, out by the fence, under the stars, drinking warm beer out of red plastic cups. And I looked at him and thought, *I love him*. Just like that. Usually when you fall in love, you don't know how or when. It just happens. It's an evolution." He refolded her napkin and handed it back to her. "But with Tom, I was conscious of the exact moment that I realized it. The feeling was so strong that I couldn't deny it, and it's something I'll never forget."

"That's so beautiful. Did you tell him right then and there?"

"Later, back at my house. When he said it back, without hesitation…" he said, too choked up to continue.

"Look at the two of us; we're pathetic," she said. "Me all choked up, you on the verge of tears. Now all we need is Tommy to walk in and crack some jokes." She handed him a packet of tissues from her purse. "I told you, Tommy has more depth than you give him credit for."

"Yeah, well, three years later," he said, somewhat composed again, "your brother still refers to the night we met at the Pink Parrot as 'the one-night stand that went horribly wrong.'"

"That's my brother. And that ring tells me you've already made up your mind." She closed the lid and handed the box back to him. "So, when are you going to pop the question?"

∾

At the Espresso Royale Café on Newbury Street, Megan sat in a green velvet club chair that was squeezed into a corner of the room by a window. Her double latte rested on the edge of a small round table next to a new journal, which she'd purchased that morning at Papyrus, and her Mont Blanc fountain pen, a graduation present from her parents. She stared at the shiny black writing instrument and the leather-bound book as if they would do the work for her. As if the thoughts in her head could be interpreted by the pen, coerced by the book, and somehow magically inscribed on the paper, captured there for posterity. Or at least for her to review and reflect upon at some future date. But her thoughts spun too fast for the book or the pen to grasp. Or maybe they didn't care, preferring instead to enjoy the view out the window and the smell of chocolate-colored Guatemalan beans being ground to a fine powder by a goateed barista in training.

"Hello?" she said into her new cell phone when she heard its unfamiliar ring. "Hello!" she said again, holding the device away from her to read it, as if she were an elderly person who'd forgotten her reading glasses. She pressed a couple of buttons randomly and repeated the greeting a third time. The light on the face of it went dead. She put the phone on the table next to the other useless implements. It began to buzz again.

"Where *are* you?" Cosimo asked when she answered.

"Where are *you*?" she said.

"Did you just hang up on me?"

"I may have, but not on purpose. I haven't figured out this new contraption yet."

"I don't like being so far away from you."

"It's two hundred miles. You're in Manhattan, not Nepal."

"You're in a mood. Anything I've done?" he said.

"No, of course not. I've just got a lot on my mind. When are you coming back?"

"As soon as I can. Why don't you come to New York for the weekend?"

"I can't," she said without hesitation.

"We'll stay at the Four Seasons. It'll be like before. Only better. Here we have theater and martinis the size of small swimming pools." He waited for a response but there was none. "Here we have me."

"And *here* we have *me*," she said.

"Why is it always a contest with you? Why can't you ever give in to an urge or a suggestion? Why can't you say, 'Sure Coz, that would be fun? I'll check the train schedule.'"

"I'm just practical, I guess." She moved the pen in her hand around and around in aimless circles on a white paper napkin. While she waited for Cosimo to respond, she started writing down numbers—one, two, three, four—for no apparent reason. "Are you still there?"

"Yes," he said.

"I'm afraid that's just how I am. Before I make a decision, I need to examine my options, prepare for all possible outcomes. I'm hearty, East Coast peasant stock. We don't do anything on a whim."

"And that's *all* I do," he said.

"Where's the stability in that?"

"And where's the fun in being so practical?"

"Seems as if we're at a stalemate."

"You act as if this is some kind of game," he said. "This is not a game...this is my life."

"Our life. I mean, lives," she said.

"This is true. And if that's the case, shouldn't we find some way to compromise?"

And while they agreed on that point, neither would make any concession during that convoluted conversation. So, Cosimo stayed in New York and spent the weekend on Long Island. He crashed with his friend Jeremy at his parents' place in East Hampton. He spent Saturday morning alone on the beach, reading his battered copy of *The Man without Qualities*, and on Sunday he joined Regina aboard Diane and Barry's yacht to discuss hawking a new sportswear line on QVC. And while he was doing that, Megan remained in Boston. She visited her parents in Brookline, cleaned her apartment again, watched a romantic comedy with Lauren, and worked on her lesson plans for next semester. The world was back to normal. At least for a while.

Chapter Twenty-Three

It was three o'clock in the morning in New York, and Cosimo had been tossing and turning for hours. He lay alone in his bed, wide awake, the suede duvet and the linen top sheet twisted in knots and wrapped around his arms and legs. He stared vacantly at the Venetian chandelier and tried to use that to hypnotize himself into slumber. An array of pillows were stuffed here and there, around and under his head and limbs. The jumbled layers made his mattress look more like a bunker than a bed. More frequently than not, there comes a moment during the night when he has to decide if he'll continue the charade of trying to fall asleep, or if he'll raise himself up and succumb to whatever it is that his demons have planned for him. This night, he could no longer bear the inundation of thoughts that accompanied his sleepless-ness: not the montage of images that flickered and flashed at lightning speed through his consciousness or the hopes and regrets that came and went in his frontal cortex, like tides ceaselessly crashing against a rocky shore. He bolted upright with an urgent need to be somewhere else, anywhere else. Trapped in the bedding, he struggled to break free. After a few seconds of furiously thrashing his arms and legs, he finally freed himself from the confines of the comforter and the sheets. Once liberated from the linens, he reached over to the nightstand and opened the top drawer. It was empty. He closed it and opened the drawer below. Also empty.

He searched the room, even though he knew it was futile. At one time or another, he had hidden pills everywhere, behind pictures and in cabinets, under furniture and in clothes, taped under sinks, rolled into socks, and tossed into chandeliers. But he remembered that he had recently ferreted out every pill and capsule he could find and poured them down the sink, hoping once again to alleviate his reliance on them, to reduce his impulsive need to reach for them at the first sign of stress. He wanted to believe that it was merely their physical presence that lured him into taking them, that the maxim "out of sight—out of mind" was actually a truism. All he wanted was to be normal and, for once in his life, to not feel like a patient.

He raced over to the sock drawer. "There's a thousand pair in here. I must have missed at least one," he said out loud, praying that the gods of sanity would hear him and take pity on him. His hands moved quickly, first looking for any sign of a hard plastic vial, then pulling the pairs apart, hoping to find anything, even a stray tablet or two. He stood frozen in front of the Biedermeier bureau with all of the drawers open, a pile of unpaired socks at his feet, and experienced an episode of déjà vu.

A few minutes later, he was staring at his reflection in the bathroom mirror, wondering what had come over him.

What possible set of circumstances could have deluded him into thinking that tossing out every single one of his pills was a good idea? His eyes were bloodshot, his face unshaven, and his voluminous, curly hair wandered off in all directions. He opened one of the vanity drawers and withdrew a bottle of eye drops and a pair of scissors. He ran his fingers through his hair. He admired it one minute and wished it were straight the next. One instant he was reveling in its luxuriousness; the next he was cursing its coarseness. The reflection of his fingers entwined in his thick crop of ringlets reminded him of Maria-Carmella's comment earlier that day: 'You're starting to get a little shaggy, dear, don't you think?'

"*Do it.*"

He looked around to see who or what had said that.

"*Do it.*"

It was softer the second time, almost a whisper.

"*Do it…DO it…DO IT!*"

The last one was a command, an order from an illusion uttered sotto voce. The first of the silken curls landed on the marble floor in the shape of a chocolate question mark. More locks dropped at an accelerated pace as the voice and the snip-snip-snip of the scissors got faster and faster. "*Do it. Doit. Doitdoitdoit.*" Then he stopped abruptly, put the scissors down, and brushed the stray hairs from his shoulders.

The mirror that had previously displayed the vision of a sleepless prince now reflected the image of a crazy person: the wild eyes, the pallid complexion, the hair not so much cropped as mutilated. While he knew that he had certain mental disabilities, he had never considered himself to be a lunatic, to be delusional, to be psychotic. Certain doctors may have, but he didn't. But the person staring back at him in the mirror looked disturbed, unstable, insane. In a few hours, a new crew would be arriving at Regina's flat to commence filming an elaborate television commercial on her terrace as part of her multifaceted Regal campaign. Regina had convinced Cosimo that a cameo role in her commercial would be good for both their brands, even though he didn't think of himself as a brand yet.

He sat on the granite counter and ran his hand along the interior of the sink. He gathered up the few clumps that had not landed on the floor and then ran the tap to rinse his hands clean. As he watched his curls disappear down the drain, he envisioned all the money that he might have earned with his own proposed fragrance line, "Royalty," spiraling down with them. As the imaginary cash funneled its way down the pipes, he heard his mother's voice again: "Don't you think…don't you think…don't you think?"

He reached into the open drawer and retrieved a pair of clippers. He attached the smallest trimmer head and began to make smooth, even arcs, starting at his forehead and moving back toward the middle of his neck. The few scattered clumps of hair that were left on his crown soon joined the pile of clippings that had accumulated on the floor. Finished, he rinsed his head under the faucet and dried it with a hand towel. Back in bed, he switched on the light, picked up the phone, and called his psychiatrist. He left a detailed message with the service regarding refills for lithium, valium, Wellbutrin, and a few others. Frenzied and spent, he fell backwards onto the mattress, the phone still in his hand, and immediately drifted into a deep slumber.

The kisses started out tender, luscious, lingering, and then became more intense, more intent. Her tongue glided across the light trail of fur on his flat stomach, darting in and out of his bellybutton and across the smooth ripples of his torso before she followed the trail further south. The roughness and the wetness of it tingled and excited him. He lightly placed both of his hands on her head, cupping each side of her blond scalp in one of his palms, and moaned as her tongue lightly touched his member, teasing him, taunting him, entreating him to beg for it. When he did, she gave him what he wanted, taking him in her warm, moist mouth before resuming the teasing licks and tender kisses across his stomach.

She gave him one more long, last lick before stopping and moving up to his chest.

"Did you like that?" she asked, biting one of his nipples to the cusp of pleasure and pain.

"God, yes. Couldn't you tell?"

"I know something that will make you feel even better."

"Not possible," he said, trying to catch his breath, "not possible."

She got off of him, maneuvered herself off the mattress, and retrieved an object from an overnight case that was on the floor. She stood at the edge of the bed and began to slowly and seductively, one by one, drape long strips of silky cloth over Cosimo's taut stomach. Each one she let dangle over a different body part, allowing the smooth tip of the material to caress his flesh before laying the crimson sashes over his skin.

"I want to tie you up," she said, eyeing the mahogany posts of the headboard.

Cosimo silently shook his head.

"You trust me, don't you?"

"It's not that; it's—" he started to say, but she cut him short by grabbing his member and slowly stroking him.

"Okay. Whatever…whatev…stop…stop…"

Penelope removed the strips from his stomach and chest and began to tie each of his arms and legs to the four corners of the bed. His limbs tightly secured, she leaned over and kissed him on the mouth. Her kiss was deliberate, aggressive, curt.

"Goodbye, sweetheart. It's been fun." Penelope blew him a kiss and gave a smart little wave of her hand as she evaporated into the night.

"Wait! Wait! Don't leave me like this," he pleaded to the fading apparition. He lay there for hours, or so it seemed, falling in and out of sleep, chilled in his nakedness by an open window. And it was through that open window that she arrived, more beautiful, more radiant, more powerful than ever. She nonchalantly made her way to the bed and then affectionately, tenderly kissed him all over his face while carefully avoiding his lips.

"I love you," he said. "I love youuuu," he repeated as his voice faded to nothing.

"I know you do. I know," Megan whispered as she started to untie him. "How did you come to be in this position?"

"I don't know. I don't know. I don't know," he heard himself repeating as he emerged from a deep sleep to an empty room. He massaged his right wrist with his left hand as if there had actually been a restraint there to chafe him. He rubbed his eyes and squinted at the phosphorescent clock over on the night table. The illuminated numbers read 3:45 a.m.

Regina and Cosimo were sitting at a rectangular glass table in her kitchen, drinking coffee and discussing the previous day's photo shoot. The session had taken several hours longer than she had anticipated, and she was still fatigued from all the commotion, from all the decisions, from having to be on and animated the entire time. Leibovitz had been intent on documenting her every move, each nuance of expression, especially those contradictions when Regina looked other than she was. What Annie wanted to capture—Regina in haute couture and curlers, smoking a cigarette, and drinking a tumbler of scotch—and what Regina wanted her to capture weren't exactly aligned. It was that kind of constant tension that had made it a particularly unpleasant afternoon for her. But her fatigue didn't show. It was only 7:00 a.m., and she looked as if she'd already sat for hair and makeup. And somehow Cosimo managed to look presentable, too, in spite of the night that he had had.

"You really like it?" he said, rubbing his hands over his newly mown scalp.

"I was disappointed at first, for about thirty seconds. You have...*had* such beautiful hair. But this gives you an edge, a look of untamable wildness. I like it. You'll start a new trend."

"Yeah, psych-ward chic," he said. "Look, I don't want to ruin this for you. I don't have to be in the commer—"

"I said I like it. I want you in it. Okay?"

"You want him in what?" Maria-Carmella said, striding into the kitchen, her hair pulled up in a beehive and a pair of oversized tortoiseshell sunglasses balanced on her head. She was more businesslike than usual, dressed in a black Donna Karan suit and a camel-colored Givenchy cashmere coat.

"Good morning, Mother. I want him to be in the video. Coz is going to help me pitch my perfume," she said as she dipped biscotti into her coffee. "I wanted to introduce you to a few people yesterday, but you left rather quickly. Is everything all right?"

"Everything's fine, dear," she said. "Just a last-minute call from Erick at Chase Manhattan. He wanted to discuss our latest acquisition. And naturally I had to inspect it myself to make sure it made sense for our portfolio."

Cosimo got up from the table, tightened the belt on his silk robe, and ambled over to the sink. He removed a china cup from the cabinet and placed it on the counter next to his own that he was about to refill.

"Coffee, Mother?" he said.

"No, thank you, dear. I'm on my way out. Papers to sign, contracts to approve, that sort of thing, you know."

"What did we get, Mother? A manufacturing plant? A cruise ship?" Regina asked. "It's not another office building, is it?" She winked at Cosimo, hoping to entice him into playing the game. "A new Gulfstream, maybe?"

Cosimo knew that Regina had no real interest in the family business, that she simply pretended to, somehow effortlessly and naturally, for Maria-Carmella's sake. And as much as he wished that he was capable of doing that himself, to please and appease his mother, he just couldn't bring himself to play that game, to feign interest in a topic he cared little about.

"No, dear, it's a..." Maria-Carmella paused to drag it out, as if she were having great difficulty uttering the words, as if the very syllables themselves were physically painful for her to pronounce. "A condo," she said. "We've bought a... condominium."

"A condo?" Regina looked perplexed.

Cosimo was still standing at the counter looking down at his feet when the timer on the Viking range went off. He opened the oven door and removed an omelet pan.

"For you? Is it for you?" Regina asked. "You found an apartment in Manhattan?" She gave Cosimo a smug smile, which seemed to imply that she thought that her plan of strategically placing real estate brochures around her flat had finally paid dividends.

Cosimo faked a cough to keep from laughing at Regina's blatant disregard for pretense. She seemed so thrilled at the thought of having her apartment back that it didn't occur to her how that question might be interpreted by their mother.

"No, dear. Boston. It's a condo in Boston," Maria-Carmella said.

"Boston? Why Bos..." Regina began, and then she tried to downplay her response, to take it back. She tilted her head to see Cosimo's reaction out of the corner of her eye. But Cosimo, in a rare display of composure, showed almost no emotion; his hands were stuffed into his pockets, his face a blank slate, his eyes staring down at his slippered feet.

Maria-Carmella let the silence in the room thicken while she occupied herself searching for an item in her purse. When she found whatever it was she'd been looking for, she snapped the bag shut.

"Yes. Erick, with his flow charts and projections and historical data, seems convinced it's a good investment. We're getting it for, how did he put it...a steal. A lovely penthouse overlooking the Commons," she said, slowly moving her focus from Regina to her son. "Isn't that right, dear?"

"Mother...I can...it was...you said—"

"That's what I thought. Articulate as ever. Unfortunately, it's too late to get a refund on those elocution lessons. That money could have offset some of those nasty," Maria-Carmella said, swallowing hard again and contorting her face into a grimace, "maintenance fees."

"I was going to tell you. It's not like it was a secret. I didn't think that—"

"You never do, do you? *Think*, that is."

"But you said...before I left...that I—"

"I also said that we would talk, but I misspoke," she said in a treacly voice. And then she added, not so sweetly, "Now *I* will talk, and you will listen. *Capiche?*"

Regina slid her chair away from the table and reached for her coffee cup.

"Sit down!" Maria-Carmella said. "You too!" was another edict; that one bellowed across the room at a cowering Cosimo.

He stood there, frozen, part of him wanting to pour himself another cup of coffee, part of him needing to drop everything immediately and do as he was told. He abandoned the idea of a second cup and did as he was commanded. He sprinted to the table, his adrenaline pumping perfectly fine even without the infusion of more caffeine.

"You're both adults, I'll grant you that. But is it necessary for me to remind you that you are where you are, *who* you are, and that you have what you have because of me?"

"I can't speak for Coz, Mother, but I am—you know that I am—*very* grateful for all your support, especially with the start-up costs for the clothing line. But I must ask you," Regina said, holding her hands out, palms up for emphasis, "at what point, under what circumstances, will you consider our debts paid? At what point do we stop being your indentured servants?"

Cosimo remained still in his chair, perfectly quiet. His mouth was dry, his breathing uneven. He knew that his sister was purposely speaking on his behalf and risking a great deal to do so, but the idea filled him more with animosity than with gratitude. He was pleased to have someone stand up for him, but her self-assurance mocked him, and her presumption that he needed a buffer, and that she be it, was arrogant. And as much as it pained him to admit it, he was still grateful that she was there to deflect some of the artillery fire.

"When I'm dead and buried. Is that soon enough for you?" Maria-Carmella said, glaring at Regina.

Then, with excruciating slowness, with a deliberateness that seemed laden with subtext, she transferred her stare from her daughter to her son. Out of habit, Cosimo's hands felt around in his pockets for pills that he knew weren't there. Couldn't possibly be there. And even if they were, it was too late to take them. There was nothing he could do, nothing he could say, nothing he could swallow that would prevent him from feeling the full impact of her blow.

"Can *you* wait that long?" she said, lightly, casually. And because of that, because of the softness of her delivery, it was even more damaging, was even more impactful, was even more intense. An innuendo clearly spelled out.

"I was just checking, Mother," Regina said, a sheepish grin spreading across her face and an embarrassed little laugh escaping her lips.

Maria-Carmella continued to stare at Cosimo.

"And you? What were you thinking? What could have possibly been going on in that little head of yours?"

"I was thinking that I needed a place to live," he said, believing that to be a satisfactory answer and an adequate reason.

He was also thinking that if he had to wait for her to die before he could stop being an indentured servant, he would kill himself.

"It never occurred to you to discuss a four-million-dollar expenditure with me first?" she said. Her query lingered in the air like a stale aroma. "What do you know about Boston real estate? What, pray tell, do you know about *any* real estate market?"

"I know enough to have gotten the place for four hundred thousand below asking," he said, assuming again that that was a good enough reason.

"That is beside the point. Another Arabian, a new Maserati, Giorgio's entire fall collection—all right. But we discuss an expenditure of this magnitude. You know that." Her comments were greeted with silence. "Yes, I have given you carte blanche. But dare I say...even carte blanche has its limits." Maria-Carmella's eyes shifted back and forth between her two children. She exhaled deeply and added, "As...do...I."

"Mother, other than what I've already said, I was comfortable with the decision because I knew I could turn around and sell it if I had to." He studied her face for any subtle change in attitude, for any sign he was getting through to her. "Is that what you want me to do, Mother, sell the place?" His tone more antagonistic and confrontational than he meant it to be.

"Calm down, Coz," Regina said, patting his arm. "She didn't say that. Did you, Mother?"

Maria-Carmella opened her purse again and retrieved a pair of leather gloves.

"I've scheduled a party for the thirtieth of January," she said. "I've reserved the ballroom at the Plaza, and I've secured Reneé to organize the affair. If you have any questions, please direct them to her. Obviously, I expect the two of you to be there. *Especially* you," she said, looking at Cosimo.

"It's been years since you've thrown that kind of gala," Regina said. "What's the occasion?"

"We're announcing Cosimo's engagement to Annabella. All of the Bollettieris will be there, and, of course, the press." Maria-Carmella watched Cosimo's mouth try to form words, but all she saw was a bubble or two escape from the center of his lips. To Regina she said, "This could be a great opportunity for you to garner some exposure for that new fashion venture of yours. I'll have Reneé print out the guest list tomorrow, and then you and I can discuss a strategy."

She stood, donned her jacket, and slipped on her gloves, deliberately drawing out the process, adjusting one finger at a time. She picked up her purse and then turned as if she were about to leave, her artillery dispensed, the skirmish over. She stopped, shifted her body, and addressed Cosimo.

"Consider the condominium my wedding gift to you," she said, and then she gracefully pivoted on her Manolo Blahniks and walked out of the kitchen, her stiletto heels clicking and clacking as she traipsed out of the apartment. Regina and Cosimo sat there in silence, neither able to look at the other. She drummed her fingers on the thick glass tabletop, and he leaned back in his chair, his arms crossed tightly over his chest, his right foot nervously tapping the floor. A clock in the living room chimed the hour. The sound that the timepiece's clapper made as it struck the bell was amplified by the silence that it encountered. That faint echo of the passing of time filled Cosimo with an undeniable sense of despair.

Chapter Twenty-Four

The next several months passed uneventfully. Cosimo successfully made the transition to living in Boston, but he continued to lobby for Megan to relinquish her apartment and move in with him. Or at least stay there on a regular basis and allow him to cover her rent until she felt secure enough to make their cohabitation permanent. That would have to qualify as their second major fight. He'd had a few embarrassingly short meetings with Terrance and Simon, but no progress was made, and a fragrance designed specifically for Cosimo was no closer to being packaged and shipped to retailers than when they'd first mentioned the concept to him months ago. They assured him that as soon as Regal was shipped and on the shelves, they would start making headway on Royalty, or whatever it was they would call his proposed cologne.

Megan was teaching another class of college freshmen about columns and caryatids, about the difference between the Venus of Willendorf and the Venus de Milo, and how to tell a Monet from a Manet. And while she complained about her students—"Can you believe one of them actually thought Art Deco was a person?"—even situations like that were rewarding for her. As hard as it was to try to educate people barely out of puberty, being allowed to share her knowledge and passion for art, or watch her students get excited about a lecture on the Bauhaus, invigorated her and gave her a reason to get out of bed in the morning. While she had refused to give up her apartment, she was spending most of her time in the penthouse, including one rather frosty morning in March when the subject of cohabitation came up yet again.

Cosimo turned off the shower and stepped out of the glass enclosure. He walked over to the mirror, placed a towel on his head and rubbed vigorously. While his hair was getting thicker and fuller each day, the curls resurfacing in miniature, it was still a far cry from his trademark ringlets. He examined his reflection and decided he preferred his hair that way—short, with no need for combs, messy products, or blow-dryers. He made a mental note to call Diego's to schedule an appointment for a trim. He put on a robe and went to the kitchen. He took a carton of milk from the Sub Zero and espresso beans from the cupboard; then he ground the beans, heated the milk, and carried the streaming latte back to the bedroom, where Megan was beginning to stir.

"What time is it?" she asked.

"Seven thirty. Here, this should wake you up."

She took the cup from him and placed her hands around it to draw on its warmth.

"Is it cold in here?" she asked.

"Yes, a little. I haven't figured out how to adjust the thermostat yet. It has like thirty buttons," he said, sitting down on the bed. "What shall we do today?"

"I don't know about you, but I've got a class to teach in two hours."

"I can audit."

"Oh no. That's all I need is you in the back of the class-room, making funny faces."

"Funny faces, yes, but with hand puppets and balloon animals."

"No thank you," she said, smiling as she inhaled the aroma of an expertly prepared latte. "I thought you were picking up the new car today?"

"Yes, it'll be ready this afternoon."

"Why don't you go for a drive, then? It's supposed to be sunny."

As she sipped her coffee, a small dab of foam clung to the top of her lip. He took the towel he had wrapped around his neck and used it to wipe the froth away from her face. She backed away at first but relaxed when she realized what he was doing.

"Don't forget about tonight. We're having dinner at Tom and Gregg's."

"I won't," he said as he reentered the bathroom.

"I also have a four o'clock class today," she said, raising her voice to make sure he could hear her. "Why don't you meet me at their place around seven?"

Cosimo returned to the bedroom carrying a small plastic bag filled with cosmetics.

"I've been living here for three months, and this is all you leave here?" he said.

"I travel light."

"You know what I mean."

"Cosimo, I can't have this conversation again. I'm not ready to give up my apartment." Her bare arms shivered from the cold. She made a move to put the cup down but continued to hold on to it. "Look at me, I don't even know where to put this. I'm afraid to set it down on your nice furniture." She took a section of the morning newspaper and placed it on the nightstand and placed the cup on top of that. She grabbed the cashmere blanket from the foot of the bed and wrapped it around her shoulders. "My apartment may not have a spectacular view, but I know how the heat works. There's one dial," she said, holding up her index finger for emphasis. "One!"

He tossed the plastic case with her toothbrush and miscellaneous essentials onto the bed and went back to the bathroom.

"Have fun at work," he said, his inflection contradicting his statement. The thud of the lock clicking into place was the exclamation point on his comment.

"Coz, I'm sorry. I didn't mean to sound so harsh."

She called out his name several more times, but he continued to give her the silent treatment. She gathered up a change of clothes and her cosmetics bag from the bed and headed for the guest room. She returned to the master bedroom only to find Cosimo still locked in the bathroom. She decided that hollering through a locked door was a little beneath her, a little too George and Martha. So she did the only other thing she could think of: she put her thoughts down in writing.

Coz,

    I feel bad about this morning. I'm sorry if I hurt your feelings. I know that you just want to be with me as much as possible. But I need a little more time before I can relinquish my old life. Please try to be patient. I care for you more than you know. Call me. I've got a break at 3:00 p.m. I'll see you at Tom's at 7:00 p.m. I left a slip of paper with their address and phone number on the dresser.

    Meg

Cosimo stayed in the bathroom until he heard her leave for work. When he finally did emerge, he saw that she had picked up his clothes, put away the dishes, and made the bed. He lay facedown on the comforter and closed his eyes. After his meltdown in the bathroom and the incident with the scissors several months earlier, he had resumed his regimen of pill popping. And ever since then, he had been taking all his medications at the recommended dosage and at the designated times, and he had stopped drinking alcohol except for the occasional glass of wine. But even so, his mind still raced with thoughts of what might have been or what might yet be. There was a constant ache in the pit of his stomach that felt like loneliness, emptiness, blackness, despite the fact that Megan was spending several nights a week with him in the penthouse.

He wanted to get up, to get out of bed, but he couldn't. There was a weight on him, in him, and it was unforgiving. Even the thought of driving his new Lamborghini that afternoon failed to cheer him up. The one thing that did give him a chuckle was knowing that the housekeeper would be there in a few hours, and that she would ceremoniously unmake the bed, change the linens, and then remake it according to her standards. But the implication of Megan's gesture was not lost on him. It was the thought of her doing that for him, and it was that thought alone that gave him the will to raise his heavy head from the pillow and get out of bed at all.

A note on the kitchen counter in Megan's looping cursive reminded him that she loved him, even though she hadn't written (or said) the words "I love you" yet. He knew that she did because she was still there, even though he was unpredictable and prone to outbursts and childish displays of emotion. And while he was capable of verbally expressing his love to her, he was not very adept at demonstrating it with actions. He knew that he had to accept her weaknesses along with her strengths in the same way that she had to tolerate his.

Her note provided him with the impetus he needed to call the dealership in Framingham and confirm the delivery of his new car. That was the way he had to navigate his way through life, one moment at a time, one rationalization at a time, always hoping for that one big push, that next reprieve—for *some* reason, for *any* reason to live. It was exhausting for him. But it was all he had ever known. He was able to endure that existence because he remained, although he couldn't comprehend why or how, fatally optimistic and blindly hopeful that someday, one day, any day now, his pain would stop.

～◦～

Tom and Gregg's place was in the south end of Boston

in an area known as Blackstone Square. It was a six-story building in the middle of a row of brownstones. Its crumbling façade overlooked a park that had, as its central element, an ornate shell-shaped fountain that hadn't been operational for thirty years. The park was ensconced on three sides by buildings that were centuries old; their pedimented windows, heavily bracketed cornices, and Mansard roofs stood in stark contrast to the glass condominiums and purpose-built lofts being erected in other parts of the city.

On the fourth side of the square was Washington Street, a busy road that was once the main artery for the city's MBTA Orange Line. For decades it had been overshadowed by a raised metal platform that supported the Terror Train (labeled that by an old *Boston Globe* headline about a holdup at gunpoint in one of the cars) and was considered by many to be an unsafe neighborhood. And even though the rusted and graffitied trestle had been torn down years ago, and the area had become considerably safer, the street was still dominated by convenience stores and liquor shops that served as sleeping alcoves for the homeless.

The neighborhood, while still slightly shabby, was on its way to becoming the next section of town to be gentrified, mostly by gays and young married couples. Gregg bought the building in the mid-1980s after it had been abandoned for several years. It was a wreck and uninhabitable, but the price was right. He slowly, laboriously began tearing out sheet rock, stripping the wood floors, and replacing the windows with double glazing to help insulate the place from the noise and the cold. Five years later, the floors were stained ebony, the previously prehistoric kitchen was resplendent with granite countertops and white lacquered cabinets, and the walls, once water-stained and crumbling, were redone in rich soothing shades of Venetian plaster.

"I'm still astonished that you did all this by yourself," Megan said as she looked out onto the green patch of grass across the street.

"You say that every time you come over," Gregg said, handing her a glass of wine.

"She's easily impressed," Tom said from his seat on the sofa.

"Smack him, would you?" she said to Gregg.

"I have," he said, shaking his head. "It doesn't do any good."

"Are those drug dealers over there?" she asked. "Are they selling crack in front of your house?"

Tom got up off the sofa and peered out the window.

"Him? That's Bob. He only sells pot," he said as he sat back down. "Come, sit. I haven't seen you in weeks."

"I'm going to use the facilities first, if you don't mind," she said, placing her glass on a table.

"You know where it is," Gregg said.

"Don't use the little soaps," Tom added. "Those are for guests."

"What am I, chopped liver?" she said as she closed the door behind her.

She flicked on the lights, and a pale pink hue filled the room. As she moved the handle on the sleek silver faucet, she began to chortle.

"Dornbracht," she said to the shiny piece of metal.

She instantly knew the name of the manufacturer of this little spigot. She recognized it from one of the many tear sheets that Cosimo's designer had shown them. And as irrelevant as this knowledge seemed, it bothered her. On one hand, the faucet was a work of art that she could appreciate for its quality and its aesthetics. On the other, it was a utilitarian piece of equipment that not everyone could afford. A few months ago, it would have been just another faucet. Now it was a Dornbracht with a certain cachet and a hefty price tag attached to it. Once you knew what it was, it was difficult to look at that shiny metal object without making certain assumptions, and consequently judgments, about its owners.

Instead of using the bar of antibacterial soap that was resting in a masculine-looking dish on the basin, she reached for one of the little soaps in the drawer, just for spite, just for fun. As she removed the small individually wrapped bar, she noticed something behind it, something made of glass and metal, something filled with fluid that looked like blue water, something that compelled her to take a closer look. Her discovery was a small glass bottle wrapped in a light metallic mesh with a dark-blue seal in its center. It was filled with an azure liquid and had an atomizer on top. She squeezed the atomizer, and the scents of lavender, citrus, and jasmine filled the room. There was another scent, an underlying aroma, rich and light at the same time, that she couldn't quite place. She reentered the living room, still holding the bottle.

"Where did this come from?" she said.

"You like?" Gregg asked.

"Yes, I do. There's an underlying aroma that's…I don't know…captivating."

"That's an endorsement if I've ever heard one," Tommy

said. "She never wears that stuff. Oh, maybe she'll splash on a little Jean Naté now and again, but not perfume."

"By the way," she said, glaring at her brother, "I opened up all the little soaps in there. I hope you don't mind?"

"That unrecognizable scent is the Italian bergamot oil," Gregg said. "It combines with the other scents to create a fuller bouquet. Take it. I get tons of samples like that."

"Are you sure?" she said, admiring the bottle of Regal.

"What are we going to do with it? It's a promotional sample from Neiman's to get the salespeople excited about it. It won't be available in the stores for a few more weeks."

"For once I'll be the first on my block!" she said, spritzing a little on her wrist.

Gregg went over to the entertainment center and riffled through a drawer.

"They gave us a DVD, too, with some selling points, a preview of the commercial, stuff like that," he said, "but I can't seem to find it."

Through an open window, they heard a loud, rumbling noise out on the street.

"What the hell is that?" Tom said. "It sounds like the Blue Angels."

"Oh, that's probably Coz in his new Lamborghini Roadster. He likes to rev the engines on his cars." She walked over to the closet and slipped the bottle of perfume into her coat pocket. "Is that him? A silver two-seater?"

"He's trying to maneuver into a spot that's too small," Tom said.

"He'll never make it," Gregg added.

"He'll make it," she said, pouring herself a glass of Pellegrino. A minute later she walked over to the door and pushed a button on the intercom. "Come on up, Sweetie. We've been holding dinner for you."

～

Tommy placed several large slices of tiramisu on dessert plates and dusted them with cocoa powder from a sterling silver canister. Gregg poured a bubbly pink dessert wine into a set of crystal glasses that had been handed down to him from his great-grandparents.

"None for me, Gregg," Megan said.

"What about the tiramisu?" Tommy said. "Do you have any idea how many stores I had to go to to find ladyfingers?"

"That I wouldn't miss for anything," she said. Then, tilting her head in Cosimo's direction, she added, "I guess I'm the designated driver this evening."

Cosimo shook his head no. His eyes were tiny slits, and his head continued to bob long after he'd made his point.

"You don't know how to drive that car," he said with a slur. "It is not like your Mustang. I will teach you this weekend."

"Oh, you have no idea what I'm capable of," she replied.

"You'd better listen to her, Cosimo," Gregg said. "I have seen her in action, and I can assure you, that girl is resourceful." He cupped his hands around his mouth and pretended to whisper, "I think she's with the CIA." He topped off Cosimo's wine glass as he whispered, "I'd tread carefully with her if I were you."

Megan was aware that her brother was being unusually quiet. He seemed to be observing her interactions with Cosimo, trying to interpret the dynamics of their relationship inherent in their touches, their glances, their stance.

That was the first time that she had wondered about how they looked as a couple. She speculated that the two of them seemed unconventional together, mismatched. But then, so were Tommy and Gregg. It was hard for her to contemplate for an extended period such an illogical, complicated subject as relationships. So she meditated on other things, like the impending taste of tiramisu and a summer evening not so long ago when it felt as if the past didn't exist, and the future didn't matter; a perfect evening with no regrets.

Downstairs Cosimo sat on the front stoop, holding his head in his hands. Megan paced the sidewalk in front of him, tossing his keys into the air and catching them again and again. He raised his head just long enough to ask her to stop making so much noise.

"Why did you let me drink so much?" he said in a way that didn't blame her but didn't absolve her either.

"You're a big boy. Besides, it wasn't my turn to watch you."

"What does that mean?"

"Nothing. Really…it meant nothing. I'm just tired. And cold."

She started walking toward the Roadster. He remained on the steps of the brownstone and, believing she would fail to start the car, waited for her to slowly return with the keys still in her hand and her ego a little deflated.

"Aren't you coming?" she said.

When his only response was to lean his head against the stone railing and close his eyes, she got into the car and engaged the engine. Instead of an apology, what Cosimo heard was the loud, rumbling *Prrrr, prrrrr, prrrr* of his brand-new Gallardo Superleggera. Megan easily maneuvered the coupe out of its tight spot, roared the engine, spun the tires, and sped down the street. After racing around the block, she rounded the corner and pulled up in front of Cosimo, still on the steps, still half asleep. She lowered the window on the passenger side.

"Get in. You'll freeze to death out there."

Cosimo struggled to his feet, slipped into the passenger seat, and buckled himself in.

"How did you…?" he said.

"My dad owned an automotive repair shop for a while. He let me move the cars from the garage to a parking lot down the street when they were finished working on them. Over the years I drove everything, and I mean everything. I can fix a flat, change the oil, and replace the fan belts on almost any car." She shifted the controls from neutral to first gear. "Hold on," she said and pressed her foot to the floor. It took just a few minutes to arrive at the Parkhurst Plaza, where Megan expertly maneuvered the car into the garage and eased it into Cosimo's dedicated spot.

"I will never doubt you again," he said.

"Good idea," she said as she closed the driver's side door with a thud that only a six-figure car can make.

Chapter Twenty-Five

Two days after that dinner, Tommy left an urgent voice mail for Megan. His message, which seemed intentionally opaque, insisted that she call him back right away.

"Why so cryptic?" she asked when Tommy answered.

"What are you doing? Right now? This very minute?"

"I was getting ready to—"

"Get over here. I found the Regal perfume commercial on the DVD that Gregg misplaced. It is going to blow your mind."

"OK, now you're starting to freak me out. Tell me right now why you're being so weird."

"I can't. You have to see it," he said, hanging up before she could object.

She hailed a taxi, and when it pulled up in front of Tommy's building, she found him anxiously waiting for her on the front steps.

"What took you so long?"

"I spoke to you like five minutes ago. This better be good."

Megan followed him upstairs. He took two and three steps at a time and was breathing hard when she caught up to him. Megan was familiar with Tommy's bursts of energy, by his total consumption with whatever was happening at a given moment, his *crises du jour*. In fact, Cosimo's mood swings often reminded her of her brother. Tommy closed the door behind them and double locked it.

"What's *that* all about?"

"Nothing. I just feel the need to be cautious and a little protective of my big sister today, that's all." He pointed to the sofa. "Have a seat. I'll be right back."

She heard the clinking of glasses and then the rumble of ice cubes being dispensed by the refrigerator door.

"Here," he said. He handed her a glass filled with ice and clear liquid. "Vodka. You're going to need it."

"Why so dramatic? What's got you whipped up into a frenzy?"

"This," he said, holding up a thin, clear plastic compact disc cover. "I found it mixed in with the classical stuff. It wasn't even in its own case. Imagine my surprise when I go to play Scheherazade and find *this* instead?" He held the disc up in front of her face. She recognized the Regal logo on the CD from the bottle they had given her the other day.

"A perfume ad?"

"That Gregg, he never puts anything back where—"

"You drag me across town, make me cancel my plans, have me—"

"I didn't tell you to cancel your plans."

"Oh, just play the damn thing!"

"Watch," he said.

He inserted the disc into the player and aimed the remote control at the flat-screen TV.

✌

Light classical music plays as the black screen fills with brightly colored images. A camera attached to a helicopter whizzes through the Manhattan skyline. It swoops and glides over the trees of Central Park and then soars upward once again, hovering over the top of a prewar apartment building. The camera telescopes in, panning a rooftop terrace and a cocktail party already in progress. A tuxedoed waitstaff is serving a well-heeled crowd fluted glasses filled with the bright, bubbling amber color of champagne. The instrumental music that has been playing softly in the background gradually increases in volume and tempo. A handheld camera, stationed in the middle of the tony guests, captures bits and pieces of dialogue, the clinking of glasses, and the hushed tones of people sharing loosely guarded secrets. The camera moves quickly, effortlessly among the glitterati while glass skyscrapers shimmer in the background. The throng parts, and the camera zooms in on a raised platform draped on three sides with billowing white fabric. Standing in the center is a statuesque woman with thick brown hair cascading over her shoulders. She is wearing a cream-colored evening gown appliquéd with hundreds of faceted crystals that twinkle and sparkle in the afternoon sunlight. Off to the right, a six-piece orchestra sets the mood. Horsehair bows move furiously back and forth across the varnished wood and steel strings of the violins. A piccolo player's nimble fingers move energetically across a short silver tube. The seated cello player playfully

plucks the instrument's strings with his right hand while occa-
sionally and dramatically spinning it with his left.

The woman on the platform reaches for a bottle that is
resting on a pedestal in the shape of a Corinthian column.
She holds the blue bottle up, admires it, and then squeezes
the atomizer twice in the direction of her exposed neck,
releasing a fine mist into the air. One infinitesimal spray on
each side of her long, lean, tanned throat. She returns the
bottle to the pedestal, and the camera goes in for a close-
up. When the camera pulls away from the bottle and back
to her, she is seated in a winged-back chair upholstered in
purple mohair. To her right stands a handsome young man
in a black-and-blue damask dinner jacket accessorized with
ripped, faded blue jeans and high-top Converse sneakers.
His hair is excessively short, his smile devious, and his eyes
a mesmerizing green. The woman whispers the word "Regal"
in the direction of the telephoto lens. The camera comes in
for a close-up of both of their faces. The gentleman leans
in and says, nonchalantly and directly to the camera, "It's
as sophisticated as you are." The view changes abruptly
back to the helicopter's perspective as it quickly soars above
the crowd until the people are once again tiny specks. The
screen fades to a royal blue, and in cream-colored script,
these words appear:

Regal
Let Loose Your Inner Princess!

Tom pressed a button on the remote control, and the
screen went dark. Megan took a sip of vodka. The tinkling
of the ice in her glass was the only sound in the room. She

looked straight ahead at the blank screen as she swirled the frozen cubes around in her cocktail.

"Is this Ketel One or Belvedere?" she asked.

"You're kidding me, right?"

Megan took another sip.

"Can I have a little more ice in this?" she said, extending the glass to him.

"Oh, I can't take it. Say something!"

"I'm thinking."

She paced the rectangular living room while taking frequent sips from her glass. She stopped and rested her hand on the back of a chair.

"It's a commercial, that's all it is," she said. "Why would Cosimo tell me about that? It could have been filmed a year ago, for all you know. I'll bet half the time those things get shelved, and no one ever sees them."

"What about his short hair? That was fairly recent, wasn't it?"

"A coincidence?"

"Not likely."

"He said he did some modeling when he was younger. Maybe when he was in New York, an old friend asked him to do it as a favor?" She opened the player and retrieved the DVD, but the only things on it were the logo and the tag line. "I'm not sure what you think the implications of this are."

Tommy walked over to his sister and took her hand.

"It gets worse," he said.

"Tommy, it's a commercial. For perfume. What has it got to do with anything? Why do you think this has anything to do with me?"

"Sit down. I'll be right back."

Tommy ran down the hall to a bedroom that served as his home office and returned with a stack of newspapers and magazines. He sat down next to Megan on the sofa.

"I'm sorry I'm being so dramatic and secretive," he said. "Okay, maybe I'm enjoying it a little. But still, I care about you. If I didn't, I would have blurted it out over the phone."

"I know. But you needn't worry about me. Coz would never do anything to hurt me."

"Maybe not intentionally. But how do you explain this?" he said, holding up an old issue of the *Star*.

"I'll never understand why you read that crap," she said, shaking her head.

"Because I'm shallow. Now *look*! What do you see?"

"Britney Spears? And that one, I don't know, George Clooney?" She pointed to their images as she looked up and down the page. "And her, that one, the Amazon. She looks kinda like that woman in the perfume commercial."

"And do you happen to know who that is?"

"Seriously, me? You're lucky I recognized George Clooney."

"Her name is Regina. She's a clothing designer." Tom shuffled through a few of the papers and pulled out another issue. "Here's another picture of her," he said, holding up *The National Enquirer*. "In this one from a few months ago, there's a photo of her with her date resting his head on her shoulder. I know it's a little out of focus, but you can't tell me that's not him."

"Who?"

"Well, if you were to take a closer look and the time to read the article, you'd find out that her date for the evening was none other than her brother, Crown Prince Giuseppe Garibaldi di Sorrento."

"*Giuseppe?*"

"That's all you have to say? Are you not connecting the dots?"

"You're trying to tell me that Cosimo, *my* Cosimo, my sweet, damaged, albeit wealthy Cosimo, is a member of the Italian royal family? It doesn't make any sense."

"Have you ever met his sister?"

She shook her head. Tommy's question made her realize how unusual it was that Cosimo, while having acknowledged that he had a sister, had never once mentioned her by name.

"I didn't think so," he said. "Look, you can't deny the name, the profile, the…" He paused, shook and lowered his head, and then continued. "I knew he looked familiar. I just knew I had seen him someplace before. I didn't say anything, but it was driving me crazy. And then when I played that disc—"

"But that guy's name is Giuseppe," she said. "Maybe it's a cousin? Or a coincidence?"

"If he wants you to move in with him so badly, tell him you will. But that first you'd like to meet his family."

"What? That's ludicrous. It's not like he's asked me to marry him."

"Not yet. Do you have a better idea? How else could you find out the truth?" He placed the DVD back in its case and the case back into the drawer. "I know," he said, "you could go through his cell phone."

"Or," she said.

"Or what?"

"Or I could ask him."

⌒

Cosimo was tossing and turning, trying to force himself, rock himself, will himself awake. Getting out of bed any morning was hard enough for him, but on this particular day, he was suffering the repercussion of mixing alcohol and Ambien in his already heavily medicated system. He vowed never to do it again, to make a fresh start. No more alcohol, no more…He stopped midthought. Even he was sick of hearing his own sales pitches, his promises to stop indulging in certain behaviors, or his vows to embark on some new regimen that might temper his demons and move him in the direction of sanity. But even if he failed, he knew he had to make the effort. If he gave up on himself, Megan might, too. His arm reached out and searched the other side of the mattress. He found nothing and no one. The bed was empty but for Cosimo.

The alarm clock went off, but he ignored it. He had deliberately and strategically placed it on a table on the other side of the room so that he would have to get out of bed to turn it off. Mistakenly having tuned it in to a heavy metal station, he endured twenty minutes of electric guitar solos before getting out of bed and yanking the plug from the wall.

He showered, but he didn't shave. He put on a new pair of Hugo Boss jeans that were shredded and paint-splattered and a green cotton shirt that he'd purchased at a local boutique because the salesgirl had said it made his eyes sparkle. He brewed himself a double espresso and sat down at the breakfast table. He twisted a lemon peel into the cup and finished it in a few quick sips. Then he stood at the sink and rinsed out the cup and wiped down the counter while he pondered his options for the day ahead. The morning mail was on the counter, and in it, the latest edition of *Boston Magazine*. As he flipped through the pages, he came upon an aerial photograph of a cluster of faded blue-gray saltbox homes in Marblehead. He hadn't taken the Lamborghini out for a drive since the day he'd brought it home, since dinner at Tom and Gregg's. Those iconic images of New England life, some tiny, some grand, all of them bordered by miles of greenish-blue water, tall sea grasses, and soft beige sand, enticed him into taking a short drive up the coast.

He went to the closet to get his wallet and keys, only his keys weren't in their usual spot. He looked on the floor, under the bed, and in his coat pockets; he failed to find them anywhere. He was mentally walking through the apartment when he remembered that Megan had driven the car last. He searched around her nightstand, but his keys were not there. He went to the hall closet to check the coat she'd been wearing that night. He dipped a hand into one of the pockets, and there they were. But there was also something else nestled there among the keys, something odd, something large, something hard, something cold. He removed the keys and then reached back in to retrieve the other mysterious object. He couldn't tell what it was from the way it felt, but the instant he saw the glass container emerge with the Mediterranean blue liquid inside, he knew that it was a bottle of Regal.

The room began to spin. He stumbled over to the sofa, unable to take his eyes off the mesh-encased vessel. His mind stuttered with thoughts. How? Where? When?

Why hadn't she said anything? He couldn't begin to comprehend the situation, but he knew that it wasn't good.
While he hadn't intentionally kept the campaign a secret
from her, she had obviously been keeping her awareness
of it a secret from him. And because he cared for her, he
worried that her fury would make Maria-Carmella's look
amateurish. A lifetime of his mother's sneak attacks and
direct confrontations had made them practically expected,
even routine. They were dreadful but endurable. But he
knew, even without prior experience, that if someone he
loved and needed were to be upset with him and confront
him, it would feel like a hole in the earth was opening up
and threatening to swallow him whole, to consume him
completely. He gripped the glass tightly, his pupils riveted
to the bottle. He could feel his pulse quicken, his breath
accelerating, his head throbbing. He was drowning and suf-
focating and being crushed all at the same time.

"Why didn't I tell her?" he cried out to the empty room.
"Now she will never understand why I didn't." Then he
became angry. He wondered what kind of game it was that
she was playing. How long she had known? Why hadn't
she said anything to him? And he wondered what it was
that she wanted. His fear mutated into rage as he began to
realize that the woman he loved was playing games with
him, manipulating him, keeping secrets from him.

A couple of hours later Cosimo was still sitting on
the sofa, the blue bottle lodged in his hand and his mind
flip-flopping between anger and fear. He raised the bottle
above his head, cocked his hand back, and prepared to
launch it across the room. Just as he was about to propel
it toward the living room wall, he heard a key in the front

door. So, instead of smashing it, he stuffed it in between the cushions and picked up a copy of *New Englander Monthly*. He tried to look casual, nonchalant, as if he'd been relaxing there for a while with his feet up, listening to Beethoven, engrossed in an article about fish hatcheries.

"I didn't expect you to be here," Megan said. She walked over to the couch, bent forward, and gave him a perfunctory kiss.

"I thought you had a meeting this afternoon," he said.

"It got rescheduled. Any good mail? Anybody call?"

"Like who?"

"Oh, I don't know… my parents, perhaps? My brother? *Regina?*"

"I think I know where this is going."

"That's not the response I was hoping for," she said, hanging her jacket over a chair.

"Where did you get this?" he said, digging the bottle out from between the cushions and holding it in his outstretched hand with the Regal logo pointed directly at her.

"Gregg gave it to me the other night. He said it was a free sample from work, from Neiman's. Why? What do *you* know about it… *Giuseppe?*" She stood there behind the divan, looking down at him, her eyes wide, her lips pursed, her arms crossed.

He motioned for her to join him on the sofa.

"What I know is that nothing can change the way I feel about you. I've been sitting here not knowing what to say to you, not knowing what to expect. And I kept coming back to the realization that nothing matters to me more than you. Nothing."

"Money?"

"Say the word, and I'll give it all away."

"What about your crown?"

"I can explain."

"You should have done that a long time ago. It appears as if you've been having fun at my expense. Why the double life?" she said, joining him but sitting as far away as possible. "Are we some kind of sociological experiment for you? Manhattan bistros one day, slumming with me and my brother the next?"

"Is that what you think?"

"Why didn't you tell me?"

"I would have, but after seeing your reaction to the Four Seasons and then to this apartment...I couldn't. I couldn't bring myself to utter those words. What should I have said? Yes, I'm fabulously wealthy, and by the way, I just happen to be a member of the Italian royal family—heir to the throne, in fact. Here, let me show you our family crest."

"That would have been the honest thing to do. The *noble* thing."

"What does some bogus title I've been shackled with have to do with anything? With us? It was an accident of birth. Believe me, I'm a prince in title only. The throne and any power it came with are ancient history."

"I know it's hard to comprehend that I'm content with my status quo, but I am," she said. "To pay for college, I cocktail-waitressed at the Marblehead Country Club. Those people with their Jaguars and their tennis lessons and their Rolex watches, all sitting around the pool sucking down Gin Fizzes and smoking cigars, were the meanest, loneliest, most disagreeable people I have ever met." Then as an afterthought she added, "Oh, and they were also the cheapest."

"Well, I for one hate Gin Fizzes," he said.

"With the other guys I've gone out with, my choices for date night were a double feature at the Rialto or an evening at the Bowl-A-Rama wearing rented shoes. And should we invite Betty and Jim or Sue and Todd? Not, should we go skiing in Zermatt or sail the Greek islands, and should we invite the Duke and Duchess of Blah-Blah-Blah or Beyoncé and JAY-Z?"

"Beyoncé and JAY-Z I don't know, but the Duke and Duchess of Blah-Blah-Blah are a lovely couple. I think you'd like them."

She offered a half-hearted laugh at his joke but then quickly brought the conversation back to the issue at hand.

"It's the money, *Giuseppe*, if that's your real name."

"Yes, it's my real name, and I'm proud of it. It's just that no one, family and friends anyway, ever calls me that." He placed the perfume bottle down on a sofa cushion. His hand was now free to grasp the medallion that hung around his neck, to feel Orion's relief and the diamond star substitutes reassuringly press into his flesh. "What do you mean, it's the money?"

"There's never enough," she said. "You keep buying bigger and bigger houses to fit in, to keep up with your friends. Then you need a Manhattan pied-à-terre to feel like you've 'made it.' Then it's a boat, a Cezanne, a *Lamborghini!* It never ends."

"I think what you say is true," he said, "for some people. But I am not some people. I am Cosimo, or Giuseppe, or whatever it is you want to call me. I am the man who loves you."

"Then explain to me the need for a closet full of designer clothes, a penthouse at the best address in town, and a two-hundred-thousand-dollar sports car!"

He was unable to look at her. He picked up the bottle of Regal again and began rotating it around and around in his hands. He absentmindedly fingered the mesh and picked at the blue plastic logo.

"That whole game of one-upmanship infuriates me," she said. "I don't ever want to have to impress someone else with what I have in order to feel good about myself." She leaned her head against the back of the sofa and watched the blue bottle as it twirled around in Cosimo's palms. "Maybe it's genetic. My palate can't tell the difference between a ten-dollar bottle of Gallo and…I don't know…name something expensive. I wouldn't be able to pronounce it, much less tell it apart from a jug of French Colombard in a blind taste test." She reached out to stop him from playing with the bottle. "And I *prefer* things that way…simple, uncomplicated."

"Okay, let's say I renounce my title and give away all my money. In a few years we'd be living in your one-bedroom apartment, having to make the choice between fixing the car or buying our children shoes. To save money we'd eat pasta and frozen pizza every night. And then one of us gets sick, and because we don't have health insurance, our meager savings go to pay the hospital bills. And those are the *good* years." The medallion on the bottle he'd been nervously picking at came loose and fell to the floor. "So, like your theory about having money, *not* having it can be equally tragic." He picked up the imitation sealing wax, wet the back of it, and stuck the plastic logo onto his forehead.

She looked away and tried not to smile, tried not to laugh at his ridiculous behavior, at his knack for turning something serious into something less fatal. She hated that he had the ability to defuse her so easily. And yet she knew that that was one of his charms. That it was one of the reasons, although she had yet to admit it even to herself, that she loved him.

"You know what's funny?" she said. "I don't know if I feel like laughing or crying. Somehow, time and time again, you confuse me. You manage to make me question the very ideas and ideals that I've always lived by. I'm not sure if that's a good thing or a bad thing."

He wrapped an arm around her waist and rested his chin on her shoulder.

"You shouldn't leave me because of that." He took the logo from his forehead, wet it again, and placed it on to hers. "You should leave me when I *stop* making you question everything."

"Who said anything about leaving?"

"I assumed that was where this conversation was headed."

"Maybe it is, but I don't recall having said that."

Chapter Twenty-Six

Megan didn't leave Cosimo. And of course, Cosimo didn't leave Megan. Not physically, anyway. He simply became less and less emotionally available to her. Part of that was due to his on-again-off-again affair with prescription drugs. It was difficult for him to remember to take them when he was feeling good, and it was even harder for him to remember (or care) to take them when he was feeling bad. It seemed to him that this pattern reflected a major design flaw inherent in the medications themselves: if you were too depressed to care about taking them, or so out of it that you couldn't remember that you *had* taken them, what good were they?

The other reason he was unavailable to her was that he was bored out of his mind. As much as he loved her, he also loved his diversions. Not other women, but other cities, other countries, new restaurants, white sand beaches, Manhattan nightclubs, moussaka in Mykonos, an opening at the Donmar…anything but another stroll along the esplanade or another dinner at Aquitaine (although he was rather fond of their French 75s). He was well aware that all relationships are based on compromises, and he was fine with that. He didn't need *all* of those diversions. He just needed some of them. At least occasionally. He was used to a constant change of scenery, to picking up and flying off wherever and whenever the mood struck him. And while he was aware that stability was an aspect of life that he might benefit from, he couldn't help but feel that he was experiencing too much of it all at once. Maybe, he thought, he should ease into it: a few weeks in Boston, one in Spain, another week in Boston, two in the Maldives; that sort of thing.

He was also self-aware enough to know that those thoughts occupied his mind so that he didn't have to think of other things, the ones of substance, the ones that seemed like a matter of life and death. Like the fact that his nuptial day to Annabella was fast approaching. Maria-Carmella had been adamant about it, and the timing of the extravaganza seemed supremely important. While she had not said it in so many words, he knew that she would freeze his accounts, cut off his generous allowance, and refuse to support him in any fashion if he failed to follow through with the marriage. She had, at Cosimo's insistence, agreed to provide him with the sum of $20 million in exchange for the deed. But even at that, he was second-guessing himself, wondering if he should have asked for more since they were at a stalemate: she needed him, and he needed the money.

It was a decidedly dark period for him, precipitated in part by a purposely unannounced visit he'd made to Terrance in his Madison Avenue office. Caught off guard, Terrance was forced to admit that he had been stalling, that he'd been reluctant to give him the news because he and Simon had been hoping that they could change the collective mind of the board of directors who had decided that the winds had shifted. They had come to the conclusion that American consumers would not be interested in a fragrance for men that was based on the same principles as a fragrance for women, and that the idea of a prince and princess as icons was a misguided one. Any plans that had been made for Royalty were being shelved indefinitely. Cosimo, who was instinctively good at reading between the lines, knew full well that indefinitely, in that instance, meant permanently. And that was why, a few days later, he sold his soul to the devil for a measly $20 million.

By then, Megan knew everything. Almost. While Cosimo had been forthcoming about his mental condition in the past, it was always sugarcoated, always expressed in a way that made his disorder seem like a mild inconvenience, like a migraine or acid reflux. But he finally sat her down and explained, in detail, its impact on his life and the various ways it was likely to challenge both her and their relationship. As for his family, she knew now that in addition to being wealthy, they were royal, although both of those dynamics still remained obscure concepts to her. And Cosimo was content to keep them obscure (and her as far away from his family and their eccentricities as possible) because of her obvious contempt for the affluent.

The one thing that she hadn't been informed about was the arrangement he had with his mother: marriage to one gelato heiress in exchange for $20 million. Cosimo did what he always did in situations like that: he ignored them and hoped they would go away. To some degree Megan understood Cosimo's rationale and why he hadn't been forthcoming with every aspect of his life. He had been right; there had never been a good reason for them to discuss finances. And how exactly does one broach the subject of royalty without seeming like a pompous, elitist jerk? Other than that, nothing he had said or done (or not said or done) was that egregious. She laid down a few ground rules, mostly around money and cohabitation, and tried to live as normal a life as one could with a wealthy, blue-blooded, bipolar boyfriend.

She cared for him more than she had ever cared for anyone before. And it was because of that that she understood his trepidation about disclosing certain information—information that might be misconstrued or overreacted to. She understood this because events in her own life had taken such a dramatic turn that she'd found herself in the compromising position of having to keep a secret of her own from him.

Cosimo flipped through a copy of *Men's Vogue* while he intermittently sipped a weak, acidic double espresso. A limp strip of lemon peel dangled off the saucer's edge. He grimaced as he took another sip, a silent commentary he shared with the other patrons in that just-like-every-other-Starbucks on Newbury Street. He contorted his face into a painful expression and hoped that someone would see him, save him, deliver to him a scalding hot demitasse of real coffee, with real flavor, with a strip of lemon on the side that didn't have the taste and texture of a deep-sea sponge.

Megan plopped herself down into a green velvet club chair that was angled next to his and expelled a heavy, world-weary sigh.

"How hard is it to make a decent cappuccino?" she said. "I mean, really?"

Megan's peeved expression failed to reveal if her question was rhetorical or not. Cosimo simply shrugged his shoulders. He was still hoping that someone would deliver a fresh espresso to him, along with their sincere apologies and biscotti on the house.

"This is all your fault, you know," she said.

"Why is it my fault?"

"You've ruined my palate, Giuseppe. You and your Miele espresso machine with the ice-cold filtered water and the imported beans, ground to a perfect chestnut-colored powder."

"Let's go back to my place, then." He took a bite of a currant scone and grimaced again as he spit it out into a green paper napkin.

"No. I refuse to be a prisoner in that penthouse of yours. I want to be out in the world, watching people, being with people…enjoying life." She broke off a piece of his scone and, before popping it into her mouth, added, "*Living* life."

"What you want, then, it would seem, is to have it both ways."

Megan covered her face with her hands and groaned. "What did you say to me?" she said, incensed that he, having been the one who'd thrust that lifestyle upon her, would now be the one chastising her for having become accustomed to it.

"Nothing. I said nothing."

"That's what I thought."

They sat there in silence, but only their own. The baristas continuously banged metal against metal, the patrons shuffled newspapers or spoke too loudly into cell phones, and the noise emanating from the speakers in the ceiling was anything but soothing background music. It was not a relaxing place to be.

"We should go to Florence," he said. "There they know how to make coffee. There is this wonderful little place on via del Como. It's small, about the size of a schoolboy's foot-locker, and it's on a busy street, but their coffee..." Cosimo pinched his thumb and forefinger together, brought them to his lips, then slowly moved his hand away while making the sound of a kiss, "it's *magnifico!*"

"Yeah, let's do that," she said. "I'll have to swing by my apartment first to pick up a few things. Then on the way to the airport, I'll call the school and tell them that I won't be in for... what, a few days? A few weeks? How long would you say we'll be gone?"

He took his napkin and shoved it into his espresso cup. The remaining coffee seeped into the paper, dampening it, darkening it. He pushed it away and stood.

"Fine. We'll just spend the rest of our lives here, walking *up* Boylston Street, *down* Newbury Street, observing and enjoying..." He took his magazine from the table and stuck it under his arm. "Excuse me, *living* life." He hovered there as he waited for her to say something, for her to stop him from leaving. When it became evident that she would do neither, he pointed to her cappuccino and said vehemently, "Better drink up. I wouldn't want you to be late for work on my account."

He knew he shouldn't leave. Not after having said that, and not with that tone of voice. It was one of the most challenging aspects of his illness, that rage that he couldn't control. That inability to stop himself from doing or saying something that he knew might have fatal consequences. He had to rely on other people to know the rules of the game, to intervene, to remain detached enough to see past his meltdown. He was pouting like a petulant child as he shoved the café door open with such force that it swung back on him, demanding that he push it open a second time in order for him to leave.

As he reached the end of the block, the John Hancock building cast a dark shadow over him and his side of the street. He wondered what it would feel like to fall from the top of that tower, watching his reflection in the blue plate-glass windows as he plummeted faster and faster toward freedom. He peered over his shoulder to see if she had followed him out of the café. There were a dozen or so people moving in his direction, but none of them was her. He wondered, *Does she not know how to play the game? Or does she know and not want to?* He lingered at the corner of Newbury and Arlington Streets without his compass, without the one new constant in his life that kept him tethered to the bigger picture. And then, he did the only thing that he was capable of in that situation: he went back to his apartment at the Parkhurst Plaza and buried himself under the covers of his freshly made bed.

Megan watched the napkin in Cosimo's abandoned cup get darker and darker until it was completely saturated. She took the remainder of his scone and shoved it into the middle of the soggy paper. She rubbed her hands back and forth against each other to remove the residual powder and crumbs. She discarded the white plastic lid from her to-go cup and took a sip of her drink. It was lukewarm, with too much milk and too little foam. She grimaced. She adjusted herself in the chair while she waited for him to come back, but she was unable to get comfortable. Yes, she thought, he could be petulant and unpredictable, but he'd never been mean or hostile before. Surely he'd realize he was out of line and come back for her. There wouldn't be an apology— there rarely was—but that had ceased to matter to her. *That's one of the perks of being in a relationship*, she thought. *Some things are just understood; they don't require an explanation.* But she couldn't always be the one going after him, even if she had been a bit curt herself. She couldn't always be the one negating her own feelings to accommodate his fluctuating moods.

Her watch informed her that she had a half hour before she needed to leave for work. A half hour can seem like an eternity during a lover's quarrel. But she wouldn't go after him. She wasn't going to call him. Not again. Everything has its limits.

Chapter Twenty-Seven

Megan set the grocery bags down on the kitchen counter and unpacked their contents. She picked up a carton of milk and, on her way to the fridge, stopped to push the playback button on the wall phone. There was only one message. It was from Regina Garibaldi.

Tommy sat on the living room floor of Megan's apartment, sifting through her CD collection. He was looking for a recording to listen to while they cooked dinner together. As his fingers flipped through the hard plastic covers, he rolled his eyes and shouted, "Don't you have any music from this century?"

Megan stood in the archway between the kitchen and the living room, her arms crossed over her chest, her face an expressionless mask.

"*Wham*? You've got Wham?" Tommy said, holding up the pre-felon photo of George Michael. "What am I going to do with you?"

"Come in here."

"Why—is that where you keep the good stuff? Abba? The Gogos? *Bananarama's Greatest Hits?*"

"Now!"

Tommy put the CD down and pushed the play button on the stereo. The old Sony fiver, previously loaded by Megan, spun around and landed on a Nat King Cole disc. As Tommy headed for the kitchen, Nat's mellifluous voice began to croon about some mysterious someone who was "Unforgettable."

"Listen," she said. She pushed the button on the phone again.

"Megan, this is Regina, Cosimo's sister. I was hoping we could talk. I'll be in Boston on Tuesday. Can you meet me for lunch? My number is two-one-two, eight-o-two, forty-one-fifty-six. And please, don't tell Cosimo that I called. It's imperative that I speak to you, and equally imperative that he not find out about it. I will explain all when we meet. *Ciao.*"

"The woman without a name apparently has a phone number," Tommy said.

"What could that mean? 'It's *imperative.*' Is she kidding me?"

"I doubt it. There was no levity in that voice," he said. "Are you going to call her?"

"I don't see that I have a choice." She pulled a pad of paper and a pen from a drawer and wrote down the number. Then she erased the message.

"It does seem rather curious that Cosimo has kept her a mystery, and now here she is being equally mysterious," he said. "It's like they're living in a Dashiell Hammett novel."

"And how did she get my number?"

"Doodoodoodoo, doodoodoodoo," Tommy sang, attempting to replicate the eerie theme song from *The Twilight Zone.*

Megan slumped down into one of the oak chairs at the breakfast nook, rested her elbows on the table, and placed her head on her hands.

"I have nothing to wear to have lunch with Regina Garibaldi." She waited for Tommy to contradict her, but he didn't. "See, this is what I mean. This is what I've been trying to tell Cosimo. All of a sudden I'm worried that my clothes are too pedestrian, my hairstyle too plain, my mannerisms too boorish." She spread her hands out in front of her and uttered a noise that conveyed exasperation. "At the very least I'm going to need a manicure and highlights."

"And Mother's pearls," Tommy said. "You should borrow those. And a pillbox hat if she has one," he added, and struck a regal pose.

"It's not funny," she said as she started to laugh.

Megan traipsed about her apartment, looking for someplace comfortable to settle into while she called Regina Garibaldi back. The loveseat sat too low and compressed her diaphragm. The side chair by the window was too firm and the upholstery too scratchy to relax in. The high-back stool at the kitchen counter, oddly enough, was the only place where she could sit and not feel that her body or her mind were being impeded. She dialed the number on the slip of paper, all the while hoping Regina wouldn't answer. But she did.

"Regina? Hi, it's Megan."

"Megan, so good of you to return my call. And so prompt. I hope I wasn't too terribly cryptic? I didn't mean to leave you with the impression that anything was wrong."

"No, I didn't hear that in your tone at all. It never occurred to me."

"Good. I thought it was time we meet. Are you free for lunch on Tuesday?"

"Yes, I have—"

"Wonderful. I'll have a car pick you up at your apartment at eleven thirty. *Ciao.*"

"But you don't—"

"Brockton Way? We've got all that. Anything else?"

The thought of Regina picking her up in front of her apartment building, on trash day no less, was unimaginable.

"Yes. Can you pick me up at my brother's place instead? It's—"

"Of course. Tom's, then. Eleven thirty."

The words "How did you know?" formed in Megan's mouth but never became audible, because she assumed, with all of her money and connections, *how* she knew. She just didn't know *why* she knew.

"Thanks. I'll be waiting."

～

Three dresses hung on a metal rolling rack outside of a fitting room in Neiman Marcus. Marion, a short, waifish-looking saleswoman dressed in a wild-print Roberto Cavalli blouse and black gabardine slacks, carried three more designer dresses draped over one arm. She reached out and repositioned the garments on the rack so that they were evenly spaced.

"I'm afraid we're down to these three, love," she said to Megan. "Why don't you try this one on next?" She handed her a Derek Lam sheath dress in black and cream with a ruffled-edge bodice. "I'm going to put these other ones away. I'll be right back."

Megan held the dress stiffly in her outstretched hand as if it were an intruder she was trying to keep at bay. Lauren scrunched up her face and said, "Un-uh, too matronly. Try the black one on. I'll bet you that's the one."

Megan carefully hung the Lam dress on the rack and flipped over the price tag on the black Dolce & Gabbana. Her gasp was loud enough that Marion heard it on the retail floor. Lauren was seated on an upholstered bench flipping through a copy of *Marie Claire* and bobbing her head in rhythm to the music on her iPod. Momentarily oblivious to all else, she didn't hear Megan's audible expression of shock. Neither did she see Megan's look of shock and awe. Megan tried to get Lauren's attention by carefully and loudly enunciating each syllable.

"It's—se—ven—teen—hun—dred—dol—lars!"

Lauren's response was to hold up a page of the glossy magazine and point to a model with long brown hair in a beaded evening gown holding up a perfume bottle. Megan repeated herself, this time making each word an independent sentence.

"Seventeen. Hundred. Dollars!"

"It's not disposable," Lauren said, as she hit pause on her iPod. "It's an investment. You'll probably wear that dress twenty or thirty times. That's like, what, sixty bucks per wearing?"

"That's not helping."

"You at least have to try it on." Lauren stood and physically corralled Megan toward the swinging doors of a small, well-lit cubicle.

Megan said nothing as she entered the fitting room. She did, however, make a number of audible grumbles and moans as she tried to wriggle into the D&G Jackie Duchess satin dress. She reemerged with her hand on the back collar, holding the tag out for Lauren to see.

"Are you sure this is a size six?" she rasped as she held her stomach in.

Lauren ignored the question and led Megan over to the trifold mirrors.

"You look gorgeous. Tell me that dress is not worth seventeen hundred dollars."

Megan stepped on to the carpeted platform used by tailors and admired herself in triplicate.

"It is pretty stunning, isn't it?" She moved her hands up and down the dress slowly, smoothing out wrinkles, adjusting the waistline. She pinched it at the hemline and said to Lauren, "Feel this."

Megan and Lauren simultaneously said, sounding like an imitation of an imitation of Barbra Streisand, "It's like buttah." Megan was still laughing when Lauren said, "You should absolutely get it."

Megan took a deep breath and reexamined her likeness in the mirrors.

"It feels so…so…" Megan continued to search for the right word, as there were so many that fit the situation: Glamorous? Sexy? Spontaneous? Foolish?

"Extravagant?" Lauren offered.

"Yes! Exactly." Megan tugged on the sleeves and repositioned the collar. "Should I?"

"Yes. It'll totally be worth it. It'll make a much better impression on his sister than that beige thing you've been wearing for years."

Megan took one more look at the price tag.

Marion entered the fitting room again with two new outfits draped over her arm.

"How's that working out for you, love?"

Megan surveyed herself one more time in the tight-fitting, gorgeous, and outrageously expensive dress. "I'll take it," she said, reaching for her purse.

"Now what about shoes?" Marion said as she palmed Megan's Visa card.

☙

Tommy stood at the window and watched the seagulls dart and then dive in the park across the street. He leaned his head against the wooden frame and let out a yawn.

"Are we keeping you up?" Lauren asked.

"No. You're just boring me, that's all," Tommy said.

"Don't you two start," Megan said, wiping off her third shade of lipstick that afternoon.

"Why is *she* so bitchy today?" Tommy said. "I thought she was the nice one in this group." When neither of them responded to his comment, he opened the window and stuck his head out.

"Holy crap!" he said as he summoned the two of them over.

"What?" Megan said, smearing her last choice of lip

color, Max Factor's Split Personality, on to her chin because of Tommy's shriek. "What is it? What's happening?"

"There's a limo pulling up downstairs that's the size of a small cruise ship." He craned his neck to get a better look at it. He motioned to Lauren. "Come here. You've got to see this."

She walked to the window and looked down but seemed unimpressed.

"How many people does she think she's picking up?" he said.

"Okay, it's official; I'm freaking out," Megan said as she passed the lipstick tube to Lauren. "Can you see? Is there a woman in the car? Or is it just the driver?"

"Chill, sis; you're starting to make *me* nervous."

"Tell me!" Megan demanded.

"The windows are all black," he said. "All I can see is the driver in the front seat."

"You'll be fine," Lauren said, wiping the red wax from Megan's mouth and reapplying. "Go like this." She pursed her own lips in demonstration and held a tissue up to Megan's mouth.

Megan's phone rang. She snatched it from the kitchen counter and tossed it to Tommy.

"Nice catch," Lauren said.

"Answer it," Megan screamed, her hands balled up into fists.

"Walker residence," Tommy said, attempting a British accent.

"You idiot," she whisper-yelled. "They know it's a cell phone."

"Fine. Be your own damn assistant."

He tossed it back to her. His underhand pitch brushed the tip of her outstretched hand. She fumbled to catch it but it tumbled to the floor. None of them made a move toward the device, and it quickly evolved into an unofficial game of statue as each of them gaped at the tiny LCD screen casting a yellow light on the white carpet. Lauren finally bent down to pick it up.

"Honestly, the two of you," she said.

She wiped the phone off on her sleeve and spoke into it.

"She'll be right down."

In the hallway of the Four Seasons, Megan's shoes sank into the plush carpet as she made the interminable procession from the elevator to the presidential suite. She paused in front of a large door and waited for a chambermaid to pass before knocking. She gave the door three sharp raps. She was poised to knock again when a tall woman with green eyes and long, lustrous hair the color of dark cocoa opened the door.

"Megan, Regina," she said, extending a flawlessly manicured hand. "Please, come in." Regina led her into a room that was part sitting room, part dining room. The table was set, and a bottle of wine was opened and breathing in the center.

"I hope you don't mind—I took the liberty of ordering lunch." She gestured for Megan to take a seat.

"This is lovely, thank you." Megan smoothed out the backside of her dress and sat down. "You shouldn't have gone to all the trouble."

"No trouble at all. Wine?" she said, holding a bottle of Pouilly Fuissé over a glass. She started to pour before Megan had a chance to answer. "It's the least I could do. I appreciate you coming down here on such short notice. *And* I appreciate your discretion where my brother is concerned." She flashed Megan a conspiratorial smile.

Megan was enthralled by Regina's movements: her hand gestures, her facial expressions, the graceful dance that her body performed in time and space. Her entire being exuded a sense of elegance and finesse that captivated Megan to the point of distraction. She was so entranced by the way Regina held the goblet, her nails painted a bright, shellacked red, her fingers adorned with numerous thin gold bands, her hand seeming to welcome and embrace the nesting glass, that she lost track of their conversation.

"Sorry, what was that?" Megan said, embarrassed by her lapse.

"I was saying that relationships are complicated things." Regina raised her glass and gracefully, sensuously, masterfully inhaled the bouquet. "Toss our mother, their titles, and my brother's psychological disorders into the mix, and you can see how you'd have to be a pretty strong individual to go the distance."

"What exactly do you mean by 'go the distance'?"

Regina continued as if a question hadn't been asked.

"It's clear to me why my brother is attracted to you. You're lovely, obviously smart, and, it seems, quite dedicated. I understand that you worked your way through Harvard. Graduated magna cum laude, didn't you? That must have been quite a challenge."

"Yes…and no. My parents, deeply religious and hard-working people, raised me to believe that what doesn't kill you makes you stronger."

"Sometimes," Regina said. "And sometimes what doesn't kill you leaves you paralyzed and wishing that it had." She leaned forward as if she were about to share something confidential. "You seem nice enough. But I wonder…what is it that you hope to gain from a relationship with my brother?"

Megan leaned in to intentionally mirror Regina's body language.

"Hope to gain?" she said quietly, incredulously. And then she repeated it, louder, more defiantly. "Hope to *gain?*"

"Don't get me wrong. I simply want to make sure your expectations are not out of line with reality." Regina leaned back in her chair and took a sip of wine. "If it's fame you're after, Cosimo shuns the limelight. If it's a title you're looking for, well, as long as Italy remains a republic, no woman will metamorphose into a princess. Now, as far as money—"

Megan pushed her chair back, stood, and threw her napkin down on the table.

"It appears that this conversation is over," she said.

She picked up her wine glass, took a quick, infinitesimal sip, then set the glass back down on the table. It took all her restraint not to douse Regina with the remaining liquid. She took a second to compose herself, then picked up her purse and stepped away from the table.

"Thank you for the wine. I'll see myself out."

"Please, sit down," Regina said.

"How dare you imply that I—"

"Megan, sit down, please. If you can't handle a little confrontation from me, you are in far deeper water than I suspected."

Megan slowly returned to her seat, but her body language and the tight grip she had on her purse made it clear that she was prepared to bolt any second.

"It *is* beginning to feel as if I've wandered into a shark tank," she sneered.

"That's more like it," Regina said. "I knew there had to be a bit of spunk in you."

"What gave you the impression that I'm after anything? Your brother introduced himself to me. He pursued me. He even made the move to Boston without asking or telling me. I have never—"

"Good for you for standing up for yourself. If you're going to have a relationship with my brother, that's one personality trait you'll find quite useful. As for your integrity, well, that may or may not be a blessing. Honesty, while admirable, is highly overrated. And transparency, well, that's just a fool's game."

"Then why were you—"

"It wasn't a test, if that's what you're thinking. At least it wasn't meant to be." Regina topped off Megan's wine glass. "There is much about you that I like, based on what my agents have told me, anyway. Let me put your mind at ease by assuring you that I have no intention of coming between you two. Quite the contrary. Cosimo loves you, and that is what is most important."

"And how would you know that?"

"Because he's done his best to keep you a secret. Even from me. Of course he's entitled to his privacy, but he often lets his emotions override his intellect, and that's what frightens me. While I've tried to put myself in his position, I am considerably less romantic and quite a bit more cynical than he is, particularly when it comes to matters of the heart. And because of that, he frequently uses me as a sounding board, as the voice of reason. But not this time. As for you, I worry that you have no idea what you've gotten yourself into."

There was a knock at the door, and Regina excused herself to answer it. After escorting the room service waiter in and inspecting to see that everything had been prepared to her satisfaction, she rejoined Megan.

"I apologize for having to dine in my room, but I'm sure you understand. I couldn't be seen with you in public."

"Okay, *now* the conversation is over," Megan said, hoping her tone conveyed that she was only kidding. Sort of. She couldn't remember a time when she felt more awkward or uncomfortable. The whole lunch-with-a-princess-at-the-Four-Seasons thing was strange enough. But Regina's insinuations made her so nervous that she found herself taking frequent sips of water and fondling the silverware.

"Sorry," Regina said. "I see how that might be misinterpreted. It's just there are photographers lurking around every corner. It would be dreadful if Cosimo found out about our tête-à-tête by reading it in some rag. Do you love him?" she asked as she watched Megan twirl a butter knife over and over on the linen tablecloth.

"I'm not sure how to answer that," Megan said, placing her hands in her lap to force herself to stop fiddling with the cutlery. "You've put me in an awkward position since I've yet to admit that to him. But yes, I guess I do. Against my better judgment."

Megan provided Regina with a capsulized version of their romance, from a chance meeting in a Parisian café to the alarming unveiling of his lavish penthouse. She informed her that, until recently, Cosimo hadn't exactly been forthcoming with the details of his affliction, and that what little knowledge she had about his disorders she'd acquired in undergrad psych classes and from her own observations of his erratic behavior.

Regina gave Megan her own theories about Cosimo's condition and empathized with her for having to deal with that on top of everything else. Then she handed her a dossier that contained the information her investigators had gathered on her. She said she should consider that proof she had no ulterior motive and nothing to hide.

"Why would I want to discover something terrible about the woman my brother loves?"

"Quite frankly, I'm not accustomed to having people compile dossiers on me, so I'm reluctant to speculate on your motives," Megan said. And then once again she found herself moving a piece of silverware around the table to have something to do with her hands.

"I have to admit that your background check did uncover one rather disturbing piece of information. The one black mark against you is your brother, Tommy," she said, placing her hand gently on top of Megan's to get her to stop spinning the spoon. She quickly added, "I'm kidding. Really, I'm just having a little fun with you. Nursing is a very noble profession. You must be very proud of him."

"I don't know that 'proud' is the right word, but yes, even though he has his own version of crazy, and there are days when I'd like to kill him…" Megan pinched her thigh under the table to help her maintain her composure. She had slipped into her comfort zone too easily. What was it about those Garibaldis? She wanted to retract the word "crazy," the word "kill." They were not likely to endear her to Cosimo's sister. "The truth is," she continued, "I couldn't ask for a better sibling."

"Now, here comes the hard part," Regina said.

Megan pinched her thigh even harder and made a conscious effort to control her breathing, to pay attention to the conversation, to brace herself. But for what?

"What I am about to tell you will be difficult for you to hear. But if you love Cosimo, you will look beyond mere appearances."

"I understand that our worlds are decidedly different," Megan said, pausing while a waiter placed a salad of seasonal fruits in front of her. "What I fail to comprehend, though, is the need for such manufactured intrigue and drama."

"I wouldn't say *need*, Megan. Our world, as you say, includes many things that are foreign and thus incomprehensible to an ordinary person."

Megan bristled at the word "ordinary."

"I only use that word," Regina said, "as a way to distinguish those of us who, by providence, were destined to live with some degree of money or fame. And in our case, aristocracy. While it may look appealing to those on the outside, the negatives often outweigh the positives."

"If that was a clarification or an apology, it needs work," Megan said as she jabbed a strawberry with what she hoped was the right fork.

"What I meant was, we have obligations that require us to behave in ways that may seem peculiar to you." Regina pierced a slice of kiwi using the same type of fork that Megan used, even though it was not the appropriate utensil for that course. "Our family has inherent responsibilities that we must honor. Our name is not our own. It is a part of history, one that obligates us to a cause that is greater than who we are as individuals."

"I don't mean to be dense or rude, but is there a point there somewhere?"

"It's complicated. I'm trying to convey the information in a way that you can understand."

"As you said, I'm magna cum laude. You needn't draw me a pretty picture. So please, tell me, what exactly is your point?"

"Cosimo is getting married in a few months."

Megan laid down her fork and pushed aside her nearly untouched meal.

"I was afraid that would affect your appetite," Regina said as she bit into a slice of mango.

The waiter cleared their salads the instant Regina laid her fork across her plate. In their place he set down richly colored china arranged with thin slices of seared tuna and three asparagus stalks tied into a bundle and drizzled with white sauce.

"Before you jump to any conclusions, allow me to explain," she said, waving away the server. "It's an arranged marriage that our mother has been planning for years. Much to Cosimo's dismay."

"Why is he going through with it, then?"

"As I said, we have obligations. With a heritage like ours, one feels compelled to ensure that the bloodline is not only preserved but enhanced."

"And just who is this…" Megan failed to conjure up an appropriate word.

"Intended? Fiancée? That's of no consequence. You will find out soon enough."

"Why are *you* telling me this instead of Cosimo?"

"Also complicated. You see, I knew he hadn't told you. And that he wouldn't tell you. He loves you too much to risk losing you because of a family obligation." Regina cut a small piece of fish into an even tinier piece and tasted it. "He is notorious for ignoring difficult situations in the hope that they will magically disappear." She pierced another slice of tuna with her fork and noticed that Megan hadn't touched hers. "Eat. Eat. The chef here worked for my family for years. It was our uncle Giuseppe who taught him how to cook. I'm sure you'll find it quite tasty."

For the first time that afternoon, Regina strayed from the conversation and drifted off. Megan reached for a roll and, in the process, knocked over her water glass. Regina's reverie was interrupted by Megan's vociferous and heartfelt apologies.

"Things change … what can you do?" Regina said, jumping up and dabbing at the wet tablecloth with her own napkin. "Knowing Cosimo as I do, I suspect he is under the delusion that since you don't read the society columns, you won't find out." She took another bite of fish. "You don't, do you?"

Megan shook her head.

"But there is no way that you wouldn't have found out eventually and felt betrayed. And rightfully so. And you would have reacted accordingly, without knowing the bigger picture. The fallout from that would devastate Cosimo. You know how sensitive he is, how irrational he can be. Knowledge is power, and my sharing this with you today is the only hope I have of protecting him."

"I don't know how to respond to this revelation," Megan said as she moved a slice of tuna around and around on her plate. A minute ago it was perfectly cooked and seasoned, but now she doubted if her stomach could tolerate another bite. "Even though it seems like we're inseparable, neither of us has made any promises to the other. He's free to do as he pleases," she said.

"You must understand, this is purely a business transaction. Our two families are basically corporations. Corporations that are, unfortunately, negotiating a merger." It was obvious that the dining portion of the lunch was over. Regina stood and asked her to join her on the sofa by a window that overlooked the Commons. "My brother is in a precarious position. Financially speaking. If he were to renege on his commitment, there's no telling the lengths to which our mother would go for retribution. At the very least, she would cut him off without a cent, and he would essentially be broke."

"It's quite possible I've misunderstood him," Megan said. "Or maybe I've only heard things the way I wanted to. But Cosimo has professed, at least to me, that money..." She stopped to reconsider what she was about to say. She tried to remember his exact words, his precise expressions. She wanted to be clear that what she was about to communicate was factual and not some romanticized interpretation of how she wanted things to be.

"Yes, for Cosimo, money never has been a priority...because he's always had it," Regina said. "It pains me to say it, but he does not live in the real world. He *has*, however, always lived in a certain fashion, in a rarefied world, if you will. While he may outwardly eschew the limelight and the trappings of privilege, there's no denying that he is accustomed to them. And I fear, given his psychological disorders, he would find it nearly impossible to navigate or exist in a world without them. Need I say more?"

Megan absentmindedly fingered the seam that ran the length of her new seventeen-hundred-dollar dress. She tried to process what Regina had said along with its implications. But that was particularly difficult to do in a room at the Four Seasons. It was admittedly more painful because the decor and the view were stark reminders of the first time he had told her that he loved her.

"What am *I* supposed to do? How do *I* fit into this scenario? Or do I?"

"If you love my brother as you say you do, nothing will change. You will pretend and act as if you know nothing about this." Regina picked up a box of tissues and offered one to Megan. She declined the offer and, instead, wiped a small tear away with a finger. "I don't see why things shouldn't continue as they have. The only difference being that marriage between the two of you is no longer an option. At least for the foreseeable future."

Who is this person sitting across from me anyway, Megan wondered, *and why should I take anything she says seriously?* What had begun as a nice afternoon had morphed into an absurd one. Until a few minutes ago, Megan hadn't admitted to anyone that she loved Cosimo, so why was Regina introducing the topic of marriage? And despite having just met her, Megan couldn't help but admire her. She watched her as she crossed her legs and adjusted her posture. Her every move was a testament to how confident and comfortable she was in her own skin. Everything about her—her looks, her poise, her inflection—was the embodiment of high society. Much to her chagrin, Megan innately trusted her.

"Of course," Regina continued, "there's always the possibility of divorce somewhere down the line. Not to hold out false hope. But in the same way that mergers and acquisitions are a never-ending fact of life, so are dissolutions and forfeitures."

Megan tried to stand. She was lightheaded and nauseous. Her knees buckled under her, but she steadied herself by holding on to the arm of the sofa.

"By now it should be obvious to you that our life of privilege does not come without sacrifices. And while it might not seem like it, you have been given a rare opportunity, one that others would kill for—an entrée, albeit a limited one, into a coveted realm. But it comes at a cost, and not everyone is suited for it. You must decide for yourself if it's worth having under those conditions."

Regina's speech about the costs associated with a life of privilege gave Megan an opportunity to compose herself. She smiled, smoothed out her dress, and extended a hand.

"Thank you for lunch, Regina. I think."

Regina took hold of her hands. Megan found her smooth skin and light touch calming and comforting.

"I know it's little consolation, but you must know that whomever Cosimo marries will be jealous of *you*. They might have his name, but you have his heart." She embraced Megan and then took a step back. "I can see why he likes you," she said, slowly walking her to the door. "If this were a different time, a different place—"

"It isn't," Megan said.

Regina positioned herself between Megan and the door and stood there with both hands on her hips. But the effect was not one of resistance or aggression. While her stance looked threatening, her eyes emanated compassion.

"You can't leave until you assure me that you're all right. While you may not know me, you must know that I'm only looking out for my brother. And, by association, you."

"I get that, I do. And I'm fine, really. I'm stronger than I look," she said as she shifted her body sideways to avoid an awkward face-to-face with Regina.

"I risked a great deal meeting with you like this. If Cosimo were to ever find out—"

"He won't."

"Good. You have my number. If you need anything at all, anytime…you call me."

Megan tried to utter the words "Thank you," but she couldn't get her mouth and her brain to collaborate. She opened her mouth, but nothing came out.

"I know—it's a lot to take in," Regina said. "Go home. Get some rest. We'll talk again soon."

"I hope you'll forgive any lapse in etiquette I may have displayed today," Megan said, trying to regain her composure. Then she wondered, as she took hold of Regina's hand again to say farewell, why was she the one apologizing? And what exactly was she apologizing for?

"While I have tried to understand Cosimo's lifestyle, there's no denying I was unaware of its intricacies or its obligations." Megan shuffled her feet a little closer to the door. "And because I have seen him shun the spotlight and try to fit into my world, I never expected to find myself swept up into yours."

"I'd say we've covered quite enough ground for one day," Regina said as she opened the door. She kissed Megan once on each cheek and then escorted her into the corridor.

Once again Megan's shoes sank into the carpet as she traipsed back down the long corridor punctuated with even-numbered doors. When she reached the elevator bank, she turned to offer a final wave goodbye, but Regina was no longer there. Megan placed her hand on her stomach and wondered if her slight bulge was real or imagined. She also wondered if she had done the right thing in not telling Regina that she was two months pregnant.

Chapter Twenty-Eight

Tommy and Gregg were sitting together on Megan's loveseat discussing menu options for their upcoming wedding reception when there was a knock at the door. Nobody made a move to answer it. Then they knocked again.

"Could somebody get that?" Megan shouted from the kitchen.

Tommy grumbled something about not being hired help as he walked to the door. When he opened it, he found Lauren and Robert standing in the dimly lit hall.

"Aren't you going to invite us in?" Lauren said.

"Since when do you need an invitation?"

"I don't *need* one; I'd just *like* one. I'm trying to be civilized, but I guess I shouldn't be surprised that you don't recognize a common courtesy when you hear one," she sneered. "By the way, when did Megan start making these meetings formal and compulsory?"

"She is getting a little bossy, isn't she?" Tommy said,

bowing and making a grand arm gesture to usher her into the apartment. "Come on in. Hi, Robert, how are you?"

Megan entered the living room, wiping her hands on a dish towel.

"Tommy," she said, "you can drop the formality. He's part of the family now."

"Yeah, you might as well call me Rob; everyone else does."

Lauren flashed her two-carat solitaire in Tommy's face. Tommy flashed his one-carat Asscher cut back in hers. Lauren grabbed Tommy's hand and inspected the ring. She pretended to put a jewelry loupe up to her eye to get a closer look at it. "Not bad. Not bad at all," she said. Then, addressing Gregg, she added, "Nicely done. I'm glad to see at least someone here has a little class and style."

"If that was a compliment, it sucked," Tommy said, pulling his hand away and rejoining his fiancé on the loveseat.

"Okay, we're all here," Gregg said. "Can we get started? Megan, do you want me to write down the minutes?"

"Very funny," Megan said. "Let's see if you're still laughing when this is over."

"Can you believe it?" Lauren said. "She's been spending so much time with Tommy lately that she's turning into a drama queen herself."

Everybody chuckled a little, even Megan. But she had some pressing business to get to, so she attempted to change the mood to a more somber, more formal tone.

"Thank you all for coming," she said. "I am incredibly fortunate to have such a great group of family and friends.

And I know I was a little evasive about the purpose of our first official meeting, but I didn't want to have to go through it several times, so I thought we should discuss this as a group, since I consider you all my family."

"Oh my God, she's dying," Lauren said. "Are you dying?" She turned to Rob. "That's it, isn't it—she's dying?"

"*Now* who's being a drama queen?" Tommy said.

"Look at her; she's not dying," Rob said. "Would you let the woman finish?"

"I'm glad one of us here is level-headed," Megan said, smiling at Rob. "No, I'm not dying. Well, maybe a little on the inside, but I'm fine, perfectly healthy. I should know; I saw the doctor this afternoon. It's about my meeting with Regina. I don't know how to say it except to, well, just say it…Cosimo is engaged to be married in a couple of months…to someone else."

There were the expected oohs and ahhhs, a couple of gasps, and a bunch of questions flying at her all at once.

"Hold on," she said. "First of all, it's not his fault or his decision. His family is forcing him into it. And if he doesn't go through with it, they'll cut him off completely. He'll have no money. He doesn't even own his condo; it's part of some trust or estate that his mother controls."

"What does this mean?" Gregg asked. "Are you two breaking up? Are they going to have an open marriage?"

"You're not still thinking of seeing him, are you?" Lauren said. "Mistress is not something I see attached to your name."

"No, I don't see you as a mistress, either," said Tommy. "Madame, maybe?"

Megan tossed the damp dishtowel at her brother. He

caught it before it hit him, and then he dropped it unceremoniously on the coffee table.

"Sorry," Tommy said. "My humor used to be able to defuse a tense situation. I must be losing my touch."

"This might be a dumb question," Rob said, "but did she, Regina—did she ask you to stop seeing him?"

"No. Maybe that was her intention, but no, she never said that. Actually, she said just the opposite." She stood, and everyone else started to as well. She motioned with her hands for them to sit back down. "I'm a terrible hostess. I completely forgot to bring out the beverages and snacks." As she headed back to the kitchen to retrieve the tray that she had prepared earlier, she said, "See, I'm terrible at this. I could never be the hostess with the mostest."

"I didn't mean that kind of madame," Tommy shouted after her.

While drinking wine and nibbling on cheese and crackers, they all gave their opinions on whether or not Megan should continue to see Cosimo. The general consensus was that she should cut her losses and move on to the next phase of her life.

"Well, that should be easy," Megan said, "since I already know what the next phase is."

Her comment was met with silence and confusion.

"Okay, if no one is going to venture a guess, I'll just have to blurt it out." She opened her mouth as if she were going to say something and then stopped. "I know; we'll do charades instead. First word, first syllable…"

Tommy picked up the dishtowel from the table and threw it back at his sister.

"Normally, I wouldn't side with him," Gregg said to Megan, "but you deserve that one."

"Fair enough," she said. She raised her wine glass to the group as if she were about to make a toast. The liquid in the glass was clear and sparkling. "Not one of you has wondered why you're all drinking Chardonnay and I'm sipping Pellegrino?" She put her glass back down. She pointed a finger at Lauren and said, "If you say, 'Oh my God' one more time, just remember: I've got a dishtowel, and I'm not afraid to use it."

Tommy went over to Megan and gave her a big hug. To the group he announced, "I'm gonna be an uncle."

Gregg cleared his throat as loudly as he could.

"I mean we're gonna be an uncle," Tommy said. He twisted his body again to face Megan and his expression drifted from glad to mad. He placed one hand on his hip, and with the other, he wagged a finger in her direction. "You will go to any lengths to upstage my wedding, won't you?" he huffed and then noisily stomped out of the room and into the kitchen.

"Is he kidding?" Lauren said as she looked toward the kitchen and then back at the group. "He is kidding, isn't he?"

Tommy popped back in to the room with another bottle of wine.

"Is she really that dumb?" he said as he moved about the room, refilling glasses.

The rest of the group nodded their heads in unison.

Chapter Twenty-Nine

Cosimo was not having a good day. In fact, it was shaping up to be one of the worst days he could remember. It wasn't so much that the day itself had been so terrible; rather, it was the culmination of events from the preceding days, all converging on him at once, that made it so unbearable. It was the cumulative effect of numerous negative influences and circumstances, crashing down upon his head like a thunderbolt from a blackened sky, that caused him such intense emotional pain.

It all began a few days earlier when Terrance informed him that his only escape clause to marrying Annabella Bollettieri, the proposed Royalty fragrance line and the millions of dollars in profits they had estimated it would generate for him, was merely an idea, a suggestion, a pipe dream that was never going to materialize. On the heels of that communication was an unpleasant exchange with Megan, exposing him for the first time to the truly tenuous nature of their relationship. That conversation took place over the phone, he in Manhattan, placating his mother by half-heart-edly participating in all the hoopla prior to the wedding, and she in Boston, in an obstetrician's office where she was being prepped, unbeknownst to Cosimo, for a sonogram.

"You've been making a lot of trips to New York," she said. "Is anything wrong?"

"No, of course not. I'm just…I'm helping Regina with a few projects, that's all."

"Are you sure? You're not seeing someone else?" Megan regretted that statement as soon as the words left her lips. But on some level, she knew that she had to confront him without betraying her pledge to Regina. And on another level, she wanted to give him the opportunity to walk away from her, without regret, to do what was expected of him.

"What kind of question is that? Why would I move to Boston and then start seeing someone in New York?"

"I don't know. I can't—"

"It's ridiculous," he said. "I keep pleading with you to move in with me, and now you accuse me of seeing someone else?"

"I never said that. Well, maybe I did. It's just that you're so distant these days. And it's more than your depression. At least that's what it feels like."

"I will admit that I haven't been much fun to be around lately, but there are some family issues I'm dealing with, and I didn't want to burden you with them."

"Look, maybe you need some space. Maybe we both do."

"Is that what you want? Is that what this is all about? Are *you* seeing someone else?"

"Why don't you call me back when you've had a chance

to calm down? After we've both calmed down…and had some time to think things through?"

Megan, afraid of what she'd say next, or of what he would or wouldn't say next, hung up the phone; ending the call and possibly their relationship. Not having the child she was carrying was never a consideration. Not having a relationship with a married man was. Yet she also found it difficult to judge him for keeping a secret from her while she was concealing her pregnancy from him. Not having known how or when to broach the subject with him gave her some insight, some empathy, into his reluctance to share his predicament with her. While she had come to terms with the idea that she was going to be a parent, she was still struggling with the idea of Cosimo being married to another woman, regardless of the reason. What she couldn't understand, though, was why they were both trying to keep secrets that would eventually, inevitably, have to be revealed.

Cosimo sensed that for the past few days, there had been something bothering Megan, that there was something different about her, especially in the way that she behaved around him, toward him. She grew more distant, more reserved, and increasingly more irritable. But as usual he had not been consistent with his medications, so he'd lost all confidence in his ability to judge reality, which for him was always a moving target. She claimed that she hadn't been feeling well in the mornings. It could be that she was coming down with the flu. Maybe she'd been taking that over-the-counter cold medicine again, and that was agitating her. And of course he knew that his inconsistent moods were always a contributing factor, but there was little he could do about that. It was easier to blame Sudafed and Nyquil for her mood swings than to blame his for hers. Cosimo was hoping that any trouble they were experiencing in their relationship would magically be resolved once Megan stopped taking her daily dose of liquid cold capsules. It seemed to him that pills, that medications of any kind, were the main theme of his life, even when they were being consumed by someone else. But the final blow, the one that really did him in, had been delivered only a few hours earlier.

He was back in his Boston penthouse again when Maria-Carmella called to schedule a photo shoot in New York with his intended. Until then he had been very accommodating and cooperative throughout the long, arduous process of planning an extravaganza under the auspices of Princess Maria-Carmella Stefani Garibaldi di Sorrento. But he was running low on money, and he was wondering when she was planning to deposit the $20 million into his account. When he broached the subject of his dwindling finances, she emitted a slight chuckle. And then on top of her laughter, she called him a silly boy. And it was that dismissive and patronizing comment, more than anything else, that infuriated him. But the real nail in the coffin came when she informed him that the lump sum he was expecting momentarily was going to be parceled out over time. And only after certain criteria had been met.

"And what criteria might they be, Mother?"

"Marrying Annabella, for one thing. You couldn't possibly believe that I would hand over twenty million dollars and then just pray that you show up at the appointed hour?"

"Fair enough, Mother. What else?" His tone was angry and impatient. He was well aware that it was perilous to cross her, to adopt any attitude with her other than absolute respect and devotion. But he knew in his gut that this phone call, that this situation, was not going to end well. And at some point during the conversation, he had lost the will to care.

"Cosimo, my dear boy. I warned you that you were ill-prepared for the business world. You should have read the contract," she said with both condescension and pity. "Honestly, dear, you must start taking responsibility for your actions."

"Tell me, Mother! *What...other...criteria?*"

"Well, if you insist on knowing this very minute...you won't be getting the bulk of the money—seventy-five percent of it—until after the birth of your first child. And believe me, Cosimo, I'm handling it this way for your own good."

Cosimo simply hung up the phone. There was nothing more to be said.

He had confided to Regina that he was contemplating backing out of the marriage. It would serve Maria-Carmella right for manipulating him in such a fashion, for effectively trying to live his life for him. But he knew as well as Regina did that it was only wishful thinking on his part, that he was deluding himself as a way of coping with an impossible situation. When it came down to the wire, he would never have the courage or the audacity to publicly humiliate her in that way. And if he did, he was the one with everything to lose.

There is pain, and then there is *pain*. And he was feeling

the latter. Everything that he was experiencing was well beyond what he knew how to deal with. He was used to the agony of depression—the hopelessness, the sadness, the despair. The same with the other disorders: the bipolar, the schizophrenia, the ADD. He could handle the violent mood swings; he'd had them all his life. He knew no other. And most of the time, when he heard the voices, he was able to disregard them. But there he was in Boston, indefinitely, betrothed to a woman he didn't love and fighting with the woman he did. And there was a fifty-fifty chance that he'd have another meltdown and ultimately end up broke and alone anyway. Xanax, he thought, no matter how many he took, wasn't going to fix or relieve any of that. But it was worth a try.

He unscrewed the childproof cap and emptied the contents onto the kitchen counter. He counted each pill, pushing them away from the others as he did so. Seventeen. That should get him through the next day or two, he thought. He made a mental note to refill the prescription. He took a bottle of Belvedere from the freezer and poured a generous amount into a water glass. He popped two of the little pink pills into his mouth and chased them down with a cold gulp of straight alcohol.

He laid down on the sofa and waited for the drugs to kick in, for his anxiety to subside, for his reality to alter. He rubbed the back of his neck and tried to relieve a knot that had become lodged there during the night. It could be the stress. It could be that he hadn't had a good night's sleep in over a week. Whatever the cause, he couldn't relax because of the throbbing pain. In his dresser drawer was a bottle, one among many, that contained a few dozen Vicodin. One dose rarely had any effect on him, so he doubled it and swallowed them with another swig of vodka. He put the pill bottle into his pocket and went back to the kitchen to refill the tumbler with alcohol.

He began to feel something, although he wasn't sure what. In the past he had taken drugs to bury his feelings. To not feel the weight of depression on his slight frame. To not have so much energy and enthusiasm that he believed himself capable of anything, and then, without considering the consequences, act as if he were. Trying to get to that place where he imagined most people lived the balance of their lives, where they weren't angry, or euphoric, or unbearably sad, was always a goal and a challenge for him. But this new feeling, the one that was slowly seeping into his consciousness, made him feel warm and mellow all over. Since he was enjoying the fuzzy sensation, physically and mentally, he decided to try and amplify it. He poured himself another glass of vodka and swiftly downed half of it.

He no longer felt like lying down. He no longer felt like being stationary at all. He felt like driving, like floating, like flying. He needed to experience the power of his new car, to be cradled by the leather seats, to be enveloped by the sound of the 750-watt Monster audio system. He had the unrelenting desire to be racing down the expressway in his new Roadster with the windows down and the pungent smell of the vast, bottomless, blue sea filling his lungs.

If the combination of drugs and alcohol he had just ingested made him feel that good, he wondered, wouldn't more feel even better? He washed down another Xanax and a third Vicodin, again with vodka. He took a couple of swigs straight from the bottle and then placed it back in the freezer. He grabbed his keys and a leather jacket, although he didn't put it on. He was anything but cold. He extinguished the lights and walked down the hallway toward the elevator. He stopped in front of a small table in the foyer and picked up a pad of paper. But while he searched for a pen, he changed his mind and decided not to leave Megan a note. He'd be better equipped to communicate with her after a drive and some fresh air, after he'd had a chance to clear his head. He tossed the pad onto the table and pressed the button on the elevator panel.

The security camera in the garage monitored him walking to his car. His pace was slow and a bit wobbly, but nothing out of the ordinary. He may have appeared tired, or to have slipped and lost his balance, but he was so used to navigating his way in the world under the influence of some combination of alcohol, amphetamines, and sedatives that nothing in the way that he carried himself would have prompted a security guard to take a second look. He inserted his key card into the slot, and the metal gate rolled up. He revved the engine on the Lamborghini and maneuvered a sharp right turn onto Arlington Street.

It was a clear night, and the moon was a thin grin, almost gone. The stars, not having to compete with the moon's glow, twinkled and pulsated, individually and in clusters. He looked for the brightest one first, Betelgeuse, then lower to the belt, and then down to the nebula that is his sword. And finally to the leg, to Rigel, the pulsating blue-white supergiant. Cosimo always saw the parts separately before they revealed themselves as the whole, as Orion the hunter, blazing in the night sky, shining just a little brighter than he should.

He kept leaning his head out the window to try to locate the constellation in the heavens, while on earth, his vehicle moved forward at an unsafe speed. His quick glances became longer and longer as the twinkling lights commanded his attention. As the narcotics and the alcohol continued to commingle in his system, compromising his attention and his dexterity, he found it difficult to concentrate on either the road or the sky. He kept one hand on the leather steering wheel, loosely controlling the 640-horsepower engine, and the other on his medallion to experience in three dimensions what he could only see as light and gas in the cosmos. The radio, which was tuned into a local jazz station, no longer blasted Dave Brubeck's "Take Five." Instead, the saxophone and piano in quintuple time had been supplanted by the gravelly voice of his uncle. Cosimo was transported to a simpler time by his uncle's baritone voice, back to a familiar garden in Italy many years ago, with the villa and all that it represented far off in the distance.

He is eleven years old, unaware that his uncle is fairly certain he will not see his nephew turn twelve. Giuseppe's cancer is spreading, and there is nothing to be done. Together they stand between thin rows of dormant plants, holding a lantern and a flashlight, shivering beneath a cobalt winter sky:

"See that star, the brilliant one? That's the red supergiant, Betelgeuse. That's his shoulder." Giuseppe puts his hand on the young boy's scalp and directs his attention to the northern sky. "Now look over there, down and to the right. That's what they call a blue-white supergiant. That's Rigel. That represents his leg."

"*You said he has a belt,*" Cosimo says. "*I don't see a belt.*"

"*There, halfway between the two brightest stars,*" his uncle says. "*See the three smaller stars in a row, going up at an angle?*"

"*I see it now.*"

"*That's Orion's belt. Just below that is an interstellar cloud of dust called a nebula. That's his sword.*"

Out of habit, Giuseppe locks the gate behind them before they embark on their slow, inevitable walk back to the house. It takes a while because Giuseppe's strength isn't what it once was, and he has to stop frequently to rest, to catch his breath.

"*There are many different legends about Orion,*" Giuseppe tells him, pausing to slow his heart rate. "*But my favorite version, and the one that I believe to be true, claims that Orion was the son of three gods, each of them representing a different element: water, air, and earth. And Orion, who was sent to the heavens and composed of stars, became the fourth element, fire.*"

"*Why do you think that's the true story, Uncle?*"

"*Because, Cosimo, while it is not the largest constellation in the sky, it is one of the brightest and most recognizable. Betelgeuse is ten thousand times more luminous than the sun. And if that's not fire, then I don't know what is.*"

Giuseppe takes a small piece of tan tissue paper out of his pocket and hands it to the boy without saying a word.

"*What is it?*" Cosimo asks.

"*It is a gift, from me to you.*"

"*What for?*"

"*You don't need a reason to give someone a gift. I just wanted to; that's all.*"

Cosimo gently unwraps the paper to find a Figaro chain and a bright gold medallion.

"I had that made for you from your grandmother's wedding ring. Those eight small diamonds represent the eight stars of Orion."

"Thank you," Cosimo says as he unconsciously runs his fingers across the surface while counting each individual accent stone.

"It is forged out of gold and diamonds and history. And when you put this on, you become the fourth element, love."

"Love's not an element, Uncle."

"No, you're right," Giuseppe says, grinning at the boy's precociousness. "But love is elemental."

Cosimo puts the tissue in his pants pocket and slips the necklace over his head. It is heavy and cold, but to him the weight is a reminder of the love that exists for him, and the cold is something he must tolerate in order to experience that love.

"To me, you have much in common with Orion. I see you as a hunter, always searching, never satisfied with your latest conquest," Giuseppe says. "And while you may not be the biggest star in the galaxy, you are, and always will be, the brightest one. At least to me."

Cosimo continued to steer the car while simultaneously monitoring the sky for any sign of Orion. He added to these distractions the task of searching for a radio station that played something with a beat. But it did him no good. All the airwaves carried Giuseppe's deep timbre and the bitter-sweet memories of his privileged youth. Cosimo blotted a tear away from his eye and returned to fondling the medallion that rested against his chest. The night was a brisk one, made even colder by the wind that entered the cabin of the Lamborghini going in excess of a hundred miles per hour. He closed the driver's side window and slumped over the steering wheel to peer out the windshield and resume his search for Betelgeuse in the night sky. But the road was not straight, and the car was heading in a different direction. Orion was no longer where he had been.

Cosimo never felt the car swerve off the road. He never felt the firm tarmac give way to unsteady gravel. He never saw the tree looming up ahead, its wide trunk and towering canopy barely visible beneath a waning crescent moon. He never felt the impact of fast-moving metal against solid, immovable bark. He never felt anything ever again.

Chapter Thirty

Megan stood in front of a large vending machine laden with candy bars, cookies, pretzels, and potato chips. Her hand, filled with quarters, trembled as it hovered over the coin slot. She wasn't the least bit hungry, but she needed something to do other than stare at the clock above the nurse's station and wait for her phone to ring. She dropped five quarters into the slot and pressed the buttons marked C and 7. A spiral wire turned inside the glass case, and a package of strawberry Pop-Tarts fell to the bottom with a clunk. She retrieved the packet of pastry with icing and sprinkles and made her way back to the row of chairs stationed around the perimeter of the waiting room. She held up the package and began to read the list of ingredients. Not because she cared what was in them, but because it was another way of passing a minute or two without losing her mind. When her cell phone buzzed, she answered it before it had a chance to vibrate a second time.

"They won't let me in to see him," she said.

"Who's the floor nurse on duty?" Tommy asked.

"I don't know, some beast with red hair, bad acne, and a limp."

"That's Margaret. She's mean."

"Can't you call someone? Do something?" She stared at the rectangular package in her hand. "Do you think she could be bribed with Pop-Tarts?"

"Very funny. But no, Pop-Tarts won't do it."

She tossed the unopened packet into a trashcan. The metal flap made an eerie squeak as it swung back and forth.

"I'm afraid I won't be much help," he said. "Nurse Ratched has only one emotion, and that's indifference. Besides, she follows the protocol manual down to the letter."

Megan put the phone down and strained to hear a conversation Margaret was having with a short woman with a tall stature. She assumed it was Cosimo's mother, but since she could only see her profile, she couldn't be sure it was the same person she'd had the run-in with at the Parkhurst Plaza.

"And she despises me. I think it has to do with a Halloween costume I wore one year," Tommy continued into the void. "I was supposed to be Rita Hayworth, but she thought I was making fun of…"

"I'll call you back," she said to Tommy when she saw Regina exit the elevator and join the other woman.

Nurse Margaret reached under the counter, retrieved a set of keys, and then ushered the two women through a pair of doors marked "**No Admittance. Hospital Personnel Only.**"

∾

A half hour passed as Megan waited for Regina to reappear. Her phone rang again, but she ignored it. She couldn't, wouldn't risk being inattentive, not for a second. She might miss Regina again and, with that, her only chance to see Cosimo. The older, mysterious woman arrived first, dabbing the corners of her eyes with a small, white handkerchief. As she approached the desk, she said something to the nurse that made what little color Margaret had drain from her face. The woman waved her arms as she spoke; her gestures expressive, but also controlled. She snapped her fingers, and a tall man in a dark suit came rushing out of nowhere and stood beside her. He opened a valise and produced a thick stack of papers and ceremoniously handed them to Margaret. The woman dismissed the man with the valise and then spoke quietly to the nurse. Margaret handed the document to another nurse while pointing in the direction of the swinging doors. As the woman stepped away from the counter, her stoic and aggressive emotions dissolved, and in their place, the first sign of sniffles and tears appeared. She let two partially full elevator cabs go by before stepping into an empty one. Megan watched the lighted numbers on the metal panel change from 8 to 7 to 6 and so on, as the enigmatic woman moved farther and farther away.

Megan wondered if Regina had left the building through a separate entrance, a back door, or another bank of elevators hidden behind the no admittance sign. *Maybe there's another way in?* she wondered. She paced the floor slowly, deliberately, oblivious to the other people in the waiting room, all of them in various states of distress. She needed to do something, but she couldn't run the risk of drawing attention to herself, either. It was possible that Regina had seen her and would come back to get her, but the likelihood of that happening diminished with each passing minute. Her eyes were glued to the double doors when her attention was drawn back to the reception desk by the high-pitched squeal of Margaret castigating another nurse. When she saw Margaret turn her back to the waiting room and open a file cabinet, Megan's cerebral cortex relinquished its power to her basic instincts. Abandoning all sense of protocol, of hierarchy, of decorum, it was Megan's gut that propelled her feet toward the double doors. She gave one hard push with her hands, and the heavy doors swung open. On the other side, she breathed a sigh of relief, but her sense of triumph ended quickly. A large, bald-headed man in a dark-gray security uniform grabbed her by the arm and began to escort her back to the waiting room.

"Let go of me. You're hurting me!" she shouted.

"And who might you be?" he said, gripping her arm even harder as he pushed her up against the double doors.

"Samuel! Sam!" another voice in the corridor said.

The security guard stopped instantly. He shifted his body to face the voice that was shouting his name from the other end of the hall.

"Let her go. She's with me."

"Yes, Miss Garibaldi. Sorry, Miss Garibaldi," he said as he released his hold on Megan's elbow. Megan gave the guard a retaliatory smack and rushed down the hall. When she reached Regina, she gripped her by her shoulders and squeezed lightly.

"Thank you," she said. "I was going crazy out there. I didn't know what else to do."

Regina's response was to bite her lip and avert her eyes. Megan tried to repress her shock at seeing the beautiful, powerful woman with whom she'd recently had lunch now appear so frail, so weak, so ordinary. Her hair was pulled back in a ponytail, and her animated face, without its intricate layers of makeup, looked vacant and unfinished. Megan did her best to withhold her tears, but they came anyway, because there was no denying that Regina's disheveled appearance had everything to do with Cosimo's condition.

"How is he?" she asked.

"Not good," Regina said, barely able to get the words out.

"Can I see him?"

She nodded and led her to a room at the end of the corridor where another security guard stood stiffly at attention.

"The car was totaled. He hit a tree going a hundred and ten miles an hour." Tears welled up in her eyes, and her arms began to shake. Megan reached out to hold one of her hands. "He's in a coma," she continued, having regained her composure. "All of his vital signs are weak. It's amazing he survived at all." She stopped again, withdrew her hand from Megan's, and folded her hands in front of herself, prayer-like. Megan watched her body stiffen and straighten while her expression changed from distraught to resolute. The metamorphosis was gradual, but undeniable. Regina had visibly altered her persona from grieving sister into a member of the royal family with appearances to keep. "They're not confident that he's going to make it," she said, calmly, officially.

"Oh my God," Megan gasped and then covered her face

with her hands to stifle a scream, to ward off more tears, to camouflage her distress. She felt her knees go numb and then start to weaken. She placed one of her hands against a wall to keep from collapsing.

"You have to prepare yourself," Regina said. "Even if he does survive…" Then she simply lowered her head and walked away.

Megan opened the door slowly, as if prolonging the time before seeing him might produce a different outcome. There were no surprises in the room. There were tubes. There were machines. There were packets of fluid suspended from IV stands on both sides of his bed. There were bandages and braces and external fixators. There were color monitors in several places displaying charts and graphs and vacillating numbers in a bright neon glow. There was beeping and humming and the soft, sinister sound of suction. And there was Cosimo. Broken Cosimo. Lying in a bed with bars on it, a pulsating screen keeping track of his faint heartbeat, and all of his head and the majority of his face wrapped in gauze.

For a moment she was as paralyzed as he was. She wanted to rush over to him, but she hesitated. For the past year she had endured much and been prepared for anything. But not for this. Never this. She inched her way forward, as if moving any faster might disturb him, injure him further, disrupt the delicate balance and tear the thin thread that his life hung by. When she reached the bed, her eyes surveyed the length of his body, up and down and back again, looking for any sign that he was there, that he knew that she was there. But the only movement, the only sound in that stark unadorned room, came from the various machines that were monitoring his vital signs or breathing for him. She took one of his hands in hers, careful not to touch the tubes attached to his wrist, and for the first time in years, Megan Walker prayed.

⌇

Megan arrived at the hospital the next morning after only a few hours of sleep. When the elevator doors opened to the ICU, she immediately sensed that something was wrong. Or at least different. It was quieter than it had been the day before. The phones weren't ringing. The nurses were decidedly less agitated. And there were no security guards or tall men with valises anywhere to be found. Having already been through the double doors and been seen in the company of Regina, she confidently, though reluctantly, approached the nurses' station. There was a new woman on duty, this one pretty, cordial. After Megan inquired about the patient in room 800, the pretty nurse adopted a more formal expression and an air of secrecy.

"I'm afraid we're only allowed to give that information to members of the immediate family," she said.

"But all I want—" Megan started to say, but she was cut off by the new nurse.

"I can't. I wish I could, but I just can't."

Another nurse seated at the desk tapped Nurse Pretty on the arm and pointed to a slip of paper taped to the inside of the counter. Nurse Pretty offered a grim smile, opened a drawer, and pulled out an envelope.

"Are you Megan Walker?"

"Yes, yes, I am."

"Do you have any—"

Megan withdrew her driver's license from her wallet, placed it on the counter, and nervously inched it toward the nurse.

Nurse Pretty handed her back her license along with the stark white envelope.

"I'm very sorry," she said and then immediately shifted her gaze to another patient's chart.

Her condolence was a sledgehammer that knocked the wind out of Megan. She drifted over to the teal-colored chairs in the waiting room and sat down. She tried not to let negative thoughts creep into her consciousness, tried to believe she was overreacting, tried to keep her hands from shaking as she tore open the seal on the rectangular parcel. More than anything, though, she wished there were a few of Cosimo's antianxiety pills stashed in her purse. Inside the envelope was a note from Regina, written on heavy card stock with a blue fountain pen in a refined, controlled cursive.

Megan,

By now it's apparent that our Cosimo is gone. I wish I could have been the one to tell you, but I am sure you understand. Mother already has a team of people working on the arrangements. I'll call you as soon as I know where the services will be. I know that you have the strength to pull through this. And I pray that I do, too.

Regards, R

There was another, smaller envelope paper-clipped to Regina's note. This one contained an odd-shaped item that made a puzzling noise when the nurse handed it to her. She took a nail file from her purse and used it as a letter opener, careful not to damage the contents. Inside of that envelope was a folded piece of paper and a long, gold chain. She knew instantly, probably even before she opened it, that inside this other envelope was the medallion with eight small diamonds on an eighteen-carat gold disc. It was Orion, the hunter, the pendant Cosimo had always worn around his neck. The one that he fondled whenever he was nervous or anxious or happy. The one that she'd never seen him take off. Regina's second note was equally short and to the point:

Megan,

    In many ways this is all that is left of him. And as much as I would treasure having it for myself, I know in my heart that Cosimo would want you to have it. It was a gift from his uncle Giuseppe, whom he treasured. And I know he treasured you as well. He was going to give up everything for you, of that I'm certain. And if nothing else, I hope you find some comfort in knowing that.

    Be well, R

Regina never called about the services. She never called about anything. And Megan was too unsettled, too insecure, too afraid or embarrassed or angry to ever call her. She was all those things, and more; she was alone again. Under ordinary circumstances that would have suited her just fine. What threw her off kilter this time was the ran-

domness of it and the speed at which it happened. Megan
had always been independent. She'd never felt she needed
to be with someone just to be with someone. There were
times, usually after the dissolution of a lackluster relationship, when she even relished her autonomy and celebrated
her reclaimed sovereignty. Now, for the first time in her
life, she found herself questioning the solidity of the very
ground beneath her feet. Being alone when it had been a
choice, a decision that she herself had made, was one thing.
But finding herself alone, unexpectedly and arbitrarily, at
the hand of some capricious and unkind god, was another.
But Megan came from good, hearty New England peasant
stock; the hit she took may have knocked her down, but it
wouldn't knock her out.

She had her own private moment of reflection, a
mini-memorial service if you will, in the Boston Garden on
the bridge where he'd first uttered the words, "I love you."
She said her goodbyes to him, made promises to keep his
memory alive, and thanked him for their time together, for
the good as well as the bad that they had shared. If he was
out there, up there, anywhere, he would know how she
felt, would know what he had meant to her, would *always*
mean to her. Especially with his legacy inside of her, getting
bigger and more spirited every day. She decided she would
take a trip to Paris after the baby was born. That was where
a true farewell should take place, toasted with a café crème
at La Brasserie de l'Isle Saint-Louis in honor of their first
meeting. And a journal entry: a sketch of the two of them
in black ink, with a caption, in a bubble, that simply said,
"I miss you."

With Cosimo gone and a child on the way, Megan's

life was anything but routine. There were endless doctors' visits and mounds of books to read about child-rearing, breastfeeding, and losing baby weight. And there were the numerous things she wasn't doing, like seeing her friends or calling Regina, all of which required more energy than she could muster.

For a few weeks after Cosimo's death, Megan sequestered herself in her apartment. She rarely answered the phone, and she resisted any attempt to cajole her into a night out, a late lunch, or even a cup of tea. For a while she took comfort in the isolation, the time apart from her brother and her friends, to ponder what had happened, what was about to happen, and what it all meant. By the middle of the third week, though, she had exhausted her capacity for introspection and was once again in need of some fellowship. So she sent out a blanket email in which she apologized for her recent but necessary quarantine and requested their presence at her apartment for a long overdue family meeting.

Everyone in attendance knew that there was no set agenda for the conclave, no real rationale for a gathering other than that Cosimo was gone and Megan was probably at her lowest point and feeling untethered. That after several weeks of being cloistered away, of contemplating his passing and preparing for his progeny, she was ready for their company. And if she needed the ruse of a family meeting for reentry into the world, that was fine with them. They were delighted to have things back to normal. At least as normal as things could be with one prince gone and another one on the way. And while no one wanted to dredge up the unfortunate incidents of the past, the subject of the departed prince and his unborn child was unavoidable.

No one in the group had been able to comprehend Megan's sense of calm given all that had happened, with all that she'd had to contend with, including never having been informed as to where or when the memorial services were to take place. In addition to that, they couldn't fathom how she'd endured, without bitterness or regret, the humiliating experience of being greeted at the penthouse by two security guards who demanded that she relinquish her key, monitored her every move while she gathered up the few possessions she'd left there, and then escorted her out of the building, one on each side, as if she were a trespasser or a petty thief.

"What would I gain by making a fuss?" she said. "He's gone. Nothing I can say or do is going to change that."

"It'll help you get closure," Lauren said.

"And what about the little zygote? Aren't you going to tell anyone about that?" Gregg said.

"I know I don't carry as much weight around here as the others," Rob interjected, "but I'm inclined to agree with them. It may seem inconsequential to you now, but one day, *because* of that little zygote you got goin' on in there, you'll lament having left certain issues unresolved."

"And you?" Megan said to Tommy. "You're being awfully quiet for a change."

"Me? I got nuthin'. I can't find any humor in this situation at all," he said. "And I get it, calling them about the funeral wouldn't change anything."

"Okay, out with it," she said, pressing him to continue.

"Out with what?"

"I saw you bite your lip. There's something you're not saying. You of all people should know better than to handle me with kid gloves."

"All right. But remember," he said, pointing a finger in a sweeping motion to indicate each member of the family, "She *made* me say it." He looked over at Rob and winked. "Rob's right. I know you and you'll eventually regret it if you don't contact them. If you don't tell them about…you know…that," he said, pointing to her belly. "And they have a right to know he had a child. That he's going to have a child, as strange as that seems. Maybe they didn't before, but his death changed that."

Megan tried to think of a clever comeback, but all she could do was nod her head in agreement.

Megan opened the door of her apartment to find Regina poised there, her statuesque beauty manifest even in the hallway of her tenement building, even with a backdrop of dingy, chipped beige paint and the pulsating gray hue of a fading fluorescent light bulb. It wasn't until she saw her standing there that she regretted not having called her to tell her about the pregnancy.

"I know, I should have called first, but I was afraid you'd hang up on me."

"And why would I do that?" Megan said.

"Then you're a better person than I am," she said. "If I were you, I'd hang up on me." She patted her coat pocket with her hand. "I have something for you. I thought it best to deliver it myself."

"Where are my manners? Please, come in."

Regina sat on the loveseat and Megan in a club chair as they engaged each other with the usual small talk inherent in such situations. After a respectable and in some regards unendurable amount of time spent on idle chatter, Regina attempted to explain to Megan the circumstances surrounding Cosimo's funeral.

"This may sound rude, or blunt, or both, but it was probably a blessing in disguise that you weren't in attendance. Our mother, of course, did everything perfectly, which means over the top." She reached out to touch Megan's hand and then withdrew it the instant flesh-to-flesh contact was made. "The whole pomp and circumstance of it, the foreign dignitaries, the choir, the press…it had nothing to do with the Cosimo you knew and loved."

"I can appreciate that. But it would have been nice if the decision not to attend hadn't been made for me."

"Truly, Megan, the only thing you missed was a well-choreographed circus, a tribute to Maria-Carmella's ego, and her attempt to fool the world, and herself, into believing she was a loving, grieving mother."

Megan shrugged her shoulders to convey her confusion as well as her dissatisfaction with that response being served up as an explanation.

"The truth is, I wanted to spare you," Regina said. "And I wanted Cosimo's service to be about Cosimo."

"And what makes you think I would have wanted anything different?"

"It's not that. It wasn't you. It was Mother. I had an obligation to inform her about you at the hospital. Before we knew for certain that he wasn't going to recover. There was never going to be a good time to tell her. But there, with her son on the verge of death and her plans for his marriage evaporating…you can imagine how she was feeling. She inevitably and fervently decided it was all your fault. There would have been no way to control her hysteria if you had been anywhere near the proceedings."

"Well, that explains the security guards."

"Pardon?"

"At the penthouse. I was forced to give back my keys and remove my belongings while two of your Doberman pinschers supervised my every move."

"*Mother's* guard dogs," she corrected her. "That is a shining example of how she operates."

"Well, to be fair, it was Cosimo who inadvertently put me in that position."

"Regardless, I am so sorry. For everything. If there is any way I can make it up to you—"

"You can't," Megan said, "but I appreciate the offer. Actually, I'm glad you stopped by. It gives me a chance to set the record straight, something I hadn't been prepared to do when we had lunch. I was a little out of my element there, and because of that I neglected to tell you…I didn't articulate…" Megan was still having trouble putting into words what had happened between her and Cosimo. "I failed to mention that it was your brother who pursued me. No matter what I said or did. No matter how much I resisted him."

"As a matter of fact, you did. And you needn't say anything more. I never doubted that what the two of you shared was real, was special. And to set the record straight, even though my intentions were good, I was way out of line that day."

"So why—"

"Maria-Carmella. There are days when I think that she
is pure evil. And then there are days when I understand
her completely and think that I would do exactly what she
would in a given situation." She reached a hand into her
coat pocket. "As much as I'd like to blame someone for his
death, to help me make sense of it, to have some place to
put the anger, it was no one's fault. Cosimo was just one of
those flames that burns brightly, but only for a short while
before flickering out and going dark. And the rest of us are
left wandering around in a daze, wondering what the hell
happened to all that light."

The conversation came to a place that seemed to
require reflection, a time in which no words could have
possibly been the right words. Anything said would have
been too much. Or not enough. It was Megan who finally
broke the silence.

"What is it that's so important you felt the need to come
all the way down to the low-rent district by yourself?"

"I guess I deserve that," Regina said, withdrawing a small
velvet case from the depths of her coat pocket. "This. I
found it in his closet under a stack of sweaters while I was
cleaning out the penthouse a few days ago. I know," she
said, "it was an unbearable chore that I postponed as long
as possible." She handed Megan the little box. "There was
no name or anything on it." She removed a small envelope
from her purse. "The only way for me to find out who they
were for was to read the card. I wouldn't normally have,
but…you understand."

Megan took the box and the card and set them down
on the coffee table.

"Aren't you going to open them?"

"Of course. Of course. I just need a minute." She picked up the still unopened box and held it as if it were a rare and delicate object. "This is so very strange," she said. She gently ran her fingers over the velvety fabric. As she slowly, tentatively opened it, the tiny hinge made an eerie squeak, like a trap door being sprung open. Inside, resting on a bed of white satin, were a pair of princess-cut sapphires in platinum settings. She picked one of them up and cradled it in her palm. She held it up to the light. She briefly placed it against the pale skin of her hand and then gingerly placed it back in its box.

"They're beautiful, aren't they?" Regina said. "Cosimo had the most exquisite taste. In jewelry, in clothes, in…" She gave Megan what could only be described as a heart-felt expression. "And in women." She stood. "I'll leave you to read the card in private." She rebuttoned her coat and retrieved her purse from the table. "How far along are you?"

"I was wondering if you were going to ask," Megan said, rubbing her belly. "Can't you tell? I look like I'm about to explode."

"No, you look great," Regina said. "You look radiant."

Megan was visibly shaken by that comment. Her face instantly lost what little color it had. And while she had been quite pale before, her complexion took on a positively ghostly pallor. For a few seconds she left the room, traveled back in time, and was standing in front of a mirror in the lobby of a Parisian pensione.

"What? Is it something I said? Something with the baby?"

"It's nothing. You couldn't possibly have known. It was something that your brother said to me. It's not important."

Megan placed the earrings back on the coffee table and then took Regina's hand and placed it on top of her stomach.

"Can you feel that?" she said. "It's pretty rambunctious."

Regina shook her head. Megan was unable to read the unspoken words in her expression.

"It was kind of you to say that I look radiant, Regina, but I have never had any misgivings about my appearance, especially now that I look like a dirigible in a blue cotton smock. You're the one who looks radiant in that raw silk jacket. It's just another example of how different our two worlds are."

"Again, I'm sorry if I…" Regina said, bowing her head respectfully, apologetically.

"Honestly, it's nothing. And I'd prove that to you if it didn't defy explanation."

Megan pivoted her body sideways to provide Regina a full view of her profile.

"I'm due in three weeks."

Megan could practically see Regina mentally counting back the months in her head.

"The answer to the question that you're too polite to ask is, yes, of course it's Cosimo's."

"Do you know…"

"A boy. I'm having a boy. I wasn't sure if I should tell you or not. Or even if you'd want to know, given the circumstances. So I kept putting it off and putting it off…" She extended her hand to Regina and said, "Thank you for coming by, for the gift, for—"

Regina ignored Megan's outstretched hand and moved

in closer to give her a hug and a kiss. She took a calling card from her purse and handed it to her.

"In case you lost my number. You call me if you need anything. Anything at all."

And then she was gone.

Megan leaned against the door after she'd closed it, took a deep breath, and shut her eyes. When she opened them again, she saw, looming in front of her as if the room around it had shrunken to the size of a doll's house, a blue velvet box and a handwritten note from Cosimo. She had been living under the misguided notion that he had finally lost the ability to surprise her. But she was wrong. It seemed to her then that the surprises might never end. Some lessons take a lifetime to learn. It began to dawn on her that the lessons she needed to learn in this lifetime involved one boyfriend now deceased, a child, another prince on the way, and the delusion that she'd ever had even the slightest bit of control over any of it.

She took the earrings out of the box, put them on, and admired her reflection in a mirror on the other side of the room. Even from a few yards away, they captured and reflected the light. Their color and their sparkle made her smile, and their heft imbued her with a peculiar sense of reassurance. The two gems seemed to be radiating a kind of power or protective force field. They had a curious yet comforting effect on her, similar to the way the medallion she'd been wearing lately had made her feel invulnerable. She grasped the pendant with the relief of Orion on it and envisioned the day when she would hand it over to her son, in the hope that a few grams of gold, eight diamond chips, and numerous stories about his father would make him feel a little safer in an uncontrollable, unpredictable world.

She did not bother with the formality of properly opening the letter. She tore the envelope apart, and with the note in her hand, let it fall to the carpet. She sat on the floor, her back resting against the loveseat, and unfolded a thick piece of ivory-colored paper. Embossed on the top of the stationery with silk threads were the initials **GGC**. And at the bottom, there was a full-color replica of the Garibaldi family crest.

> *Megan,*
>
> *I saw these after our first weekend in Boston and have been waiting for the right moment to give them to you. Like you, they sparkle and are multifaceted. You were never a diamond in the rough. You are a jewel whose radiance drew me in and whose color, clarity, and depth keeps me coming back.*
>
> *I couldn't think of a better way to express my feelings than to offer you these precious stones. The sapphire is the gem of destiny, and they purportedly bring the wearer spiritual enlightenment and inner peace. May you always have those.*

There was no signature and no way to tell if he had completed his thoughts. There was nothing in the note that hinted of his early demise, or that he had any reason to believe that he wouldn't be around another day to finish what he'd started. And it was that, not the earrings, not the note, but the thought of things unfinished that compelled her to cry. That necessitated she place her head down on the coffee table and weep. And to wonder if those tears that flowed so abundantly and uncontrollably would ever stop. It was so very short, their time together. The blink of an eye, really. And yet during that brief period, Crown Prince Giuseppe Cosimo Garibaldi de Sorrento had managed to profoundly touch, to permanently impact, to incontrovertibly alter her life.

For a few days after his passing, she had felt remorse about their last communication. That their time together had ended so poorly when so much of it had otherwise been filled with great conversations and an abundance of laughter. But she realized that it was foolish to concern herself with things that were beyond her control. Back then, she thought she was making it easier for him to leave her, as he had once done for her. She wanted him to be able to marry, to fulfill his obligations, without having to worry about her. In her heart, though, she knew that you can't live your life as if the person you care about is going to die before you see them again. It was the totality of the year they'd shared together that mattered, not the random few arguments they'd had before it all came to a screeching halt.

But there was something else that mattered. Something she needed to do to stop the tears, temper the sadness, mitigate the regret. If Cosimo had taught her anything, it was that she had to go on, no matter how grim or how difficult things got; that there is an ebb and a flow to everything; and that even the darkest of moods will eventually subside, if only for a moment. And it is for those moments that you must live. As she thought about the lessons he had inadvertently taught her, the tears began to subside, partially because he'd also taught her to be silly, to do the things that brought her joy, no matter how juvenile or how inconsequential they might be.

She went to the closet and put on her parka. On her way out the door, she stopped to take another look at the earrings in the mirror and to touch the diamonds on the Orion pendant. She whispered the numbers to herself— one, two, three...seven, eight—her fingers slowly gliding over each one as she counted. And then she left her apartment. It was a long walk, and it was cold, but the minutes flew by. And even though it still seemed silly and inconsequential, it was something she was compelled to do.

It was dark now, and the wind had picked up. The bitter chill that was in the air ensured that the city streets and the Public Garden were all but deserted. It had been a while since she'd walked through that park or even thought about what had happened there among the flowers and the ponds one surprisingly warm autumn afternoon.

It was there on that bridge, in front of those swans, with the Parkhurst Plaza penthouse peeking out above the trees, that under a starry sky, and in the shadow of the Four Seasons hotel, Megan Walker said aloud, for the very first time, the words she should have spoken months before but never did: "I love you, too."

Chapter Thirty-One

Regina, her attorney, Douglas, and Megan Walker were already seated around a large mahogany table when Maria-Carmella came charging into the conference room.

"Can we get right down to your agenda, Douglas?" she said, looking up from her wristwatch to acknowledge him. "I only have a half hour before…what is *she* doing here?" Maria-Carmella pointed a crooked finger and flashed a venomous sneer in Megan's direction.

"You're late, Mother. You've kept us all waiting," Regina said, her inflection implying both irony and contempt.

"One of us is leaving, Douglas, and if you value my business, you'll call security and have this woman, this…this…sycophant escorted out onto the street posthaste."

"That's not how we're going to handle this, Maria-Carmella," Douglas said.

"No, Mother," Regina said. "I'm sure you can find your own way out."

Maria-Carmella mumbled the word "unimaginable" and began to move toward the door.

"Honestly, Mother, sit down."

"What is this all about?" she demanded. "Why is *she* here? How could you—"

"Maria-Carmella, I'm afraid I'm going to have to side with Regina on this one," Douglas said. "Please, have a seat."

"Mother, I know that you prefer…that it's easier for you to envision the world as something other than it is. But it is not." Regina walked over to her and gently placed a hand on her arm. "It is time for you to deal with the reality that Cosimo is gone and that his death was no one's fault."

Maria-Carmella recoiled from her daughter's touch.

"I'm not a child, Regina, and you are not a psychiatrist. So if there isn't anything else—"

"You can try and deny that Cosimo had a son, Mother, but that will never change the fact that he's still flesh and blood. And that he"—she pointed to the bundle in Megan's arms—"is your grandson."

Megan was sitting at the end of the conference table with a three-month-old baby on her lap. He was bundled in a plush powder-blue blanket, his miniature hands barely visible, his tiny fingers stretching and squeezing and grasping at air. She lifted a corner of the fleece coverlet away from the infant's head to reveal an olive-skinned face, a contented smile, and a crown covered in fluffy auburn hair.

"Mrs. Garibaldi, I know there are still so many things left unsaid, but I thought…*we* thought that you'd still like to meet him," she said, offering up the child as if he were a sacrificial lamb. "This is Gus."

"Prince Gus, Mother," Regina said. "Isn't he yummy? And look at that face. Look at how much he—"

"You cannot be serious!" Maria-Carmella exclaimed, and then she left the room with so much force and fury that it felt like her absence created a vacuum.

Regina paused in the doorway and mouthed an apology to Megan before dashing from the room to catch up with Maria-Carmella.

"Mother, wait."

Maria-Carmella stopped abruptly, her shoulders stiff, her back to Regina, her eyes targeting the bank of elevators at the building's core.

"I thought you'd want to know," Regina said. "You *have* to know."

Maria-Carmella shifted her stance slowly, deliberately, obstinately folding her arms across her chest.

"To know what?" she said, pronouncing each word contemptuously. "That some little harlot is trying to extort money from us? Trying to make a mockery of our name?"

"She hasn't asked us for anything. This was my idea. I'm the one who dragged her to Manhattan to give you the chance to meet your grandson. Before it's too late."

"Maybe she hasn't asked for anything yet, but you mark my words, she has a team of lawyers already lined up, just waiting for—"

"Waiting for what, Mother?"

"That is not my grandchild!" she wailed.

Regina was momentarily stunned. She could not recall ever having heard Maria-Carmella raise her voice before, much less shout. Her confrontations, while always aggressive, were also always contained and controlled. Her accusations and her threats were all the more intimidating because they were soft-spoken.

"And that name, Gus." Maria-Carmella shivered with disgust. "How pedestrian. How plebian. There is no way in hell that—"

"That woman in there," Regina said, "was going to walk away from the man she loved so that your precious, albeit delusional, dream of some goddamned dynasty could be fulfilled!" Now it was Regina who was on the verge of screaming. "That woman in there has endured nine months of pregnancy, on her own, with no financial or emotional support from us because she has principles. Because she has integrity. That woman in there is the mother of your grandson, whether you like it or not, whether you can accept it or not."

Maria-Carmella hauled back her arm to smack her daughter, but Regina blocked the impending slap with her forearm.

"Don't even try it, Mother. Are you kidding me with that?"

"There is no way that bastard in there, that *Gus*"— Maria-Carmella spoke the name as if it were repugnant for her to repeat it—"is Cosimo's child, my grandson, *or* a prince."

"Mother, there are times when even I am astounded by your degree of arrogance. And in this case, *ignorance*." Regina reached her hand into a black alligator clutch purse. "I was afraid that you'd react this way. And after everything we've been through. The one good thing that's happened this past year, besides the birth of my nephew, is that sales of Regal perfume and my sportswear line have surpassed everyone's expectations."

"I'm happy to hear you're doing so well, Regina, but that doesn't mean—"

"Save it, Mother. What it means is this."

She pulled a slip of paper out of her purse and handed it to her. Maria-Carmella took the elongated green business check and stared at it with her brows knitted together.

"Why are you giving me this?"

"It's your investment in Reggie, Mother. It's a reimbursement, as you can see, along with a substantial amount of interest." She started to head back to the conference room but stopped short. She took a few steps back to confront her mother face-to-face. "I've had enough. It stops here, at least for me. You can continue to infect everyone around you with your poison and your narrow-mindedness, to continue to try to impress or to frighten everyone with your money and your title. But I for one am done, finished."

"What has come over you? I am still your mother."

"In title only, Mother," Regina said, using her fingers to mime quotation marks for emphasis.

"What has that parvenu—"

"Stop it!" Regina screamed.

Maria-Carmella cringed as she observed the people walking past them in the foyer and down the hall, their heads tilting, straining to hear, to comprehend the cause of the commotion. She pulled her coat collar up to shield part of her face.

"I'm having your things delivered to a suite at the Plaza," Regina said matter-of-factly. "You are no longer welcome in my home."

"You're being cruel for no reason! I can't understand what—"

"I learned from the best, Mother."

Maria-Carmella said nothing; she simply stood there, plucking imaginary lint off of her Valentino jacket.

"What? Maria-Carmella dumbstruck?" Regina said. "That's a first." She was afraid of what she was about to say but equally certain that she had waited far too long to say it. "I don't want to hear from you or see you again, Mother. Not until you're ready to start acting like a human being. And not until you're ready to accept the fact that things didn't turn out as you planned. That like it or not, Cosimo did have a child with that remarkable woman in there." She pulled on the door handle and paused before finishing her thought. She had to choose her words carefully. She wanted to reach her mother, shake some sense in to her, not devastate her. Neither did she want to say something she might live to regret.

"She may not be an heiress, Mother, but in many ways, Gus's mother is far richer than you will ever be. And for the record, the child's name is not Gus; that's just his nickname." She paused before delivering the final bullet. "Yes, Mother, your grandson's name is *Giuseppe*."

Regina disappeared into the conference room, closing the door behind her with dignity and finality.

Maria-Carmella stood frozen in the lobby, equal distance from the elevator that was waiting to whisk her away and her alleged grandson, waiting for his third feeding of the day. She was unable to bring herself to walk the few steps to the double doors of Douglas's office, to a future that was different than the one she had planned. She was unable to acquiesce in any way. She could not summon the strength to pull open a door that might reveal to her, once again, an infant who might very well be the child of her child.

Regina stood next to Megan and dangled a bracelet over Gus's outstretched hands.

"That went well," Megan said.

"Frankly," Regina said, "it went quite a bit better than I expected."

"Really?"

"Sad, but true. It's not likely to happen until the little guy's in college, but she'll come around. Believe it or not, there's a soft, chewy center buried beneath that hard outer shell."

"You're kidding," Megan said.

"Well, I don't know that anyone's ever seen it, but then again, I've always been an optimist."

Chapter Thirty-Two

A year had passed, and there was still no rapprochement between mother and daughter. Regina continued to expand her brand, including, among other things, the addition of a skin care line called Noblesse. She was also preparing to launch a line of clothes for children with the intention of utilizing her favorite nephew, Gus, as a model. Megan and Regina had many discussions about using him in this fashion and, in the end, agreed that it was not so much cannibalizing his heritage as it was celebrating it. He had, after all, started out in life with a deficit.

Megan continued to teach college freshmen that Arthur Deco was not a real person and therefore was not responsible for the designs and styles prevalent in the 1920s and 1930s. And she made the occasional trip to Manhattan with Gus for photo shoots with Annie Leibovitz and playdates with his favorite aunt, Regina, since she was now using Gus's likeness in advertisements, packaging, and brochures for her newest enterprise, Toddler-Couture. For his modeling gigs in New York, Gus was paid scale and a per diem. Megan was uncharacteristically ambivalent about whether or not her child should become a minor celebrity or spend his formative years in anonymity. She had learned her lesson the hard way: his life would be what it would be, regardless of how much she tried to control or manipulate it.

Maria-Carmella had no idea what day it was. Back in Italy, the afternoons at Villa Vita Fortunata lingered like a bad taste in her mouth, each day a carbon copy of the previous one. There were no portents of meaning, no incidents to make them memorable, nothing to distinguish a Wednesday from the Monday that preceded it. How long had it been since she'd left the house, accepted an invitation, or even spoken to anyone on the phone? She couldn't remember how many weeks it had been—or was it months?—since she had stopped leaving voice mail messages for Regina. How long had it been since she discontinued the practice of checking her emails or social media of any kind? And even though her exile was technically self-imposed, it was still exile.

A sense of despair began to creep into her consciousness. In some regards that wasn't a bad thing, as despair was a reprieve from the emptiness and apathy she was currently operating under. She had never been one to indulge in self-reflection, but there, alone in her villa, with only a handful of aloof staff going out of their way to avoid her, she found herself ruminating about the past and pondering the present. For her, the future had always fallen into place naturally. It was little more than an afterthought, something that played itself out—and usually according to her expectations. But now it seemed to require anticipation, consideration, preparation, execution. She could no longer take it for granted that things would turn out as she wished, simply because she wanted them to.

When she heard the rumblings of a truck at the back of the house, she rang the miniature bell that sat on a side table. A few seconds later, Gino was standing in the entrance to her study. He wore a starched, white, unlined jacket and a blank expression on his face.

"Your Highness?"

"That noise?"

"The manure, Your Highness. The dirt that you had me order last week. It is here."

Maria-Carmella had completely forgotten that she had made such a request. At first she said nothing, not sure of what to make of the news, of the reminder that she had implemented something that took forethought and action and then lost all recollection of it.

"Of course," she said and then dismissed him with a flick of her wrist.

In the kitchen she stood by the French doors and watched two men unload a yellow dumpster of black soil into a long, rectangular plot along the side of the house. Maria-Carmella had never so much as planted a bulb before, and here she had initiated the beginnings of a vegetable garden that would be hard to miss and even harder to dismiss. Once the truck had left the grounds, Maria-Carmella walked outside and surveyed the damage. That was how she thought of it: Damage. Destruction. Disruption. But the sight of the soil was not unfamiliar and the smell of the dung not unpleasant. She had only visited Giuseppe's garden a few times, but the aroma of cow manure brought back images of him on his knees, instructing a pint-sized Cosimo about the proper depth for planting each varietal and of the use of pulverized grape seeds as both fertilizer and pesticide.

Later that same day, she called together her entire staff. She stood in front of the small group and addressed them as if they were the board of directors of some charity she presided over. Her persona had changed once again. She was no longer the harsh, dismissive figurehead that they had learned to fear and avoid. Neither was she the vacant shell of a woman that they had come to know in recent months, unenthusiastically barking out orders with less and less conviction each day. She told them of her plans and enlisted their advice. It took them a while to warm up to the idea, to this new version of their mistress. And it took some coaxing and patience on her part to get them to open up, to offer suggestions and recommendations, without fear of recrimination. But before long, the cook, the groundskeeper, the butler—all were eager to be heard, to be of service, to have their ideas entertained rather than ridiculed.

The end result of that meeting came two days later, with Maria-Carmella back in the side yard wearing work clothes that her staff had procured for her and digging holes with tools they had purchased from local shops. Too impatient to deal with the planting of seeds, she had ordered boxes of beautiful, healthy seedlings from a nursery in Castellammare di Stabia. They had arrived that morning and now rested in neat, narrow rows against the side of the house. The groundskeeper stood at the edge of the plot and offered advice but no assistance. At one point Maria-Carmella grew so frustrated with the clumsiness of the thick gloves that she ripped them off her palms and, without thought or hesitation, dug her lotioned and manicured hands deep into the soft, fertile soil. A rush of energy shot through her body as her flesh merged with the earth, as the realization of the direct connection between being and doing, of cause and effect, began to enter her consciousness. In the process of moving each plant from container to earth, she couldn't help but think back to the destruction of that other garden.

It had been a day like any other. Maria-Carmella stood poised in front of the mirror atop her vanity, trying to decide between the Harry Winston Diamond Wreath necklace and the Bvlgari Giardini Italiani one while occasionally glancing out the window. It was an annoying habit that she had—looking out her bedroom window, sometimes anxiously, sometimes angrily, always eagerly—waiting to see Giuseppe's straw hat come bobbing, cresting over the hill, late as usual. But that day he would not be coming. Nor the next day. Nor the one after that. No, today the town car that sat idling at the entrance of the estate purred only for her, for Maria-Carmella, who was running late because she was waiting for—nothing.

It had been several years since her brother had succumbed to the cancer, yet in all that time, she had never stopped anticipating his presence, never stopped expecting to see his smiling face, never stopped hoping to find one of his preserve jars on her dressing table filled to overflowing with a ragtag concoction of wildflowers and branches.

When the cook asked, a mere few weeks after his passing, if he should send his sous-chef down the hill to gather up what was left in the garden, he was summarily fired, replaced by a new cook with no connection to the garden, to Giuseppe, or to the abundant harvest that had once been produced by both. For three years after that, the small garden sat untouched with all the vegetables that were left behind, rotting and reverting back into soil.

Maria-Carmella drew tight the curtains of the window that overlooked the hillside and made her way down the winding marble staircase. Halfway down the last set of steps, she caught the eye of Mario, the groundskeeper, making his way toward the solarium. She motioned to him with the almost imperceptible raising of an eyebrow. A second later he was standing at her side, nodding in agreement to her every word. When the conversation was over, Mario placed the calls that she had explicitly and dispassionately ordered him to make. The next day, two large trucks arrived. One for digging. One for hauling. By nightfall Giuseppe's garden was no longer.

～

As the months passed, Maria-Carmella gave up all hope of hearing from her daughter. For the most part, her mail lay unopened and her phone calls unreturned. The few invitations to galas and charity events that still managed to find their way to her were also ignored. She had even abandoned her habit of reading the daily newspapers for fear they might mention Regina and reopen wounds that were beyond her ability to heal. As for her last interaction with Cosimo, she did her best not to think about it. She had never been the kind of person who dwelled in the past, nor did she have an inclination to be introspective. She was unfamiliar with the concepts of guilt, of regret, of remorse. What she did feel, however, was a gnawing emptiness, which, having experienced it after the loss of Giuseppe, she knew would eventually diminish but would never completely dissipate.

Each morning after a small breakfast, she would put on the sunbonnet that hung outside the kitchen doors and stroll back and forth along the side of the house, admiring the new shoots, the fragrant buds, and a profusion of pods, petals, and plumes that signaled the arrival of tomatoes, green beans, cucumbers, and squash. That signified the arrival of sustenance. She watered the garden daily with the attention of a nursing mother and plucked the earth free of weeds with the care and precision of a surgeon. It took her a while to relinquish old habits, to stop allowing the infinitesimal to take on grand proportions, to accept the idea that perfectionism is not a useful trait in a gardener.

The days melded together, one into the other, but this time with a consistency and a renewed sense of purpose that lifted her spirits. She stopped getting her weekly manicures and began to appreciate the unlikely beauty in hands that had toiled hard and whose rough texture and weathered appearance were a testament to, if not a celebration of, that hard work. What she found most astonishing about the entire enterprise was not that she had grown accustomed to the khakis, the bonnets, and the work shirts that she toiled in daily but that she had come to prefer them to her former attire of stiff fabrics, cumbersome jewelry, and assorted accoutrements.

The weeks merged into months, the seedlings into an abundant crop, and Maria-Carmella into the most unlikely of farmers who now had to find a use for all of that produce. Even after the staff had been sufficiently supplied with potatoes and eggplants, the garden was still bursting with an endless supply of fruits and leafy greens. It was only then that the task of tending to the garden had grown beyond her ability to maintain it. And it was then that she hired several young boys from a nearby village to come by a few days a week to help harvest the crop. Before long they were tending to it daily. They even set up a small kiosk in the center of town from which to sell the various crops. She compensated the boys handsomely for their productivity and insisted that all the proceeds from their stall be donated to the local school. It wasn't long before word spread, and Maria-Carmella found herself instructing a growing number of children about the fragile infrastructure of the garden and of the benefits of enterprise and hard work.

While her demeanor had lightened along with the season, and the staff cautiously reveled in the minor changes that occurred in the daily diminishing of tension in the household, she noticed a sense of malaise creeping back a little more each day. While she took great pleasure in the garden, in its gentle reminder of Giuseppe and Cosimo, in the questions and the admiration of the children, it occurred to her that there must be a world somewhere in between. A world that incorporated the rich and the poor and all that each had to learn from the other.

Part of her longed to be pampered once again, to be poured into a sequined cocktail dress, and to sip sherry with some oil magnate on the massive terrace of his Upper East

Side co-op. But another part of her hungered for something with more substance than she knew she could find there. She was aware that the solution to her predicament was not to be found in trading bon mots over hors d'oeuvres, but neither was it waiting for her at the other end of a hoe. She was eager to reenter a world that celebrated culture, but one that took its professed philanthropy more seriously. The small flecks of dirt that remained under her fingernails and the brown spots that were appearing on her hands after months of exposure to the sun made it clear to her that simply adding her name to the masthead of some charity or writing a large check would be insufficient. Neither of those things would nurture her or anyone else. Not in any fundamental way. She was struck with the surprising, yet undeniable, realization that it was up to her to shake things up. And with a snap of her fingers, her staff began to set things in motion. Calls were made, appointments were scheduled, and travel arrangements confirmed.

Chapter Thirty-Three

Regina was greeted by a young woman in a tailored suit as she entered the forty-ninth-floor lobby of her attorney's office.

"Good morning, Ms. Garibaldi. Mr. Scheff is waiting for you. Right this way."

Regina followed her down a long corridor decorated with geese and hunting scenes, dark wood-paneled walls, and tufted leather upholstery. It was all very masculine and reassuring. The receptionist opened the door to a corner office with a view of the Manhattan skyline.

"Douglas," she said, "nice to see you again."

"Regina, a pleasure as always," he said, giving her a friendly but professional hug. "But you know, with all those billboards for Regal scattered around town, it's like—"

"Don't remind me; I'm so sick of those things," she said as she admired the view. "Now, what's so important that you needed to see me right away?"

He pointed to a conference table on the other side of

the room. Seated there, looking rather dim, understated, and monochromatic, was Maria-Carmella. Regina, momentarily surprised and shocked by her mother's appearance, quickly regained her composure.

"You had your attorney make an appointment for you to see me?" she said.

"What can I say? I learned from the best," Maria-Carmella said without a hint of sarcasm. She motioned to the chair next to hers.

"Honestly, Mother! And *you*…" she said to Douglas, but she was unable or unwilling to finish her thought. She shifted on her heels and headed for the door.

"Please…wait," Maria-Carmella said.

"Hear her out," Douglas added. "You owe her that much."

"You've got five minutes," Regina said as she sat in the chair farthest away from her.

"I've missed you."

There was a dramatic pause, but it was not clear to Regina whether her mother's emotions were real or if they were intentional, manipulative, rehearsed.

"And I miss my son," she said. She fidgeted in her chair, clearly ill at ease with such a personal exposé. "There's nothing I can say or do that can change what happened to your brother. But I pray that I can rectify what's happened between the two of us."

"I know how difficult that was for you to say, and I couldn't be more shocked or delighted to hear it," Regina said. "If there is one thing that is irrefutable, Mother, it's that neither of us has ever walked away from a challenge."

On the conference table was a vase filled with wildflowers and twigs, an inelegant arrangement of miscellaneous stems, clashing colors, and contrasting textures. Maria-Carmella removed a bud from the centerpiece and held it in her hand. She looked at the blue iris she had taken and then lifted it to her nostrils and inhaled its subtle scent. Admiring the pale-blue flower seemed to give her the courage to continue.

"You know, Douglas, your assistant Jean had to scour the entire Upper East Side to assemble this pitiful, beautiful arrangement," Maria-Carmella said.

Regina and Douglas exchanged confused glances. Neither could surmise the purpose of that revelation or predict where it was leading.

"Your uncle," Maria-Carmella continued, directing her comments to her daughter, "on those days when he lingered in his garden long past the time he needed to be dressed and ready for some event or soiree, would, as a peace offering, gather up a ghastly combination of wildflowers for me. He'd take that sad collection of weeds and whatever else he could find, stick them in a random jar or glass, and then tie them together with a stray piece of twine or bind them with a sprig of lavender. He had a strange knack for making those misfit flowers seem almost elegant." She leaned forward and shifted the vase so that Regina and Douglas could view the other side. "He would transform the most pathetic collection of branches and errant stems into the most magnificent, fragrant arrangement and then place them on my dressing table as compensation for his tardiness. I dismissed them to his face and pretended to be irritated by his eccentricity. But being left alone with that concoction of misfit flowers while he showered the dirt off and donned his tuxedo was often the best part of my day. Those pedestrian, seemingly inconsequential bouquets would fill the place with this intoxicating fragrance." Maria-Carmella gently reinserted the iris she'd been holding back into the mix. "Shortly after our driver had passed through the front gate and we were on our way, a member of the staff would enter my room and remove them, along with the mess of stray petals and seeds they inevitably left behind. But no matter how late we'd been out, that smell, that perfume, that essence still lingered there, greeting me again upon my return."

Regina smiled with a glow of recognition. It reminded her of the many occasions she had observed her mother unconsciously toying with a wayward flower that had been plucked or dropped from a centerpiece. It was one of the few predictable habits she had. She would twirl it between her fingers, inhale its scent from a distance, and then carefully, methodically, place it to one side of her dinner plate. During the course of the evening, whenever there was a lull in the conversation, she would see her mother's eyes wander down to the white linen tablecloth and the wilting flower that grew limper and limper as the night progressed. Somehow, while the dishes and the silverware of each course were cleared, the glasses and ashtrays refreshed or replaced, that one little blossom managed to remain where it was until the very last dessert plate was whisked off into the kitchen.

"Your uncle was quite a bit older than me, and unarguably wiser, although I've come to that realization a little late in life. He was able to see in your brother what I never could." Maria-Carmella stood and moved around the table. She settled into the seat next to Regina. "I had always thought of Cosimo as being damaged in some way. Like a bird with a broken wing or a misfit flower that never quite fit in. I thought that all I needed to do was to fix it, and he'd be better. But I never knew how." She withdrew a handkerchief and blotted the corners of her eyes. "And because I couldn't fix him, I felt broken myself." She placed a hand on top of Regina's. "I spent the better part of my life trying to prove to the world, to myself, that we weren't broken. As if the act of pretending would make it so."

Regina raised her free hand to her eyes and dabbed away her own salty moisture. When Douglas made a move to leave, they silently but emphatically ordered him to remain.

"The truth is, dear, we're all broken in some regard," Maria-Carmella said. "And I'm wise enough to know I'm too old to change my ways. I will do my best to make whatever adjustments are necessary to rebuild our relationship, but in the end, you must accept me as I am."

"Thank you for that, Mother. I'm delighted you've taken the time for some much-needed introspection." Regina leaned in and put her arms around her. "I'm sorry I was so hard on you, but it seemed like my only option at the time."

"No need to apologize, dear. You neither did nor said anything wrong. And that is as new-agey and enlightened as I will ever get."

"Are you serious about doing whatever it takes to mend fences?" Regina said.

"What if I were to qualify that by stipulating... anything within reason?"

"Mother, have I mentioned that *Playboy* has been hounding me to be in their magazine? You know, a tasteful and classy layout with lots of ermine and subdued lighting."

And then, just to carry the joke a bit further, she added, "Can't you just see the photos of me scantily clad and splashing in the fountain in front of the villa?"

"Okay, you win. Anything you want." Maria-Carmella smiled at her daughter and winked at the attorney. "Douglas, now would be a good time for you to leave us alone for a few minutes."

Douglas got up and headed for the door. He hesitated before opening it, waiting for a sign from Regina that it was okay for him to go. Her calm expression was all that he needed to leave the room.

"You have something else you need to say to me, Mother?"

"There was a box in a closet that contained some of your uncle's possessions. A member of his staff gave it to me shortly after he passed away. A few photographs, trinkets, mementos, things like that. Until recently I couldn't bring myself to open the case and look inside."

"And what does that have to do with me?"

"Before he died, he made an obscure reference to a gift he'd had made for you. He said he was waiting for the right time to present it, that he wanted it to be special, memorable. He was quite ill by then and often delirious, so I never gave it another thought...until I looked in that box." She opened her purse and withdrew a clump of tan tissue paper and placed it on the table. "In spite of any flaws he may have had, he was a master of detail, his word was gold, and he always finished what he started." She slid the wad of paper slowly, deliberately across the mahogany surface until it rested a few inches in front of Regina.

Maria-Carmella saw her daughter begin to tremble,

watched her tears start to flow with both trepidation and anticipation. Regina put her hands up to her face and quietly gulped to try to refrain from crying. Maria-Carmella reached a hand out, and Regina accepted it. She gripped it tightly and then placed her other hand over them to complete the embrace, to envelope and comfort her daughter in some small, maternal way.

"Dear, I've never seen you look so overwhelmed before. I know it's a shock. It was to me, too. Discovering that he was still capable of surprising me after all this time wasn't something I was prepared for. But it's all good, dear." She released her grip on her daughter's hand, picked up the clump of tissue paper, and held it out in her open palm. "If the past year has taught me anything, it's that we all need to be a little more like Giuseppe. And that I should be grateful that my children had him in their lives to compensate them for the traits and qualities that I lacked."

Regina tentatively took the paper from her mother's palm and placed it back on the tabletop. She took a handkerchief from her purse and patted her eyes. Then slowly, carefully, she began to liberate the contents from its wrapping. As her eyes scanned the bright gold medallion with the two large diamonds that represented the constellation's two first-magnitude stars, Achernar and Acamar, she began to tremble all over again.

"It's a phoenix," Maria-Carmella said. She was moved by the fact that the gift had made her daughter speechless. It made her feel maternal, awkward, happy, and excluded, all at the same time. "Giuseppe admired your ability to rebound after any setback. He believed that to be your greatest strength and your saving grace." She made a rotating motion with her hand. "There's an inscription on the back."

Regina laid the front of the medallion on her palm and read the engraving, laughing through her tears as she did so.

Regina,
Your strength inspires me,
your presence blesses me,
your love enriches me.
Uncle G.

She turned the medallion over again and ran her fingers across the two brilliant gemstones and then along the fine, linear relief that represented the firebird constellation.

"Mother…you have no idea…you can't imagine…"

"Yes, dear, I think I can. I couldn't have six months ago, but now I can."

"And the other…" Regina said, stopping herself midsentence, afraid that mentioning it would tarnish their reunion.

"I know, dear, I know. It never would have occurred to me that you could give her Orion as a keepsake. It would have broken your heart to do so. But the instant I unwrapped this one, I knew that's exactly what you had done."

Regina kissed her mother on the cheek and then stood and took off her jacket.

"Shall we do this?" she said.

"That's why I'm here."

Regina opened the door to Douglas's outer office and approached his assistant. "Jean, could you ask Douglas to rejoin us? And if you're free, I'm sure he could use your help. We'll need someone to take notes and to draw up some contracts." She was straddling the transom of the conference room again when another thought occurred to her. "Oh, and Jean, could you bring in some fresh coffee? There's a good chance we'll be here for a while."

Chapter Thirty-Four

Megan took a sip of her espresso and then placed the cup back in its saucer. She picked up the Brasserie de l'Isle Saint-Louis menu and perused the list of appetizers. Cosimo held one of her hands with his left while he aggressively smoked a cigarette with his right. She closed her menu and, with her free hand, reached across the table to push away a few errant curls from his forehead.

"You're going to catch yourself on fire one of these days," she said.

Cosimo said nothing. He released his hand from hers and used it to light another cigarette with the one that was almost down to its filter. Megan scrunched up her face with a look of irritation. She waved a hand in front of her as if she were trying to clear away a billow of smoke that had drifted her way.

"What are you doing?" Tommy said as he approached her from behind.

"Jesus!" she said. "You shouldn't sneak up on a person like that."

"A little jumpy today, are we? What's with all the muttering and wild gestures? You look like a lunatic, sitting here all by yourself, waving your arms about, conversing to an empty chair."

"Lunacy is highly underrated. It's a lost art, really."

"You poor girl," he said. "All this stress has finally gotten to you."

She motioned for him to take a seat in the empty chair next to hers. Tommy did so, but not without making a few grand gestures of his own, comically checking first to make sure that the chair was indeed unoccupied.

"Oh, sit down already," she said. "Make fun of me all you want. One of these days you'll find out what it's like to lose someone you care about. And I'm willing to bet it won't be long before that happens, either. Gregg is bound to wake up from that spell you've cast on him and leave you for some nice young well-adjusted man who'll treat him like the prince he is."

"Oh, honey," Tommy said as he rested a comforting hand on her shoulder. "I'm serious. It never occurred to me how difficult it must be for you to be back in Paris again. All alone."

"I'm hardly alone."

"You know what I mean."

"It's funny, you know," she continued, "those traits that you hate about a person when they're here are the very things you miss most about them when they're gone."

"And what will you miss most about me?"

"Oh, Tommy, there are so many things I hate about you, I wouldn't know where to begin." She picked up a large vinyl menu and whacked him on the head with it. "Is Gregg having fun?"

"Hard to tell. He's got us on such a tight schedule. Ten to twelve, it's the Eiffel Tower. Twelve to two, it's a walk through the Tuileries and then up the Champs-Elysées to the Arc de Triomphe. From two to five, it's some exhibition at some gallery in some arrondissement that ..." Tommy trailed off, exhausted from the mere thought of Gregg's fully packed itinerary.

"It's his first trip to Paris," she said. "He doesn't want to miss anything."

"Believe me—the only way he's going to miss anything is if it isn't listed in one of those guidebooks he keeps referring to." He spotted Lauren walking toward the café. He shouted her name and waved her over. "I keep trying to tell him that if he doesn't take his nose out of those damn books, his only memories of Paris are going to be tiny four-color photographs with generic comments in small print thought up by the folks at Lonely Planet and Fodors."

Lauren set down several shopping bags, sat down, took off her shoes, and massaged her feet, groaning in pleasure as she did so.

"What do you think of that?" Tommy said, directing his comment to Megan. "Your girlfriend here brings fourteen steamer trunks for a four-day trip, and she forgets to pack flats."

"I didn't forget, numbskull. I, unlike you, always want to look my best. I'm happy to forgo comfort for style," she said, her pained expression in sharp contrast to her declaration. "Ahhh, isn't it beautiful," she added, her head shifting left to right along the banks of the Seine. "It was so nice of Regina to include us in this little boondoggle. I wish Robert could have come."

"You can thank *me* for that," Megan said. "I'm the one who suggested she shoot the Toddler-Couture commercial on Pont Neuf. And it was *I* who persuaded her that Gus needed his entire entourage with him in order to do his best work."

"Brilliant idea, sis," Tommy said. "I just love her tag line: 'Clothing that bridges the gap between who you are and who you want to be.'"

"If she's Italian," Gregg said, sneaking up behind Tommy and wrapping his arms around his neck, "why not film it in Florence or Venice?"

"It's not about being Italian. Or French," Megan said. "It's about being worldly, international, sophisticated. Paris's landmarks are much more recognizable to the general public than most other European locales. People might recognize the Ponte Vecchio, but that implies cheap jewelry, not haute couture."

"Well, I still think she should use the tag line that I came up with," Tommy said.

"And what little gem might that be?" Lauren asked, giggling.

"In Toddler-Couture, your child will always look fabulous and ready for any playdate. With stretchable waistbands and dynamic colors, poopy pants never looked so good."

Lauren burst out laughing. Megan and Gregg just shook their heads. Gregg checked his watch and tapped Tommy on the shoulder. He lifted his palms a few times in Lauren's direction. "Up! Up! We have to get going," he said. "We're already an hour behind schedule."

They all kissed Megan in that European fashion; then they gathered up their coats and parcels and said goodbye. Once again Megan found herself sitting alone under the red awning of an outdoor bistro on the Île Saint-Louis. Or just about. She looked at the empty chair to her right and said in a mockingly irritated voice, "See what you're missing, Coz?"

～∾

They appeared as if they had materialized out of thin air, magically formed, intact and three-dimensional, where before there had been nothing. Regina held his right hand, and Maria-Carmella firmly gripped his left.

"Whee!" said Regina.

She and her mother pulled on the little boy's arms and lifted him into the air.

"Whee!" shrieked Gus, who then giggled while his feet kicked at the empty space below. His curly brown hair bounced and swayed as he wriggled midair between the two women. Megan grinned, relieved to see her son again: safe, happy, embraced. Megan and Maria-Carmella regarded each other from a distance of a few hundred feet, each acknowledging the other with a tight smile. The two hadn't seen each other since their introduction at the attorney's office in Manhattan. And while Regina had informed Megan that she had invited her mother to join them in Paris so that she could spend some time with Gus, actually seeing her there, tenderly holding her child's hand, still came as a shock.

When the three of them reached the end of the bridge,

Maria-Carmella knelt down and whispered in Gus's ear. Gus nodded his head enthusiastically. Then she spoke to her daughter. Megan was too far away to hear their conversation, but she did see Regina shake her head, no. Maria-Carmella moved in closer to her daughter, placed a hand on her arm, and spoke to her in a clearly authoritative way. Megan watched for Regina's reaction but was unable to interpret what it meant.

Regina knelt down and said something to Gus, who was apparently very pleased with that communication. Seconds later, Regina and Gus drifted off to the right, toward the main street that cut through the center of the Île Saint-Louis. Maria-Carmella ambled purposefully in the direction of the brasserie and to the table where Megan was seated.

"They're going for ice cream," she said, hovering over Megan, her hands stuffed deep into her coat pockets.

"So I gathered."

"I hope you don't mind," Maria-Carmella said. "I thought it best that we speak privately." She surveyed the landscape, then sat in a chair on the other side of the table. With one hand she pulled her coat closed, and with the other, she dismissed an approaching waiter. "It's rather chilly for June, don't you think?"

"*C'est vrai,*" Megan said. "June in Paris. It's the most unpredictable month."

Megan removed a cardigan sweater she'd hung over the back of her chair and draped it over her shoulders as if to confirm her agreement. Since Regina had confided in her that Maria-Carmella had mellowed to some degree, she decided to give the woman the benefit of the doubt and try to be cordial. That is, unless she crosses a line.

Maria-Carmella reached over and lightly, barely, touched Megan's sweater.

"Cashmere. Nice. Ralph Lauren?"

"Vera Wang," Megan replied.

"It suits you."

"I wouldn't be too impressed if I were you, Mrs. Garibaldi. I dug it out of the irregulars bin in Filene's Basement."

Maria-Carmella, in a rare display of self-restraint, hesitated in a way that implied she was contemplating her next comment carefully.

"Dear, a word of advice. If I may?"

Megan nodded.

"Certain information is sometimes best withheld."

"Point taken," she said. "You had something you wanted to discuss?"

"You're very direct, aren't you?"

"Only when I need to be."

"Don't get me wrong, dear; I meant that as a compliment."

They fell into an awkward silence. Megan ran a finger around the rim of her water glass. Maria-Carmella buttoned her coat and pulled her collar up.

"We met here, you know?" Megan said.

"Paris?"

"Right here. This café. At one of these very tables."

Maria-Carmella looked down at her chair, then at the ones around her. She was visibly uncomfortable. She leaned back in her seat, and that little accommodation made them both feel a bit more at ease.

"I'm sorry my son did not think he could tell me about you. The truth is, at the time, it wouldn't have mattered anyway. Granted, I was hard on him, but I was only trying to protect him, to do what I thought was best." She turned away from Megan and stared vacantly into the murky water of the Seine. "From the day he was born, I only ever saw him as a fragile child, as a broken little boy. I was never comfortable with…never understood his weakness. I guess that drove me to be too hard on him." When she turned her attention back to Megan, her demeanor implied both contrition and acceptance. "I loved him in the only way that I knew how. But make no mistake, I did love my son."

Megan couldn't help but feel a certain amount of compassion for this woman. But when her eyes welled up, she refused to shed a tear. No matter how repentant Maria-Carmella professed to be about the past, Megan didn't know her well enough to let her guard down. To keep herself grounded, she briefly let her mind drift to the other side of the street where she knew that Regina and Gus would be standing in line, perusing the Berthillon menu of dense ice creams and exotic fruit-flavored sorbets.

"I won't pretend to know how Cosimo felt about you," Megan finally said, sitting up straight in her chair and leaning forward. "I won't insult you with some made-up story of how he told me that he loved you in spite of everything. He kept me in the dark about you, as well." She took a sip of water and then a deep breath. "What I can tell you, with absolute certainty, is that his family meant everything to him. That no matter how difficult your relationship was, *I know*, for what it's worth, that he never stopped trying to please you."

It was now Maria-Carmella's turn to keep her emotions at bay. She picked up the red leather menu again and perused it. Her eyes drifted around the pages, never landing on any one item long enough for her to be seriously contemplating anything.

"The past *is*," Maria-Carmella said. Her expression said thank you, but the words never came. "There is nothing we can do about it. It's silly to have regrets. But sometimes…"

She stood and placed her purse on the table. She reached in, pulled out a large manila envelope, and handed it to Megan. An address label on the front of it, typed in a distinctive font, displayed Megan's name along with her Boston address. In the upper-left-hand corner was the name of a New York law firm, so prestigious even Megan knew of its reputation.

"I'm afraid that's the best I can do," Maria-Carmella said. She then turned and walked in the direction of the ice cream shop where Regina and Gus were nearing the front of the line. Megan ordered another espresso. She twisted the lemon peel and slowly dragged it around the rim of the cup, her eyes focused on the envelope's gold metal clasp. She picked it up again. It was heavy. Its heft implied importance and consequence. She pried apart the thin metal fastener and pulled out a thick stack of stark white paper. She tried to read the first couple of pages, but the language was too thick with legal jargon for her to comprehend that morning. A few words jumped out at her as she perused the other pages: estate, trust, annuity, conservatorship. Her name was mentioned, as was her son's. And the words "twenty million dollars."

Maria-Carmella had handed Megan a document that spelled out clearly, and legally, the terms under which Giuseppe Cosimo Thomas Walker was to be awarded the sum of $20 million. Three million dollars was to be distributed to the conservator, Megan Walker, upon the signing and return of the enclosed documents. Another $500,000 was to be dispersed annually to Gus's conservator upon the anniversary of his birth. And when Gus reached the age of eighteen, he was to be awarded the balance: $10 million. There was only one stipulation, namely that, from that day forward, Giuseppe Cosimo Thomas Walker, whenever he addressed Princess Maria-Carmella Stefani Garibaldi di Sorrento, was to refer to her singularly and respectfully as *Your Royal Highness.** There was a small asterisk after the word *Highness*, which Megan, too shaken to continue, ignored for the moment.

The papers shook in her grip, and she dropped the stack onto the round table. Her hands covered her mouth as she tried to regain control of her breathing. She looked off to the left of the island, but she knew, even as she did so, that the ice cream shop was not visible from her seat, that the three of them were out of sight once again. She took another sip of water, picked up the document, and resumed reading the page with the large numbers and the curious asterisk. In tiny, almost illegible print, at the bottom of the page, was another little black star:

Should for any reason Mr. Giuseppe Walker be unable to comply with the conditions of this agreement, the term "Nonna" will serve as an acceptable substitute for "Your Royal Highness."

Megan was relieved that no one at the café took notice of her, even though she'd just let loose an audible laugh.

Acknowledgments

No book comes into being without a team of people behind it (editors, readers, teachers, etc.), and this one is no different. I'd like to acknowledge every one of them, but this will have to do for now.

To two individuals who encouraged and nurtured my earliest attempts at writing: Thomas Burke and Catherine Temma Davidson.

To Michelle Richmond, a terrific writer and editor. (Thanks for exorcising the ick factor.)

To my teachers and mentors at the University of San Francisco for their input and encouragement: David Booth, Lewis Buzbee, Kaui Hart Hemmings, Nina Schyuler, and Karl Soehnlein. And a special thank-you to Maximilian DeLaure for pushing me to stretch and grow as a writer in addition to his relentless lessons on POV.

To Lesley Lupo for her generous gift of time and unending encouragement.

To Jim Balgooyen, Karen Bourgeois, Andy Dallin, April Eberhardt, Nancy Mace, Carol Strayer, Julie Venkat, John Vidaurri, and all my other readers for their thoughtful feedback and unrelenting support.

CPSIA information can be obtained
at www.ICGtesting.com
Printed in the USA
FFHW021820260419
52075326-57456FF

9 780578 483122